MISS MOLE

Other Virago Modern Classics published by The Dial Press

ANTONIA WHITE
Frost in May
The Lost Traveller
The Sugar House
Beyond the Glass
Strangers

RADCLYFFE HALL
The Unlit Lamp

REBECCA WEST
Harriet Hume
The Judge
The Return of the Soldier

F. TENNYSON JESSE
The Lacquer Lady

SARAH GRAND
The Beth Book

BARBARA COMYNS
The Vet's Daughter
*Our spoons came
   from Woolworths*

HENRY HANDEL RICHARDSON
The Getting of Wisdom
Maurice Guest

MARY WEBB
Gone to Earth
Precious Bane
The Golden Arrow
Seven for a Secret

RUTH ADAM
I'm Not Complaining

VITA SACKVILLE-WEST
All Passion Spent

E. H. YOUNG
Miss Mole

M. BARNARD ELDERSHAW
*Tomorrow & Tomorrow &
Tomorrow*

EMILY EDEN
*The Semi-Attached Couple
   & The Semi-Detached House*

MARGARET KENNEDY
The Ladies of Lyndon
Together and Apart
The Constant Nymph

MAY SINCLAIR
Mary Olivier: A Life

ADA LEVERSON
The Little Ottleys

E. ARNOT ROBERTSON
Ordinary Families

ELIZABETH TAYLOR
Mrs. Palfrey at the Claremont
The Sleeping Beauty
The Soul of Kindness
In a Summer Season
Angel

ROSAMOND LEHMANN
A Note in Music
The Weather in the Streets

ROSE MACAULAY
Told by an Idiot

SHEILA KAYE-SMITH
Joanna Godden

MAUREEN DUFFY
That's How it Was

ELIZABETH JENKINS
The Tortoise and the Hare

VIOLET TREFUSIS
Hunt the Slipper

HARRIET MARTINEAU
Deerbrook

E. H. Young

MISS MOLE

With a new introduction by
Sally Beauman

The Dial Press
DOUBLEDAY & COMPANY, INC.
GARDEN CITY, NEW YORK
1985

Published by The Dial Press

Library of Congress Cataloging in Publication Data

Young, E. H. (Emily Hilda), 1880-1949.
Miss Mole.

Originally published: London : J. Cape, 1930.
I. Title.
PR6047.0465M5 1985   823'.912   84-14950

ISBN 0-385-27975-2

First published in Great Britain by Jonathan Cape Ltd.
1930

Copyright © D.H.M. Gotch 1930

Introduction copyright © Sally Beauman 1984

Manufactured in the United States of America

INTRODUCTION

This is, at first sight, a very odd book: it has an exceedingly
odd, indeed unlikely, heroine, the eponymous Miss Mole,
and an exceedingly odd style. The first impression of it is
that everything is aslant. We view a world, a society,
through the eyes of a woman, but we do so in snatches,
crookedly, as if the events were narrated glancing over the
shoulder, from the side rather than the centre, seen with a
squint. Everything is a little topsy-turvy, a little dislocated,
a little out of true. Order is not observed, deliberately. The
reader is kept on the hop, trying to piece together
connections, relationships, from glimpses, hints, mysterious jokes and allusions. We are misled, confused, no sooner
make a deduction than find it to be wrong: not for nothing
is Miss Mole an accomplished inventor of fibs. 'I don't
mean to tell you anything,' Miss Mole says to the woman
we have just discovered (at the very end of their
conversation) is her cousin, and her creator adopts the
same pose. She does tell, of course, eventually; gradually
the puzzling little pieces fall into place and the
kaleidoscopic picture connects; but she takes her time, and
she teases. So does Miss Mole. It is how she survives in life.

The novel was published in 1930, when its author E.H.
Young was fifty. It thus predates by some forty years the
spy novels of John le Carré, and his invented terminology
of the secret world. In le Carré, a 'mole' is an undercover
agent, a plant within an organisation whose true identity
and loyalties must not be discovered. As in the world of
Smiley, so here: we are not, of course, in the territory of the
thriller, Miss Mole is not working for the Russians or MI5.

vii

But she is involved in a kind of espionage: she is a spy in the house of life.

She is extremely well-equipped for the role. She is, as already mentioned, an accomplished embroiderer of the truth, a story-teller. But above and beyond her narrative gifts, she has two most excellent qualifications: she is a woman (a plain woman, of a certain age), and she is a servant. It is the next best thing to invisibility.

Miss Mole is a spinster, and a housekeeper/companion. She has a secret, connected to her past, which is not divulged fully, even to the reader, until almost the end of the novel, and she lives a secret life, a double life, compounded of enforced subservience and indomitable spirit. She has, because of poverty and past actions, to earn her living; in earning her living she has to curb her tongue. But her mind has remained gloriously free and subversive, her eye acute. Each depressing situation Miss Mole takes up has its own ideology, and ostensibly the quiet, plain, efficient spinster conforms to it. She gets the fires lit at the right time, and a good dinner on the table; she buys silk and mends her employers' second-best black dresses; she does not rebel (at first) against the tyranny of their foibles, or the pomposity of their pronouncements, or the inaccuracy of their beliefs. Apparently, she knows her place.

In reality, of course, she conforms not at all. All the time her mind keeps up its own independent and sardonic commentary on the events she witnesses, and the people she meets; she remains a free agent. And, since she has an acerbic wit, and often becomes bored with curbing her tongue, she occasionally speaks out. Then she is fired; she moves on, and the cycle begins again. It might go on for perpetuity, and probably did in the actual lives of the many domestic Miss Moles of the pre-war years. But repression and dissembling breed a contrary flamboyance

– that paradox was often remarked upon in the careers of such notorious political moles as Philby, Burgess, and Maclean. At the time this novel begins it is a phenomenon detectable in Miss Mole. She has grown bored with tactical conformity; the temptation to mock and to tease more overtly has grown, and her fortunes have declined accordingly. 'Trying to be funny is one of your failings,' her cousin Lilla snubbingly tells her at the beginning of this novel, on learning that Miss Mole is about to be dismissed yet again. Lilla, of course, is wrong; Miss Mole's humour is not only her weapon, it is her greatest strength, and no effort is needed on her part to utilise it.

Lilla, anxious to be rid of the problem of her socially embarrassing cousin, finds her a new situation, as housekeeper to the Corder family; so the framework for the book is established. The free agent burrows into the chill bosom of another family: the scene is set for satiric fireworks; Miss Mole v. the rest; truth and acerbity v. humbug. The fireworks are duly provided: E.H. Young is a sharp and funny writer with a brilliant eye for moral fudging and verbal hypocrisy, and she has a splendid foil in Miss Mole. If that were all E.H. Young gave us, we would still have a sparkling novel, but she does more than that: the book is multi-faceted, not one-sided. For Miss Mole, like many spies, is an isolated creature, the victim as well as the begetter of her own dissembling. She begins the novel alone, without father, mother, brother, sister, lover, husband, child or friend. She ends the novel a changed woman in a changed situation. The Corders – an unpromising family, whose name is not accidental – are the agency that forge for her new links with life. She returns the compliment, with interest, as it happens, and it is here, in the ground swell below the surface wit, that the substance of this considerable novel lies.

Miss Mole falls midway in E.H. Young's work. Of her mature novels, all written between the wars, three fall before it and three after it, but none of the others achieves its sureness of touch and mastery of tone. Young herself is now little known, her novels having been long out of print; but during her lifetime she was a very popular and successful novelist, her books reaching a wide audience here and in America. All were highly praised at the time of publication; *Miss Mole*, the best received but not the most popular of her works (the semi-autobiographical *William* held that distinction), was awarded the James Tait Black Memorial Prize for fiction.

It was written at a time when E.H. Young herself had, for at least the past ten years, lived a double life – one that was to continue until her death from lung cancer in 1949. She had married, in 1902, a Bristol solicitor, J.A.H. Daniell, and Bristol, where they lived, was to be the setting for almost all her novels. Her husband was killed at Ypres in 1917, and Emily Young then moved to London, taking up residence with the man she loved, and living with him and his wife (who was wife in name only) in Sydenham Hill. It was a curious ménage, and one that was to continue for the next twenty years of her life. The man, Ralph Henderson, had been a friend and schoolfellow of her husband, and he was the Head Master of the London public school, Alleyn's.* Although Henderson's wife seems to have tolerated this situation quite happily, it was, by its very nature, dangerous, and veiled in secrecy. Had it come to light, Henderson's academic career would certainly have ended. As it was, the couple avoided scandal, Henderson remained at Alleyn's for twenty years, and during that time Emily Young wrote seven novels. In 1940, after his retirement they moved to Wiltshire, alone, living

---

*A fuller account of E.H. Young's life is given in the introduction to *The Misses Mallett*.

in Bradford-on-Avon together until the time of her death. Even then they never married.

Thus E.H. Young, or Mrs Daniell as she was known in private life, was well equipped to write a novel in which secrecy and truth, propriety and individual morality, clash. Like Miss Mole she too had a secret that was potentially damaging: she lived with it for at least forty years of her life.

Propriety, in fact, stalks this novel; its dry hands and stale breath touch the lives of all the characters. We are in Bristol (rechristened Radstowe). More specifically we are in Clifton, not the rarefied heights of that desirable district, as we are in the earlier *The Misses Mallett*, but further down the hill, in Beresford Road, a territory Pooter would have found to his liking. There the houses 'give the impression that nothing unusual or indecorous can happen within their walls'. Respectability is the true religion; most of the inhabitants, however, having cast aside the church of their upbringing (Nonconformist Chapel) now claim allegiance to one that carries more social clout. The Reverend Robert Corder, whose household Miss Mole, a natural outsider, joins, is therefore something of an outsider himself. Appointed because of his charisma in the pulpit, in a desperate attempt to stop the defections from the Congregational Chapel, Corder is a man cut-off. His nearest neighbour is socially undesirable (though Miss Mole finds the gentleman in question most amusing); his parishioners are unreliable; his wife is dead; he is remote from his children. Corder, the Minister, the articulate preacher, cannot even communicate with his own flesh and blood, despite his deep affection for them. It is to this cold tight little enclave, hedged in with class obsession, bound by emotional evasion and repression, that Miss Mole comes, a tart spinster with a Past, alias a ministering angel. The clash between propriety and true morality is almost instant; the roles of sinner and Minister are reversed.

Miss Mole refuses to be bound in by the Corder household. She makes little forays – first into the lives of Corder's family, then wider afield. Her contacts fan out, enabling E.H. Young to map here the territory of the *petit bourgeois* as in *The Misses Mallett* she mapped the purlieus of the upper middle classes. With equal insouciance Miss Mole moves from the monstrous villa of her cousin, Lilla Spenser-Smith, patron and benefactor to the Corder household, to the world of seedy lodging houses, clinging precariously to the lower slopes of respectability. There, in the unlikely circumstances with which the novel begins, she meets Samuel Blenkinsop, bank clerk and 'single gent' – not a likely nor a doughty hero one would think, but then this novel is full of surprises.

It is these forays, these interventions of Miss Mole that provide the motor for E.H. Young's plot, at first sight slight, at second of considerable ingenuity. Becoming involved with the Corders, particularly Robert Corder's sad little daughter Ruth, she helps to change their lives, and in the process transforms her own. Against a background of family rebellions and secrecies a very real and often moving investigation of the nature of love takes place – familial love, romantic love and its relationship to personal fulfilment. Meanwhile, ticking away, is the time bomb of Miss Mole's own secret, also involving love, and her efforts to drown out the sound of that ticking with a series of heady inventions and barefaced lies, are very funny indeed.

She nearly, very nearly, succeeds; her ultimate failure is also – the book is beautifully balanced – her salvation. Religious terms creep in: E.H. Young avoids them, but nonetheless there is something of the morality play in this novel. The opposition of good and bad is dealt with very subtly – evil lurks in the smallest nuance, the slightest action – but the opposition is there, and the theme of the novel is transgression. Not the obvious transgression Miss Mole has committed in the past, that, weighed properly, is seen as morally justifiable; no, the transgression here is deviation from truth, whether it is to take refuge in hypocrisy, or evasion as Robert Corder does, or to take refuge in the covert, as Miss Mole does. For Miss Mole, frank though she is, honest though she is, has, like the animal she is named for, hidden herself away from the light, protected herself from the full scrutiny of others, out of shame partly, but more out of pride.

With the greatest dexterity and facility E.H. Young conveys this wilful immolation in the very texture of her writing. That squinting myopic vision, that elliptic approach so remarkable, so throwing, at the beginning of the novel, gradually changes. The style keeps step with the spiritual development of the central character; as her self-knowledge increases, so the writing moves confidently to a different, clearer, more direct mode. By the time Miss Mole is ready and able to come out of hiding and take the one risk that she, proud of her own recklessness, has never taken – showing herself, as she is, to another person – by then, the writing is transformed. It is terse, winged, immensely authoritative. The tortuousness of some three hundred and fifty pages (productive and purposeful tortuousness) is triumphantly resolved in an exchange of a few sentences.

'Well, now you know everything about me,' says Miss Mole to her rescuer, and to the reader, in the novel's penultimate moments. She has come a long journey from the evasions with which the novel began, and it has been charted with insight, compassion, a dazzling technical virtuousity, and a narrative experimentalism quite remarkable for its period. It is, by any standards, a fine, provocative novel.

Sally Beauman, London, 1983

xiii

MISS MOLE

Chapter 1

THE voice of her new friend, bidding her good night, followed Miss Hannah Mole as she went down the garden path, and the laurel bushes, as she brushed by them, repeated in a whisper, yet with a strange assurance, the persuasive invitation of Mrs. Gibson to come back soon.

'Yes, yes, I'll come!' Hannah called out hurriedly, and she glanced over her shoulder as the golden patch on the path disappeared. Mrs. Gibson had shut the front door: she had returned to the problems which ought never to have arisen in her respectable house, and Hannah, freed from the necessity for action, for the expression of sympathy and the giving of advice, was able to admire the skill she had shown in these activities, but first, because she was grateful by nature as well as appreciative of herself, she offered up thanks for the timely justification of her faith in the interest of life. That faith had been persistent, though, latterly, it had demanded a dogged perseverance, and at the moment when she most needed encouragement it had been supplied. She would not ignore the creditable quickness with which she had grasped the opportunity offered; it was, indeed, only to those with seeing eyes and hearing ears that miracles were vouchsafed, and who but Hannah Mole, at her impact with Mrs. Gibson's broad bosom, would have had the prescience to linger after her apology and give Mrs. Gibson time to recover her breath and explain why she stood outside her gate, bareheaded and in a flutter.

On the same spot Hannah now stood, a little breathless herself, through excitement and the effort to reconcile her good fortune with the small deception she had practised on her employer. The effort was not successful and she renewed her conviction that the power which controlled her life was not hampered by man's conventional morality, otherwise, she would surely have been punished and not rewarded for the lie which had induced Mrs. Widdows to send her companion shopping at the hour when she should have been mending Mrs. Widdows' second-best black dress. Yes, Hannah should have been knocked down by a motor-car or, worse still, have been robbed of her purse, for hiding the reel of silk and pretending she could not find it.

The crowded little sitting-room had been unbearably hot. A large fire blazed and crackled, the canary made sad, subdued movements in its cage, Mrs. Widdows' corsets creaked regularly, her large knees almost touched Hannah's own, for the two women sat near each other to share the lamplight, and Hannah, luckier than the canary, had found a means of escape. Too wise to suggest that she should go out and buy the necessary silk, she had merely remarked with regret that it would be impossible for Mrs. Widdows to wear the second-best dress on the morrow, and, at once, Mrs. Widdows had indignantly driven her forth with orders to return quickly. And nearly two hours had passed and the silk was still in the shop. Hannah was indifferent about the silk, for the reel she had removed from the work-basket was in the pocket of her coat, and she was twopence half-penny and an adventure to the good, but the passage of time was a serious matter, so serious that another hour or two would make no difference. She glanced up the street, and then down, and while she seemed to hesitate between duty and desire, she had already made her choice. She would go down, towards the traffic and the shops. By the light of the street lamp, she looked at the old-fashioned flat watch she carried in her handbag. It was six o'clock. Most of the shops would be shut, but there would be light and movement; tram-cars full of passengers would be leaping in their advance, like strange beasts rejoicing in their strength; people on foot would be streaming homewards from the city of Radstowe, and Miss Hannah Mole, who had no home of her own, would look at these people with envy but with the cynical reflection that some of those homes might be comparable to that of Mrs. Widdows – stuffy and unkind, or to the one she had just left– holding tragedy maliciously streaked with humour. In nearly twenty years of earning

8

her living, as companion, nursery governess or useful help, she had lost all illusions except those she created for herself, but these appeared at her command and, stirred by her late adventure, she was ready to find another in the approach of each person she met. In Prince's Road, however, there were not many people and such as there were walked quietly, as though the influence of the old terraced houses on one side of the road were stronger than that of the later buildings on the other. It was the old houses that gave its character to the street and here, as elsewhere in Upper Radstowe, the gently persistent personality of the place remained, unmoved by any material or spiritual changes since the first red bricks were well and truly laid. It was like a masterpiece of portrait painting in which a person of another generation looks down on his descendants and dominates them through the union of the painter's art and something permanent in himself. Even where the old houses had disappeared, their ghosts seemed to hover over the streets, and Hannah, too, walked quietly, careful not to disturb them. In no other place of her acquaintance did the trees cast such lovely shadows in the lamplight, and on this windless night the leaves were patterned with extraordinary, ethereal clearness on the pavement. Now and then she paused to look at them, puzzled that the reflected object should always seem more beautiful than the original, and eager to find some analogy to this experience in her mental processes.

'Not the thing itself, but its shadow,' she murmured, as she saw her own shadow going before her, and she nodded as though she had solved a problem. She judged herself by the shadow she chose to project for her own pleasure and it was her business in life – and one in which she usually failed – to make other people accept her creation. Yes, she failed, she failed! They would not look at the beautiful, the valuable Hannah Mole: they saw the substance and disapproved of it and she did not blame them: it was what she would have done herself and in the one case when she had concentrated on the fine shadow presented to her, she had been mistaken.

She pushed past that thought with an increase of her pace and reached the wide thoroughfare where the tram-cars

9

clanged and swayed. Here she paused and looked about her. This part of Radstowe was a new growth, it was not the one of her affections, but on this autumn evening it had its beauty. The broad space made by the meeting of several roads was roughly framed in trees, for in Radstowe trees grew everywhere, as church spires seemed to spring up at every corner, and the electric light from tall standards cast a theatrical glare on the greens and browns and yellows of their leaves.

At Hannah's left hand, in a shrubbery of its own, there stood a building, in a debased Greek style, whither the Muses occasionally drew the people of Radstowe to a half-hearted worship. The darkness in which it was retired, suddenly illuminated by the head-lights of a passing car, dealt kindly with its faults, and there was mystery in its pale, pillared façade, a suggestion of sensitive aloofness in its withdrawal from the road. When Hannah passed this temple in the daytime, her long nose would twitch in derision at its false severity and the rusty-looking shrubs dedicated to its importance in the æsthetic life of Radstowe – had the gardener, she wondered, chosen laurels with any thought beyond their sturdiness? – but now it had an artificial charm for her: she could ignore the placards on the enclosing railings and see it as another example of the city's facility for happily mixing the incongruous.

She stood on the pavement, a thin, shabby figure, so insignificant in her old hat and coat, so forgetful of herself in her enjoyment of the scene, that she might have been wearing a cloak of invisibility, and while she watched the traffic and saw the moving tram-cars like magic-lantern slides, quick and coloured, no one who saw through that cloak would have suspected her power for transmuting what was common into what was rare and, in that occupation, keeping anxious thoughts at bay. To-night she could not keep them all at bay, for though she was pleased with her adventure and the speculations in which it permitted her to indulge, she was altruistically concerned for the other actors in it, and it would have obvious consequences for herself. Mrs. Widdows was not a lady to whom confidences could be made or who would accept excuses, and Hannah would presently find herself without a situation. It was a familiar experience but, in this case, her contempt would have to be assumed, and she made a rapid calculation of her savings, shrugged her shoulders and took a half-turn to the right. A cup of coffee and a bun would strengthen her for the encounter with her employer and, as she sipped and ate, she could pretend, once more, that her appearance belied her purse and that she was one of those odd, rich women who take a pleasure in looking poor. She was good at pretending and she thanked God sincerely that her self-esteem had enabled her to resist the effects of condescension, of the studied kindness which hurts proud spirits, the slyer variety she had encountered, in her youth, from men, when compliance and disdain were equally disastrous to her prosperity, the bullying of people uncertain of their authority, and the heartlessness of those who saw her as a machine set going at their order and unable to stop without another. Her independence had survived all this, and it was, as she knew but could not regret, her conviction of her dignity as a human being which, more than any of her faults, had been her misfortune, but it had its uses when she demanded a bun and a cup of coffee of young women who respected richer appetites, and she went on in this confidence, and with pleasure for though this street might have found itself at home in any city, she knew what lay beyond it and she treated herself as she would have treated a child who thinks it has been cheated of a promise: there was not much further to go, the surprise was close at hand, and when it came she rewarded herself with a long sigh of pleasure.

She stood at the top of a steep hill, lined with shops, edged with lamp-posts, and the shops and the lamp-posts seemed to be running, pell-mell, to the bottom, to meet and lose themselves in the blue mist lying there. Golden and russet trees were growing in the open space which the mist now enwrapped, their branches were spangled with the lights of still more lamps, and though the colours of the trees were hardly perceptible at that distance and in the increasing darkness, Hannah's memory could reinforce her sight and what she saw was like a fine painted screen for the cathedral of which the dark tower could be seen against a sky which looked pale by contrast. Whether the prospect was as lovely to others as to her she did not know, nor did it matter; the wonder of it was that her childish recollections had not deceived her. She had stood on that spot, for the first time, thirty years ago when, after a day's shopping, she and her parents had halted for a moment before they made their descent on their way to the station, and the lights, the mist, the trees peering through a magic lake of blue, had been no more fairy-like to her then than they were now. There were things, she told herself, that were imperishable, but she smiled as she remembered how her father had attributed the fairy blue to the damp rising from the river and how her mother had sighed at the downward jolt. For the small Hannah – and she pictured herself in her queer clothes and country-made boots, with her father, gnarled like one of his own apple trees on one side of her, and her mother, as rosy as the apples, on the other – it had been a journey of delight which suffered no diminishment, for no sooner had they reached the blue and lost, in gaining, it, than they turned a corner and were in the midst of a confusion as exciting as a circus, for here huge coloured tram-cars – and Hannah never lost her love for them – were gathered round a large triangle of paving, and when one monster, carefully controlled, glided away to the sound of a bell and the spluttering of sparks overhead, another would take its place, and the first would be seen growing smaller as it gathered speed and swaying in the pleasure of its own strength. There seemed no end to these leviathans, with their insides illuminated as, surely, that of Jonah's whale had never been, and when she was hustled into one of them, with pushings from both parents, before she had had her fill of gazing, she almost lost a glimpse of the masts and funnels of ships rising, as it seemed, from the street, and though she was to learn that here a river carried in a culvert met the water of the docks, knowledge, which spoils so much, had not deprived the young Hannah, or the mature one, of a recurring astonishment at the sight.

Much had changed in the city since those days. The steep street roared with ascending and purred with descending motor-cars; there were more people on the pavements

– where did they come from? Hannah asked, thinking of the declining birth-rate – but she did not resent their presence. A throng of people excited her with its reminder that each separate person had a claim on life, a demand to make of it as imperious as her own, and an obligation towards it, a thought that was both humiliating and enlivening. And she had no miserliness in her pleasures, no feeling that they were increased by being hidden. Involuntarily, she half flung out a hand as though she invited all these strangers to share with her the beauty spread out below, and it was with regret, but a pressing hunger, that she turned into a tea-shop a few paces down the street.

Chapter 2

AT this hour when it was too early for dinner and too late for tea, the shop was almost empty and a lady who was sitting in full view of the door and who started at Hannah's entry, immediately repressed all signs of dismay and resigned herself to the impossibility of avoiding recognition. She laid down her knife and fork while Hannah, on her part, advanced with every appearance of enthusiasm.

'Lilla! What luck!' she exclaimed loudly, and then chuckled contentedly as her eyes, which were not quite brown, or green, or grey, surveyed all that was visible of the seated figure. 'Just the same!' she murmured, and her large, amiable mouth was tilted at the corners. 'If I'd pictured how you'd look if I met you – but to tell the truth, Lilla, I haven't been thinking of you lately – I should have imagined you exactly as you are. That hat – so suitably autumnal, but not wintry –'

'For goodness' sake, sit down, Hannah, and lower your voice a little. What on earth are you doing here?'

Hannah sat down, and on the chair occupied by Mrs. Spenser-Smith's elegant monogrammed hand-bag, she placed her own shabby one, with a deliberate comparison of their values which made Lilla jerk her head irritably, but there was nothing envious in Hannah's expression when she looked up.

'And your coat!' she went on. 'It's wonderful how your tailor eliminates that tell-tale thickness at the back of the middle-aged neck. But perhaps you haven't got one. Anyhow, you look very nice and it's a pleasure to see you.'

Mrs. Spenser-Smith blinked these compliments aside and remarked, 'I thought you were in Bradford, or some place of that sort.'

'Not for years,' Hannah said, peering across the table at

14

Lilla's plate. 'What are you eating? And why? Have you caught the restaurant habit, or haven't you got a cook?'

'I've had the same cook for more than ten years,' Mrs. Spenser-Smith replied loftily.

'I call that very creditable,' Hannah said, beckoning to the waitress and ordering her coffee and bun. 'I wish you'd ask her how it's done.'

'By giving satisfaction,' Mrs. Spenser-Smith replied loftily.

'And getting it, I suppose,' Hannah sighed. 'Oh well! What you get on the swings, you lose on the roundabouts, and I'd rather have my experience than her character, for what, after all, can she do with it, except keep it? And it must be an awful responsibility. Worse than pearls, because you can't insure it.'

'On the contrary,' Mrs. Spenser-Smith began, but Hannah held up her hand.

'I know. I know all the moral maxims. It sounds so easy. But then, all employers are not like you, Lilla. This coffee smells very good, but alas, how small the bun appears! Yes, your servants are well fed, I haven't a doubt, and I'm sure their bedrooms are beyond reproach. You should see the one I'm occupying now! It's in the basement, among the beetles. The servant sleeps in the attic, safe from amorous policemen. Don't frown so anxiously, Lilla. I am obviously in no danger.' She sat back in her chair and shut her eyes. 'But I can hear the ships. I can hear the ships as they come hooting up the river. D'you know what nostalgia is? It's what I was suffering from when, as you put it, I was in "some place of that sort." So I spent some of my hard-earned –'

'Don't shout,' Mrs. Spenser-Smith begged.

'It doesn't matter. With your well-known charitable propensities, I shall only be taken for one of your hangers-on – which I may be yet, I warn you. I spent quite a lot of money on Nonconformist religious weeklies, and very nearly re-established my character by reading them ostentatiously. But it was the advertisements I was after. I wanted to be in Radstowe, and Radstowe, I knew, would proclaim its needs in the religious weeklies. I took the first offer, at a pittance, too late to see the lilacs and laburnums, but in time for what,

15

I'm sure, you call the autumn foliage, Lilla dear. And,' she added sadly, 'I shan't last until next spring and it was the spring I wanted, for to-night, as ever is, I fear I'm going to get the sack.'

Mrs. Spenser-Smith frowned again, and after an anxious exploring glance which, happily, lighted on no face she knew, she said sharply, 'And you sit here, eating cakes!'

Lifting her level eyebrows, Hannah looked with amusement at her plate, where there was a scattering of crumbs. 'I was always reckless,' she murmured, and then, with an air of being politely eager to shift the conversation from herself, she asked effusively, 'And how is Ernest? And how are the children? I should love to see the children!'

'They're at school,' said Mrs. Spenser-Smith, promptly putting an end to Hannah's hopes. 'Ernest, as usual, is quite well. He overworks, of course,' she added, between pride and resignation. 'And now, Hannah, what's this about losing your situation? And do tell me the truth – if you can. Who are you living with?'

'A tall, gaunt woman with a false hair-front. Dresses in black – I'm supposed to be mending her second best at this moment. Even her stays are black and they reach from her arm-pits to her knees. Wears black beads in memory of the departed and has his photograph, enlarged and tinted, on an easel in the drawing-room. Lives in Channing Square, name of Widdows. Prophetic! I suppose that's why he risked it.'

'Don't be vulgar, Hannah. I think jokes about marriage are in the very worst taste. Widdows? I've never heard of her.'

'Perhaps that's why she's so unpleasant,' Miss Mole said gently.

The robin-brightness of Mrs. Spenser-Smith's brown eyes was dimmed with disapproval. She was not stupid, though she chose to let Hannah think her so, and she said severely, 'According to you, Hannah, every employer you've ever had was objectionable.'

'Not all,' Hannah said quickly, 'but naturally, the ones I loved I lost – through no fault of my own. They were exceptional people. The others? Yes, what can you expect? It's the what-d'you-call-it of the position, and perhaps – it's a long chance but perhaps – there are people who find Mrs. Widdows lovable.'

'You don't adapt yourself,' Mrs. Spenser-Smith complained. 'It was the same at school. You were always kicking against authority. But you ought to have learnt sense by this time and if you leave this Mrs. Widdows, what are you going to do?'

'I don't know,' said Miss Mole, 'but I really think I'll have another bun. I've got a spare twopence-halfpenny in my pocket. I earned it – by sleight-of-hand. Yes, another of those excellent buns, please, and a curranty one. Doctors,' she informed Mrs. Spenser-Smith, 'tell us that currants have sustaining properties, and I badly need them. I don't know what I'm going to do and I'm not worrying about it much. I've got a whole month for making plans and I always enjoy the month I'm under notice. I feel so free and jolly, and there have been occasions when I've been asked to stay on, after all. Happiness,' she said, a slight oiliness in her tone, 'is a great power for good, is it not?'

'Tut!' said Mrs. Spenser-Smith. 'Don't try any of that with me! I know you too well.'

Miss Mole chuckled. 'But not so very well – in Radstowe. I've been careful of your reputation. I haven't told a soul that we're related. I didn't even put you to the inconvenience of letting you know I was here. You should give me credit for that. And if I'd said I was the cousin, once removed, of Mrs. Spenser-Smith, that old black cat might have been different, for, of course, everybody knows who you are! But there, I never think of myself!'

'If you'd been entirely penniless, it would have been much better for you,' Lilla pronounced distinctly. 'I suppose that house of yours is let?'

'House?' said Hannah. 'Oh, you mean my teeny-weeny cottage.'

'You get the rent from that, don't you?'

'I suppose so,' Hannah said, smiling oddly, 'but really, my money has such a trick of slipping through my fingers –'

'Then you can't go there, when you leave your situation.

17

You'd better eat humble pie, Hannah, for what's to become of you I don't know.'

'Well,' said Miss Mole in a drawl, 'it's just possible that I might find myself in your nice red and white house, and no later than to-morrow, for I may be dismissed without warning. In your nice house, behind the lace curtains and the geraniums and the gravel sweep, having my breakfast in bed, though I'm afraid my calico night-gowns might shock your housemaid.'

'I wear calico ones myself,' said Mrs. Spenser-Smith, putting the seal of her approval on them.

'But I don't suppose your housemaid does.'

'And breakfast in bed is not what you want, Hannah.'

'That's all you know about it,' Hannah said.

'What you want,' Lilla continued, 'is a place where you'll settle down and be useful, and if you're useful you'll be happy. Now, can't you make up your mind to please this Mrs. Widdows?'

'She doesn't want to be pleased. She's been longing for the moment when she could turn me out and find another victim, and now she's got it. And I'm not afraid of starving while I have a kind, rich cousin like you, dear. And an old school-fellow, too! What I want at my age, which is your own, is a little light work. In a house like yours, you can surely offer me that. You must want someone to arrange the flowers and sew the buttons on your gloves, and I shouldn't expect to appear at dinner when there's company. You wouldn't have to consider my feelings, because I haven't got any, and if the cook gave notice, I could cook, and if the parlourmaid gave notice, I should be tripping round the damask.'

'Yes, I daresay! And spilling the gravy on it! And, as it happens, my servants don't give notice. At the first sign of discontent, they're told to go.'

'That's the way to treat them!' Hannah cried encouragingly. 'But if they fell ill, Lilla,' – she leant forward coaxingly, 'think what a comfort I should be to you! And you know, Ernest had always a soft spot in his heart for me.'

'Yes,' said Lilla, 'Ernest's soft spots are often highly inconvenient. To-day, for instance, when I wanted the car to take me home after a busy afternoon, he chooses to lend it to someone else. I have to be at the chapel this evening for the Literary Society Meeting and I should be worn out if I made two journeys across the Downs beforehand.'

'Good for your figure,' Hannah said. 'The time may come when your tailor won't be able to cope with it. So that's why you're dining out. I should like to see you at the Literary Meeting, trying not to yawn. What's the subject?'

'Charles Lamb.'

'Hardy annual,' Hannah muttered, twitching her nose.

'It's a duty,' Mrs. Spenser-Smith said patiently, yet with a touch of grandeur. 'I'd much rather stay at home with a nice book, but these things have to be supported, for the sake of the young people.'

'Ah yes, but it isn't the young people who go to them. It's the old girls, like myself, who have nothing else to do. I've seen them, sitting on the hard benches, half asleep, like fowls gone to roost.'

'They'll go to sleep to-night,' Lilla admitted, 'though,' she added as she remembered to keep Hannah in her place, 'I don't see why you should try to be funny at their expense. Trying to be funny is one of your failings.'

Miss Mole answered meekly. 'I know I ought never to see a joke unless my superiors make one, and then I've got to be convulsed with admiring merriment. I've no right to a will nor an opinion of my own, but somehow – I'm that contrary! – I insist on laughing when I'm amused and exercising my poor intelligence. Let me come with you to-night, Lilla, and I might make a speech.'

'You might make a fool of yourself,' said Mrs. Spenser-Smith, picking up her modestly rich fur necklet and settling it at her throat. 'Go back to Channing Square, at once, and do, for goodness' sake, try to see which side your bread is buttered. And, in any case, Mr. Blenkinsop's lecture wouldn't entertain you. He's rather a dull young man. What's the matter?' she asked, for Hannah had put down the bun she was lifting towards her mouth and the mouth remained open.

'Such a funny name!' Hannah murmured. She leaned
19

back and folded her hands on her lap. 'I like to co-ordinate – or whatever the word is – my impressions with other people's facts. Now, that name. I should have suspected its owner of being a dull young man, a rather owlish young man, with a Biblical Christian name. Am I right?'

'His name is Samuel,' said Mrs. Spenser-Smith, impatient with this topic.

'And he's a member of your chapel?'

'Not a very worthy one, I'm sorry to say. He's highly irregular.'

Now Hannah leaned forward, her eyes sparkling. 'You're not going to tell me he's a bit of a rake?'

The droop of Mrs. Spenser-Smith's eyelids effaced a world which had any acquaintance with rakes. 'Irregular in his attendance on Sundays,' she said coldly.

'That upsets one of my theories, but it's interesting. Are you going, Lilla? Try to find a corner for me in your red and white house. I've been past it several times. I like the colour scheme. The conjunction of the yellow gravel with the geraniums –'

'The geraniums are over,' Lilla said, 'and what colour do you expect gravel to be? I shall ask Ernest if he knows of any suitable post for you.'

'Ernest's reply will be obvious. You'd better not ask him.'

'And then I'll write to you.'

'Don't bother, don't bother,' Miss Mole said airily. 'I'll come to tea one afternoon. These,' she smiled maliciously, 'are not my best clothes – but very nearly. My shoes, however,' she thrust out a surprisingly elegant foot, 'will always stand inspection.'

Mrs. Spenser-Smith gave an unwilling, downward glance. 'Absurd!' she said. 'You've no sense of proportion.'

'Yet I risked this one,' Hannah pointed to her right foot, 'without a thought for its beauty. Fortunately, it's hardly scratched.' She looked up, her face rejuvenated by mischief. 'I broke a window with it, Lilla.'

Incredulity struggled with curiosity in Mrs. Spenser-Smith, and curiosity with her determination to deny Hannah the pleasure of thinking herself interesting. 'Pooh!' she said lightly, and then her unpractised imagination took a clumsy flight. 'You don't mean to tell me that woman had locked you out of the house?'

'I don't mean to tell you anything,' Miss Mole said sweetly, and with the smile on her lips she watched her cousin's admirable exit which was designed to show the increasing number of people in the shop that she was of very different quality from that of the person she left behind her.

Chapter 3

ALL over Upper Radstowe, in late spring-time, the pavements are strewn with flecks of colour, as though there had been a wedding in every house, for petals of pink and white, purple and yellow, lie there, dropped as a benison on the approach of summer. Before this, urged by the warm rain, the trees open their new leaves slowly, carefully unwrapping the yearly surprise which never grows stale, and the flowers which come afterwards are like happy laughter at its success. The dropping of the petals has a gracious resignation in it, for, without them, the smaller flowering trees have lost their beauty for the year; their greenness is merged into the general greenness of the summer and they have no splendour to offer autumn. Miss Mole had missed the spring in Radstowe, she had missed the almond blossom – a faint pink against a bright blue sky or rosy against a grey one – she had missed the lilacs and laburnums and the double cherry, the tall tulips in the gardens and the consciousness that, across the river, primroses were growing on grassy banks; she had seen the summer and made the best of the only season she did not care for, and here was autumn, prodigal of its gold and bronze, and there were moments when she renounced her allegiance to the spring or, rather, yoked with it a new allegiance to the autumn which was responsible for spring's increase. In spring she knew that something both exciting and beautiful would happen with each day while her pleasure in the autumn was as much anticipatory as immediate. Like a man gloating over the wine bottles with which he means to stock his cellar, enjoying the variations in the shapes and sizes of the bottles and the colours of their contents, but looking forward to the day of the wine's maturity, Hannah watched the big trees in this time of their brilliance, and with a contentment which was

22

not of the eye alone, saw it lying in heaps at their feet. She was a farmer's daughter; she had a feeling for the earth and liked to see it nourished, and though she had been dowered with a constant desire for beauty, and found it sufficient in itself, there was an added satisfaction in knowing it was feeding what it came from, and so, when she wandered about Upper Radstowe that October, finding unexpected little streets, paved lanes and winding paths or flights of steps, leading from the Upper to the Lower Radstowe; when she strolled down the long Avenue where, on one side, well set back from the road, there were large houses screened by one row of the elms, and on the other, screened by the opposing row, a stretch of tree-laden grass ending in a cliff which bound the river; when she walked on the Downs dotted with well-grown hawthorn bushes which were almost insignificant in that expanse, where the sense of the river, out of sight, was always present and the voices of the ships came with challenge or complaint, she could feel that while her own affairs were in a sad condition, those of the earth were doing well and beautifully.

Until she was fourteen years old, she had only seen Radstowe in snatches of a day, when her parents had business in the city and allowed her to accompany them, and there had been torture as well as pleasure in the expeditions, for her father would linger at the cattle market and her mother spend an unreasonable time in the shops. It was maddening to know that there were intricate miles of river and docks to be explored, ferry-boats awaiting her at the cost of a half-penny a journey, broad bridges spanning the water, narrow ones, without railings, across the locks, big ships with sacks of flour sliding into their holds, slow-moving cranes dangling their burdens with apparent unwillingness to let them go; it was maddening to see these things only in glimpses or in a desperate sally from which she was recalled by the anxiety of her mother or the anger of her father and by her own premature knowledge that these two were, in effect, younger than she was and must not be distressed. In a vague way, she was always sorry for them: there must have been a few years during which they represented authority and wisdom, but, within her memory, they were a little pathetic in their

23

slowness and in their silences which were only broken for the utterance of what they thought were facts, and physically they seemed very old – they were both in middle life when Hannah was born – while she could afford to postpone her explorations.

This capacity for waiting and believing that the good things were surely approaching had served Hannah very well through a life which most people would have found dull and disappointing. She refused to see it so: it would have been treachery to herself. Her life was almost her only possession and she was as tender with it as a mother with a defective child: there was no doubt it would improve, the big miracle would happen and, meanwhile, there were the smaller ones such as this chance to rove at her will through Upper Radstowe, to cross the suspension bridge and reach the woods covering the high banks on the southern side of the river, or to go further afield – and Mrs. Gibson was astonished at her energy – and find the real country where the wind smelt of apples and damp moss. It was the first such chance she had had, for though, in her fifteenth year, she had been sent to school in Upper Radstowe, her excursions were necessarily restricted and never solitary, but she learnt to love the place and she kept her childish wonder, she grew familiar with the colours of the changing seasons, she accepted the frequent rain without resentment and she could never be grateful enough for that spasm of emulation which had induced her father to send his Hannah to school with his rich cousin's Lilla. In doing this he outraged his belief that what he called a fancy education was a stumbling-block to a plain farmer's daughter, he stretched his resources further than they would easily go and Hannah had often wondered what obscure antagonism had flowered in so unlikely a manner and with such advantage to herself. It was the one impulsive action she remembered in a man as little given to eccentricity as one of his own turnips, but she had seen turnips grown to odd shapes, and something comparable to these distortions had happened in the case of Farmer Mole. She had stayed at the school until she was eighteen, for she was not to leave a day before Lilla did, and this was an extravagance which, she suspected, gave her father a grim pleasure, while it set her mother clucking over the continued difficulties of Hannah's wardrobe. How was she to have a dress for the dancing class, another for Sundays and still another for afternoons unless Mrs. Mole, with the help of the village dressmaker, could alter some of her own clothes? Fortunately, in the days when she was married, materials were made to last, and among the strange gar- ments Hannah took to school were a black watered silk, a prune-coloured merino, and a delaine patterned with large pansies. They lasted a long time, and as Hannah remained thin, though she grew to a moderate height, and her mother's wedding garments were voluminous, there was always enough stuff with which to lengthen the dresses: they suffered strange partnerships, separations and reunions: they were a thorn in the flesh they covered, but Hannah was never seen to wince. It was Lilla who did that and Hannah enjoyed seeing her do it, yet she had an amused affection for this cousin who had such an air of dignity and importance, such a fixed view of what was proper, even in her teens. With her sanguine colour and her bright eyes, for which she had an evident admiration, with the clothes which were too rich and fashionable for a school-girl, and her slight pomposity, Lilla was as ludicrous to Hannah as was Hannah's appearance to everybody else. But the offen- sive laughter of these convention-ridden young people stopped there. She saw to it that they should laugh at the rest of her only if she chose, and now, when she was nearly forty, she could appreciate the cleverness – she would not call it courage – which she had shown at fourteen, in per- suading scoffers that those dreadful clothes were the symbol of her high difference from themselves.

Hannah often walked past the plain-fronted white house from which the sound of piano practice still came in the strange, discordant, yet satisfying jumble which gave her a glorious sense of liberty. She had soon been released from the bondage of her own hopeless efforts, and when she heard scales tripping lightly from one direction, stumbling and starting again from another, while The Merry Peasant took advantage of the pauses, or the Rachmaninoff Prelude assured him he was of no importance, she tasted again an exquisite pleasure of her youth. It was a house which just missed character. It stood four stories high in the middle, there was a lower wing at each side and a walled garden encompassed it. At the front there was a wrought-iron gate for visitors and mistresses and, at the back, a door for everybody else, but the glory of the gate had departed: it was rusty and needed paint, and the house itself was shabby. The houses in Upper Radstowe had a way of growing shabby and when Hannah stood at the gate, peering in, she fancied that thus the ghosts of the eighteenth century must stand and look at their fine houses going to decay, let out in flats, with the gathered perambulators and bicycles of the inhabitants cumbering the stately entrance-halls. No doubt they found a mournful enjoyment in their memories and exalted them, and the difference between those ghosts and Hannah was that she had a present which did not suffer from comparison with the past. She had no illusions about the wonderful happiness or the misunderstood misery of her girlhood: she had been alive and interested then, as she was now, and if the possibilities of her future were limited by the exigencies of time, this limitation had its value, since what was going to happen must be nearer than it had ever been before. She must be within shouting distance of the rich old gentleman who was going to leave her a fortune, or the moderately rich one who would leave her a competency. Again, lessening her demands of Fortune, she might meet, at any turn of the road, the perfect employer who would appreciate Hannah Mole and keep her as a friend of the family when the need for her services was past and who, to the brief announcement in *The Times* of Hannah's death, would add a little tribute of affection. She would be the confidante of the young people as they grew up, the wise and humorous counsellor.

She roused herself from these visions which were passing across the discoloured front of her old school. She was on her way to visit Lilla and she must at least pretend to be practical, she must concoct the mixture of truth and falsehood suitable to that lady's palate. A week had passed since their meeting in the tea-shop and for all but a few hours of that week she had been lodged in Mrs. Gibson's house, she

26

had been under the same roof as Mr. Samuel Blenkinsop. That would have to be explained and Hannah neither wished nor intended to tell the truth. It involved the private affairs of other people and it was always pleasant to deceive Lilla and to tease her. Moreover, it was doubtful whether the truth would appear to her as probable. She would merely tell Hannah to edit her stories more carefully. And truth, after all, was a relative good: it had to be adulterated and adapted, like a drug, to the constitution of each individual, and Hannah would describe neither her first nor her second visit to the house in Prince's Road.

She had called there after meeting Lilla, and the little maid in her large cap, who still showed signs of her agitation earlier in the evening, had led her into Mrs. Gibson's comfortable presence. Mrs. Gibson's anxieties were incapable of disturbing a basic serenity compounded of mental sluggishness, good nature and physical well-being, and though she was still somewhat shaken, she was in no danger of collapse. She was glad to see Hannah again. Everything was going on as well as could be expected, but Mr. Blenkinsop was upset, and a chat was just what she needed.

'And why should Mr. Blenkinsop be upset?' Hannah demanded. 'He hasn't tried to kill himself and he isn't married to a man who has! He isn't the baby of an unsuccessful suicide! He ought to count his blessings – and I'm one of them. If it hadn't been for me –'

'I know!' said Mrs. Gibson. 'So quick, you were, too! And how you ever thought of breaking the window – But there, Mr. Blenkinsop is very respectable and he was always against me letting the basement as a flat. He said we'd get undesirables, and there,' Mrs. Gibson pointed downwards, 'sure enough, they are.'

'If it hadn't been for me,' Hannah persisted, 'there would have been an inquest. How would Mr. Blenkinsop have liked that? I'm no more used to suicides than he is –'

'Certainly not!' Mrs. Gibson said courteously.

'But I tried to give Mrs. Ridding the impression that there was nothing unusual about it. It was the least one could do, but much more than he did.'

'It was a pity he came along when he did,' Mrs. Gibson

27

sighed. 'It's true I was looking out for him. It was either him or a policeman, until you bumped into me, and then I'm sure there was no need for anybody else. I'd been shouting myself hoarse through the keyhole, but what was the use of that when he'd locked the door on the inside? And that poor young thing! And the baby crying! Dear, dear! Well, let's hope it will be a lesson to him. He's in bed now and I'm going to coax her up here for a bit of supper.'

'And what will Mr. Blenkinsop say to that?'

'I'm hoping he won't find out,' Mrs. Gibson replied simply. 'When he settled down here after his mother died, he hoped I'd see my way to keeping other lodgers out. He pays well, but I made no promise. I like a bit of company.'

'Then,' said Hannah, 'will you take me in to-morrow? I can't pay like Mr. Blenkinsop, but I promise not to put my head in a gas oven. It may be for a few days, or a few weeks. I don't know. I shall be out of a situation.'

'Why,' said Mrs. Gibson, mildly astonished, 'I thought you must be a lady with an independence.'

'Plenty of independence, but it doesn't fill my pockets.'

'Well I never!' Mrs. Gibson exclaimed. 'You see, I noticed your shoes. I was always rather noticing. And then, with you being so prompt and managing – but still, I do admit, it's comfortable to know you're one more like myself.'

Chapter 4

THIS was the story which had to be re-arranged for Lilla's benefit, but Hannah trusted to the inspiration of the moment and wasted no time which could be spent on the beauty of the October day. The sun shone with the peculiar brightness of autumn and, in passing through the trees and gilding them, it seemed to borrow as it gave and strike the heaps of fallen leaves with added strength. The streets had the white, swept appearance given by the east wind, chimneys and roofs made sharp lines on the blue sky, and sounds of voices, footsteps, cars and carts and horses, had an unusual resonance. Michaelmas daisies and dahlias flowered in the gardens, there were berries on the rowan trees, the world seemed to be flying every flag it had, and, when Hannah crossed The Green, the fall of a chestnut sounded stealthy, as though its descent were a little shameful in the general glory. It lay among the leaves, a glossy roan, bursting from its green, spiked shell, and she stooped to pick it up, but left it lying there. When the children came out of school one of them would find it and, for her, to remember the feeling of that polished ball was just as good as to handle it. Indeed, she thought, it was better, for the good thing remembered or hoped for had a blessed superiority over the thing grasped, and she fancied that God, finding the decent order of his plans upset by the wilfulness of the creatures for whom He made them, had been tenderly inspired with this idea of compensation.

'And a good thing, too!' she muttered, glancing at the clock on the otherwise conscientiously Early English Church.

There was no time to go round the hill and look at the river: she must go down Chatterton Street, which had a turning into Channing Square, and risk encountering Mrs. Widdows. The risk was not great. She would be dozing,

29

poor thing, over the fire in the stuffy little sitting-room, while the woman she had dismissed with contumely – that was a good word, though Hannah was never sure how to pronounce it – was taking a part in this fine pageant. She realized that her contribution was purely spiritual: there was nothing ornamental in her appearance and her clothes were always of a useful shade, but she held up her head and walked briskly, enjoying the snap of twigs and the sibilance of leaves under her feet.

The narrow road she was following widened at its juncture with several others. The Avenue was stately on her left hand, another road, shaded by trees, came curling up from the river: on her right, a broader one skirted that edge of the Downs which she could reach by the short ascent in front of her, and the ends of all these roads were held together, as in a knot, by a drinking-fountain for men and beasts.

It was hard to believe that the big, sprawling city was so near. This was a place for leisure, for genteel strolling, for long crocodiles of school-girls who must partake of the elegant beauties of nature among their other forms of nourishment, and ladies in small bonnets and bustles should have been walking under the trees. Here there was no impingement of new on old or of shabbiness on prosperity, and Hannah would have felt less affection for this part of Upper Radstowe, lovely as the trees made it, if it had not grown out of the older one and if she had not known that her own country, wild under its demureness, grey-rocked under its springy turf, lay just across the water.

The Downs were not the country, but they came as near it as they could. They stretched away, almost out of sight, rimmed by distant roads and houses on all sides but the cliffed one, and great trees as well as hawthorn bushes grew there. A double row of elms marched straight towards Lilla's house and, as Hannah walked in their dappled shadows, she heard the thud of hooves and the creak of leather and the jingle of steel, and it seemed to fit the mixed character of the Downs that these riders should be on hired horses, that the sheep, industriously nibbling, should have dirty fleeces, and that voices thick with the Radstowe burr should come from the throats of youths kicking a football. But always, even, it seemed to Hannah, when it rained, the clouds sailed higher over that part of the world than elsewhere, and she had heard Lilla say that, except on Saturdays and Sundays, the view from her windows had almost the appearance of a private park. Unfortunately, Lilla's house, which was already discernible as a red and white blot beyond the trees, could not be mistaken for one of England's stately homes. It had been built for Ernest's father towards the end of his life, and the attempt to produce something like a small Elizabethan manor house had been frustrated by his determination that there should be no misunderstanding about its origin, and below the flat gables of the top story, bow windows and a porch bulged on the ground floor; the tiles were the reddest procurable and white stucco concealed the bricks. The garden was separated from the road by its own width of greensward guarded by posts and chains, and this indication that the Spenser-Smiths had more than enough garden to spare was callously interpreted by urchins as an invitation to swing on the chains. Even Lilla's ointment had a fly in it, Hannah thought, beaming on a culprit who had expected a frown, and she blinked affectedly, for her own amusement, when she opened the gate and met the full glare of white and red and yellow under the sunshine.

The doorstep was spotless, the knocker gleamed, potted chrysanthemums were arranged in tiers in the porch, and Hannah had her nose against a flower and was savouring its sweet bitterness, when the door opened. From the parlour-maid's point of view, this was a bad beginning, and either in punishment or on her quick estimate of this caller's place in the world, she took Hannah to a small room which had a feeling of not being lived in. Here the humble and the suppliant sat on the edges of the chairs; here were kept the books which were not obviously the right ones for the Spenser-Smiths to possess. The classics, Hannah guessed, were displayed somewhere to advantage, and these were the pickings from book-stalls, children's books and those by writers of whose eminence and respectability Lilla was not assured.

Hannah took down a volume and prepared to wait, but Lilla, apparently, was anxious to know the worst as soon as possible, and after tactfully showing annoyance that Hannah should have been left in a room without a fire, she took her cousin into a drawing-room bright with gay cretonne, a wood fire and sunshine, and asked cheerfully if this were her free afternoon.

'Well, yes, as you might say and in a manner of speaking, it is. And a very nice afternoon, too. It will help us through the winter, as they always say. And this is a very nice room. You see, Lilla, all's right with my world.'

'I'm very glad to hear it,' Mrs. Spenser-Smith said with reserve. She had had some experience of Hannah's high spirits. 'Are you going to stay to tea?'

'If you press me like that, dear, of course I will. Time exists for me no longer, unless I'm hungry, and there are ways of misleading one's stomach. By staying in bed till ten o'clock, I can manage on a cup of tea till the middle of the day; you're giving me a free meal and I shall be in bed with a book before the pangs begin again.'

'For goodness' sake,' said Lilla, who had rung the bell, 'don't talk any of your nonsense while Maud's bringing in the tea. And afterwards, you'd better tell me what you mean by it.'

'I mean,' said Hannah, when the ban of silence was removed, 'that I'm resting at present, as we say on the stage. Remark the pronoun, Lilla. I was on the stage once, you know. In a crowd. And they let me wear my own clothes!'

'Then, if I were you,' said Lilla, 'I should be careful not to mention it. How you could do it! But I don't suppose you really did. And true or not, if you say things like that, what's going to become of you?'

'It was a virtuous crowd,' Hannah said meekly. 'We were all booing a bad man. You can't ask more than that. I booed for a week and they picked up another shabby female in the next town.'

'I don't want to hear about it,' Lilla said. 'For your own sake, you'd better not tell me what you know I shan't approve of.'

'Ah,' said Hannah, 'what's your little scheme?'

32

Lilla tightened her lips. 'I don't know that I'm justified in having one.'

'That doesn't matter in the least, dear.'

'It matters to me,' she said, and then, with a quick change from the noble to the practical, she asked sharply, 'Did you get a month's wages?'

A little shamefaced, Hannah nodded her head. 'I did. I managed to be unbearably irritating without being actually rude, so she could neither keep nor rob me. It took some doing, I can tell you. And I was longing to be rude – personally abusive, you know – but there, I don't suppose you do; you're so genteel.'

Lilla pushed a cushion behind her back, wreaking on the impassivity of down the annoyance which would have made as little permanent impression on Hannah. 'And where are you staying now? You didn't go the same night, I suppose?'

'No. The next morning – in a cab.' She spoke slowly and her eyes had the fixity of careful thought. 'A horse cab, with a beery, bottle-nosed old man on the box.'

'I don't want details.'

'They're part of the story, and old bottle-nose is the knight-errant. It's a pity his type is dying out. They know a lot about life, those old men, and I like them. They always believe the worst and they don't mind a bit. He knew what had happened at once and I'm sorry to tell you that he winked at me. No, I didn't wink back, but I let him know that I knew how, and then I told him I wanted some cheap lodgings and he said he knew the very place for me. And so he did. He took me to a house in Prince's Road, quite near your place of worship, dear, and I'm sure you'll feel quite happy about me because Mrs. Gibson is a member of the congregation. I would have let you know sooner, but I've been so busy in the free library, looking at the advertisements.'

'Nothing,' said Lilla after a pause, 'could have been more unfortunate.'

'Why? I call it very lucky. Only a pound a week for a bed-sitting-room, a shilling in the slot for the gas fire, and a share of Mrs. Gibson's dinner for practically nothing. She's

33

far too generous, but I try to help her and she says she finds my conversation very bright.'

'Most unfortunate!' Lilla repeated. 'And why that cabman should have taken you to one of the houses I should have wished you to avoid, is more than I can understand.'

'It seems quite respectable,' Hannah murmured. 'Mr. Blenkinsop lives there, you know.'

'Of course I know it! But I suppose you don't see much of him?'

'As much as I can,' Hannah answered cheerfully. 'But he's rather a shy bird. And if you're worrying about what I've told these people, you can set your mind at rest. The name of Spenser-Smith has never passed my lips. Mrs. Gibson wouldn't feel at ease with me if she knew I had such grand connections.'

Lilla assumed the expression with which she tried to counter Hannah's attacks. It was almost, but not quite, blank. She gave the cushion another push and said, 'I was thinking of this silly way of talking about theatres. It doesn't do, Hannah. It may be bright,' she made the word astonishingly acid, 'but it will be remembered against you. The fact is – mind, I'm not sure about it, but I do want you to be careful – there's a chance that I can get you a post as Mr. Corder's housekeeper.'

'Who's he? Oh, I know. The minister. Does he want one?'

'No,' said Lilla, compressing her lips again, 'but I think he ought to have one.'

'Then he's doomed,' said Hannah. 'Thank you, Lilla. I take this very kind. What's the salary?'

'Nothing's settled. You mustn't count on it. Mr. Corder is a widower and he's talking it over with his daughter.'

'Oh, he's got a daughter.'

'Two,' said Lilla. 'Ruth is still at school and somebody ought to look after her. The other night at the Literary meeting –'

'Was Mr. Blenkinsop amusing?' Hannah interpolated.

'No. He didn't seem to be thinking about what he was saying.'

'No wonder!' Hannah murmured. 'But go on, dear, go on. At the Literary meeting –?'

34

'Ruth had a large hole in her stocking. It looks so bad. Ethel's useless, she's always at the Mission, and I've been thinking for some time that they ought to have a responsible woman in the house. There's only a skimpy little servant and there's a young man cousin who lives with them – Mr. Corder's son is at Oxford and, between you and me, Hannah, I make that possible – and I don't think it's quite nice, but I wasn't going to suggest anything until I could recommend somebody. There are plenty of women in the chapel who would jump at the chance, but I was fond of Mrs. Corder –'

'Say no more, dear!' Hannah exclaimed. 'I understand it all! You want a good, solid sand-bag to fill up the gap; you want a watchdog, of no breed or beauty, but warranted to bark; your affection for the poor woman's memory is stronger than his and you're not going to let him forget her altogether. Quite right!' Hannah's thin, odd face was glowing, her eyes, greener than usual, shone. 'It's not complimentary to me, but it's magnificent and I'll bark like fury. And they say women are not loyal to each other! Why, already I feel like a sister to Mrs. What's-her-name myself!'

'Don't be ridiculous,' said Mrs. Spenser-Smith. 'I liked Mrs. Corder well enough. She was rather a nonentity, compared with him, poor little woman, but I believe she did her best, and when I see that Patsy Withers making eyes at him –'

'I'll remember the name,' Hannah said.

'You haven't got the post yet,' Lilla said sharply, 'and I don't believe you're really fit for it. I've stretched a point, Hannah. I don't suppose you could produce a written character which Mr. Corder would look at twice, and goodness knows what you've been doing all these years, and if you go, I do hope you'll remember that I've practically guaranteed you. And, by the way, I've said nothing about our relationship. I thought it wouldn't be fair to either of you. I want you to go there on your own merits. I mentioned this to Ernest and he quite agrees.'

Hannah smiled with pleasant maliciousness and said nothing, but she gave the impression of being ready to say a good deal and Lilla went on hastily. 'I'll let you know what happens. I shall see him at the week-night service.'

'But won't he want to see me?'

'Not necessary,' said Mrs. Spenser-Smith in her best Spenser-Smithian manner.

'Not advisable, you mean! I daresay you're right. What sort of man is he? Is he brisk and hearty, or one of those gentle paw-folders?'

'That isn't funny, Hannah, it's vulgar; I might say irreverent. Do try to remember you're a lady.'

'But I'm not. I come of the same stock as you do, Lilla, and we know what that is. Simple yeoman stock, and my father often dropped his aitches and so did yours. I know you don't like remembering it, but there's the fact. I happened to be educated above my station – though you, of course, were not! – and there are times when I revert – revert, Lilla! But I'll try to behave myself and I'll keep my eye on Patsy. Thank you for the tea, and now I'll go back to Mrs. Gibson and cobble up some of my underclothes, though I hope they'll be a matter of indifference to the Reverend Corder.'

'There you are again!' Lilla said with a sigh, and she offered her cool, rosy face to be kissed.

'It's only a bit of fun between us girls!' Hannah cried, and as she brushed her cheek against her cousin's, she added, 'You're a good soul, Lilla. I always liked you.'

'Oh, go along with you,' Lilla said good-naturedly, and gently urged her to the door. There was no knowing what generous foolishness Ernest would commit, if he found her in the house when he came home.

Chapter 5

THE wind had risen strongly as night came on and Hannah crossed the Downs under swaying branches and swirling leaves. The football-players, the riders, the children had all gone home; lamps edged the roads, but, where Hannah walked under the elms, there was a stormy darkness. The branches creaked lugubriously or with shrill protest, and those which still kept their leaves were like great flails, threshing the winds, maddened by their sterile efforts, for it was the wind, threshing harder, that produced the harvest, whipping it from the trees and driving it before him. Hannah was driven, too; a wisp of a woman, exhilarated by the noise and the buffeting. Lilla's comfortable, bright room seemed unreal to her, Mr. Corder was the invention of an idle moment and Hannah Mole had no past, no future, only this breathless present when the wind would have had her go westwards and she was making for the south. For ten minutes or a quarter of an hour, until she reached lower ground and the shelter of the streets, where the wind did its best with the trees in the gardens but found their weaker resistance a dull affair, she had that freedom from care which is the reward of exciting physical effort; but in the comparative quiet of Chatterton Road she became conscious of the self which needed money for food and clothing and, absurdly, she saw it handed to her by Mr. Corder on one of his own offertory plates. She shook her head and made a grimace of refusal. She had a prejudice against Nonconformist ministers, she pictured Mr. Corder according to the pattern in her mind, ignorantly unctuous, pretending to a humility which was patently absent, and she had a moment of rebellion. She could see herself clearly enough with other people's eyes: she was drab, she was nearing, if she had not reached, middle-age, she bore the stamp of a

37

woman who had always worked against the grain, she was, in fact, the ideal housekeeper for Mr. Corder. She admitted that no one sitting in his dining-room and mending his woven underwear at a table with a rusty little fern in the middle of a green serge cloth, could look more suitable than Hannah Mole. Who would suspect her of a sense of fun and irony, of a passionate love for beauty and the power to drag it from its hidden places? Who could imagine that Miss Mole had pictured herself, at different times, as an explorer in strange lands, as a lady wrapped in luxury and delicate garments, as the mother of adorably naughty children and the inspiringly elusive mistress of a poet? She could turn up her own long nose at these fanciful excursions, without convincing herself of their improbability. The desires, the energy, the gaiety were there, but they were ruled by an ironic conception of herself which did not seem inconsistent and which was also the armour she assumed against the world when it was not willing to be friendly. And, after all, as she told herself, quelling her useless rebellion, the things she wanted, if she had them, would soon turn into those she wanted no longer and – here was God's happy idea of compensation again – she found a wealth of amusement in going about disguised, while because her clear-sightedness was not kept entirely for the weaknesses of others, she had to own that she who had been a failure in the lot forced on her, was not likely to be a success in any one she chose. She was a vagrant and with the vagrant's advantages, the readiness to move on, the carelessness of possessions, she had to support the inconvenience of being moved on before she was ready to go and of finding herself poorer than was comfortable. Now both these conditions had befallen her. Few things, she thought at that moment, could be more distasteful than leaving the house, where she was treated as a friend, where she had a sly, lazy pleasure in listening to Mrs. Gibson's platitudes and a keener one in discomfiting Mr. Blenkinsop by waylaying him on the stairs and forcing him into conversation; a house which she could leave at her caprice for a saunter round Upper Radstowe or a long walk on the other side of the river, to which she could return with the certainty of a welcome, and she must resign all this for the

38

sake of mending Mr. Corder's daughter's stockings and keeping herself fed and clad.

Yet it was better to be Hannah Mole than to be Lilla who could see herself as one person only, and that was Mrs. Spenser-Smith, who had never broken a basement window to save a man from gas poisoning, dragged him from the neighbourhood of the oven, and then consoled the baby who was crying, neglected, in his perambulator: better than to be poor little Mrs. Ridding with that strange look on her face. It was the look, Hannah thought, of someone who had braced herself for approaching an inevitable catastrophe and seen its postponement with despair. The look had no more than flashed across her face but Hannah had seen it and she could recall it plainly now, in the darkness. 'Oh, for money!' Hannah moaned, not thinking of herself. Money could cause neurotics to be cured or, if it failed in that, it could enable a young widow to bring up her boy, and Hannah began to desire it passionately. She had heard Lilla speak with grand disparagement of it, but that was just what Lilla, who had always had it, would take care to do. Money was one of the best things in the world, used properly, used by Miss Hannah Mole, and all the way down Prince's Road she was buying annuities for people like herself, settling some thousands of pounds on Mrs. Ridding, and sending people Christmas cards and valentines in the shape of five-pound notes.

When she reached Mrs. Gibson's house she saw a light in the basement kitchen and, through the mended window, which was open, she could hear Mrs. Ridding singing. Hannah's big mouth drooped. She heard that singing every morning before Mr. Ridding went to work and every evening when he came home, but never at any other time of day, and it hurt her that anyone so young should be so unhappy and so brave. She was ashamed of her own discontent and her concentration on herself. What happened to her, who had lived more than half her life and had some fun in it and, yes, one mad, romantic interlude, was of very little importance now, but Mrs. Ridding was a girl and Hannah's large, erratic heart was aching for her. And there was nothing she could do. Her funds of advice – which she

39

did not take herself – of drollery, of encouragement, were of no use, for Mrs. Ridding was very bright and cold with the witnesses of that sordid scene in the basement, even with the woman who had comforted and bathed the baby. Hannah wished she could bath the baby again. Mrs. Gibson had been much impressed by her handling of him; Mrs. Gibson, in fact, admired everything Hannah did, and perhaps it would be salutary for her to live with a man who was much more likely to admire what he did himself.

Hannah turned the lock with the latchkey Mrs. Gibson lent her and found Mr. Blenkinsop hanging up his hat in the hall.

'Oh, good evening, Mr. Blenkinsop!' she exclaimed girlishly. 'You're rather late, aren't you?'

Mr. Blenkinsop looked at her severely through his spectacles. 'Purposely,' he remarked significantly, and stood aside to let her pass up the stairs before him.

Hannah went ahead meekly. She had not yet found the manner to which Mr. Blenkinsop would respond. She had tried to deepen the impression which her prowess in the basement kitchen must have made on him, she had hinted that she, too, had an interest in literature and Charles Lamb; she had asked foolish feminine questions about banking, which was Mr. Blenkinsop's profession, but nothing stirred him. He remained grave, solid, and as monosyllabic as language and bare courtesy would allow.

'Sickening!' she said to herself, straightening her back, for she knew that the view, from below, of a woman ascending the stairs is often unfortunate, but when she had turned on the light in her room and looked at her reflection, she forgave him, though she had not done with him yet. Mr. Blenkinsop was clearly not a reader of character or a connoisseur of human rarities, and there was no reason why he should encourage the attentions of this woman with the satirical nose, a rather sallow skin and eyes of no particular colour, yet she felt as uneasy as a soldier in a hostile country who has left an unconquered fortified place behind him. She wished she had introduced the subject of Mr. Corder; that might have roused him and instructed her at the same time. Forewarned was forearmed and Mrs. Gibson's views

40

would be of no value. To her, all reverend gentlemen were good and most of them were awful; they were like the stars; they shed their light, but they were unapproachable. However, though there was no doubt about what she would say, her way of saying it might be amusing, and when Hannah had changed her outdoor dress for an old silk one which looked well enough by artificial light, she tapped on Mrs. Gibson's sitting-room door and popped in without waiting for a summons.

'Oh, there you are, dear,' Mrs. Gibson sighed. 'Always so cheerful!'

'What's the matter?' Hannah asked, for Mrs. Gibson's voice was melancholy and she was sunk in her chair as though she had been pushed there.

'He's been at me,' Mrs. Gibson said, 'about the Riddings. He's just this minute left me. It's either them or him, he says. What d'you think of that? I'm sorry to say it, but I call it unkind, unkind to me and to those poor things down there. Now, what would you do yourself, Miss Mole, dear? Would you turn them out? No, I know you wouldn't. Stand-offish as she is, considering everything, if you know what I mean, I can't help feeling I've got a duty by her. I can keep my eye on her. And there's that baby. I never had one of my own and, if you ask me, the motherly ones are those that never had any.'

'Ah,' said Hannah weightily. Her thoughts, straying from Mrs. Gibson's problem, were pursuing this idea. She had believed it was her own and she was surprised to find that it was also Mrs. Gibson's. 'But you had a husband,' she said.

'Well, of course, dear. And I was a good wife to him. Those are his own words.'

'I was wondering,' Hannah said, 'if the best wives are the ones who are not married.'

'Oh, my dear, I don't hold with that kind of thing!'

But Hannah was trying to find proofs for her theory that non-realization was the highest good.

'I don't mean what you mean,' she said.

'I'm glad of that,' said Mrs. Gibson. 'There's too much of that kind of thing nowadays – so I'm told.'

'Dreadful, isn't it?' Hannah murmured back.

'And anyhow, there's no question of that here, I'm thankful to say, but he tells me there'll be trouble again; he says he doesn't feel the same about the place. He says he needs quiet after his day's work.'

Hannah made a loud, derisive noise. 'Work! Chasing money with a little shovel! It's like playing tiddleywinks! And quiet!' She held up a hand. 'Listen, Mrs. Gibson. There's not a sound.'

Mrs. Gibson nodded complaisantly. 'A well-built house. I don't know where he'd find a better. And then, you see, I knew his ma. At the sewing-meeting. I don't go now, dear. I've enough to do with the mending at home and Mr. Blenkinsop's very hard on his socks, but in the old days, with Mrs. Blenkinsop and Mrs. Corder, I went. And now she's passed away and little did I think then I'd ever have her son for a lodger. She was a gloomy woman, I must say, but all the same, there it is.'

'And Mrs. Corder – what's she like?'

'Dead, too, dear. Yes. Pneumonia. It's a terrible thing. Here to-day and gone to-morrow. Only ill for a week. Poor man! I'll never forget the funeral.'

Now Hannah made a vague sound of sympathy. 'A loss to the chapel,' she suggested.

'Well' – Mrs. Gibson, who had been growing drowsy over the fire and her reminiscences, tried to sit more upright and her voice was almost a whisper – 'well, I don't know about that. People used to say things. She was never at the Sunday evening service, and that didn't look well, did it?'

'Tired of hearing him talk, perhaps.'

'That might have been it,' Mrs. Gibson said with unexpected tolerance. 'A wife feels different to anybody else. But at the sewing-meeting, now and then, she'd be funny rather. Absent-minded,' she added, triumphant at finding the right word.

'Thinking of him,' Hannah suggested again.

'Ah, now, you can't have it both ways!' Mrs. Gibson cried cunningly.

'No, but you can think in heaps of them,' Hannah said,

42

and she gave her nose the twist which could mean disgust or a bitter kind of satisfaction.

Mrs. Gibson wisely ignored these possibilities. 'And then, he'd come in and give us a look round, as cheery as you could want.'

'I know,' said Hannah.

'And laugh! He was full of his jokes.'

'I know,' Hannah repeated grimly. How was she going to meet those jokes, or were they less frequent in the family circle? She was convinced that his wife had hated him, and while Mrs. Gibson rambled on, Hannah was either gazing into a future full of dislike for that hearty man or re-constructing the married misery of Mrs. Corder.

'How I've been talking!' Mrs. Gibson said at last. 'And you haven't told me what I'm to do about Mr. Blenkinsop.'

'Tell him he ought to be ashamed of himself,' Hannah said, rising from the hearthrug, and she went away, leaving Mrs. Gibson disappointed, for the first time, in the resource-fulness of Miss Mole.

Chapter 6

BERESFORD ROAD and Prince's Road meet at a point just below Albert Square, and as they are both on the western side of Nunnery Road, where the tram-cars go up to the Downs and down to the city, they can claim to be in Upper Radstowe, but, except for that terraced row of houses on one side of what the errand boys call Prince's, they might belong to any other mid-Victorian suburb. The houses in Beresford Road are just emerging from the basement era. Their kitchens are still a few steps below the level of the sitting-rooms, but they have been raised from the cellarage whence a sturdier, or dumber, race of servants was content to ascend a long flight of stairs an innumerable number of times a day. Some of the houses are surrounded by their own gardens; others look like one house and are really two, with their entrances deceptively placed at the side; they give, and want to give, the impression that nothing unusual or indecorous can happen within their walls, and the red bulk of Beresford Road Congregational Chapel proclaims that Nonconformity has been received into the bosom of respectability. Perhaps the great days of the chapel are over. It was built for the benefit of those rising families whose incomes permitted a removal to this part of Radstowe and whose religious convictions had not changed with their fortunes; at a time when there was still something faintly defiant in marching a large, decently clad family to chapel in the face of church-goers who had never dared anything for freedom, but now that the church had amiably acknowledged dissenters as men and brothers, the only flavour left in Nonconformity was the unpleasant knowledge that its supporters were still considered socially doubtful. Big families were now out of fashion: many of those girls and boys who had regarded Sundays as half festival, half penance, who had been glad to wear their best clothes over the prickly discomfort of their clean under-garments, and to watch their acquaintances through the boredom of the services, had moved on to what was called a better part of Upper Radstowe, reared two or three children and quietly seceded from the faith of their fathers. The bolder spirits, who still went anywhere, went to the Unitarian Church, but Upper Radstowe was not the right soil for Nonconformity, which flourished more abundantly on the other side of Nunnery Road, and the appointment of Robert Corder to Beresford Road Chapel, fifteen years ago, had been an attempt to stir the sluggish ground with the chemical of a vigorous personality. His predecessor had been a gentle old man who preached patiently to the shining empty pews and could not be expected to lure young people to hear him, while Robert Corder was a bold, upstanding figure and the sight and sound of him advertised the vitality of his faith. He could be seen, striding about the streets, leaping on to moving tram-cars and off them, rushing to and from committee meetings, always in a hurry, yet always willing to check his speed for a few words with his acquaintances, and these words were cheery, optimistic and delivered in a loud voice, unless a quieter sympathy was called for. A member of his chapel brought him to a halt; a deacon could divert him from his course, and then he would stride on, still faster, making up for time which, as he often and merrily told these waylayers, was not lost, but had gone, before he knew it.

These were habits and occupations with which Miss Mole was not yet acquainted. From the window of her bed-sitting-room she could see the roof of the chapel and she had noticed it as a warm patch of red among the other roofs and the trees. She was a specialist in roofs and from many high windows in Upper Radstowe they could be seen in every shape and colour. They slid down the steep slope to Lower Radstowe, red, grey, blue and green, and spread like a flower garden over the city. There were old red tiles in close neighbourhood to shining slates, there were mossy green roofs squeezed between the walls of higher houses and, with all these variations in height, there were trees overtopping chimneys and chimneys sending their smoke

45

into other people's windows, but this could not be seen from Hannah's room. Her view of the newer part of Upper Radstowe was ordinary enough, and she had made the most of the chapel roof until it had suddenly changed into a portent. She liked it no longer, yet she looked at it more often: she imagined herself sitting under it, a small drab speck against the varnish, and, during the days which passed before she heard from Lilla, she spent some time in Beresford Road, feeling like a conspirator or a private detective. She tried to get into the chapel and found, as she expected, that the doors were locked. 'This,' she said, addressing the ivy which grew round the porch, 'is enough to drive anybody to Rome, and I've a good mind to go there. I suppose the place is so ugly that they daren't let anyone see it unless there's one of their entertainments going on, and then they've got each other's hats to look at. Not,' she added, 'that there can be anything much in the way of hats.'

She would have been very gloomy if she had not been enjoying her prejudices and her prophetic powers. She was sure the red roof was painted blue on the inside, like the firmament, and sprinkled with opaque golden stars: she had seen Mr. Corder's house, No. 14 – a long stone's throw from the chapel and on the other side of the road – and her forebodings had been justified. It was one of the coupled houses, with an asphalt path running up to the inconspicuous door. There were a bow and a flat window on each of two floors and a small one, like an eye, in the gable. Hannah had strolled past the house adventurously: at any moment Mr. Corder might appear and it would be hard to look like a woman with a right to be in the road. She was not curious about him: it was the house she was concerned with, and if she could put her head inside its door she would know, at once, whether she could be happy in it. That, however, was further than she dared to go and she had to content herself with an external view, finding nothing hopeful in the lace curtains and the plot of grass edged with laurels and confined by iron railings. The architect of that house had been no artist. It was an ugly house, yet its twin, next door, looked infinitely more habitable, though the venetian blinds were askew. Dusty-looking red curtains, clasped by brass

46

chains, draped the lower bow window and a bird-cage containing a canary reminded Hannah painfully of Mrs. Widdows. No. 16 was quite as unattractive as No. 14 to the eye, but Hannah would have felt happier if the red curtains had belonged to Mr. Corder.

She was startled the next morning, when she passed again, to hear a harsh voice bidding her good day and, standing on tiptoe to peer over the privet hedge which grew above No. 16's railings, she saw a parrot in a cage in the middle of the grass plot. The bird leered at her for an instant and then with an insulting expression, pretended it had never seen her, though she offered it the usual complimentary remarks.

'Fond of birds?' asked another voice, and a face popped over the privet hedge, close to her own. 'Picking up the dead leaves,' said its owner, showing her a handful, 'and giving Poll an airing at the same time. Can't let him out alone, 'cos of the cats. Even my own cats. Jealousy, I suppose. Now you'll tell me that a bird is always a bird to a cat – and they'd eat Minnie, that's the canary, there, if they could get her, I haven't a doubt, but – and I've made a study of this – it's not food they're after with Poll. It's the human voice that upsets them and he's remarkably chatty at times. The human voice, coming from the wrong place. It's natural, when you come to think of it.'

Miss Mole had discovered why No. 16 was a fitter habitation for her than No. 14. She recognized something native to herself in this elderly man who could fall into conversation with a stranger, something congenial in his battered old face and his roguish, disrespectful eye. As much as she could see of him was arrayed in a sleeved woollen waistcoat, a high stiff collar, and a red tie pierced by a pin with a diamond and opal horseshoe head, and he had the look of a man who would wear his cap in the house.

'That's very interesting,' she said, dropping back on to her heels, while he pressed closer to the hedge to get a better sight of her, and his humorous, rather watery eyes seemed to be comparing her unfavourably with all the fine-looking women they had rested on.

'Saw you yesterday, didn't I?' he asked. 'Shaving at the

47

time, up there,' he jerked a thumb backwards 'and saw a woman at the chapel door. "That's a new thing," I said to myself. Couldn't make it out at all, so I kept my eye on you. Seemed funny to me.'

'It would have been funnier if I'd got in,' Hannah said with a sniff.

'Ah, not my idea of fun, but if you want to get in,' he jerked his thumb sideways and his tone made large allowances for human vagaries, 'you'll get the key, I dessay, next door. Parson lives there. Went out half an hour ago with his coat tails flying. Pretended he didn't see me,' he gave Hannah a slow wink, 'but I could tell him a thing or two if I liked. Only, as it happens,' he sank out of sight and his voice came muffled through the hedge, 'I don't like.' She could hear him gathering up more leaves.

A farewell seemed unnecessary, to go without one seemed rude, and she murmured something to which he made no response, but he had brightened her outlook; to live next door to a man who could tell Robert Corder a thing or two, to discover what those things were would be an alleviation of the dreariness she anticipated, and when she opened Lilla's letter with the news that Mrs. Spenser-Smith had had her way and that Miss Mole would be expected in Beresford Road on the Tuesday of next week, Hannah could think more lightly of her bondage and face the fact that there were not many pounds left in her purse, but she made a wry face at Lilla's much-underlined conclusion in which she pointed out that with fifty pounds a year, her board and lodging and the rent from her house in the country, Hannah would surely be able to lay something by for a rainy day.

'About enough to buy a cheap umbrella,' Hannah said, flipping the letter across the table before she tore it into little pieces in carefulness that the secret of her relationship to Lilla should be kept.

For Mrs. Gibson the next few days had a noble sadness in them. She was to lose Miss Mole but could not grudge her to the exalted state of being housekeeper to Mr. Corder, and Miss Mole knew she would be welcome at any time if she liked to drop in for a cup of tea. Mrs. Gibson gazed admiringly at this woman who had appeared out of nowhere

48

to save Mr. Ridding's life, to keep out the policeman and avert an inquest and who betrayed no nervousness at the prospect of living with a minister, a man whose jokes, as Mrs. Gibson recognized, were comparable to passing froth on a pool of unknown depth.

Hannah's own sadness was shot with a sense of adventure. She was prepared for every kind of dullness and annoyance, she was prepared to be sent adrift again on a world that did not want her, but her belief in approaching good was irrepressible: there was the man next door with his cats and his parrot and his canary and, for all she knew, he might be the one who was to leave her a fortune; there would be the fun of watching Lilla's secret anxiety and careful condescension, and she was in the place she loved with the chance, if she behaved herself, of finding primroses on the other side of the river, in the spring.

Yet she wished she could have had a little longer with Mrs. Gibson, for Mrs. Ridding was still unfriendly and Mr. Blenkinsop was still the fortified place she had left behind her. She understood the nature of Mrs. Ridding's defences and respected them, but she itched to tease Mr. Blenkinsop with feints of attack. In daily expectation of another ultimatum, Mrs. Gibson was treating him as though he were seriously ill: she whispered if she encountered Hannah on the landing outside his rooms, took special pains with the cooking of his food and carried it to him herself lest the blundering of the little servant should distress him, and this both angered Hannah and gave her the opportunity she wanted.

On her last evening, she went into the kitchen and picked up the tray.

'He won't like it!' Mrs. Gibson gasped.

'He'll have to lump it,' Hannah said vulgarly. 'What about your poor legs, as you call them?'

There were no limits to Miss Mole's audacity: Mrs. Gibson could not cope with it and she looked at Hannah with the mournful, helpless interest she had once experienced when she saw a man go into a cage of lions.

Mr. Blenkinsop was sitting by the fire in a large sitting-room heavily furnished with his mother's mahogany. In front of him was a chessboard on a stool and his hand was

49

poised above one of the pieces. He did not look up and Hannah felt as if she had carelessly entered a church while a service was in progress. The proper thing was to slip away and trust the appetizing smell of cooked meats to creep through Mr. Blenkinsop's absorption, but, instead of doing that, she said crisply, 'Dinner is served, sir!' and taking a step forward, she added, 'So that's what you do in the evenings! It must be a great resource.'

Mr. Blenkinsop looked astonished and then frowned. 'It needs concentration,' he said pointedly.

'That's what I mean,' Hannah replied obtusely. 'I've brought up your dinner because Mrs. Gibson's legs ache.'

'There's no reason why Mrs. Gibson should do it.'

'Fear,' said Hannah, 'is one of the strongest human emotions.'

'I'm afraid I don't follow you,' Mr. Blenkinsop said with marked politeness.

'The poor dear is afraid of losing you.'

'She knows how to keep me.' Mr. Blenkinsop took his seat at the table and unfolded his napkin. 'And really,' he went on, indignation mastering courtesy, 'I don't quite understand why you should interest yourself in the question.'

'No, you don't understand,' Hannah said gently. 'And I make no apology. I'm speaking, as it were, from my deathbed. *Moriturus te saluto!* To-morrow, you'll be glad to know, I'm moving on. I'm going to live with Mr. Corder – as his housekeeper – oh Lord!' A faint gleam of interest passed across Mr. Blenkinsop's face and she took advantage of it. 'Yes, think of that!' she cried. 'I'd rather live with the Riddings. Why don't you teach Mr. Ridding to play chess? That would keep him out of the oven! And what an inconvenience for you to find new lodgings! And Mrs. Gibson's heart will break! Stay where you are, Mr. Blenkinsop, and think of me to-morrow at this time, when you're here in your comfortable room and I'm in a strange land. But perhaps I shall see you sometimes at the chapel. That will cheer me up.'

'Not very likely,' Mr. Blenkinsop said, firmly nipping this bud of hope, and he applied himself to his dinner with an unmistakable air of dismissal.

Chapter 7

MRS. GIBSON's greengrocer undertook to deliver Miss Mole's
box at the home in Beresford Road and thither, in the dusk,
Miss Mole walked, following the cart and feeling that this
was her own funeral and she the solitary mourner. Slowly
the cart creaked down the road and slowly Miss Mole
walked after it, and it seemed to her that her old trunk was
her coffin and that the solitary mourner was her own ghost.
A little wind was driving the fallen leaves along the pavement, there was a rustling of the bushes in the gardens, the
tired pony's steps and the turning of the wheels were dismal
sounds, and she wished she had gone to the expense of hiring
a cab and arriving with some appearance of eagerness. This
was a very melancholy procession, a detachment of an
army of women like herself who went from house to
house behind their boxes, a sad multitude of women with
carefully pleasant faces, hiding their ailments, lowering
their ages and thankfully accepting less than they earned.
What became of them all? What was to become of herself?
Age was creeping on her all the time and she had saved
nothing, she would soon be told she was too old for this post
or that, and, for a second, fear took hold of her with a cold
hand and the whispering of the dead leaves warned her that,
like them, she would be swept into the gutter and no one
would ask where she had gone, and her fear changed into
a craving that there should be at least one person to whom
her disappearance would be a calamity. 'No one!' the leaves
whispered maliciously, while a little gust of laughter came
from the bushes, and at that, Hannah paused and looked
disdainfully in their direction. She was not to be laughed
at! She was not to be laughed at and she refused to be
frightened! Her head went up and she walked more quickly,
to get level with the cart, and the ruby glow in No. 16's

bow window applauded her spirit. It was pleasant to think he was in there by the fire with the parrot and the canary and the cats. He would be surprised when he saw her flicking a duster from a window of No. 14, and Hannah liked surprising people. This was something to look forward to and she was not depressed when she saw no welcoming lights shining from Mr. Corder's house.

The greengrocer shouldered the box, Hannah followed him up the asphalt path and rang the bell. There was a glimmer of light in the hall, but no one could be heard stirring in the house.

'Seems as if they're all out,' the greengrocer said, and whistled under his breath.

Hannah rang the bell more loudly, the greengrocer cocked his head with polite attention, and now they heard the sound of someone running down the stairs.

Half an hour later, when Hannah was kneeling in front of her box, she fancied she could still hear that sound. It had struck her ear, at her first hearing of it, with a strange significance, as though Fate itself were coming to let her in, yet when the door was opened it revealed no more than the figure of a small, thin girl who did not know how to greet a stranger or to apologize for the necessary absence of her elders and the neglect of the servant who should have answered the door.

Hannah made a mental note about that servant and another that this girl, who must be the one who had holes in her stockings, was not at all pleased to see her, and she answered reserve with reserve, but when the greengrocer had struggled upstairs with the trunk and Ruth had found a box of matches and lighted the gas in Miss Mole's attic bedroom and, doing her best, had gone to the window to pull down the blind, Hannah forgot to be dignified and called out, 'Oh, don't do that! I want to look. It faces nearly south, doesn't it?'

It was a dormer window, the one she had seen from the road, and she felt like a pigeon peering from a hole in a dovecot. The house was set higher than she had thought and, over the opposite roofs, she could see thousands of twinkling lights and the dim outline of more roofs and chimneys. And

52

this was a view which would be no less lovely in the morning, when the spires and towers of Radstowe's innumerable churches and the factory chimneys with their pennons of smoke would clear themselves from the wide-spread huddle of buildings. She turned her head a little to the right and the wind came straight across the hills from the place where her pink cottage stood in its little orchard, and it was characteristic of Hannah to accept the pleasure and ignore the pain of the wind's reminders, to overpay the greengrocer and to smile as she told Ruth she was going to unpack.

Cheerfully she looked about her when she was left alone and she decided that she liked this narrow room with its sloping walls, and then, with the wariness of an old campaigner, she examined the blankets, which were clean, and the sheets, which were rather coarse, and thumped the mattress critically.

'Lumpy,' she said, frowning a little. But never mind! She had the view from the window, she thought she would be able to hear the ships hooting up and down the river, and not far away there was the real Upper Radstowe with its old streets and crescents, its odd passages and flights of steps, and she unstrapped her box, forgetting she had seen it as a coffin.

The size of the box erroneously suggested that Miss Mole's wardrobe was extensive. There was still plenty of room in drawers and cupboards when she had laid out and hung up her clothes, and there was still a good deal left in the box, for Miss Mole's treasures travelled with her and the chief of these was the model of a sailing-ship miraculously enclosed in a pale-green bottle. She took it from its wrapping of cotton wool and gazed at it tenderly when she had put it on the narrow mantelpiece. She liked to see it sailing all alone, never getting any further and never losing its gallantness, and it brought back memories of her very early childhood when it stood on the parlour mantelpiece, far out of her reach, a mystery in itself and a hint of greater mysteries. It was connected with the few sights, sounds and smells that remained to her of those days; heavy bees buzzing among the pinks on a hot afternoon, a turn in the garden path where danger lurked behind the hedge of box, the

53

crackling of her starched pinafore, the rattling of milk-pails and the creaking of her father's corded breeches.

She had a lot to be thankful for, she thought. It was good to have such clean country memories and it was astonishing how solid a background they made to life. Consciously or unconsciously, they were there, and, however murky and sordid some of her experiences had been, her roots were in wholesome earth and she had sprouted among sweet-smelling things. No one loved streets better than Hannah Mole, but she had a secret satisfaction in her knowledge of matters on which these townspeople depended and which they took for granted, and it gave her a feeling of permanency, of something more real than anything else in her restless flittings about the world and her changing views of what she was or might have been.

She had finished dressing herself for the latest part she had undertaken when a knock came at the door and the thin little girl appeared again, evidently unwilling to be the messenger who summoned Miss Mole to supper. She was a little breathless, but whether with nervousness, indignation or the ascent of the stairs, Hannah did not know.

'She wants feeding up,' she thought, as she smiled with determined brightness, and she promised herself that the day would come when this child would be glad of an excuse to knock at Miss Mole's door. Even now her eyes had lighted on the bottled ship with a quickly hidden interest, and of that, too, Hannah made a mental note.

Her bedroom had been a pleasant surprise; the rest of the house was what she had known it must be. The hall smelt faintly of the morning's cooking, the gas was protected by a lantern of red and blue glass, and though, when she entered the dining-room, she missed the green serge cover on a table which was laid for supper, the rusty fern was there, under a three-armed chandelier. One of these arms was fitted for incandescent gas which bubbled inside a frosted globe; the others were neglected and stood out gauntly like withered branches on a tree, but the room was further illuminated – though it still seemed rather dark – by an ordinary gas jet on each side of the fireplace, and these flames gently hissed in their globes of pink and white.

54

She noticed these things with a glance of her practised eye, and she had no time to verify her suspicion that there was cold mutton on the table before her hand was seized by a young woman who pranced to meet her.

In her nervous or happy moments, prancing was Ethel Corder's gait and, indeed, she reminded Hannah of an awkward-tempered colt. There was a display of teeth and eyeballs, a look of half-playful viciousness for which her physical peculiarities were chiefly responsible. Her pale, scanty hair started growing too far back and there was a deficiency of eyebrow, yet her plainness had a certain feverish quality which attracted and held the attention.

'Someone's been knocking her about in the stable or stealing her oats,' Hannah thought, while Ethel volubly explained that an emergency committee meeting had engaged her father and herself. 'I shall have to be careful. And the little one looks like a starved donkey. It's lucky I was brought up on a farm.' She wanted to stroke and reassure them both, to tell them she could make them plump and happy if they would trust her. She wanted to stop the gas from bubbling like a turkey and hissing like a pair of geese. She saw there was plenty here for a farmer's daughter to do, and though this might not be the place Hannah Mole would have chosen for herself, it was the one that needed Hannah, and she was turning the cold mutton into a savoury hash for to-morrow's dinner and getting rid of the rusty fern, when the voice which had cheered many a sewing-meeting bade her good evening.

'So this is Miss Mole,' he said, nicely fitting his tone to the one suitable for an emissary of Mrs. Spenser-Smith who was far from being Mrs. Spenser-Smith herself, and Hannah, prejudiced already, thought she saw him quickly appraising her as a useful nobody.

With the best will in the world it was impossible to think the same of him. His height, his handsome head of dark chestnut hair just flecked with grey, the pointed beard of a lighter colour, his suggestion of great physical energy, dominated the room, and with a stiffened back, but a crestfallen spirit, Hannah had to admit that Mr. Corder, too, was something of a surprise.

55

Meekly, she took her seat opposite to Ruth, the servant brought in a dish of damp potatoes, and Mr. Corder took up the carving-knife and fork. Ethel had fallen silent and Ruth seemed determined not to speak. She looked crossly at the mutton on her plate and at Miss Mole on the other side of the table, but she bent industriously over her food when her father began to talk.

'This is a fine old city, Miss Mole,' he said, 'full of historic associations, and we have one of the finest parish churches in the country – if you are interested in architecture,' he added, with a subtle suggestion that this was not likely.

Hannah longed to ask what effect her indifference would have on the building, but Mr. Corder did not wait for reassurance about its safety.

'Ruth must take you to see it, some day. On a Saturday afternoon, perhaps, Ruthie?'

'I play hockey on Saturday afternoons,' Ruth muttered.

'Ah, yes, of course, these games!' Mr. Corder said good-humouredly. 'Well, Miss Mole may find her way there herself. The Cathedral is not so good. I don't care about the Cathedral, but we are rather proud of our Chapter House. It may surprise you –' He interrupted himself. 'By the way, what has happened to Wilfrid? Wilfrid is my nephew and he is supposed to be studying medicine at the University,' he told Hannah. 'Do you know where he is, Ethel?'

Ethel's eyes goggled nervously. 'He had an engagement,' she said in haste, and Hannah suspected that Ruth's smile had been calculated to make her sister exclaim angrily, 'It's perfectly true, Ruth! He told me about it yesterday.'

'And I knew he'd have it a week ago,' Ruth retorted coolly, and Hannah realized that this rude little girl was hinting that her cousin had taken care to avoid Miss Mole's first evening.

Robert Corder lifted his eyebrows and managed to look bland as he said, 'I think Ruth shares my opinion about the genuineness of Wilfrid's engagements. However, we need not waste our time over Wilfrid. I was saying, Miss Mole, that you may be surprised at my interest in ecclesiastical architecture, but whatever our religious differences may be, these buildings are a common heritage, and when I first

56

came to Radstowe, fifteen years ago, I made a point of seeing everything of interest or importance, and very valuable the knowledge has been to me. I have been able to wake a civic pride in a great many people, I believe, but not, I'm afraid,' he said playfully, 'in my own children. You know the saying about the prophet! I'm pretty sure Ruth has never been inside St. Mary's – eh, Ruthie?'

Ruth flushed an angry red and said she hated churches.

'Ruth is a stout Nonconformist, Miss Mole, but we mustn't be narrow. And there are other beauties in Radstowe. "A thing of beauty is a joy for ever." You recognize that, Ruth, Ethel? And there are other interests. Radstowe was once the most important port in England, but with the increase in tonnage she has lost her place. The big ships can't get up the river. It is a tidal river – most picturesque in its gorge – you must be sure to see that, too – but the channel is very narrow, with large deposits of mud.' And at some length and with what accuracy Hannah could not judge, he explained how these deposits were made. 'Dredging goes on, but does very little good. It is a great misfortune for our trade.'

'Yes,' said Hannah, deciding to be dumb no longer as she could not be deaf, 'but it's well worth it. At low tide the mud is beautiful. All the colours of the rainbow, and it makes such a nice promenade for the gulls.'

Mr. Corder was like a horse bewildered by a check in full gallop. 'So you have seen our river?'

'Oh yes,' Hannah said lightly, 'I've known Radstowe all my life.'

'Ah, really –' said Mr. Corder, and suddenly Radstowe became of very little importance. 'Ruth, will you ring the bell. I think we are ready for the pudding.'

Chapter 8

FAMILY loyalties and disloyalties are like currents in the sea: they intermingle, jostle each other, change places and are diverted or united according to the strength of the obstacles they meet, and Hannah, sailing alone, like her bottled ship, on this unknown ocean, found that her little craft, which might be upset at any moment, was quite robust enough to affect these currents. Ruth, undoubtedly, had been embarrassed by her father's instructive monologue, but she could not tolerate his discomfiture by a stranger, though the stranger's intention might have been innocent, and in the mild amiability she showed him until the meal was over and the few remarks she made to Ethel, who seemed to have missed what Ruth resented, she proclaimed her allegiance to the Corder clan.

Her tongue was always Hannah's danger and its readiness had sometimes been her undoing. She could control the expression of her face, but the temptation of a quick reply or a disconcerting statement was too much for her, and she would have been superhuman if she had resisted this one, and remarkably careless of her future if she had not tried to disarm suspicion by a quietly sensible demeanour while her duties were explained by Ethel and they made a tour of the house together.

When they returned to the dining-room, Ruth had her homework spread out on the green serge table cover, and a young man, with his shoulders wedged under the mantelpiece, was warming his back at the fire. He was rather a beautiful young man, Hannah thought, as she looked at his slenderness and the studied carelessness of his dark hair, but one, she decided the next moment, who would have to be kept in his place, for he was returning her glance quizzically, and the lift of his eyebrows condoled with her while his

58

smile invited her to share his amusement at the alien atmosphere in which he and she found themselves. This was drawing a bow at a venture, but he was safe enough, for if the arrow missed its mark no one need know where he had aimed it, and Hannah's demure response *to* his greeting did not discountenance him.

'I've been trying to make Ruth tell me about you,' he said gaily, 'but she's like David Balfour. She's an awful poor hand at a description.'

'I didn't tell you a single thing!' Ruth cried.

'And now, methinks, you do protest too much.'

'But I could tell you something about yourself! I knew you'd begin showing off at once!'

'No, no,' Wilfrid protested genially. 'I was only letting Miss Mole know that this is a cultured household – as indeed it ought to be. We have *Familiar Quotations* on our bookshelves and they save a deal of trouble and hard work.'

'If you're hinting that Father hasn't read as much as you have –'

'I didn't mention the uncle, dear child,' Wilfrid said gently. 'But all the same,' he dropped his pose of an ironical young man and became a natural one, 'all the same, I'll bet you he hasn't. Bet you anything you like. I don't blame him. He's a busy man. He's the kind of man *Familiar Quotations* was made for, and he'd be a fool if he didn't take advantage of it.'

'He's got more sense in his little finger –' Ruth began. She looked as if she was going to cry. 'It's you that's the fool! And I don't know how I'm going to get my homework finished with so many people in the room! I shall have to do it in my bedroom. And I don't care if I do catch cold,' she said, in answer to Ethel's expostulations, and from the door she gave half a glance at Hannah. 'It won't be my fault, anyhow.'

Ethel looked anxiously at Hannah. 'I don't know what's the matter with her,' she said. 'And I don't know what Miss Mole will think of us,' she said to Wilfrid.

'No, I don't suppose we shall ever know that. Well, I'm sorry I teased the child. Is the uncle in?'

'Yes,' Ethel was anxious again, 'and I said you had an engagement.'

'So I had. An important committee meeting of the Medical Students' Temperance Society – if he wants to know.'

'Oh, Wilfrid! Really?' Ethel clutched the blue beads round her neck and smiled with an alarming joyfulness.

Wilfrid dropped his eyelids. 'But if he doesn't want to know,' he said drawlingly, 'it wasn't!' and he slouched gracefully out of the room.

'Dear me!' Hannah said. They were the first words she had spoken and she wished Wilfrid could have heard them. It was the only possible comment and she thought he would have appreciated it in her own sense.

Ethel interpreted it as astonishment, and she hastened to explain that Wilfrid was a dreadful tease but he did not mean to be unkind. He did not realize how much she was in earnest about temperance reform. Or perhaps he did – what did Miss Mole think? – but liked to pretend he could take nothing seriously. She wished he was not a medical student. They were rather a wild lot, yet the doctor's was a noble profession and that of a medical missionary was the best of all. She had wanted to be a missionary herself – in China – but, when her mother died, it seemed to be her duty to stay at home.

'And now I've come, and if I turn out all right, perhaps you'll be able to go after all.'

Ethel gave what was equivalent to a violent shy, keeping her eyes, meanwhile, on the object which had alarmed her. 'I don't know,' she said. 'I do such a lot for Father. And I have a Girls' Club at the Mission. I'd given up all idea of going away.'

'The missionary field, as they call it, or the stage,' Hannah said. 'It's generally one or the other, in one's teens, not that I ever fancied myself at either. But all the world's a stage, as you'll find in *Familiar Quotations*.'

'And, in a way, a missionary field, too,' Ethel said eagerly. 'And perhaps it's really harder to stay at home.'

'I shouldn't be surprised,' Hannah said. 'Oughtn't I to be darning, or something?'

60

'Oh, not on your first evening, Miss Mole! The basket's in that cupboard and I'm afraid you'll find a lot of socks in it.'

'All the more reason for starting, then. And you said Mr. Corder likes his tea at ten o'clock?'

'And biscuits.'

'And biscuits,' Hannah repeated. 'Keeps him awake, I should think,' she said, rummaging in the mending-basket.

'Yes, there's plenty to do here.'

Ethel shied again. 'I'm always so busy,' she said, fidgeting with her beads, while Hannah thrust a thin, probing hand into socks and stockings. 'I'm so glad you've come, Miss Mole, and I knew I should like anyone recommended by Mrs. Spenser-Smith.'

'Did she choose the servant for you, too?' Hannah asked casually.

'Oh, no! She's one of my girls. One of my club girls. So she always has to go out on Wednesdays, Miss Mole. That's the Club social evening. And it's the week-night service at the chapel, so Father and Doris and I are all out and we have a high tea that evening.'

'Sardines, I suppose?'

'Not always,' Ethel said simply, and Hannah, who had been ready to suggest that these piles of mending should be shared and Ethel's restless hands employed, felt herself softening towards this young woman who wanted to approach and would be scared by a sudden movement. She went on with her darning, behaving as she would have behaved with the nervous colt, pretending she was not watching it and letting it get used to her presence before she advanced, and she could feel Ethel gaining confidence though her fears kept jerking her back.

Aloud, she said cunningly, 'I'm afraid I've frightened everybody else away. Do you think your sister ought to be sitting up there, in the cold?'

Ethel showed the whites of her eyes, but, this time, she did not jump. 'I think we'd better leave her alone, Miss Mole. Nobody knows how to manage her. Mother did.' And now it was Ethel's turn to look ready to cry. 'And she gets on with my brother – everyone does – but she doesn't seem to want me to be kind to her.'

61

'She doesn't look very strong.'

'Perhaps that's it,' Ethel said hopefully, and it occurred to Hannah that here was another someone else who was not happy unless everybody appreciated her, and this one had less than common skill to evoke the admiration she wanted. Hannah was inclined to think that this was a feminine craving, the result of work in which the personal element was supreme, but she was to learn that in this household there was no one who was free from it. Robert Corder, it was true, made no efforts: he had found they were unnecessary and he accepted, as his due, the particular kind of adulation given to a man in his position and was astonished only if it was denied him, and when Hannah had seen him in his chapel, after a service, petting, and being petted by a docile flock, it was easy to understand why he treated her with marked coldness. She had tripped him up on her first evening in his house, and while his vanity and her appear-ance could persuade him that this was an accident, he was careful not to get in her way again. It was also easy to under-stand why Lilla had introduced the watch-dog. Miss Patsy Withers, a plump, fading, but still comely blonde, would have made a soothing companion for the Reverend Robert, a woman who would always say what she meant and, still more commendably, mean the thing most likely to please him, and when Hannah dusted the large photograph of the late Mrs. Corder which stood on the minister's desk, she wondered if that lady had ever puzzled her husband. She looked capable of a silence which was certainly not due to any lack of ideas, and the more Hannah examined that face, the more she liked it, and the more she was convinced that Lilla's loyalty to the dead was a romantic way of expressing her determination to keep her own place as leading lady in the chapel.

It amused Hannah to see Lilla walking down the aisle to her prominent pew, to meet her in the porch and receive an appropriate bow and sometimes even a handshake, and Hannah always took care to respond discreetly, but with a glance or a pressure which brought a wary look into Lilla's eyes. It was hard to watch Ernest taking round the offer-tory plate and not to smile at him: it was harder not to encourage the kindness he was ready to bestow on her. His greetings were a little too enthusiastic to be those of her patroness's husband, but, in the general cheerfulness of that porch and the heartiness with which the sharers of a spiritual banquet mingled before they separated for their more private and material feasts, this brotherliness was not likely to attract attention.

Each Sunday morning Hannah sat under the blue be-spangled roof and she looked in vain for Mr. Blenkinsop. She would get a series of nods from Mrs. Gibson, and some-times a whispered word, but their confidences were ex-changed when Hannah dropped in for the cup of tea she had been promised, and she knew that Mr. Blenkinsop was still in Prince's Road and that no further misadventure had dis-turbed his peace. Mrs. Gibson said it did her good to see Hannah sitting in the minister's pew, with Ruth on one side of her and that handsome young man on the other. She liked to see a young man at chapel. While his mother was alive, Mr. Blenkinsop had been as regular as anyone could wish, and now he only went occasionally to the evening service, but, for all that, he was as steady as he could be and she was not the one to judge people entirely by their chapel-going.

'No, indeed,' Hannah said seriously, 'but I shouldn't enjoy the services so much if Mr. Corder's nephew was not there.' She did not tell Mrs. Gibson how neatly he some-times paraphrased the hymns and sang them in her ear, or how his elbow met hers during the sermon or the extem-porary prayers. Wilfrid was one of Hannah's many diffi-culties and few joys for, in the Corder household, he alone flatteringly suspected something of her quality and acknow-ledged it by paying her attentions she did her best to repress, because, as she had early discovered, to be favoured by Wilfrid was to irritate Ethel and to be implicated in Ruth's determined scorn of him. Ethel was friendliness itself when no one else was troubling about Miss Mole, but she was a bad sharer, in Hannah as in Wilfrid, and when Ethel was upset Ruth seemed to take pains to irritate her, while Wilfrid teased them both in turn with bewilderingly quick changes. The truth was that Ethel openly, and Ruth

63

secretly, admired him for his looks, his nonchalance, and his disregard for all they had been taught to consider sacred, and Hannah was mortified and amused to find herself in the same condition, though her sight was clearer. Under his obvious faults, he was a lovable young man, and for her what was his most lovable quality was the quickness with which he sought her eye when his uncle was at his most ministerial, while those nudges of his elbow in chapel were his indication that, in spite of all rebuffs, she could not deceive him. She could pretend to be the plain Miss Mole, keeping house for Mr. Corder, doing her work efficiently, presenting an imperturbable obtuseness to Ruth's continued hostility, meeting Ethel's gusts of friendship quietly and ignoring signs of jealousy, letting slip her opportunities to cap Wilfrid's wit with her own, but, so those nudges and those glances warned her, failing to deceive him.

This was heartening to Hannah. It lightened a task which could only be done well if she persisted in seeing it as a game in which Wilfrid's appreciation and the improvement in the meals were the only points she had yet scored. She would score again when she had made harmony out of these discords and when she had persuaded Ruth that an interloper could be a friend, but she had to play with a cautiousness which was alien to her or lose the game.

Why did she take this trouble? she sometimes asked herself. Was it for the sake of the game itself or in a belated realization that, somehow, her future must be assured, that with youth behind her she could not afford more failures? She could not answer her own questions but, day by day, as she dusted Mrs. Corder's photograph, she liked to fancy that between her and this woman there was some sort of pact which she was trusted not to break.

Chapter 9

IT was a long time since Hannah had lived with a family. After an exhausting experience in which she had battled with half a dozen riotous children, an ailing mother and a father who tried to be confidential about the trials and disappointments of marriage, she had taken a post with an old lady in the hope of comparative leisure and, like an actress who makes a success in a particular kind of part and finds it difficult to get another, she had seemed doomed to old, invalid and lonely ladies for the rest of her life. She had naturally been suspected of inability to deal with the young after an existence of picking up dropped stitches, fetching clean pocket handkerchiefs and reading aloud, though Hannah could have been eloquent about the wearing nature of such work. Often she had looked at a charwoman with envy, desiring healthy labour with brush and bucket, and for her folly in not hiring a bedroom and letting herself out by the day, she blamed what must have been an odd lingering desire for the gentility she affected to despise. She would have made an admirable charwoman: that vulgar strain in her which Lilla justly deplored, so unsuitable in a companion or a housekeeper, would have been a positive recommendation in a charwoman, and she pictured herself, going from house to house, energetic, good-humoured, free of speech, the perfect charwoman of fiction, with a home which was all her own and none of these tangled personalities to deal with. Well, she would tell herself with a sniff, she might come to it yet, but women in that walk of life were not liable to be made the heirs of rich old gentlemen, and towards that pleasant prospect Hannah still pretended to be gazing. She had seen no one in the chapel who answered to the description, and though she had waved a duster out of every window, she had not met No. 16's roguish leer. A sparkling October had given place to a damp November and the weather, she supposed, was bad for parrots and for gardening. She sometimes saw No. 16 trundling towards the back gate, she heard him calling in the cats at night, but she had no time to plan encounters, for she worked as hard as any charwoman and had to adapt herself to new and difficult conditions.

In her other situations where there was a man of the house, he had left it at a reasonable hour in the morning and could be trusted not to reappear until the evening: there was no such regularity in the movements of Mr. Corder. The absence or presence of his hat and coat was the only surety that he was out or in, and it became a habit with Hannah to glance at the pegs as she went through the hall and to feel her spirits rising or falling with what she saw there, another unwilling confession that his personality was not negligible. Hannah's somewhat toneless singing, which contrasted so strangely with the quality of her speaking voice, was generally silenced when he was in the house; he damped down the tempers of his daughters and Hannah wondered if he knew they had them; he stifled conversation, for he was ready with information on all subjects, and opinions which differed from his own either amused or angered him, yet hardly a day passed without a caller, someone needing help or advice, an ardent chapel worker with some difficulty to be solved, a deacon on a mission of importance, and the voice which came from the study was not always Robert Corder's, and though he might lead the laughter, there was response to it, and people went away looking happier than they had come. Nevertheless, Hannah would make a grimace at the study door as she passed. She was sure Mrs. Corder, from her place on the great man's desk, was listening gravely to what he said and making her acute, silent comments, balancing the counsels he gave against what she knew of him and yet, more tolerant than Hannah, refusing to judge him harshly.

She had made of Mrs. Corder a person like herself, with more wisdom, more kindness and more patience, qualities she must have needed in excess, Hannah thought grimly, for she who prided herself on her willingness to accept the

66

good and bad in men and women as easily as she accepted their physical and mental parts, was deliberately antagonistic to Robert Corder. The swing of his coat-tails vexed her as probably the swing of her skirts vexed him; she would not believe in the boasted broadmindedness of a man who sneered at opposing views or waved them aside, and whose small, tight mouth she could discern under the moustache which masked it. Like most childless women, she exaggerated the joys and privileges of possessing offspring, and Robert Corder seemed unaware of them. He was not an unkind father; he was amiable enough and ready to expand under the affection he had made it impossible for them to show him, but he seemed to Hannah to treat his daughters as an audience for his sentiments and the record of his doings and to forget that these girls had characters, unless they happened to annoy him. While Hannah chafed under his bland assumptions, she enjoyed watching for corroborative evidence of the estimate she had made of him and he rarely disappointed her, for, when things went well with him, he had to talk, and it was then that Wilfrid's eyes sought hers and with the tiniest droop of an eyelid, lift of an eyebrow or face of unnatural solemnity, sent his message to her across the table.

Hannah took a penitential pleasure in controlling herself. If she asserted her personality before she had established herself firmly, even Lilla's patronage would not save her. She had to persuade Robert Corder that she was useful before she let him suspect her of a mind quicker than his own, and she behaved discreetly, for she had her compact with Mrs. Corder to keep, she had her own powers to prove, and, though she would have laughed at the idea, she had the zeal of a reformer under her thin crust of cynicism. She wanted to fatten Ruth and see an occasional look of happiness on her face, to ease Ethel's restlessness and get some sort of beauty into the house. She could not change the ugly furniture – and there Mrs. Corder had badly failed – but friendliness and humour and gaiety cost no money; they were, in fact, in the penniless Hannah's pocket, waiting for these difficult people to take them, and Hannah bided their time and her own.

67

She found that Ethel's labours at the Mission were not so arduous as the state of the house implied. She had bursts of feverish activity, she was constant in her attendance at the Girls' Club and she sometimes helped her father with his correspondence, and then, for a whole day, it would seem she had nothing to do, and she would shadow Hannah about the house, as though she dreaded loneliness, watch her as she worked, without offering to help, and spend the evening turning the pages of a book, making fitful conversation, repairing, or making changes in her rather tawdry clothes. She had a misguided passion for colour and for ornaments, and the jingling of her beads was the constant accompaniment to her restless movements. Ruth, frowning over her lessons, would beg her to be quiet and one night she asked why the drawing-room fire should not be lit, so that Ethel and Miss Mole could sit there and leave her in peace.

'We can't afford a fire in every room in the house,' Ethel explained.

'Doris has one to herself, Father has another, why should the rest of us have to share one? And anyhow, it's Miss Mole who manages the money now, so you needn't interfere!'

Miss Mole said nothing. This remark was probably intended as a jeer at Ethel, but, at least, it recognized her own existence, and a small smile must have come on her lips, for Wilfrid, entering at that moment, gave a clap of his hands and cried, 'I've been wondering who you were ever since the happy hour when I first saw you and I've found out at last! Good evening, Mona Lisa. And don't pretend you don't know it's you I'm talking to!'

Hannah looked up, then down. 'It's the long nose,' she said.

'Not a bit of it! It's the secret smile. It's all the wisdom of the world.'

Ethel was at a loss and seemed distressed. Ruth glanced up curiously for an instant and then bowed her head over her books and shielded her face with her hands.

'I can't remember, for the moment,' Ethel said, 'who Mona Lisa is.'

'A plain woman,' Hannah said.

68

'Then it's very rude of Wilfrid,' there was relief in Ethel's voice, 'to say you're like her.'

'On the contrary,' he said, 'she may be plain, but she's the most fascinating woman in the world.'

'Oh!' said Ethel blankly, and, after a moment's fidgeting, she went out of the room.

Wilfrid nodded towards the door. 'She's gone to look her up in the dictionary!'

'No, she hasn't,' Ruth spoke dryly. 'She's gone up to her room and she'll be opening and shutting drawers and banging things about for hours and I shan't be able to go to sleep.' Her voice rose painfully. 'Why haven't you more sense?' she cried. 'If you want to say things like that, why can't you say them when she isn't here?'

For the first time in weeks, Hannah forgot to be on her guard. A feeling of great mental weariness, of physical sickness, overcame her. The work slipped from her hands and she leaned back in her chair, shutting her eyes for a minute. It seemed to her horrible that Ruth should have so clear an insight into Ethel's nature, and such bitter experience of it, that Ethel's nature should be what it was. At Ruth's age, Hannah had just gone to school in Upper Radstowe, with an intimate, frank knowledge of sexual processes, acquired by living on a farm, and was discovering that matters which her father had not scrupled to discuss in her presence were the subjects of sly whisperings in the school. The shock she suffered was different from the one to which Lilla piously laid claim, for Lilla was disgusted by physical details and Hannah was disgusted that anyone should consider them unclean, and she had been spared Ruth's irritating contact with a mind subject, no doubt unconsciously, to the dictates of the body.

The crudity of this thought was distasteful to Miss Mole; the truth of it was worse. It was all very well to talk about civilization's benefits to women and the preservation of their chastity, but what was happening to the minds of countless virgins who would never be anything else if they wished to be thought respectable? And while Ruth, like Ethel, was probably in ignorance of causes, she, too, was the unfortunate victim of effects.

69

Hannah sighed, and raised her eyes to find Ruth looking at her with a startled interest, and to wonder, under that look, whether her policy of self-effacement was the right one.

There was a fire in the drawing-room the next evening and there was a feeling of holiday in the house. Robert Corder was speaking at some meeting outside Radstowe and would not be back that night, and Hannah prepared a supper of surprises, such as they could not often have, for he was a hearty eater and needed solid fare. The family had the grace to recognize her efforts: Ethel pathetically did her best to pretend she had no grudge against Wilfrid or Miss Mole, Ruth openly enjoyed the food, Wilfrid forebore to flatter or to tease, and Hannah told herself that this was a very good imitation of a temporarily happy family.

When the meal was over Ruth was left in the dining-room to do her work, as she had desired, in peace, but Hannah lingered to repair the fire and gather up the mending which was her nightly occupation.

'Now you'll be all right, won't you?' she said cheerfully.

Ruth's small, worried face became more strained. 'I didn't say I wanted to be alone,' she said, and Hannah realized that her apparent sullenness was embarrassment. 'I only wanted to be quiet. You sit so still. You're not like Ethel. And she'll be happier, alone, in there with Wilfrid.'

'And I'd rather stay here,' said Hannah, and neither of them spoke again until Ruth pushed her books aside and said she was going to bed.

'Good night,' Hannah said, with a cool nod and smile.

Ruth stooped to the fire and warmed her hands and then, with a little catch of her breath, she went away.

'I shall get her yet!' Hannah said to herself.

At some time during that night, she woke with a start. She had been dreaming a variation of a dream she often had. The scene was always the same. Somewhere in the neighbourhood of her cottage, in one of the low-ceilinged rooms or in the orchard, she was supremely happy, bewildered, or in great distress, and to-night trouble had been predominant. She thought the pain of it must have waked her, or her own cry, but as she lay, trying to compose her-

self, she heard a sound outside her door and the turning of
the handle.

'Who is it?' she said and, under the influence of her dream,
her voice was not quite steady.

'It's only me, Miss Mole. I thought I heard funny noises.'

Hannah fumbled for the matches and lit the candle by
her bed. Ruth stood in the doorway, clad only in her nightgown, with her feet bare, and in the uncertain light she
looked like a little wraith with frightened eyes.

Hannah swung herself out of bed. 'Get in, quick!' she
cried. She threw the bed-clothes over Ruth and put on
her own dressing-gown. 'What is it?' she asked briskly.
'Burglars?'

'I don't know.' Ruth's teeth were chattering. 'I'd been
dreaming.'

'Ah – so had I,' Hannah said.

'I'd been dreaming – and I expect I'm being silly, but I
wish I needn't sleep in that dressing-room. It's bad enough
when Father's there, but to-night his room was so empty or
so – or so full. And I couldn't find the matches to light the
gas, and I thought I heard someone moving, so I ran up
here. I'm sorry, Miss Mole.'

'Don't mention it!' Hannah said, making a funny face
and sitting on the bed. 'If it's burglars, I propose to stay
here. No good interfering with them. Might cause bad
feeling. We'll give them a few minutes to help themselves,
and when I think they've gone I'll go and look for them.'

Ruth laughed, and it was the first time Hannah had heard
her do it naturally. 'I don't suppose it was burglars at all.
They wouldn't come to a house like this, would they? But
I don't want to go back to that room, Miss Mole.'

'You shan't. I'll go. We don't mind each other's sheets,
do we? And you'll feel happy up here, won't you, with my
little ship on the mantelpiece, and you'll go to sleep?'

Ruth nodded. 'Where did you get your little ship?'

'Off the mantelpiece in my old home in the country. I'll
tell you about it some day.'

'Whereabouts in the country?'

'Over the hills – but not very far away.' She was silent
for a minute or two, looking down. 'Well,' she said, 'I

should think they've gone by this time. Good night. Promise you'll go to sleep.'

'Won't you be frightened yourself?'

'Not a bit. I met a burglar once and liked him. I'll tell you about that, too, in the day-time. I shall have to put out the candle, you know.'

'I know. I don't mind. Miss Mole —' darkness made this confession easier — 'I don't believe I really believed there were burglars at all.'

'No. It was a bad dream. I was having one myself. I'm glad you woke me. I'll buy some night-lights to-morrow. The matches are never where you want them.'

'And they go out when you're in a hurry. And Miss, Mole —' this was still more difficult —'you won't tell anybody will you?'

'But, of course I shall!' Hannah said with a mocking seriousness. 'The first thing I shall do in the morning is to tell Doris, then your sister, then your cousin, and when your father comes home he shall hear all about it.'

Ruth laughed again, a little ghostly sound, and Hannah, as she went down the dark stairs, said to herself triumphantly, 'I've got her now!' but with her triumph a little dismay was mixed. She knew the hampering nature of possessions.

Chapter 10

SEEING those two at breakfast, the next morning, no one would have guessed that their relationships had changed. Ruth was too shy, Hannah was too wily, and they were both too cautious, to behave differently. Hannah did not want to press her victory home. The enemy would surrender unconditionally before long, and there was no need to augment Ethel's jealousy. In Ethel's view, Wilfrid, of course, had been talking nonsense when he implied that Miss Mole was the most fascinating woman in the world, but his nonsense usually had enough truth in it to make it sting or soothe, and poor Ethel, who could not hide her feelings, was hurt and puzzled. What made a woman fascinating to Wilfrid? she seemed to ask, as she looked from one to the other. To Ethel, at twenty-three, Miss Mole was almost old and had certainly passed the age when she could hope to be attractive. She was not good-looking, yet when she was in the room Wilfrid always watched her. Ethel liked Miss Mole and would have liked her better if Wilfrid had not liked her at all: she gave the house a feeling of safety: if it caught fire, if anybody was ill, Miss Mole would know what to do, and things had been more comfortable since she came. Ethel was grateful for her freedom from the harassing business of planning meals and trying to make Doris do her duty without disturbing their common bond in the Mission, and being reported as a stern mistress to other members of the Girls' Club. There was every reason why Ethel should have been an inefficient housekeeper, and every reason why Miss Mole should be a good one. At forty, all distracting desires, ambitions, hopes and disappointments must have passed away, leaving the mind calm and satisfied with the affairs of every day, a state for which Ethel sometimes envied Miss Mole, more often pitied her, while always she tried to believe

73

that Wilfrid's flattery was a new way of winning Ethel's
attention to himself.

Naturally, no one saw Miss Mole when she was alone in
her dove-cot and no one was privy to her sleeping or her
waking dreams. They were all too young or too self-
absorbed to understand that her life was as important to
her as theirs to them and had the same possibilities of adventure and romance; that, with her, to accept the present as
the pattern of the future would have been to die. This was
the attitude of hope and not of discontent and what Ethel
saw as the resignation of middle-age was the capacity to
make drama out of humdrum things. Here was a little
society, in itself commonplace enough, but a miniature of all
societies, with the same intrigues within and the same
threatenings of danger from outside. It had its acknowledged head in Robert Corder, who, sure of himself and his
position, had no suspicion that his rule was criticized by his
second-in-command, or that his subjects might rebel. In one
of his public speeches, or in a sermon, he would have des-
cribed the home just as Hannah saw it, as a small community in which personalities were stronger than theories
of conduct, resilience more enduring than rigidity; he would
have said there was no life without change and struggle,
and, becoming metaphorical – Hannah enjoyed composing
sermons for him – he would have likened young people to
plants which must be given space and air, and their elders
to the wise gardeners who would not confine or clip until
the growth had attained a certain sturdiness, and he would
have meant everything he said, and believed he followed
his own counsels, but in his home he had planted his seed-
lings within a narrow compass and assumed that all was
well with them. It was enough that he had given them good
ground and it was their privilege and duty to prosper. He
cast an eye on them, now and then, saw they were still
where he had put them, took submission for content and
closeness for companionship. Doubtless, he wanted them to
grow – Hannah gave him credit for that – but he would
have resented any divergence from the shape he liked himself and though he did not flourish his shears openly, everyone knew they were in his pocket. There was a general

conspiracy to keep them there; and the struggles took place underground. He was a busy man and he was not likely to look for what was hidden.

Other people, as usual, knew more about his family than he did, and he took his place at the supper-table one evening, wearing an expression that boded trouble. He always tried to translate his anger into grief and this produced a look which demanded recognition, or threatened to turn sour and, as it was better to meet him half-way than to sit in an awed silence, Ethel asked anxiously if he felt unwell.

'If I did,' he said, 'I hope I should be able to hide it. I have had a distressing experience. Two, in fact.'

'But it was the Education Committee Meeting this evening, wasn't it?' Ethel asked.

'Exactly,' he said. He looked coldly at Wilfrid. 'I want to talk to you after supper. And as though one misfortune were not enough, I met Samuel Blenkinsop on my way home. I had not seen him since he gave his very dull paper on Charles Lamb, and I must own that he had the decency to seem embarrassed.' He looked round the table, waiting for his cue, but no one risked a question or a comment. To ask why Mr. Blenkinsop looked embarrassed would be to admit stupidity: a comment made at this dangerous moment when some disaster was hanging over Wilfrid's handsome head, would certainly be the wrong one, to be silent was almost an affront, and if the younger people heard, in Hannah's voice, a gallant attempt to save the situation, she knew it herself as the result of an irresistible curiosity.

'You mean,' she suggested, 'he was ashamed of his paper. He'd been trying to forget it and when he saw you the horror swooped on him. I know the feeling.'

'I mean nothing of the sort, Miss Mole.' He paused to look a little inquisitively, but more repressingly, at the maker of this rather surprising speech. 'He would be fortunate if he had nothing else to be ashamed of.'

Swiftly she had to readjust her view of that stolid young man, working out chess problems in his quiet room, and, before she knew it, she had said incredulously, not unhopefully, 'Has he robbed the bank?'

She was conscious, at once, of consternation in the room,

75

like a thin fog through which the familiar appeared slightly distorted. With a stealthy movement, Wilfrid had taken his handkerchief from his sleeve and was wiping his nose very thoroughly and Ethel was looking from her father to Miss Mole, uncertain and frightened of his reaction, half-suspicious of her intention; the quick little frown of Ruth's anxieties had come and gone. Evidently, this was considered a frivolous question to ask of a man who was in earnest; it had a levity unsuitable in Miss Mole and to the occasion and all she could do now was to look inquiringly stupid.

Mr. Corder's grief had been re-translated into an astonished anger. 'If that was meant to be humorous, Miss Mole, I'm afraid it is not successful.'

'No, no, it wasn't!' Hannah protested. 'But –' now that she was attacked, she was at liberty to strike back and there was a gurgle of laughter under her voice, 'it would have been funny if he'd really done it!'

'Oh, Miss Mole!' Ethel gasped.

'Out of character,' Miss Mole explained neatly, holding up her small head.

'So you are acquainted with Mr. Blenkinsop?' Robert Corder asked slowly, as though he were on the track of a crime.

'I've seen him –' Hannah began, and Robert Corder interrupted her with a betraying sharpness.

'Not in the chapel!' he said, and she knew it was only pride that prevented him from asking the questions she did not mean to answer.

She had had her little fling and it had done her good, though she feared Wilfrid would suffer for it, and while the interview in the study was taking place Ethel was looking at her resentfully.

'You shouldn't make Father angry'! she exclaimed.

'Did I?' said Hannah. She was holding out a spoonful of a treacly concoction of malt she had persuaded Ruth to take and, under her little air of command, she was afraid Ruth would refuse it, in token of loyalty to her father. She was wonderfully relieved when Ruth docilely put her lips to the spoon. 'Good girl!' she said. 'I always used to spit it

76

out. Dozens of bottles were bought for me and not a speck of it did I swallow. Kept it in my mouth – and ran.'

'If Wilfrid gets into trouble with Father, he'll be sent home,' Ethel mourned, 'and he isn't happy there. His mother doesn't understand him.'

'I shouldn't think she understands anything – except prayer meetings.'

'Ruth! How can you be so naughty?'

'I don't care. She's a horrible old woman and she smells of camphor. All Father's relations are horrible, and Uncle Jim's the only decent one we've got.'

This diverted Ethel. 'Wouldn't it be lovely if he came for Christmas!' she cried, but Ruth would never share her raptures, and Ethel began pacing the room again in her suspense.

Wilfrid, however, returned cheerfully. 'It's all right!' he said, 'nothing worse than idleness. No lies necessary. But it's confoundedly awkward to have the uncle on all these committees. He'd met the Dean – as well as Mr. Blenkinsop. What's old Blenkinsop done? You weren't tactful, Mona Lisa, but you were funny.'

'Was I?' Hannah said. 'It was Mr. Blenkinsop who seemed funny to me – picking the locks, running off with the bags of money –'

'But he hasn't!' Ethel exclaimed. 'I don't think you ought to say such things.'

'If he had,' said Hannah, solemnly, 'I should be the last person to breathe a word of it.'

'Then you'd be quite wrong!'

'Poor Ethel!' Wilfrid said tenderly. 'It's no good crossing swords with Mona Lisa.'

'You're all very unkind!' Ethel cried. 'Making fun of everything, when Father's so upset. You don't know how he feels it when anyone leaves the chapel. It's like – like a personal insult.'

'Ah, yes,' Wilfrid said sympathetically, 'he'd take it like that, of course,' and he looked at Hannah who was cautiously unresponsive. 'But is that all poor old Blenkinsop's done? Lucky fellar! Still, it's a poor heart that never rejoices and a dull one that doesn't take the chance, and I

77

find the chapel distinctly entertaining. I love hearing Mrs. Spenser-Smith telling everybody she's got a silk petticoat when she swishes down the aisle, and seeing poor old Ernest's agonies when the widows drop their mites into the plate, and many a time I've seen him slip past them before they could do it. I like old Ernest.'

'I like them both,' Ethel said, and, forgetting her grievances, she added eagerly, 'I wonder if they'll have a party this Christmas.'

'If they do,' said Ruth, 'I'm going to have a bad cold in the head. I hate their parties.'

'And my duty to my mother will keep me at her side during the festive season. Honestly, I'd rather see her crying over the Christmas pudding and hear her telling fibs about my father and wishing I were like him – and we all know he was a bit of a scamp, and that's why I hold his memory dear – than go to one of those – you know the word I want to use, Mona Lisa – well, one of those parties.'

'Miss Mole won't believe you. She knows Mrs. Spenser-Smith.'

'But I've never been to one of her parties,' Hannah said.

'I wonder if she'll ask you!'

'I should hardly think so, and I should have to stay at home and look after Ruth.'

'Which is far better,' Wilfrid murmured. 'Well, I've promised to turn over a new leaf and I'm going to do it, beside my cheery little gas-fire, so farewell! But I'm always forgetting to ask you something. Who makes my bed?'

'I do,' said Hannah.

'Then, what's happened to my mattress?'

'It was there this morning.'

'I know it's there, but it's different. It's lumpy.'

'They get lumpy in time,' Hannah said.

'It's done it in jolly quick time, then.'

'But it's a new one!' Ethel said. 'It's got a red and fawn ticking, hasn't it, Miss Mole?'

'Green,' said Hannah. 'Mine's red and fawn.'

'Then you've got the wrong one. We'll have to change them.'

'And give Mona Lisa the lumps! What are you talking about?'

'I'll go and look at them now,' Ethel said.

'Miss Mole's the housekeeper!' Ruth cried hastily.

'But I bought that mattress,' Ethel said, going off with a jingle.

'She'll pull the bed-clothes off and forget to put them on again!' Wilfrid exclaimed, going after her.

'Did you change them?' Ruth asked softly, and Hannah nodded. 'I thought so!' Ruth said with a chuckle.

Chapter 11

If Hannah had chosen to look for them, she could have found as many reasons and excuses for Robert Corder's peculiarities as for those of Ethel and Ruth. Robert Corder himself did not seek excuses; he saw his troubles as the faults of other people and it did not occur to him that the chief of his difficulties was that he had been born too late. Thirty or forty years earlier, he would have been a happier man. It would not have been necessary, then, to make the mental compromises he found so bewildering; he would have been set firmly on the infallibility of his creed and his authority as its exponent would have been unquestioned. Life would have been simpler to direct and consequently simpler to live. It was the knowledge that infallibility of book, of man and of creed was increasingly denied, and with a strength under which one must bend or break, that took the full sweetness out of his position, and being a man of great energy but no intellect, he felt bound to give the appearance of keeping abreast of modern thought, while his mind resented, and did not really make, the effort. In the days when to doubt or to question was bad manners, if it was not sin, his work would have offered him everything he wanted – adulation, security of mind and station and the loyal following of that army of men and boys it had always been his ambition to lead. Self-confidence, physical strength, a manly exterior were his, but the army was merely a handful of old soldiers, suspicious of changes, and raw recruits, and of this disappointment, with its implication of failure in himself or his teaching, his encounter with Samuel Blenkinsop had reminded him. Those people in his chapel who kept the old simplicity and to whom he was God's vicegerent, were his inferiors, as he knew too well: most of his flock were his inferiors and this contributed to his comfort, but a few were his equals in ability, if not in state, and these accepted new ideas rather too quickly for the Reverend Robert, who liked to point the way himself, or else they took the Gospel with a literalness which was not practical. If Mrs. Spenser-Smith had not been a level-headed woman, her husband would have given all he had to the poor, without considering their deserts. Fortunately, Mrs. Spenser-Smith and the Reverend Robert were of one mind about deserts, of which agreement a luxurious arm-chair in his study and a son at Oxford were proofs. There is no union, however, which does not involve chafing at times, and the pride he took in casually mentioning the son at Oxford was offset by his annoyance that Howard should have a privilege his father had missed and could have put to better use. Undeniably, a part of Howard's life was an unknown world to Robert Corder, and while this did not prevent him from criticism and informatory observations, it put him at a disadvantage for which he blamed his benefactress and subtly punished Howard.

And now Mrs. Spenser-Smith's anxiety for the general welfare of the family had brought Miss Mole into the house.

He glanced with a frown, to which he quickly added a sigh, at the handsomely framed photograph on his desk, another of Mrs. Spenser-Smith's gifts. He did not like that representation of his wife. He preferred the little one on his bedroom mantelpiece in which her soft face looked at him hopefully above the stiff collar and tie, and under the hard straw hat of her youth. It told him that he was indeed the man he believed himself to be, while this photograph, of a much later date, had suffered some distortion of expression in the enlarging process on which Mrs. Spenser-Smith had insisted. It vexed him that people who had not known her should imagine that faintly humorous, patient look was hers. Miss Mole, for instance, must have received a false impression, if she was capable of receiving any impression at all, and about this Mr. Corder's opinion wavered. She seemed stupid, outside her sphere. She had been stupidly frivolous – or was it merely tactless? – tonight, but he was disturbed by her remark, ridiculous in

81

itself, that it would be out of Samuel Blenkinsop's character to rob a bank. They were unlikely words from the Miss Mole he knew and they had been uttered with a crispness and an assurance which, to quote her own expression, were out of character.

He turned to the letters on his desk. He was wasting time over a matter to which he would not have given a thought if Wilfrid's idleness and Blenkinsop's desertion had not upset him. He was, of course, well abreast of his times in his views about women, and it would have horrified him to learn that he could not judge a clever or a plain woman fairly. A clever one challenged him to a combat in which he might not be the victor and a plain one roused in him a primitive antagonism. In failing to please him, a woman virtually denied her sex and became offensive to those instincts which he did his best to ignore.

His letters were soon answered. He might have prepared a sermon, but he was in no mood for it. His interview with the Dean rankled in his memory, his interview with Wilfrid had not given him the satisfaction he expected. Wilfrid, even when submissive, suggested an amused superiority, impossible to notice and therefore impossible to deal with. Samuel had been heavily courteous, but uncommunicative, in reply to the rallying reproaches with which Mr. Corder had met him. In these days a young man showed no pleasure at being treated as an equal, he seemed to expect it, and, after all, Mr. Corder reflected, Blenkinsop must be well on in the thirties. A different method might have been better, he decided, and he had no desire to be another man's conscience. He had done his duty in the way of reminder, but he was not a tradesman seeking custom, and that brought his thoughts back to Wilfrid, his sister's son. She had made a marriage to which her father was opposed and it had turned out badly, but the surprisingly snug profits of the parental drapery business had been left to her. The elder Corder had been just as strongly opposed to Robert's entering the ministry: to the small tradesman, it seemed a costly business, with years of paying out money for which he would get no return, and Robert, as stubborn as his sister, had financed himself with immense difficulty and labour and some timely help from good Nonconformists who were attracted by the handsome, eager young man. Robert Corder considered his rebellion, unlike his sister's, justified by its intention and its results which his father had not had the generosity to acknowledge, while he had rewarded her, who had merely followed her inclination, and left her in a position to pay her brother for his care of her son. Irritated that he could not afford to get rid of Wilfrid and lose the money, he took a turn up and down the room, glancing at the clock. Ruth must have forgotten to say good night to him. Hurt by his favourite daughter, angry with Wilfrid, Blenkinsop and Miss Mole, he could not settle down to read or to write, and Hannah, entering punctually with the tea-tray, found him standing in front of the fire with his hands in his pockets.

'Always punctual!' he said with deceptive cordiality.

'I try to be,' Hannah said modestly, putting down the tray. 'But what a miserable little fire!' She knelt down to replenish it. 'Men,' she said, as though to herself, while she was busy with poker and tongs, 'are chillier creatures than women, but I've never met one yet who could keep a fire in. There must be some reason for it.'

'Perhaps we have other things to think of.'

'I hope so,' said Hannah easily.

He wished he had neglected her remark. He did not want to make a precedent of this conversation, but he could not let her have the last word. 'And then, we pay for the coal,' he said.

Still on her knees, she turned and looked at him and, suspecting a hint of amusement on her foreshortened face, he went on, with authority. 'And, in this household, we have to be economical. I notice that, for some reason or other, Ruth has a night-light in her bedroom.' He was glad to have a definite fault to find. 'That seems to me both pampering and wasteful. I don't understand this innovation. She has been used to going to sleep in the dark.'

'Yes,' said Hannah quietly, 'and waking up in it.'

'And waking up in it – certainly,' he said.

'It's not good for her,' Hannah said decidedly.

He did not like her familiarity with his hearthrug. 'Won't

83

you sit down?' he asked. 'I think we had better discuss this matter.'

'I'll just sweep up the hearth first,' she said, and he thought it was extraordinary that no woman could give her whole attention to a subject.

But it appeared that Miss Mole had been thinking while she swept, for when she had finished and sat down, she said at once, 'You have made me responsible for the expenses of the house. If I keep within my allowance, as I have done, so far, I don't think it's fair to criticize details.'

'It's not really a question of the money, Miss Mole,' he said irritably. 'It's a question of training. I don't want Ruth encouraged in her nervousness. I hoped she was growing out of it. Often, when – when her mother was with us, she would come into our room and wake us, saying she was frightened. What is she afraid of?'

'Bears, perhaps,' Hannah said thoughtfully. 'When I was a child, I was troubled by a most persistent and accomplished bear. And there was no way of escaping him. He could climb perpendicular walls; he could unlock doors. It's no good pitting reason against things that are not reasonable in themselves – like fears.'

'So,' he said, 'you are a student of psychology!'

Hannah let that sneer pass. 'Bears,' she said, still in her quiet tone and looking at the fire, 'or wolves. There was another time when I knew a wolf would catch me if I wasn't on a certain stair before my bedroom door banged behind me. The wolf was half a game, but the bear was a real bear.'

'But this is ridiculous, Miss Mole. You're not going to tell me Ruth fancies there are wild animals in her bedroom!

'In the middle of the night? I could fancy it myself! And Ruth's young – and old – for her age.' She looked up at him. 'What about ghosts?' she asked. There was another question on the tip of her tongue but, in loyalty to Ruth, she would not ask it. Not once had Ruth spoken of her mother, there was no photograph of her in the dressing-room, and what Hannah wanted to know was whether Ruth had loved or feared the dead woman who had known, perhaps with love, perhaps with sternness, how to manage her.

'Ghosts!' Robert Corder snorted. 'I would rather it was bears!'

'I expect she would too,' Hannah said promptly, and stood up. 'Bears or ghosts, the night-light will keep them off.'

'I'm not satisfied about it,' he said. Miss Mole was taking too much for granted. 'And Ruth knows I'm near her.'

Hannah loosed her folded hands and raised her shoulders. 'You are the master of the house,' she said, quite unnecessarily, he thought, 'but I ask you,' her hands came together again, 'to let her have the night-light. I warn you not to take it from her. Ruth isn't strong, but I can look after her if I'm given the chance.'

'That is partly what you are here for.'

'Then give me the chance,' she said, smiling, rather startlingly, for the first time.

'I'll think it over,' he said, turning towards his tea-tray.

'Thank you,' she said quietly, and he was vexed that she should thank him. Had there been something ironical in her tone?

He sat, stirring his tea, considering their conversation and searching for offence in her share of it. She had been a little too talkative with her stories of her childhood. She was gaining confidence, he supposed, and might prove to be one of those chattering women if she was encouraged. Her hint of understanding Ruth better than he did was annoying. But it was true that Ruth was not strong. She caught cold easily – like her mother. He would think it over, he told himself, but he knew that Miss Mole would have her way. He was not going to run a risk and be blamed if harm came of it, and she might be right. Mrs. Spenser-Smith had spoken of her experience. He felt puzzled about Miss Mole and wished he had not mentioned money. Parsimony was not one of his failings and it had been unfair to himself – the result of his upsetting day – to talk as though it were.

Chapter 12

RUTH'S door was open when Hannah went up to bed and there was no light in her room. Had Mr. Corder been up and blown it out, in the cause of discipline? She was ready to rush downstairs and upbraid him, when a sharp-whistled note called her in.

'I got into bed,' Ruth said slowly, 'and the matches weren't on the table so I couldn't light the night-light and I thought I'd wait till you came up.'

'If you got out of bed to open the door, why didn't you get the matches at the same time?'

'The door wasn't shut,' Ruth said.

'I see,' said Hannah. She admired the strategy and the adroitness of Ruth's explanation and she had to control the gratified twitching of her lips as she lighted the guardian lamp. 'But, in future,' she said severely, 'I shall light it myself when you go up to bed.'

'Ten minutes after would be better. Then you can turn out the gas, too. I don't like turning out gas. I have to get out of bed again to see if I've done it properly. Several times. Did you do that?'

'There was no gas in my home. Lamps downstairs, candles upstairs. And on a very moony night, I didn't light my candle. We don't pull down our bedroom blinds in the country, and the lady could look in if she liked and I could look out and see her trailing her skirts over the tree-tops. And the owls used to hoot as she went by.' She straightened the quilt over Ruth's motionless little body. 'Go to sleep. Good night.'

'Just shut the door for a minute, please, Miss Mole,' Ruth said quickly.

Hannah obeyed, and as she turned back to the bed she was thankful for the nights of her childhood in the bare bedroom with the sloping roof and the open window free of these lace curtains and venetian blinds and she was sorry for Ruth who was saying slowly, 'I don't believe I've ever heard an owl.'

'Not in Beresford Road, I'm afraid.'

'No, not owls.' She looked at Hannah as though she meant to say something, and then decided to say something else. 'Do you go to your home when you have a holiday?'

'It isn't mine any longer. It was sold when my father and mother died, twenty years ago.'

'Twenty years! Then,' said Ruth, shutting her eyes and creasing her forehead, 'I suppose you've got used to it by this time,' and Hannah knew Ruth was thinking about death and about her mother, and the question it had been impossible to ask Robert Corder was answered.

She felt a sharp pain in her throat, yet she could envy Ruth a love which, in all probability, had been without a blemish. The memory of it was something to be cherished, and such a memory had been denied to Hannah Mole.

She heaved a deep sigh. 'I don't think getting used to things is the right way to deal with them,' she said. 'I think –' she was talking more to herself than to Ruth, 'I think that's wasting them. You've got to use them all the time.' She changed her tone and said cheerfully, 'And I didn't lose the whole of my home. I kept a tiny bit of it, a little cottage and an orchard. I couldn't bear to let it go and that's all I could afford to keep when the debts were paid.'

'Then you can go there, in your holidays, and hear the owls again.'

'Well, no, I can't very well,' Hannah said.

'Why not?'

'It's let.'

'Oh, I see. What a pity. But you get the money for it.'

'That's the idea,' Hannah said.

Ruth sighed regretfully. 'I'd like to hear those owls, Miss Mole –' there was the pause Hannah was beginning to know – 'do you like parrots? I hate them.'

'You're full of hates, child. What's the matter with parrots? God made them, I suppose.'

87

'Yes, but he made Mr. Samson too. When you were in the country, you hadn't any neighbours, had you?'

'Cows, sheep, horses, pigs, the owls –'

'But not a parrot or Mr. Samson. I wish he didn't live next door. He always tries to talk to me when he sees me, over the hedge of the back garden. And once he asked me to go into the house. He said he'd got a kitten for me. So I said I didn't like kittens, but really, Miss Mole, I adore them. But I was frightened of him and sometimes I dream about him. But I used to find – I mean, if you talk about nasty things to somebody, they stop worrying you.'

'And how long has this been worrying you?'

'Oh, ever since – about two years ago when he tried to give me the kitten.'

'Poor old man!' Hannah said.

'I think he's an old beast.'

'There you are again! Is there anything you happen to care for, besides kittens?'

'Lots of things,' Ruth said.

'Well, I should like to hear about them, some time, for a change. And I daresay Mr. Samson's lonely too.'

'Too?' Ruth repeated with a catch of her breath.

'Yes. Like me,' Hannah said. 'Good night.'

A surprising answer for that little egotist and a good exit, she said to herself with satisfaction. It would do Ruth no harm to learn that other people, even those middle-aged people who seem so secure to youth, could suffer like herself, and Hannah doubted whether, until this moment, anyone in the house had given Miss Mole a thought detached from some personal connection. Her comfort and happiness, for which the family might have felt some responsibility, was either assumed or ignored. She could well believe that Robert Corder considered any inmate of his house a fortunate person, but even to Wilfrid, who was as much an alien as herself, she was only a kind of mirror in which he could study his own reflection, while Ruth's growing curiosity was only a love of hearing stories. This lack of interest was not flattering, but it had its advantages – like everything else – she told herself, as she entered her dark bedroom and went to the open window.

88

She knelt down and, laying her hands on the sill, she rested her chin on them. The roofs of the opposite houses were wet with a shower the clouds had dropped as they scurried before a harassing little wind, like ships sacrificing their cargo under pursuit, and the wind that chased them brought to Hannah's credulous nostrils a damp smell of apples and moss. Far away, against the dark sky, sweeping in ascending fields from the docks of Radstowe, she thought, or imagined, she could see the high ground hiding her own country. It lay snugly behind that barrier, with its little farms and orchards, its flat lands criss-crossed by willow-edged ditches and cupped by hills. It was a country that satisfied two sides of Hannah's nature. She loved the homeliness of the farms and cottages, washed with pink or white, each with its big or little orchard where spotted pigs rooted in the long grass: she loved the hills groined with pale limestone and their solitary moor-like tops where the heather became black with distance, but it was in the mingling of the familiar and the unknown that she found her chief delight. They seemed separate, but they were one: the homesteads and the fields were only flesh on the bones of earth and the same heart was beating under the grey rocks and the apple trees, just as Hannah's heart was beating alike for the woman who wanted her own fireside, and the one who wanted to wander, the one with a sane desire for love and its obligations and the other who had learnt to fear anything in the nature of a contract.

Her own fireside was over there, behind the barrier, and if she ever sat at it again it would be alone, or with a dog or cat for company. It was ten years since she had been inside the house and since then she had seen it only once, coming upon it stealthily and peering through the apple trees to make sure of its existence outside her dreams. She had taken care not to intrude on the tenant, lest he should think she came in search of the rent he never paid, but she had seen that the house was really there, a little flat-fronted cottage, badly needing another wash of pink, with a plume of smoke very blue against a cold grey sky. That was five years ago and anything might have happened to it since then. It hurt her to think of it neglected, perhaps deserted. It was cruel

89

to ignore it, absurd to own property about which her pride forbade her to ask questions; she was acting with recklessness of the future when she might want her home, but she had been a fool and she must pay for her folly.

The folly had had its sweetness and she remembered the sweetness and folly together, the precious and the worthless, without any sense of incongruity. All life could be likened to that episode, and all human beings, and the worst sorrows came from the failure to accept imperfection, knowing it for the alloy it was and yet, by some strange spiritual alchemy, seeing it as pure gold.

'Like a wedding ring,' Hannah said, twisting her lips ironically.

A little spatter of rain fell between her and those memories. She looked from the dim line on the horizon to the lights of Radstowe, far below on her left hand, and she thought they were like the camp-fires of innumerable explorers in a strange and dangerous country. Each man tended his own fire sedulously and to one, as to Hannah Mole, what lay beyond the ring of light was hopeful adventure; to another, as to Ruth, the justification of his fears was in the darkness.

Hopeful adventure, even here in Robert Corder's house! She was grateful to Fortune who, in making her a servant, had remembered to give her freedom and happiness in herself. She might have been meek and dutiful and dull inside as well as out, or she might have been discontented and defiant. She was lucky, she thought, as she knelt there with her face towards the cottage which might be crumbling and her back to the narrow room which held everything else she had, for the chief of her possessions, as she knew, was the power to see those lights as camp-fires, and herself as an adventuress. She was not sure she told the truth in saying she was lonely. Yes, lonely and tired too, sometimes, and chilled by the thought of poor and solitary old age, but these were moods that passed and there remained for her good company the many natures in her own thin body. And the rich old gentleman was steadily approaching.

The thought of him reminded her of Mr. Samson, who had offered Ruth a kitten, and withheld information from Robert Corder. He seemed to make a habit of talking to

people over hedges; she would give him another opportunity, she decided, and very busy with her inventions about
him, she undressed swiftly. He might be a bad old man,
but he might be a rich one, and if he was so free with his
kittens for a little girl, she said to herself in the vulgar manner that made Lilla wince, he might be equally free with
his money for an older one.

'Upon my word,' she said aloud, 'I believe I'd marry
anyone who asked me – except Robert Corder,' and she
chuckled as she got into bed and chuckled again when she
remembered that she was lying on Wilfrid's mattress.

That was a dishonourable trick, she supposed, but it did
not prevent her from sleeping well. It was not the first she
had played in the course of her career and it would not be
the last. Each week she took threepence from the house-
keeping money to put in the plate on Sunday, and she owed
Mrs. Widdows exactly a penny halfpenny, the price of a
reel of silk. But what did Mrs. Widdows owe her in the
form of kindness? And why should she pay for listening to
sermons she could hear for nothing from Robert Corder on
any other day of the week? These rigid codes of conduct
were made for people who did not know morality when they
saw it. It was immoral for the hardest-worked person in the
house to lie on the hardest bed: it would be wrong for Mr.
Corder's housekeeper to let the offertory plate go by without a contribution, but it was worse to rob the poor in the
person of herself. She was quite happy about the weekly
threepence and quite safe, for, to do Robert Corder justice,
he did not interfere with her expenditure or overlook her accounts, and she recognized his little outburst for what it was,
but there might yet be trouble with Ethel about the mattress.

Strange that, in a world where pain seemed inevitable,
there should be trouble about a mattress! Yes, it seemed
inevitable, not for her, who knew how to protect herself,
but for nearly everybody else: for little Mrs. Ridding with
that enigmatical look on her face, for Ethel, busy with her
suspicions, for Ruth with her fears, even for Mr. Blenkinsop
with his frustrated desire for peace.

She fell asleep, thinking of Mr. Blenkinsop with the bags
of gold under his arms.

Chapter 13

RUTH had not learnt to accept imperfection. She saw it all round her and she was in a constant state of rebellion against it. She saw it in herself, in her father, in Ethel, in the house and in her circumstances. Nothing, to her mind, was what it should have been. The loss of her mother was not included in this criticism. That was a disaster for which there was no expression. She did not join it to these minor but persistent frets as a cause for discontent. It was too big for comparison or connection with anything else she knew. It came from outside and, in a way, it remained outside, as a black, cold cloud would have been outside her body, but it had emptied her life of all that had been soft and gracious and amusing in it. Her father had told her that God, for His own good purposes, had taken her mother to Himself and, unwilling as she always was to believe in His decisions, she had to submit to this one. No power but God's was great enough to bring about so terrible a catastrophe, and she did not wonder that He wanted her for Himself. It was selfish to take her, but it was natural, and she had to endure the loss patiently because she was helpless under it. The things against which Ruth rebelled were those which might so easily have been different, and her mother's death had not created them; they had merely become more apparent and some of them were actually easier to bear without her. The closeness of her contact with her mother's mind had doubled her embarrassment when her father was didactic or petty and Ethel was unreasonable: the quick sympathy which both tried to hide had magnified the importance of what they both deplored: they suffered for and wanted to protect each other, and Ruth could be more stoical when it was only her father and sister and not her mother's husband and daughter who offended her. The tension of one side of

Ruth's life had slackened a little when her mother died, while, on another, it had tightened. Now that she need not be careful to pretend, now that she could neither love nor laugh – and it would have surprised Mrs. Corder's acquaintances and, perhaps, her husband, to know how often she had made Ruth laugh – she could concentrate on her dissatisfactions. She had her ideal of what a home should be. The mother in it would be her mother, but the father would be different. If it was necessary for him to be a minister of religion, he would be the vicar of the Established Church, and the church itself would be old and dim and beautiful and people would not shake hands across the yellow pews and talk intimately about their ailments and their children. They would do that, if they must, in the sunny churchyard, and quietly, with the hush of the service on them and the influence of stained glass and carved stone. The house would be old too, with a cedar on the lawn, and several dogs, and inside there would be pretty and precious things, things which had belonged to ancestors, portraits and old silver, and the ancestors would be admirals and generals and judges. The sons of that house would go to public schools and universities and no one would think it necessary to mention it; the girls would have beauty and beautiful clothes and gracious love affairs: they would not giggle with young men, like Ethel, or be cross with everybody, like Ruth: there would be order in that household and quiet servants. She was not sure whether the father would be more like a country gentleman than a vicar, interested in agriculture and sport, or whether he would be vague and gentle, with some absorbing hobby which made him lovably absent-minded, but she knew he would never embarrass his wife and children, he would neither be effusive nor condescending with his parishioners, and his children need not hesitate to ask anyone to tea. School life and home life could merge into each other safely and though, like all vicars, he would be more or less of a public character, he could be trusted not to say things at which his children's friends could sneer.

These were the surroundings and the conditions Ruth wanted and her mother had not taken them with her. Ruth had wanted them almost as much while she lived, and in default of the unattainable, she posed at school as a stout Nonconformist and a despiser of aristocracy who was fiercely loyal to her humble Puritan forbears. There were girls in her form who went to Beresford Road Chapel and, while her father preached, Ruth was listening with those girls' ears and framing replies to criticism, though with much criticism she had not to deal. The girls were as ready as their parents to admire, Ruth had her reflected glory, but she could not risk the loss of it by introducing these admirers into the home. Her father had his place in the pulpit, Ruth had hers in the school, where, with her defiances and the humour her family never saw, she was considered an amusing and original character by her contemporaries, but how would she appear to them when her father called her Ruthie and teased her and made rather foolish jokes in his desire to put the young people at their ease and to show that he could be a jolly, ordinary man? Their conception of her would be changed; she would be different too, and she could never again be the self which came most naturally to her at school.

It would have been simple in the old Vicarage; in Beresford Road it was impossible. She kept her two lives apart, despising herself for snobbishness and lack of courage, but keeping the place she had made for herself and living almost freely for half her time. No one there would have suspected her of the fears that assailed her at night or of yearnings for beauty within and without. She was a hard worker and though this keenness and an odd sense of fair play constrained her from being tiresome in class, these virtues were forgiven for the sake of her readiness to see and mimic the peculiarities of her superiors; the Ruth who strolled homewards with her friends was gay and impudent, or downright and cynical according to her mood and the impression she wished to make, and very different from the one who, later on, brooded over the supper-table, and to a Ruth who, one day, was showing off more successfully than usual, it was terrible to turn and see the approaching figure of Miss Mole, clad in a very old-fashioned ulster. It might have been a handsome, and it must have been a sturdy garment when it was bought: it had a character which the oncoming of dusk

94

and the drizzling rain could not disguise: it gave Miss Mole a waist where waists no longer existed and a breadth of shoulder out of all proportion to her thin frame; it was impossible not to notice it and it was all Ruth could do to sustain her mirth under the sound of those rapidly-approaching footsteps.

The figure passed; Ruth felt a nudge at each side of her; someone giggled and Ruth continued her chatter, but when she parted from her companions, she began to run, drawing sharp breaths through her piteously-parted lips. She was like Peter: she had denied her friend, and if those girls ever saw the ulster again and recognized Miss Mole as the wearer what would they think of Ruth? They had nudged and giggled and she had not said a word. She ought to have called out to Miss Mole and stopped her, but she had been afraid of ridicule. She had not only committed a disloyal act, but one which might be discovered, and in that bitter moment she learnt that secret sin could be forgotten, while sin revealed to the world could be remembered for ever. All she could do now was to hurry and wipe away some of the stain.

Going home was not quite as bad as it had been for the last two years, she was not so anxious to linger in the streets, her habit of running past the next-door house and entering her own with a rush, was an old one, and Miss Mole, lighting the hall gas, showed no surprise at Ruth's breathless entrance, though her sharply benevolent eyes may have seen more than the dampness of Ruth's clothes as she said briskly, 'Don't stand about in your coat. And you'll change your stockings, won't you?'

'What about you, Miss Mole?' Ruth said faintly. 'You're wet too.'

Miss Mole patted the abominable ulster. 'It can't get through this. Do go and change or you'll have a cold and it seems a pity to waste one when there isn't a party to dodge.'

Ruth's smile was wan. Miss Mole, revealing herself as a person of humour and understanding, was simply making things worse for her. She went towards the stairs where there was more shadow. 'Did you come across Regent Square?'

'Yes. I'd been for a walk round the hill to look at the river. Lovely it was, too, in the rain. The mist was thick on the water and there was a tree on the other side like a torch blazing through a fog. But the leaves will be dropping under this rain.'

For a moment, Ruth was held from her purpose. She wished Miss Mole would go on talking like that. She said things differently, in Ruth's experience, from other people and in a different voice. She had spoken of a moony night, and beauty and peace had stolen over her listener, and now Ruth felt the chill danger of thick mist and the joy of seeing light ahead. The necessity for confession seemed less pressing, the world of vision became of more importance than the one of facts, and while she was persuading herself that it would be easy and kinder to be silent, she began to speak.

'Miss Mole,' she said, 'I think I saw you. I mean – I saw you. But you went past so quickly and I was too late. You know how things happen. I ought to have shouted to you at once, but it would have looked so funny to the other girls if I'd recognized you when you were nearly out of sight, so I didn't – but I feel so mean.'

'Mean?' said Hannah. 'I'm grateful. When I'm in this ulster, I'm supposed to be invisible. I know what it's like. I ought not to wear it at all, but it's thick and it's an old friend. If you'd stopped me I should have died of shame. Thank goodness you didn't. I won't run the risk again, except in the dark. Now will you kindly go and change those clothes? You ought to have worn your mackintosh. It's high-tea night and when I was up on the hill I suddenly thought of mushrooms and I bought some on the way home. We'll have them with scrambled eggs and you can come and help me if you like.'

Ruth was childish in some ways, but she was not stupid. She could see that Miss Mole's words might be tactful as well as true. She had not dared to ask whether Miss Mole had seen and avoided her and, if so, whether it was for her own sake or for Ruth's. The confession had not been a full one, but, after Miss Mole's expressed horror of the ulster, how could she mention it? That would have been easing her soul at the cost of Miss Mole's feelings and though it was convenient to say no more, it was not necessarily wrong. Less and less, as she grew older, did she believe that the unpleasant things were the good ones and, as she slowly changed her stockings, she gave way willingly to the belief, which had been reluctant until to-day, that Miss Mole could be trusted with her omissions as safely as with her fears. She felt, rather than thought, that Miss Mole's mind could overleap gaps and understand how they came there, and when she went down to the kitchen, she felt stiff and awkward in the consciousness of a surrender she had been determined not to make.

Miss Mole was skinning the mushrooms, and when she had shown Ruth how to do it they sat at the kitchen table together and worked busily.

'I've been thinking about clothes,' Hannah said, and Ruth, though she turned red, decided that it was a good thing to talk about them at once, before the thought of the ulster became a solid barrier against the subject. 'I've always liked them, and never had what I wanted. When I went to school, we weren't all dressed alike, and I was a scarecrow – but much more noticeable. The only thing to do was to pretend I had an original taste in dress and the other poor things hadn't, and I've done that ever since, except about my shoes and stockings. I'm extravagant about them, so I have to go short elsewhere.' She glanced down at the shoes she had been too hurried to change. 'There isn't a better pair in Radstowe, but I broke a window with this one once,' she said carelessly.

Ruth looked up. 'What did you do that for?'

'It's one of the stories I can't tell you, but it was very sad – and exciting.'

'Can't you tell me, really? You're always talking about stories and not telling them. There's the one about the burglar –'

'Ah yes, but there's so little time. You have to work in the evenings and then you have to go to bed, or there's someone else in the room.'

'To-night would be a good night,' Ruth suggested, 'and I haven't so very much to do. Unless Wilfrid's going to be in?'

97

'No, he'll be out.'

'Oh well, then –!' Ruth exclaimed.

'We'll see. You have to be in the right mood for telling stories. But do remind me to ask Ethel if she knows any old woman who would condescend to wear that ulster.'

'Oh, Miss Mole,' Ruth almost pleaded, 'I shouldn't give it away, if you like it.'

'I don't. I merely master it.'

'But you said it was an old friend, and there must be yards and yards of stuff in it. Perhaps you could have it altered.'

'No, I'm not brave enough to show it to a tailor. But I think I'll keep it. It's good enough for wearing to the pillar-box on a dark night, but I won't wear it anywhere else,' she said, and now Ruth knew that Miss Mole could forgive everything she understood, and that she probably understood everything.

Chapter 14

For once, Hannah's hands were idle. She lay back in the arm-chair by the dining-room fire with a book on her knee, and Ruth, glancing up from her work, now and then, saw that her eyes were often shut. She looked different like that; younger and, though Ruth did not find words for her thought, more vulnerable. Her dress of dark-red silk was not fashionable and it was old, but the skirt of it and her silk stockings shimmered in the firelight, the buckles on her slippers sparkled, and her idleness and her elegant feet gave Ruth a feeling of satisfaction and of approach to the ideal life in the Vicarage, where everybody changed for dinner, and no one was in a hurry. Her mother, whose resistance to evening meetings had not been complete and who might be called out at any hour on missions of mercy, had seldom worn a dress unsuitable for sudden excursions, and this had offended Ruth's sense of fitness and added to the restlessness of a home in which everybody was expected to be doing good outside it.

All stuffy things had been implied, for Ruth, in the name of housekeeper; stuffy frocks, thick stockings, a prim face and an oppressive sense of duty, yet here was Miss Mole looking, for all her lack of fashion, like a lady who belonged to a world unconnected with chapels, where beauty and leisure were expected and attained. It was a peep through a door Ruth had always wanted to open, and she said quietly, 'I like it when you're not darning.'

Hannah opened her eyes for a moment. 'Half asleep,' she said drowsily and shut them again. This was not the truth, for her mind was busy, but Hannah was not scrupulous about truth. She was not convinced of its positive value as human beings knew it, she considered it a limiting and an embarrassing convention. The bare truth was often dull and more often awkward, while lies were a form of imagination and a protection for the privacy of her thoughts and, in a life lived in houses which were not her own and where she was never safe from intrusion, it was necessary to have this retreat.

Now, behind the veil of her sleepiness, she was wondering if she was altogether glad of Ruth's change of front. It was what she had been working for and she found, once more, that gain was often loss. She had won Ruth and that exciting campaign was over. It had been conducted with a skill of which, unfortunately, only she was aware, and of which she could not boast, and her reward was a possession needing care and involving obligations. She was growing fond of Ruth and, ten years ago, she had promised herself future freedom from soft emotions. They were more trouble than they were worth, but vanity was her weakness. She strove for admiration and found she could get nothing without giving something else. She saw that she would have to resign herself to being fond of Ruth, she had gone too far to withdraw, but there she would have to stop: she must not saddle herself with the whole family and, indeed, it was not likely that she would have the chance. Robert Corder and she were naturally antipathetic, though he had been amiable this evening, praising the mushrooms, with perhaps a covert suggestion that the kitchen was her sphere and she would do well to stay in it, while Ethel was so much divided against herself, dragged in one direction by religion and in another by mundane desires, that no one else could put the parts together and handle them.

'I've nearly finished,' she heard Ruth saying, 'I'm nearly ready for the burglar story.'

'It's not a good one for this time of night.'

'Oh, Miss Mole, you said you liked him!'

'So I did, but then I've got queer tastes. And I'm afraid you've scamped your work.'

'But it's such a chance – when everybody's out.'

'Oh well –' Hannah said, hastily gathering her thoughts. 'It was when I was living with an old lady who wore a wig. People without experience of wigs believe they simplify life. They think you just take them off and put them on. Nothing of the sort. A wig needs as much care as a pedigree Pekinese and I know, because I've looked after both. I lost a situation once because a woman heard me telling her nasty little dog what I really thought of it, but it did me good, and the dog too, I daresay. Well, anyhow, this old lady had a wig, in fact she had two, because they had to be sent to the hairdresser, now and then, to be tidied up, and they were bright gold. She was rich, and I suppose she liked the colour. But she wasn't a bad old woman. I was fond of her. Well, one night – it was a lonely house, simply asking for burglars to walk into it – and I ought to have told you that one of the wigs had come back from the hair-dresser that very evening, in a registered parcel, and I'd left it, unopened, on the landing table where the bedroom candles were put. It was that kind of house.'

'Ah,' said Ruth, 'the burglar thought it was jewels!'

'Wait a minute. I saw my old lady into bed and into her nightcap and I longed to tell her how nice she looked when she wasn't tricked out in the yellow hair –'

'But it must have been awful when the wig was off and the cap wasn't on! I don't think I could have stayed there.'

'I didn't stay long. The old lady died. She was going to leave me some money, she said, and I think she meant it, but she died first. It's a way old ladies have.'

'Did she die of fright about the burglar?'

'She didn't know there'd been one, because he took noth-ing. Nothing!' Hannah repeated impressively. 'And all through me! If she'd known that, she might have given me the money there and then.'

'And you didn't tell her?'

'I haven't told a soul until to-night. And I'd better warn you that the story's got a moral.'

'Of course it has. And the moral's that you mustn't be too modest.'

'That's always been one of my failings,' Hannah said with a wink. 'But this story's hanging fire a bit, isn't it? I'll cut it short. I woke up in the night and heard a rustling sort of noise. "Mice!" I said to myself, but it wasn't exactly a mousy noise. So I listened and my heart began to thump and, very quietly, I got out of bed. I turned the door handle without making a sound, and then –' she sat up to illustrate her action, 'I threw the door open – like that – and what do you think I saw?'

Ruth shook her head. She knew she was not expected to reply.

'I saw the burglar, looking at himself in the mirror, with my old lady's wig on the top of his head!'

'Then,' said Ruth slowly, 'there must have been a light on the landing.'

'Yes, there was,' Hannah said quickly. 'He'd turned it on. And that's where you're supposed to laugh and you haven't even smiled.'

'I'm thinking about the light. He can't have been a good burglar.'

'He wasn't. He was a funny one. I laughed and he laughed and, after that, we felt we were friends, and he went away like a gentleman, saying he was glad he'd met me. And the moral is that we must be ready to laugh on the most terrifying occasions. Now, I call that rather a good story and a good moral, and you don't seem to like it a bit.'

'I'm rather worried about it,' said Ruth, and she looked frowningly past Hannah's head, 'because, if it was a house that had bedroom candles, would the landing have had electric light? I really do like the story, Miss Mole, but I can't bear not to get things clear. Now, if he'd had an electric torch –'

'Yes,' said Hannah gloomily, 'I ought to have thought of that, but it wouldn't have done. You see, the drama of the thing is opening your bedroom door in the dark, simply shaking like a leaf, as they say, and finding a blaze of light and a burglar standing in front of a looking-glass with a wig on his head. The bedroom candles were a mistake.'

'Miss Mole,' Ruth said solemnly, 'did you make it up?'

Three times Hannah slowly nodded her head, catching her lip like a naughty child. 'If I'd had more time,' she began apologetically –

'If you'd had more time, I shouldn't have found out,' Ruth said, and the anxious look, which troubled Hannah,

102

returned to her face. 'And I suppose it isn't true about your cottage and the owls.'

'Every word of it,' Hannah said. 'And the old lady and the wigs are true, but what was the good of them without the burglar? You wanted a burglar and I had to give you a nice one.'

'But have you ever known a nasty one?'

'No, but I can make one up.'

Ruth smiled feebly. 'Ethel would think it was dreadful.'

'I wouldn't have told it to Ethel,' Hannah said quickly, and Ruth's smile broadened.

'She'd think it was lying.'

'Not lying. Fiction,' Hannah said.

'Yes, fiction,' Ruth agreed willingly. 'But how,' she cried, 'am I going to know when it really happened and when it didn't?'

'Ah, that's the fun of it. You've got to find out and, next time, I shall be more careful.'

'And did you break the window with your foot?'

'Yes, that was true.'

'And you can't tell me about that?'

'You wouldn't like it, though it had its funny side, I must admit. I'm afraid you wouldn't see it. You're not very good at laughing.'

'No. But I'm glad it's true about the cottage,' she said contentedly.

'Are you?' Hannah asked rather wearily, and she sank back in her chair and shut her eyes again.

Ruth felt a little uneasy. The quality of Miss Mole's relaxation had changed. She was no longer a lady of leisure, but one who was tired, and, perhaps, unhappy, and Ruth had a peep through another door which led into the places where Miss Mole's spirit had wandered.

She cleared her throat and said in a small voice, 'Miss Mole, are you all right?'

'I'm doing my best,' Hannah said, smiling, but keeping her eyes shut.

'I mean, do you feel ill, or something?'

'I don't feel ill, but I do feel something.'

'A pain?'

103

'A kind of pain.'

'Well, would you like anything?'

'Heaps of things,' Hannah said, and now she disclosed her eyes which were bright and merry. 'I want a small fortune to begin with. Fetch me that, if you can. If you can't, you'd better go to bed.'

'Not yet. Let's talk about it. If you had it, what would you do?'

'Pack my box. No offence meant, but wouldn't you do it yourself?'

'I suppose so,' Ruth said, trying to be reasonable and not hurt.

'I'd pack my box, but I'd leave you my little ship, for remembrance, and a good home. I should want a good home for it. It would be an awkward thing to take into the Arabian desert, for instance. You want ships of the desert there, not bottled ones. However, I'm not sure that I should go to Arabia. I've never been able to eat dates. London first, and new clothes of the very best cut and quality, and while they're being made, for I'm not going to have anything off a peg, I'll go into travel agencies and ask questions of young men who don't know the answers.'

'How do you know they don't?' Ruth asked sharply.

'Because I've tried them. Many an afternoon I've spent, leaning over one of those counters. You get all the uncertainty of foreign travel without the expense. But I won't make things too difficult for them at first. I'm going to Spain. I've never been there though it's full of my own castles.'

'And of mine,' said Ruth.

'Yes, I wonder there's any room left in the place. Let's go and see. Will you come with me?'

Ruth nodded. 'I'd love to.'

'Good,' said Miss Mole. 'I can easily afford it. And after that, where shall we go? Not Italy. Too much culture and too many spinsters like myself. We might pick up a little boat at Marseilles and go jogging down the Mediterranean. And we wouldn't come back until we wanted to, and we'd begun to wish we hadn't so much time on our hands. But we'd see South America first.'

104

The loud ringing of the front-door bell shattered the visions they were sharing of Creole beauties, vast mountain ranges, immense rivers and impassable jungles.

'There!' Ruth exclaimed. 'Somebody's come to spoil it!'

'Only the postman,' Hannah said airily, 'with a registered letter from my lawyers, about the fortune.'

There was the chance that something exciting was going to happen with every knock or ring, and though few people would have applied the adjective to Mr. Blenkinsop, who was standing on the doorstep, Hannah felt laughter rising in her at the sight of him.

'I call this very kind,' she said brightly. 'Do come in.'

Raising his hat, Mr. Blenkinsop asked if Mr. Corder was at home.

'Mr. Corder?' Hannah said, pretending to be disappointed. 'No, he's out.'

'I'm sorry,' said Mr. Blenkinsop, turning to go.

'Wait a bit!' Hannah cried. 'I haven't seen you since I carried up your dinner. But I've heard about you. Come in, and I'll tell you what I've heard.'

'Thank you, but I wanted to see Mr. Corder. I'll come another day.'

'You won't find him in on a Wednesday. It's the week-night service.'

'Stupid of me,' Mr. Blenkinsop muttered.

'Mr. Corder will consider it a sad lapse of memory. I don't think I'll tell him you came.'

'It's a matter of indifference to me,' he said.

'Yes, that's what he'll realize, I'm afraid. I've looked for you every Sunday, Mr. Blenkinsop.'

'I don't quite see why you should trouble.'

'I have a tenderness for Mr. Corder's feelings.'

'Oh,' said Mr. Blenkinsop, 'so you've settled down.'

'You can put it that way if you like. I wish you'd come in, but it's a nice night, after the rain,' she said, looking skyward. 'What bright stars!'

'Yes, very bright.'

'But it's cold,' said Miss Mole.

'Don't let me keep you,' said he, but he did not move, and Hannah went on conversationally. 'Yes, it's cold, but

I suppose we ought to call it seasonable. It's funny about that word. It's only cold, never hot, weather that's seasonable. Now why? I find words very fascinating.'

'I'm afraid,' Mr. Blenkinsop said stiffly, 'I mustn't stay here and discuss etymology.'

'I thought that was beetles,' Hannah said innocently, 'and we can have a practical study of them in the kitchen, if you like. I seem doomed to have trouble in kitchens. And that reminds me – How are the Riddings getting on? You know, I feel I haven't been properly thanked for that evening.'

'Thanked!' Mr. Blenkinsop exclaimed, staring at her malignantly. 'What I want to know is why on earth you wanted to do it. And as for thanks, whose did you expect?' he demanded, and with those words he marched away.

She had roused him at last, but she thought his fervour somewhat disproportionate to the slightness of the inconvenience he suffered.

Chapter 15

THAT night Ethel left the Girls' Club in the charge of Miss Patsy Withers and another helper and went home earlier than usual. She had a headache and felt miserable. It was cold in the tram-car, after the heat of the Mission Room, and she wanted to be in bed with a hot-water bottle and something warm to drink, and she wished, as she wished more often than anyone suspected, that she could find her mother at home. Ethel's loss was of a different nature from Ruth's. For Ethel, her mother had been a quiet voice and a kind hand, a voice never raised in expostulation and a hand that knew how to put a pillow under an aching head. When she was overwrought and her mother applied physical remedies, it did not occur to Ethel that in this refusal to reprove or advise, this assumption that her child was ill, her mother was doing all she could to treat her mentally. Ethel's life was so fiercely subjective that her mother, for her, had hardly existed objectively. Perhaps no one and nothing existed for her in that sense and inevitably she became the prey of every misadventure. Now she sat huddled in her corner, trying to keep her eyes shut to ease her headache, but each time the tram-car stopped she had to open them to see who was boarding it or alighting: she had to make a quick comparison of each woman's clothes with her own, to wonder if she could twist her hat into the shape of the one opposite, or train her hair to fall over her ears like that of the girl who had just come in, and under this eagerness to be doing something, this restlessness which had its value, there was a weariness of the Girls' Club and a sense of futility.

Doris had not been there, Doris, her favourite, who had been elevated to service in the Corder's household, and was supposed to adore Miss Ethel. There had been laughter of a familiar kind when her absence was mentioned and Ethel had felt sharp tears spring into her eyes, as though she had been struck. They were laughing because they knew more about Doris than she did, and they were glad because the favourite was proved disloyal.

Ethel told herself she was too sensitive, but that was her nature. She was hurt and she was anxious and her head throbbed more violently as she pictured Doris wandering in the darkness with a young man and imagined, with the inaccuracy of theoretical knowledge, the probably disastrous progress of that courtship. She would have to speak to Doris, and she knew that, in such matters, Doris would see her as a child in arms and feed her with appropriate sops. She had felt sure of her influence over the girl, and her certainty was taken from her. Life, for Ethel, was something like walking across a bog, leaping from what looked like a solid tuft to another and finding many of them shaking and some sinking under her, and she lost her nerve, and then her judgment, at each mistake. Doris's absence and the girls' laughter had made the friendliness of Patsy Withers the more welcome, and, in a gust of grateful confidence, Ethel had talked about Miss Mole and detected a gleam of pleasure in Patsy's eyes when she told the puzzling story about the mattresses. It had been rather silly to tell her, Ethel thought, but then, she was so impulsive; she was sensitive and impulsive, and no one understood her now except Howard – and Wilfrid, when he was not teasing her. She had an unbounded admiration for her father, but she wished he had more time and patience to spare her. He had a way of making her difficulties seem very small in comparison with his own and of suggesting that he had cares enough already. There was Miss Mole – Ethel felt guilty again at the thought of her – who always listened with interest, but how could anyone be sure she was not another of those tufts? And there was God, she remembered hurriedly, and she looked askance at her neighbours, as though they had divined her forgetfulness. No one was looking at her and she shut her eyes again, saying she would pray, she must have more faith, and with that thought, or because the tram-car stopped at the place where she intended to get out, her troubles became less pressing.

She could have gone on to the halt at the end of Beresford Road, but this one was at the end of University Walk and once, as she walked back from the club, Wilfrid had overtaken her there and they had gone home together, by way of Prince's Road, because Wilfrid had said it was more romantic, and then he had spoilt her happiness by asking why she walked so slowly.

Wilfrid was one of Ethel's tufts, but so bright, so alluring that she could not believe it would betray her, and she had found her own way of explaining its instability. It was not altogether satisfactory and she knew it, but it served for consolation when her faith in herself and in the charms she hoped she possessed, was tottering. Wilfrid and she were cousins and when he was unkind to her it was when he remembered that relationship. He had to repress her feelings and hide his own under his banter. It was noble of him, but Ethel would have been happier if there could have been one passionate scene which would have become a sacred memory, casting its pale light over the rest of their barren lives, and thinking of Wilfrid thus, hoping to hear his gay voice behind her and trying to walk as she would like him to see her walking, she followed the route they had taken together, up Prince's Road, dim and wide and quiet, with the shadows of bare branches outlined on the pavement in the lamplight.

The drizzling rain of the afternoon had stopped, there was a starry sky above her, and though she was not moved by beauty, the influence of the place and hour was soothing and she went slowly, forgetting her troubles, hardly thinking, but letting little plans and hopes – her dress for the Spenser-Smiths' party, the altering of her hat, a cup of cocoa beside the fire and a few words with Wilfrid before she went to bed – flit in pictures across her mind, and then, at the angle made by the junction of Prince's and Beresford Roads, she stopped for a dreadful moment before she turned and ran.

Like Ruth, earlier in the day, she was strangling her sobs – and she was happier than Ruth, because she was not pursued by her own disloyalty, but she was also more miserable, because, with what she called Wilfrid's faithlessness, her world was darkened. The stars had gone out when she saw him a few yards ahead of her, beyond the turning, holding a girl's hand as though, when she offered it in farewell, he could not let it go. There was no mistaking Wilfrid's bare head and his slim figure leaning backwards as he held the girl's hand at arm's length, to see her better, perhaps, or to draw her to him, and as Ethel ran, she was caught by a greater pain than that of seeing Wilfrid's alliance with another, though the two were mingled; it was the primitive pain of being undesired by any man and the conviction – acknowledged in the moment's misery – that no one would ever hold her hand in that half-playful, lingering grasp.

Centuries of loneliness seemed to pass over her before she reached the garden gate and saw, through her blurred eyes, one bulky figure, standing there, changed into two. She rushed past them. She had left Wilfrid, holding a girl's hand, to find Doris in a young man's arms, and they had both betrayed her. She sped up the path and banged the door in the face of Doris who was following behind her; she flung open the door of the dining-room and saw Ruth and Miss Mole smiling at each other across the hearthrug and for an instant she stood there before she turned and went stumblingly, noisily, up the stairs to her room.

The sight of her, distraught and angry, remained like a material object in the doorway, and when Hannah looked at Ruth she saw that her face was white.

'Oh, what can have happened now?' she moaned.

Hannah had no answer ready, and a knock at the front door called her to open it. There stood Doris, her head flung up, her meekly virtuous expression changed to one of defiance.

'He's a steady, respectable young man,' she said, 'and if he wasn't it would be all the same! I've as good a right to walk out as anybody else, and more chance than some I I could name, and so I'm willing to tell her at her convenience.'

'Bless my soul!' Hannah said mildly, looking the little maid up and down, and what she left out of her voice, she put into that cool glance. 'You trot up to bed and I'll talk to you in the morning,' she said, and Doris went. Hannah twisted her nose in satisfaction. It was a good thing there was some one capable of command in a house inhabited by one young woman who was distraught, another who was defiant, and a child who looked ready to faint.

'Life in the happy Nonconformist home!' she thought. 'This would do Mr. Blenkinsop a power of good,' and she stepped outside the door and a few paces down the path, to taste the freshness of the night before she went back to Ruth. She could still see Ethel's face clearly against the darkness. It was the face of one who ragingly but helplessly had watched murder done, and almost mechanically, but with a grim smile, Hannah cast her eyes about for the corpse.

Something swift and dark curveted past her feet and, at the same moment, she heard the thick voice of Mr. Samson in its nightly call of 'Puss, Puss, Puss!'

'Your cat's here,' she cried back, and she crossed the grass plot and looked over the dividing hedge of laurel to see Mr. Samson standing where the parrot's cage had been. 'Your cat's here, in the garden,' she said again.

'That you, Miss Fitt?' he said in a rumble. 'Catch her for me, can you?'

'Catch an eel!' Hannah said, making a dart for the kitten who was amused by the clumsiness of these human beings.

'Gently does it,' Mr. Samson advised. 'You've got a good voice for calling a cat. I'd come and catch her myself, but I might be caught by the Reverend – Ha, ha! Got her? Good! Hand her over. This'll bring on my bronchitis again, I shouldn't wonder. Haven't been outside the house for a week, but I've had my eye on you, out of the window. 'Tisn't much I miss. I've seen you running in and out, looking so perky, and off to the chapel on Sunday! Well, when you feel like it, Miss Fitt, just come in and have a talk and a look at my cats.'

'Shall I? Perhaps I will, but I must go back now and look after my little girl.'

'What, the scared one? Ought to be in bed.' Mr. Samson growled.

'And you've got my name wrong,' Hannah said. 'My name is Mole.'

'That's a silly kind of a name,' he said indignantly. 'I'll stick to the one I've given you – Miss Fitt! See the joke? That's what you are and if you don't know it you'll soon find out.'

'Oh – I see!' Hannah said, and laughed so clearly that a young man, coming whistling down the street, stopped his own music to listen.

Wilfrid was by her side when she reached the door and he slipped his arm into hers. 'What's the meaning of this, Mona Lisa? I heard sounds of revelry and girlish laughter. Clandestine meetings with our godless neighbour?'

'Catching his cat,' Hannah said.

'Useful things, cats,' said Wilfrid. 'And dogs. I suppose the uncle isn't in yet, but you've been running it rather close, you know. And don't try to look severe, because you can't, with love's young dream all over your face.' He shut the door and looked round the hall as though he scented trouble. 'Ethel in?' he asked carelessly.

'Yes,' said Hannah, and she gave him a sharp look.

He shrugged his shoulders and spread his hands. 'It's not my fault, Mona Lisa,' he said languidly, but there was dancing laughter in his eyes. 'How did I know she'd come home by Prince's Road?'

'I don't know what you're talking about,' Hannah said, and she went into the dining-room where Ruth was crouching by the fire, her face as sharp as a rat's.

'You left me alone in the house,' she complained bitterly. 'You needn't have done that, need you? And Ethel might have come down and killed me.'

'Don't be ridiculous. Come along to bed.'

'But you don't know, you don't know! This is the first bad one she's had since you came. I can't go into that room and listen to her banging. She'll do it for hours and I can hear her.'

'What am I to do with you all?' Hannah asked sadly.

'And we'd had such a happy evening,' Ruth went on. It's no good being happy. It's better to be miserable all the time.'

'And still better to be brave. Think of me and the burglar!'

Ruth was not to be comforted. 'That's only a story. This is a bad dream that keeps coming back.'

'My poor lamb,' Hannah said, 'you shall sleep in my room if I have to sleep on the floor.'

'Can I?' It was pitiable to see how the sharp face softened.

'And you'd better be quick about it,' Wilfrid said through the open door. 'I can hear the uncle marching up the path.'

Hannah paused to give him a nod of gratitude as she hurried Ruth up the stairs. There was nothing seriously wrong with that boy: he had the kindest heart in the house, but it was not the house he ought to have been in.

Chapter 16

LEAVING a defiant maid-servant and a nervous child on the top landing, Hannah descended to the one below, where she found Wilfrid waiting for her in his bedroom doorway and listening, between apprehension and amusement, to the sounds in Ethel's room. These were the banging of drawers and the rattling of their handles under the shock, and Ethel's footsteps thudding stubbornly across the floor, and Wilfrid made a gesture in their direction, and whispered, 'Come in for a minute.'

'I can't. I must get your uncle's tea.'

'Let him wait! He's been to the Spenser-Smiths' and had a jolly good supper. He came back in their car. I heard it at the gate. He'll be purring like a well-fed cat. As for you, Mona Lisa, you look like a stray one.'

'I do feel rather lost. I think I'll ask Mr. Samson if he's got room for me among the others.'

'And it's all my fault,' Wilfrid sighed, dramatically running his fingers through his hair. 'But why the deuce shouldn't I walk home with a girl? It's no more than common courtesy. And if I held her hand a bit longer than was necessary, what's that to Ethel?'

'Nothing at all I should think. Don't distress yourself,' Hannah said coldly. 'There's been trouble with Doris.'

'All right, Mona Lisa, all right! I can see you're thinking I'm a conceited puppy. Have it your own way. But that doesn't account for her running like a hare when she saw me. And what's Doris been doing?'

'Walking out with a young man, I believe.'

'And I caught you flirting with old Samson! My word, we have been going it! Wouldn't the uncle be pleased! He's a bit morbid about intercourse between the sexes. Of course he approves of marriage, but the preliminaries make him sick. I call it an objectionable characteristic. How did he get married himself? But then, anything the uncle does is on a higher plane! I suppose,' he said slyly, 'you haven't noticed that?'

Hannah's face lost all expression. That was her answer to Wilfrid and her own resistance to temptation. 'And what about your own preliminaries, as you call them?' she asked. 'Are you engaged to the young woman?'

'Engaged! Don't be simple!'

'Well, in my young days, if we held hands we meant something by it.'

'Oh, we meant something, I assure you. And how dull your young days must have been, poor Mona Lisa.'

'No,' said Hannah, 'they weren't, because I wasn't. It isn't the days that are dull, it's the people who can't see them properly. What on earth do you think I should do in this house if I couldn't make amusement for myself?'

'Oh, come, I do my best, but you've got a professional conscience. I admire you for it, but it doesn't deceive me. Not in the least. Let's exchange views about the uncle, Mona Lisa. It would do us both all the good in the world.'

'I can't stay long enough,' Hannah said. 'But I'll tell you one thing you'll like.' She smiled at him very sweetly. 'There's a remarkably strong family likeness between you and him. Not in the face. In the character,' and with that, and a spiteful little grimace across her shoulder, she left him, and forgot her mendacious triumph as she heard Ethel shut her wardrobe door with a vicious bang.

What was she to do with this family? she asked herself, as she ran down the stairs. And why should she stay? She was not so old or so useless that she could not get another post, but she remembered Ruth, snuggling under the bedclothes and saying childishly, 'Whatever did I do without you?' and she remembered her compact with Mrs. Corder.

'I'll make a job of it,' she said, rapidly preparing Mr. Corder's tray, and she carried it into his study with secret pomp, as though, in this ritual, she dedicated herself to the family's service.

Robert Corder made a handsome figure, standing on the hearthrug, with his head thrown back and some of the urbanity, fit for a visit to the Spenser-Smiths', still beaming from him, and at the sight of him, Hannah's faith in her resolutions failed her. She could deal with hysteria, she could help those she pitied, but, in the presence of this man, could she sustain her character of industrious nonentity? Something alive seemed to turn in her breast. It was the demon of mischief who lay there; he was stretching himself in lazy preparation for action and, if she was not careful, he would presently express himself in speech. Perhaps, she thought, a little, a very little, liberty would be good for him: if she kept him too quiet, he would suddenly get out of control, and there would be an end to her high endeavours for the family. The best thing, she decided swiftly, was to be natural: that would satisfy the demon and it was the golden rule for manners, but if she obeyed it at this moment, she would throw the teapot at Mr. Corder's head. She had had a tiring day and he stood there, like a large healthy animal waiting to be fed, and made no movement to relieve her of the tray.

'If you would kindly take those books off the table,' she said politely, 'I shall be able to put this down.'

He looked at his watch before he obliged her. 'Half-past ten,' he said.

'Is that all?' Hannah said pleasantly. 'I thought it was about eleven,' and before he had time to make one of the several retorts that must have occurred to him, she exclaimed, 'And now I've forgotten the biscuits!'

'Don't trouble about them, Miss Mole. I had supper with Mr. and Mrs. Spenser-Smith.'

She recognized the cue for a murmur of congratulation or envy, but she chose to miss it. 'Then, if you don't want them, I'll say good night, Mr. Corder.'

'Just a moment, Miss Mole. Mrs. Spenser-Smith expressed some surprise that you had not been to see her. I think it would be courteous to pay her that attention.'

'Then I'll try to pop in some afternoon, when I'm having a walk.'

Robert Corder's quick little frown, like Ruth's, but different in its causes, came and went. 'Her At Home day is the first Friday in the month.'

'Does she have an At Home day?' Hannah asked with a wide smile. 'I thought that was unfashionable. Then I can't go till December.'

'You misunderstand me,' he said gently. 'It might be better for you to avoid that day.'

'Yes, they're dreary occasions, aren't they? Thank you for telling me. Good night.'

She knew she would be called back when she reached the door.

'Another thing, Miss Mole. I shall be asking a gentleman to supper next week. I think Thursday would be the best day. He has just taken up the ministry of Highfield Chapel – a small place, but I suppose he considers it promotion – and I feel we ought to do what we can to welcome him. You will bear that in mind, won't you?'

'Yes,' Hannah said. 'Do you want anything special to eat?'

'I can safely leave that to you, I'm sure. In fact, I think I ought to say how much I appreciate the care you have given to our meals.'

'I'm glad you're pleased,' she said sincerely. If he was not obtuse, he was generous, and she smiled as she spoke; then her eyes, leaving his face, fell on that of Mrs. Corder who was listening attentively to all they said, and Hannah persuaded herself that Mrs. Corder was glad to think of Ruth, upstairs in the dovecot, and trusted Hannah to do what she could for Ethel. 'And, by the way,' Hannah said, 'is the minister married?'

Mr. Corder's annoyance expressed itself in a somewhat sickly smile. 'Always the first question!' he exclaimed. 'But is it of any real importance to you, Miss Mole?'

'Of great importance,' she replied, 'because I suppose, if he is, he will bring his wife.'

Robert Corder turned away quickly. 'No, no, he's not married,' he said.

She looked at his back almost tenderly. The poor man could not open his mouth without betraying himself and though she had said nothing at which he could reasonably take offence, perhaps she had given him something to think about, and her demon had had his little outing and she had

117

a soothing draught to offer Ethel when she carried up a cup of hot milk and knocked at her door.

It was a little while before she gained admittance. She had the impression that everything Ethel possessed was being hurriedly concealed in drawers and cupboards and, when she entered, there were still signs of disorder in the room.

'Don't worry about Doris,' she said at once. 'I'll have a few words with her in the morning. It will be easier for me than for you. And drink this while it's hot.' She tried to avoid looking at Ethel's scarred face, but Ethel showed no more shame than she had shown control. 'I'm all in favour of walking out, but I should like to know something about the young man.'

'She ought to have told me!' Ethel exclaimed. 'I've been so good to her!'

'Yes,' Hannah said, 'it's a mistake to be good to people, if you're hoping for reward, because you won't get it. It would have been better for both of you if you'd tried to train her. You'll feel ashamed of her, to-morrow week, when she slams the dishes on the table. Did you know your father is asking a minister to supper?'

Ethel, who had been restive under reproof, rolling her eyes and threatening to bolt, steadied herself as Hannah produced this carrot. 'A minister! Who is it?'

'I don't know,' Hannah said carelessly. 'Some young man who's got a new cure of souls – if you have such things in your denomination. Anyhow, I hope he'll cure them.'

'Then it must be the new minister at Highfield Chapel.'

'That's the man. We shall have to kill the fatted calf, I suppose,' Hannah said, and she wished it was possible to put a love potion into the ginger-beer which was the Corders' festal beverage. Ethel loved, and married to a minister, would be a useful member of society, and he must have his fatted calf, so he must think Ethel had cooked it and, in the meantime, a week of tranquillity for the family was assured.

An hour later she lay in Ruth's bed, considering the events of the past day. She thought of them, one by one, extracting from them all their savour, whether sweet or

118

bitter. There was her walk on the hill overlooking the water, with the bright tree showing through a grey mist which seemed to darken when the wings of a swooping gull flashed through it: there was the sound of unseen ships hooting or booming at the turn of the river and, at her will, she had been able to imagine them as huge amphibians, calling to each other as they floundered in the water and sought the hidden banks, or she could acknowledge them as the sirens of ships which were coming home from distant places or setting out on fresh voyages, and standing up there with the soft rain on her face, she had marvelled at the richness of human life in which imagination could create strange beasts though facts were sufficient in themselves, while she, who had the privilege of these experiences, had no ache or pain in the whole of her lithe body and no more troubles than were good for her.

She had a feeling of sovereignty while she stood there; she could make what she liked of her world. She was more than a sovereign; she was a magician, changing ships into leviathans with some tiny adjustment of her brain, and, in addition, she had a freedom such as, surely, no one else in all Radstowe could claim, for she was in possession of herself and did not set too great a value on it.

In this high mood, she had swung down from her perch above the rocks and kept her fine content until she came upon Ruth, near Regent Square, and remembered her old ulster and realized, with a pang, that a part of her belonged to Ruth. She had given it willingly and could not withdraw it and she had increased her gift before the day was over.

It had been the most eventful day of her sojourn with the Corders and, in an existence like hers, where excitements outside herself came seldom, it seemed wasteful to have such a walk, to seal her friendship with Ruth, interview Mr. Blenkinsop, witness Ethel's abandonment and Doris's impudence, talk to Mr. Samson over the hedge and get a compliment from Robert Corder and news about a minister, in one day.

'This is extravagance,' she murmured.

There were no more sounds from Ethel's room, and as Hannah turned on her other side to sleep, she saw that the door communicating with Robert Corder's room was framed in gold. Then that border slowly changed its shape, widening at the top and side, and his figure was silhouetted against the light. She lay still and stiff and shut her eyes. She heard him advance a step and felt his silent, swift retreat. He shut the door as quietly as he had opened it and the gold band was round it, as though it had never stirred.

'What will he make of this?' she wondered, pressing her mouth against the pillow. There would be trouble in the morning, but it would be something to tell Lilla when she paid her call, avoiding the first Friday of the month. Yes, with some amplifications, it would make a very good story, and while she amplified it and planned a fit and reasonable reply to any complaint Robert Corder might make, she felt a new kindness for a man who could steal into a room so gently to look at his little daughter.

Chapter 17

THE shadow that fell on Hannah the next morning was not the one of Robert Corder's displeasure. It was a darker one that hung over her all the week and, on the evening of the supper-party, she slipped out of the house and walked swiftly up the road. At the top of it, she stood still and, drawing a deep breath, looked back. The road was empty. There was nothing to be seen, and she had not expected to see anything, except the lighted windows of the houses and the street lamps which stood like sentinels who were tired of keeping unnecessary watch and did not recognize a fugitive in Miss Mole, and there was no one to notice her as she paused with her back against the railings of a garden and a wry smile on her lips. She was thinking that, until this moment, she had not run away from anything since the days when she had believed in the clever bear and pretended a wolf was coming after her.

'Drat the man!' she said, recovering her jauntiness.

She had shut her door in his face, ten years ago, and that was a heartening memory, and if she avoided him now it was for reasons which he would be the last person to understand. And, if she had stayed, what a pleasantly-shocking little talk he and Robert Corder, closeted in the study, would have had about her! She could imagine the shakings of heads over Mr. Pilgrim's revelations, the pursings of lips, and Robert Corder's sudden, angry realization that he would have to face an awkward situation. She had spared him that, for the present, and it had been easier than she dared to hope when the name of Mr. Pilgrim fell blastingly on her ears. It was Mr. Pilgrim for whom she had been so ready to kill the fatted calf – but it was she who was the prodigal! It was he who was the eligible bachelor of her hopes and, characteristically, she had time to be sorry for

121

Ethel before she began to consider herself. Even Ethel could hardly be enthusiastic about Mr. Pilgrim after she had seen him, and Ruth and Wilfrid were already in dismay at the prospect of an evening with a strange minister. They enraged Ethel with their prophecies of how he would look and what he would say and, in spite of Hannah's distress, she longed to prompt them. They wondered if he would be content to discuss ministerial affairs with Robert Corder, a possibility at which Ethel rolled anxious eyes, or whether they would be expected to help in his entertainment, and it was then that Wilfrid opened the door for Hannah by thanking his God they had her to rely on. 'And if he's not the man I take him for, he'll think she's a rare bird to find in Beresford Road. But if he is, and I'm afraid he is, then it will be she who'll get all the fun. So you'll enjoy yourself, Mona Lisa if no one else does, and you must do your best for us.'

Ethel was affronted as, no doubt, Wilfrid meant her to be, and her anger against him, assuaged by the imminence of Mr. Pilgrim, returned in force. She had been keeping her father's house, she reminded him, for the last two years and this was not the first time they had received a guest. He was trying to make Miss Mole think he did not know how to behave – he was always praising someone to annoy somebody else – and, as a matter of fact, it would be easier for her without Miss Mole. It was very difficult to be the hostess when there was another woman there, older than oneself. It made her nervous. They had had the Spenser-Smiths to supper and Mrs. Spenser-Smith had said how nice everything had been.

'That was because she talked all the time. This Pilgrim fellow may stammer, or something, and then the uncle will have to do the talking and that'll be the last visit Pilgrim pays here. You mark my words! It's better to have Miss Mole in the hand than to drive Pilgrim into the bush.'

'Oh, how horrid you are!' Ethel cried. 'Of course he doesn't stammer. How could he preach?'

'Perhaps he can't.'

'And you're disgusting about Father, and perfectly ridiculous about Miss Mole.' Ethel's voice was getting beyond

122

control. 'Why should you think she's such a brilliant con-
versationalist? I've never noticed it.'

'Ah, she's like old Samson's parrot. She can do it when
she chooses. But then, I know I'm prejudiced about her.'

Hannah raised her head from her darning and looked
coolly from one to the other. 'I don't know what your
manners will be like on Thursday,' she said quietly, 'but I
hope they won't be what they are now. You needn't continue the discussion, because I happen to be engaged that
evening.'

'Oh, I say, what luck! Can't you be engaged to me?'

'But, Miss Mole –' Ethel began and her face was stilled
by her rapid calculations.

'If you're thinking about the cooking, you needn't worry
about that. I shall leave the supper prepared and, as you
say, it will be easier for you without me, and for everybody
else.'

'It won't. It'll be much worse,' Ruth muttered, and
Ethel, preoccupied with a new thought, could only dart a
glance at this second ally of Miss Mole's before she asked –
'But what will Father think?'

'I don't know,' Hannah replied simply.

'And I don't mean to be rude, Miss Mole –

'But you succeeded,' Hannah said.

'I'm sorry, Miss Mole. It was only because Wilfrid made
me so angry. And I don't think Father will like it. And
suppose Doris makes mistakes?'

'She will,' Hannah said pleasantly, and she could have
added the assurance that Mr. Pilgrim would not know.

It was clear that her mind was made up and though
Robert Corder resented Miss Mole's engagement, in a place
unnamed, and let her know it, he also let her know, but
without intention, that he was secretly relieved, for a housekeeper, like a son at Oxford, was a good thing to mention
casually, but an irritation in the flesh, when she happened
to have a trick of misinterpreting the most obvious remarks.
It was this which had obliged him to ignore his discovery
of her in Ruth's bedroom and he felt mentally securer when
she was out of the house.

She could divine all this with the acuteness which was

partly natural and partly an acquired habit of self-defence, she could see him on the brink of asking what her engagement might be and retiring, as usual, under cover of some unnecessary orders, and now, just before the guest was due, she had run up the street to find a temporary refuge with Mrs. Gibson.

As she turned into Prince's Road she reflected sagely on the sequence of events and the difficulty of deciding that this one was good and that one evil. If she had not deceived Mrs. Widdows and gone out to buy the reel of silk, she could not have saved Mr. Ridding's life, and while Mr. Blenkinsop seemed to regret this preservation, it had been the means of providing Hannah with a shelter in her time of need. It was impossible to please everybody, and even the menace of Mr. Pilgrim, which had been darkening her life for the past week, might prove to be one of those clouds with a silver lining, but no one could really know until the end of time, when each little action and its consequence would be balanced in the scales, and she was sure the adjudicator would not be aggrieved, though he might be astonished, at the result. She was conscious in herself of a tolerance which must be a dim reflection of a greater one; she refused to be harsher with herself than she was with other people or than her vague but tender God was with all the world, and she had recovered her spirits when she saw the lighted window of Mrs. Ridding's basement kitchen and rang the bell of Mrs. Gibson's front door.

There was always a strangely muffled feeling in that house. If there was still trouble in the basement, it did not penetrate into Mrs. Gibson's comfortably-furnished rooms, and as Hannah ate her supper and listened to Mrs. Gibson's gentle and contented talk, she felt as though she were under the influence of some mild narcotic. Mrs. Gibson's voice rose only when she pressed Hannah to eat. She thought Miss Mole was looking tired. She had been out to choose the chicken herself and Miss Mole must eat as much as she could.

'You're a lady, Mrs. Gibson, if ever there was one,' Hannah said. 'I don't know anybody else who would have taken so much trouble for me.'

124

'Oh, my dear!' Mrs. Gibson exclaimed. It saddened and flattered her to think this was true.

'Yes,' Hannah went on, 'if Mrs. Spenser-Smith had asked me out to supper, she would have given me yesterday's mutton hashed. Quite good enough for Miss Mole! She'd keep her chickens for the people who could afford them. It's the way of the world, but you don't belong to it. You ought to be in Heaven, Mrs. Gibson, and I hope you won't go yet. You had all this to see to and Mr. Blenkinsop's dinner as well.'

Mrs. Gibson nodded her head in satisfaction. 'Mr. Blenkinsop was very obliging when I told him you were coming. He said he'd have his dinner early and then it would be out of the way.'

'Ah,' said Hannah, 'he was afraid I'd take it up to him!'

'I don't know, dear. He's got a kind heart, really. What do you think he did on Sunday? Took Mr. Ridding off for a walk in the country!'

'And lost him?' Hannah suggested.

'No, dear. Mr. Blenkinsop isn't the man to lose things. He's very careful. If there's a collar missing, he knows it, and he'll get Sarah to tighten up his trouser-buttons when they're nowhere near coming off.'

'I call that very delicate,' Hannah said.

'Yes, but it vexes the girl sometimes, though I must say he makes it worth her while. Well, off they went with a packet of bread and cheese apiece, and they didn't come back till dark. It would do Mr. Ridding good, he said, and give that poor little thing a bit of a rest.'

'Is that what he called her?'

'It's what I call her myself.'

'And how did he know she needed a rest?'

'Anybody that looks at her can see that,' Mrs. Gibson said. 'She's always putting the baby in his pram when Mr. Blenkinsop goes off to business. I thought there might be trouble about that. "Leave him out at the back," I said to her, but she said how was she to hear him crying when she was in the kitchen, so we risked it – behind the bushes – and Mr. Blenkinsop hasn't made any complaint, though prams weren't what he expected when he came here.' She sighed gently. 'And I didn't expect them myself. But things are going on very comfortably and we must hope for the best. Now, Sarah's going to clear away, and we'll have a nice cosy time by the fire.'

At half-past nine Mrs. Gibson had begun to nod and Hannah knew it was time for her to go. She went upstairs to fetch her coat and hat, wondering how she should spend the hour before it was safe to return to Beresford Road. She decided to walk round the hill and down the Avenue and see how many leaves were hanging on the trees and, if Mr. Pilgrim still lingered, she might be able to get upstairs and into her nightgown before she was seen.

She felt rather desolate and she felt angry. She was sacrificing some of her independence to that man whom she ought to have outfaced, but she could not have him defiling the poor little remains of her romance, and she did not want to be separated from Ruth. Which of these motives was the stronger, she did not know. She kept the memory of her short-lived happiness in a place of its own, which was all she could do for it; she rarely looked at it, but she would keep prying eyes from it, if she could, and the memory of Ruth's thin face, at once so childish and so mature, seemed to encourage and commend her. Nevertheless, she was conscious of the loneliness, in which she pretended to rejoice, when, through his open door, she saw the warm glow of Mr. Blenkinsop's shaded lamps cast on the dark landing. He was not the man to sit in a room with the door open and, before he came back, there would be time, she thought, for a peep. It would suit her acid humour to see in what comfort Mr. Blenkinsop passed his evenings, while Hannah Mole, threatened by her past, had to wander in the streets. In the unlikely possibility of Mr. Blenkinsop's having a past he need not be afraid of it. He had, according to Mrs. Gibson, a nice little income from his mother, and he was a man, and to men a past could be forgiven, even, if repentance followed, by a Nonconformist minister, while Hannah was a woman for whom repentance had no practical results. In this unfairness, she found what consolation she needed, for though what she had done was folly, it had been done fearlessly and she was too proud to feel regret.

She was advancing for her peep when Mr. Blenkinsop appeared in the doorway. 'I thought that was your step on the stairs,' he said.

'And I did my best not to make a sound! I know you don't like being disturbed.'

'It's quicker than other people's,' he said, 'and, as a matter of fact, I was just going to have a little walk. I generally have one at this time of night, so perhaps you'll allow me to see you home.'

'I wasn't going home, as you call it, yet,' she said. 'When I have a night out I make the most of it. I'm going round the hill and down the Avenue.'

'I don't think you ought to do that alone.'

'I shan't be alone if I'm with you. But no!' she cried repentantly, 'I won't spoil your walk. I'll go by myself. Let's start at opposite ends and I'll meet you at the top of Beresford Road, to show you I'm not murdered, and you can deliver me at the door.'

'That would be a very silly thing to do,' he said.

'But I like doing silly things.'

'And I don't,' he said firmly, following her down the stairs.

'Ah, you ought to learn,' she said, seeing him plainly now, in the light of the hall, and she thought he looked too set and stolid to learn anything she could teach him. Spectacled and grave, he waited while she said good night to Mrs. Gibson, and they set off together without a word.

Hannah found it difficult to talk to Mr. Blenkinsop when she could not see his face. The sight of it made her feel merry and ready to be absurd; his mere bulk, keeping pace with hers, deadened her faculties, and he seemed to have nothing to say himself. In silence they crossed Regent Square and went through the little alley to the street where stately Georgian houses began when the shops ended, and so reached the Green, and the lamps lighting the little paths.

'I think this is much sillier than walking separately,' Hannah said and, looking up at him, she had the gratification of seeing him smile unwillingly. The smile only lasted for a moment.

'But you are safer,' he said.

'If you want to be safe, you'd better be dead.'

'I don't agree with you,' Mr. Blenkinsop said.

'Good! Let's argue about it.'

'I don't see anything to argue about.'

'Then tell me about the Riddings.'

'You're very curious about the Riddings.'

'Of course I am. Are you teaching him to play chess.'

Mr. Blenkinsop cleared his throat. 'Yes, I'm trying,' he said bashfully, and then, angrily, as though it were Hannah's fault, he exclaimed, 'That girl will break down herself, if she doesn't get some relief!'

Hannah was content to be silent for the rest of the walk. She had plenty to think about and so, apparently, had Mr. Blenkinsop, and she believed they were both thinking of Mrs. Ridding; and though, apart from her interesting thoughts, it was, as she had said, a silly walk, she enjoyed the feeling of his unnecessary protection and she was touched by his courtesy.

When she parted from him at the gate, she saw that the doorstep was illumined as it could not be unless the door was open, and in the hall she found Mr. Corder. She had feared to find Mr. Pilgrim too, and her smile of relief was a new thing to the minister.

'I have just been out to look for you,' he said.

'How kind of you! Then I suppose you saw me coming down the road with Mr. Blenkinsop.' He had not expected this frankness and she felt that he was disappointed.

'Mr. Blenkinsop?' he repeated.

'Yes. I've spent the evening with Mrs. Gibson and Mr. Blenkinsop saw me home.'

'Ah, Mrs. Gibson. I hope you had a pleasant time. Don't trouble about my tea, Miss Mole. I have had to make it myself.'

Chapter 18

A FORTNIGHT later Hannah walked across the downs to pay her call on Lilla. Robert Corder had again reminded her of this duty and she was willing enough to perform it. The shadow cast by Mr. Pilgrim had receded, and though she could still see it like a storm-cloud that might, or might not, break, the sky immediately above her was clear and she felt light-hearted. She had found something very whimsical in the comparative indifference of the family towards a visit which, to her, had been so portentous. At breakfast, the next morning, Robert Corder had made some of those kindly, disparaging remarks of which he was a master. He hoped Mr. Pilgrim would not find city life too much for him after the less exacting demands of the country: fortunately for him, the chapel was a small one, with a congregation of simple-minded people and no intellectual influence there, or in the wider interests of Radstowe, would be expected of him. In other words, though he did not use them, Mr. Pilgrim was not likely to sit on any committees with Robert Corder.

Wilfrid's glance at Hannah was a comment on these bland remarks and a description of the evening's entertainment. Ethel looked thoughtful and subdued and Ruth was occupied with a letter which was spread out on her knee and sheltered by the table.

When she looked up her face was radiant. 'Uncle Jim's coming for Christmas!' she cried.

'Indeed?' Robert Corder said coldly.

'Good man,' Wilfrid muttered, and Ethel, whose pleasure was spoilt by the fact that Ruth conveyed it, turned to him sharply, saying, 'He's no relation of yours!'

'That's why I like him,' Wilfrid retorted.

This little flurry passed unnoticed by Robert Corder. He

was looking hurt. 'I have heard nothing about this visit,' he said.

'Oh, but you will. He's going to write to you.'

'Is that a letter from him?'

'Yes,' said Ruth, ready to protect it.

'I never ask to see your letters, as you know,' her father said, and waited unsuccessfully for a moment. 'But I think it would have been better if he had written to me first, and I don't know that it will be convenient to have him. You must remember that we have a room less than we had last time he came, and there will be Howard at home, too. There will be extra mouths to cook for and I think Miss Mole ought to be considered in this matter.'

'Oh, Moley –!' Ruth exclaimed, and turned scarlet.

Here was another annoyance for Robert Corder. 'That is not the way to address Miss Mole,' he said. 'Miss Mole, I would rather you did not allow it.'

'But she doesn't! I mean – it just slipped out. Miss Mole, two people wouldn't make such a terrible lot of difference, would they?'

'With due notice, I can feed a regiment,' Hannah said grandly.

'There!' said Ruth, looking at her father boldly.

'Of course she can,' said Ethel, less in support of Ruth than in depreciation of Miss Mole. 'I've done it myself and nobody thought anything of it.'

'Yes, we did. We thought a lot, because we couldn't eat the Christmas puddings. You didn't fill the basins and the water got in. Don't you remember?'

'Ruthie, Ruthie, that isn't kind. Ethel did her best. Now don't get excited, but run off to school or you'll be late.'

'But I am excited and there's plenty of time. And Wilfrid will be away for the Christmas days and you know you always make him and Howard share a room when they're here together, and what difference will Uncle Jim make? You can't not have him, when it's the first Christmas he's had at home for years. But it won't be the last! He's left the sea!'

'Left the sea?' Robert Corder repeated, and he looked towards the letter which Ruth was putting in her pocket.

'Retired, said Ruth, enjoying her private information. 'He says he thinks he'll buy a little farm,' and she disappeared before her father could make it difficult for her to keep her letter to herself.

'Well, well,' he said, tolerantly. 'I suppose we must forgive a bluff sailor for his rough and ready manners. No doubt I shall hear from him before long.'

'And you'll let him come, won't you?' Ethel begged.

Robert Corder decided to become the indulgent father. 'I see I shall have an unhappy Christmas if I don't,' he said playfully and Hannah made a mental note of this weakness which, in anyone else, she might have called amiability.

It was plain that he did not care for Uncle Jim, who was Mrs. Corder's brother and, with Mr. Blenkinsop's affairs already developing in her mind, Hannah began busying herself with Uncle Jim, his sister and her husband, and seeking any information she could get, though she could manage very well without it.

While she crossed the downs, keeping to the paths for the sake of Lilla's carpets, thinking that a grey sky was lovelier than a blue one, that the bare trees were exquisite against it and that the proper place for leaves was the ground, she was imagining little past scenes between Uncle Jim and Robert Corder, and clumsily tender ones between Mr. Blenkinsop and Mrs. Riddings. She did not trouble about the construction of her dramas: she saw pictures and framed sentences; she saw Uncle Jim with a protective arm round his sister's waist and heard Mr. Blenkinsop saying solemnly, 'Yes, since that very first evening –' She imagined Uncle Jim as a modern buccaneer, bronzed and bearded, and though she feared he would not actually have rings in his ears, it would be surprising not to see them there, and suddenly, the actors in her little scene became Uncle Jim and herself. Those flashing eyes of his pierced below her plain exterior and recognized a kindred spirit, and he would carry her off to sea, for really, it was absurd for a sailor to think he could turn farmer, but if he persisted, she would be there to help him, and they would adopt Ruth and live happy ever after.

'H'm,' Hannah said in self-derision. She had arrived at Lilla's chain and posts, and the windows of the red and white house were looking at her with coldly-practical eyes. Her fancies could not live under that gaze. The bold buccaneer would choose a buxom wench for partner; Miss Mole must continue to trust in the rich old gentleman, and she was wondering whether Lilla knew anything about Mr. Samson, when the severe parlourmaid opened the door and, making no mistake this time, took Hannah to the drawing-room.

'You're looking very well, Hannah,' Lilla said, taking the credit to herself.

'And you're looking more like a robin than ever, dear,' Hannah said, making the usual peck at her cousin's cheek. 'It's nice to see you in your natural habitat, or whatever they call it. You have such an exalted expression in chapel that I hardly know you, though of course, I'm proud of our slight acquaintance.'

'Now, don't begin your nonsense, but tell me how you're getting on.'

'I shouldn't like to boast,' Hannah said, 'until I hear what Mr. Corder has told you.'

'Very little. Naturally, as I recommended you, he wouldn't like to make any complaints to me. And perhaps there are none to make,' she added generously. 'How do you think you are managing yourself?'

'Splendidly! Almost too well, I'm sometimes afraid. I'm glad to have you to confide in, Lilla. I'm rather worried and I want your advice.'

'Then it's the first time you've wanted anybody's,' Lilla said dryly, and her bright eyes hardened with suspicion.

'Thank God, I've never had the same need to!' Hannah exclaimed. 'You'll hardly believe me, Lilla –'

'You may be sure of that, but, whatever it is, just talk about something else till the tea has come in.'

'Yes,' said Hannah, 'that's the kind of thing it is. And I hope it's a good tea, because I've been rather mean with ours lately. Saving up for Christmas. We're going to have Mrs. Corder's brother with us. Do you know anything about him?'

'I believe he's a sailor of some sort. I think he calls himself a captain, but not, of course, in the Navy.'

'No, if he had been, I should have heard of it. I don't much mind about his profession. It's his character, his impressionability, his income, I'm after. And his age. That's rather important, but he can hardly be a stripling.'

'Really, Hannah – Now, let me show you these little bags I'm making for Christmas presents,' she said brightly as the maid came in. 'Pretty, aren't they?'

'Very pretty,' Hannah said, wondering which one she would get. Lilla's presents to people like herself would be of the hashed-mutton variety, and Hannah was glad. A handsome present from Lilla would have been difficult to accept and, so far, she had not been put to that inconvenience.

'I thought one of these would do very well for Ethel Corder.'

'She'd love it, but give her a gaudy one, and put a modest little cheque inside.'

'I don't think I need reminding of that,' Lilla said coldly. 'First and last, I do a good deal for the Corders.'

'And Ethel's devoted to you. If I wasn't devoted to you myself, I should get rather tired of hearing your name. And little does she suspect that you and I were practically fed at the same bosom. Figuratively speaking, Lilla, figuratively speaking! And I've heard Mr. Corder use that expression himself.'

'Not about human beings,' Lilla said, 'and I don't like it.'

'But between us girls!' Hannah protested mildly. 'You must give me a little licence, and that reminds me of another thing I want to ask you. Do you know an old man called Samson, who lives next door to us in Beresford Road? Keeps a parrot and dozens of cats.'

'I've heard the parrot and a very objectionable noise it makes. Isn't he a common old man with a red face?'

'Yes, gloriously common,' Hannah said. 'That's why I like him. I'm common myself. There's no need to think before you speak, with him. It does me good. I've made friends with him, Lilla, you won't be surprised to hear. He's had bronchitis lately, and I've been doing his shopping for him, and if there are any coppers in his change he lets me keep them for my trouble, on condition that I don't put them in the plate on Sunday.'

133

'Then, if that's the truth, and I don't suppose it is, I think you're very unwise. Isn't there anybody else to do it for him?'

'Not a soul, poor old dear. He looks after the house himself, and very neat and clean it is, in spite of the cats.'

'Then it's still more unwise, but, of course, I don't really believe you'd take the man's money.'

'That's the truest part of a perfectly true tale. Funny, isn't it? It pleases him and I don't mind a bit. It doesn't often come to more than twopence halfpenny, because I do some juggling with sixpences and threepenny-bits.'

'Well, you'd better be careful. You were not engaged to look after the neighbours and, from what I remember of the man, I don't think Mr. Corder would approve of the acquaintance.'

'Ah,' said Hannah, 'that's where I score. I happen to have a trump card up my sleeve and out it will come when it's wanted, I confess I'm looking forward to the moment.'

'Oh, well,' Lilla sighed, 'it's no good talking to you. You'll go your own way and you'll come to grief and it will be most unpleasant for me.'

'We have to bear each other's burdens, dear,' Hannah said quietly. 'And I'll have another crumpet, if I may. They're so beautifully buttery.'

'Very indigestible, I'm afraid. I daren't touch them.'

'And a crumpet that isn't swimming in butter is about as much use as a ship in dry dock. I'll try that little aphorism on Uncle Jim – if it is an aphorism. I'll look it up. If you want to give me a Christmas present, Lilla, give me a dictionary.'

'Mr. Corder must have dozens of dictionaries.'

'Well, they're not mine – yet,' Hannah said.

Lilla pretended not to hear this remark. 'I'm going to give you one of these little bags. And now,' Hannah was waiting for this, 'what do you want my advice about?'

'No, no, I'm not going to worry you, but,' she leaned forward eagerly, 'I must just ask you one question. Have you ever heard that Mr. Corder walks in his sleep? That's my one hope, Lilla. Did Mrs. Corder ever complain of that, among other things?'

134

'Mrs. Corder never complained of anything. Why should she?'

'There's a skeleton in every cupboard. Now I wonder how that saying arose. We go on, using these expressions, part of our common heritage, Lilla –'

'I wish you wouldn't harp so much on being common, but just keep the fact to yourself.'

Hannah put down her cup with a shaking hand. 'You shouldn't make me laugh when I'm drinking. Oh, Lilla, what a treasure you are! All right, I won't. But it's part of our heritage, all the same, and neither you nor I know where it comes from. Now, the kind of dictionary I want is the kind that will tell me things like that. I'm afraid it will be rather expensive.'

'I don't see what you want with a dictionary, and I haven't a skeleton in my cupboard and I don't believe there's one in Robert Corder's. You'd better speak plainly, Hannah.'

'I'll speak as plainly as I can without being improper, though, really it wasn't so very improper because I pretended to be asleep, as any nice woman would, but imagine my horror when Mr. Corder opened my bedroom door and came and had a look at me. It wasn't a long look, and I don't wonder, but a look it was! Now, how can you explain that?'

'I can't,' Lilla said slowly, 'but I'm sure you can. It's no good trying those tricks on me, Hannah, and if it had really happened you wouldn't have told me. I hope you won't try them on anyone else. In the first place, they're vulgar and, in the second, they're not funny.'

Hannah looked disappointed. 'I thought it was very funny at the time. I must have told it badly. I haven't been very successful with my stories lately. And it would have been funnier still if I'd just opened an eye and winked at him. I meant to put that in when I told you and I forgot. Well, I must go back and call on Mr. Samson. He would have seen the joke. The good jokes, Lilla, are the ones in which character and circumstances conflict humorously and Mr. Samson would appreciate this one.'

'For goodness' sake, don't tell him!' Lilla exclaimed. 'If he thinks you're that kind of woman –'

'He knows exactly what kind of woman I am, which is more than you do, Lilla dear.'

'But what's the real explanation?' Lilla asked, almost wistfully.

'Family secrets, family secrets!' Hannah said. I've kept yours and I'm going to keep the Corders'.'

Chapter 19

IT was pleasant to see Ruth looking happier and Hannah subdued a sort of jealousy of Uncle Jim, whose advent had succeeded where her own presence had failed, and she determined to be happy too. It was pure wastefulness to spoil the present because the future might hold trouble, and everything conspired to help her. Ruth was less quarrelsome with Ethel, and Ethel, perhaps exhausted by her outburst, seemed more peaceful and more enthusiastic about the club, though Doris had definitely deserted it in favour of her young man. There were Christmas festivities to be arranged, both there and at the chapel and, when she chose, Ethel could be as thorough in her work as in her grief. Hannah herself had more than enough to do with her own preparations, but she found time for a visit to Mr. Samson, now and then. That disreputable-looking old gentleman, who seemed to have been all over the world and to have tried all trades, who distrusted all men and most women with a good-humoured cynicism, whose chief prejudice was against parsons of every denomination and who had settled down in Beresford Road as though in obedience to some unsuspected craving for respectability, was the perfect antidote to Robert Corder. He was, in fact, in many ways, what Hannah would have been if she had been a man, and in his freedom from any received set of opinions, in his loose, but not offensive, tongue, in the stories he told her and, above all, in his appreciation of herself, she found a relief which, no doubt, had its subtle effect on the Corder household. Her demon of mischief, getting its exercise in talking to Mr. Samson and provoking his thick chuckle of amusement, had a less persistent desire to tease Robert Corder. It was impossible to resist puzzling him when the opportunity came, but she did not go out of her way to do it, and she could feel that he was inclining to think of her as the right woman in the right place. This, in itself, was irritating, but the contrast between his view and Mr. Samson's, between the careful face Robert Corder knew and the one she could show Mr. Samson, between the self-conscious propriety of the minister and the old man's lively disregard of it, was a secret delight. If Mr. Samson's stories were true, he had known many women intimately; he talked of marriage with knowledge, though he did not mention a wife, and whatever his experiences had really been, they had produced what, to Hannah, seemed a sane apprehension of the relationship between men and women, giving due, and often humorous, importance to its physical side, but accepting it as naturally as he accepted food, and refusing to make a definite cleavage between male and female, anywhere. Mr. Samson, clearly, had not deliberately thought this out, nor did he express his opinions: like his red, puffy face and his wicked old eyes, they were the fruit of life as he had lived it, and though the fruit was ripe, it was not rotten. Ruth need have had no fear of him; indeed, as Hannah discovered, she had every cause to trust him, and Hannah herself could enjoy his approval of her remarkably neat legs and feet without feeling obliged to assure him of her inherent modesty. Hannah had no modesty in Robert Corder's sense which implied a perpetual and restraining consciousness of her sex. She was not anxious to forget it; she was as feminine as anyone else and she had suffered too much from being treated as a machine, but she was a human being more abundantly than she was a woman, and this was what Mr. Samson understood.

She had her superstitious moments when she feared she had too many sources of happiness. She had the friendship of Wilfrid and Ruth and Mr. Samson, she was looking forward to the arrival of Howard and Uncle Jim, and she had Mr. Samson's stories to remember and her own to concoct. These were a pleasant accompaniment to her household tasks. She could read when she was in bed, and she read late into every night at the expense of Robert Corder's candles, but while she stoned the raisins for the Christmas puddings, dusted or darned, she was busy with her own romances in which sometimes Robert Corder and his wife, sometimes the bold buccaneer and herself were the the chief actors or, more often, Mr. Blenkinsop struggled with the puzzling emotions she had created for him. She took most pleasure in the Blenkinsop story, for she could make it either comic or pathetic, and Mr. Blenkinsop was a subject to her taste. She could see the man who believed in safety being drawn into those dangerous, dim regions of pity where, as he groped his way, he would suddenly find himself on the frontier of a world still more dangerous and more attractive. As Mrs. Gibson said, he had a kind heart and it was touched by that spectacle of a slip of a girl pretending she had no troubles. Hannah, too, felt every admiration for Mrs. Ridding, but Mrs. Ridding had a baby, and a neurotic husband was a price worth paying for it. For the sake of one good baby Hannah would have paid more than that and there were times when she felt vexed with Mr. Blenkinsop. Because Mrs. Ridding was the first woman of his acquaintance who had faced a difficult situation bravely, he would naturally think she was the only one there was and, flattered by the belief that he had made this discovery for himself, he was ready to credit her with every other good quality, as a man, finding a new continent, would refuse to see a fault in it. She could now understand his resentment at the unnecessary preservation of Mr. Ridding, yet – here was the vicious circle again – if Mr. Ridding had been left to die, Mrs. Ridding would, in all likelihood, have disappeared from Prince's Road or, if she had remained, Mr. Blenkinsop would have considered her fortunate and taken no further interest in her, and it seemed to Hannah that her own mistake in life always had been, and still was, her refusal to feel any sorrow for herself or to suggest herself as a subject for sorrow in other people. In her attempts to attract Mr. Blenkinsop's attention, with sprightliness, intellect and ignorance, she had omitted the one method which would have been successful. Then she caught sight of her image in the glass and remembered that pathos without beauty is merely irritating, that a woman with a long nose could not be touching in her sadness, and at this point she neglected her stories for philosophical speculations on the effect of noses on destiny. In a woman, the perfect nose, in its appearance and its effects, was rather delicately cut, and very delicately tilted, while the suspicion of a droop had a tendency to produce tragedy unless its owner was a determined person, like herself. She had no theories about men's noses. In the comparative unimportance of a man's features, she reluctantly found proof of some sort of superiority in the other sex, and when she tried to remember the details of Mr. Blenkinsop's face, she could recall no more than a clear skin, an impression of solid worth and a pair of spectacles.

She was as glad, then, as she was astonished, when, on another Wednesday night, he gave her an opportunity to look at him. She was alone in the house, for Ruth was at some school festivity and Hannah was working at a party frock which was to be a surprise for her. One of Ruth's objections to the Spenser-Smiths' parties was the inadequacy of her clothes and the grandeur of Margery Spenser-Smith's, and Hannah, who had known worse than inadequacy in her own, was determined that her child should be as prettily dressed as Lilla's.

She frowned at the interruption when the bell rang, but she smiled when she saw Mr. Blenkinsop. 'You have a very bad memory,' she told him. 'It's Wednesday night and Mr. Corder isn't in.'

'Is anyone else at home?' he inquired.

'Only me,' Hannah said. 'Would you like to leave a message?'

'I'd rather come in, unless I shall be in the way.'

'Not at all, and if you're handy with your needle, I can give you plenty to do. But I expect,' she said, looking at him gravely, 'you can't manage anything more complicated than buttons.'

'I haven't even got a needle. Mrs. Gibson makes that unnecessary.'

'Mrs. Gibson spoils people. You'll miss her when you leave her.'

In the act of following Hannah into the dining-room, Mr. Blenkinsop stood still. 'Who said I was going to leave her?'

'There was murmur about it, wasn't there? A kind of subterranean growl? Come and sit down. And I thought you might have come to the conclusion that it was the best

140

thing to do. If I had a little capital, I'd start a boarding-house, for what they call single gentlemen, myself, and I'd look after you like a mother, Mr. Blenkinsop.'

'But I haven't the slightest intention of leaving Mrs. Gibson.'

'Oh, well, Mr. Blenkinsop, you're the best judge, of course,' she said primly, picking up her sewing.

'Certainly I am,' he said stoutly. 'And as for starting a boarding-house, that would be a very silly thing to do.'

'Why? If I can manage this family,' Hannah said impressively, 'I should make child's play of the single gents.'

'You're too young,' Mr. Blenkinsop said, frowning a little.

'Young!' Hannah's laughter, the sound which had silenced Wilfrid's whistling as he came down the street, was like a mockery of her own derision. 'Why, how old do you think I am?'

'About my own age, I suppose.'

Hannah shook her head. 'Centuries older, Mr. Blenkinsop. Perhaps only a few years, as we count time, but while you've been behind your bars in the bank I've been pushing my way into other people's houses and being pushed out again. Great fun!' she added hastily. 'I'd rather be allowed to run wild and pick up my living than be kept in your gilded cage. And the only thing I don't like about Mr. Samson –'

'Who's Mr. Samson?'

'Nobody seems to know Mr. Samson and he's an extraordinary character. I really think I like him as well as Robert Corder,' Hannah said thoughtfully. 'But he keeps birds in cages, and you know about the robin redbreast in a cage, don't you, Mr. Blenkinsop? He puts all Heaven in a rage and that's how I feel when I think of you in the bank. From the first moment I saw you, looking through the kitchen window – I'm sorry, I didn't mean to refer to that again – you reminded me of a bird. My favourite bird,' she said, but she would not tell him what that was and, as she looked at him, she decided that he was not so owlish as she had thought. The spectacles gave him most of his solemnity, his firmly shut mouth seemed to mark his determination to support them, and Hannah wished she dared ask him to take them off.

'You talk a lot of nonsense, don't you?' he asked patiently. 'Does Mr. Corder understand it?'

'I shouldn't think of trying to find out,' she replied. 'Mr. Corder's mind moves in different spheres from mine and I just accept the fact.'

She smiled trustfully at Mr. Blenkinsop, who said, 'I should hope it does.'

'So does Mr. Corder,' Miss Mole said demurely and, to her great surprise, Mr. Blenkinsop let out a modest burst of laughter.

'I didn't know you could do it,' she said.

'What?' Mr. Blenkinsop asked, preparing to be affronted.

'I didn't know you could laugh and I don't know why you did.'

'Because you meant me to,' he said mournfully, 'and I haven't had many chances.'

'You should make them.'

'And I'm worried.'

'Ah!' Hannah said. 'Can't you balance the cash properly, or whatever it is you do in a bank?'

'I can't balance Mr. Corder's religious views with my own.'

'Is that all? Who could? I shouldn't worry about that. I doubt whether he knows what his are.'

'But I'm a member of his church.'

'You can retire, I suppose?'

'I'm going to,' said Mr. Blenkinsop. 'When my mother was alive, I let things drift. It didn't seem worth while to upset her, but lately I've come to the conclusion that I'm not honest. The last sermon I heard him preach, on the subject of marriage, well, to put it plainly, it made me sick.'

'Too lax?' Hannah suggested.

'Too idiotic,' Mr. Blenkinsop said resignedly, and Hannah, taking a long time over her next stitch, asked carefully, 'When was it? I must have missed that one.'

'Oh, one evening, a few weeks ago.'

'I see,' Hannah said, and she paused in her work to connect Mr. Blenkinsop's views on marriage with the complicated love affair of which she suspected him. 'And you've come to-night to tell him what you think?'

'No. I don't want to lose my temper. I'm going to write to him. Argument would be a waste of time.'

'Well, I'm glad you've warned me. It will be a stormy day, I'm afraid.'

'Will it really? I'm sorry. But don't you think I ought to do it?'

'I don't feel so keenly as you do about marriage, Mr. Blenkinsop.'

'I didn't say I felt particularly keenly.'

'No, you didn't say so,' Hannah said, with an irritating smile.

'That simply happened to be the subject that brought things to a head. I differ fundamentally from Mr. Corder and the doctrines he has to teach.'

'Exactly,' Hannah said, 'so you'd better declare your independence as quickly as possible. You'll feel more comfortable, won't you? How's the chess getting on?'

'I knew you'd ask that, sooner or later,' he said, trying not to smile.

'And the country walks?' Hannah persisted. 'You want to hide your light under a bushel, but Mrs. Gibson brings it out. You're doing good by stealth and blushing to have it known.'

'No,' said Mr. Blenkinsop with an effort, 'I'm afraid my motives are not altogether unselfish,' and he looked as if he would have said more if he had not heard someone entering the hall.

Hannah hastily put away her sewing and wished she could do the same with Mr. Blenkinsop. 'Every room,' she said, looking at him with twinkling eyes, 'ought to have two doors. If this is Mr. Corder, what are you going to do?'

'I shall say good evening and walk out.'

'And what about me?'

'You?'

'He won't approve of finding a young spinster like me alone in the house with a single gent.'

'Then he'll have to put up with it,' Mr. Blenkinsop said, and Hannah was telling him that so bold a spirit was wasted on a bank when Robert Corder opened the door.

143

Chapter 20

MR. BLENKINSOP would have been more tactful and more chivalrous if he had explained his presence by pretending he had been waiting for this arrival. He did nothing of the kind and, after shaking hands with Robert Corder, he went away and Robert Corder, looking hurt, retired to his study. It was his habit to go there at once, when he came home, unless he heard sounds which roused his curiosity, and he was very curious, from some other part of the house, and Hannah wished she had instructed Mr. Blenkinsop to talk in whispers. She was sorry his visit had been cut short just as he was beginning to be interesting and though it was a little puzzling that he should seek her out, Hannah, who was not modest, could make it natural enough. Mr. Blenkinsop, bewildered, and troubled by a new situation, had instinctively turned to the person who could understand it. And she could understand everything, she thought, in a kind of ecstasy. She knew that Robert Corder was now trying to decide whether he should ask questions and risk the evasions which he could not believe were snubs, or find the outlet he wanted in a reprimand, and he would not know what he was going to do until he saw her. That she would presently witness the solution to this problem was some compensation for Mr. Blenkinsop's departure, and at a suspicion of rebellion against the necessity for making her visits to her old friend on the sly and receiving those of her young one under the shadow of Robert Corder's displeasure, she reminded herself that these conditions prevented dullness. There had been peace between her and Robert Corder for the last two weeks and she told herself that she had no wish to break the truce, but she was not going to turn the other cheek: that was part of his profession, not hers, and when she took his tea into the study and saw him writing at his desk, she

144

thought he was obeying the command laid on him, for he raised his head and thanked her, and she felt disappointed, but until she was actually through the door, she could not be sure he had nothing to say to her and it was when she was about to turn the handle that she heard him speak in a high, questioning tone.

'And Ruth?'

'Ruth?' Hannah repeated.

'Have you forgotten that she is at the school concert to-night? Or did you remember it very well?'

'Very well,' Hannah replied.

'I see. Well, Miss Mole, there is, of course, no objection to your having visitors, as long as they don't interfere with your duties, but I thought it was understood that you were to fetch Ruth.'

To be attacked on the subject of her duties, which were always punctiliously fulfilled, for, as Wilfrid said, she had a professional conscience, to receive suggestions that she was neglecting Ruth, was more than Miss Mole could bear, and she made no effort to keep the anger out of her voice as she replied quickly, 'Then you made a mistake. Wilfrid offered to fetch her for me.'

'That was very obliging of Wilfrid,' Robert Corder said smoothly, 'but I don't care to have my daughter's safety dependent on a young man who isn't scrupulous to keep his promises.'

'It isn't too late to start now,' Hannah said, with a glance at the clock.

'Then, Miss Mole, I shall be glad if you will go.'

'I'm sorry to refuse, Mr. Corder, but I couldn't insult Wilfrid like that.'

'Wilfrid?' he said coldly.

'That is what he has asked me to call him. I don't distrust him and I won't behave as if I do.'

'But, at my request –'

Miss Mole shook her head, smiling as she would have smiled at a child who could not be blamed for his stupidity. 'I wouldn't kick a puppy at anyone's request.'

'Puppy is a good word in this connection,' he said, and Hannah realized that his temper was very bad and that

145

though he seemed impervious to anything but petty slights to his own dignity, he might have troubles worthy of sympathy.

'It was an unfortunate word to use,' she said lightly. 'I meant any young thing. Wilfrid will keep his promise, Mr. Corder, and Ruth will like being fetched by him. It isn't every girl who has such a handsome cousin. And,' she went on quickly, as he frowned, 'your daughter was anxious that the house should not be left.'

'And you were anxious to see Mr. Blenkinsop.'

Miss Mole was deaf to this interruption. 'She didn't want Doris and her young man to be waiting about in the street. I should have thought the atmosphere of Beresford Road would have a sobering effect, much more sobering than the Downs, where I suppose they wander.'

'Miss Mole, I dislike this sort of talk.'

'But they do it, you know.'

'And I was not aware that Doris,' he overcame his repugnance with difficulty, 'that Doris had what you call a young man.'

'Yes, he's quite young,' Hannah said simply. 'He's the grocer's assistant. You see, when he called for orders –'

'I don't wish to hear about it. I dislike the idea very much.'

'Yes, Doris isn't particularly attractive, is she? I shouldn't have chosen her myself, but there's no accounting for tastes, as they say, and I think she has improved a little under the influence of the grocer's assistant's love. And he's highly respectable – at least, they've both told me so, and the grocer himself corroborates. I've made inquiries. He's rather a friend of mine.'

'You seem to make friends rather easily, Miss Mole.'

'Yes, isn't it lucky for me?' she said brightly, and then, as though she noticed his clouded brow for the first time, she asked in her softest voice, 'Have I done anything to annoy you?' and immediately perceived that the frontal attack was the one for Robert Corder. A patch of red showed on each cheek and he fidgeted with the papers on his desk.

'I did hear something to-night which disturbed me a little,' he confessed, and Hannah, glad that he was not look-

146

ing at her, braced herself for the shock. 'And then,' he went on, 'I am disappointed in Samuel Blenkinsop. He neglects the chapel, but he visits my house when I am out of it and goes off without a word. I don't understand it.'

Hannah's body slackened suddenly and she found that all her muscles ached. 'Do you mind if I sit down?' she asked.

'I shan't keep you a moment, Miss Mole, but yes, sit down, of course. Can you tell me, as you seem so intimate with Blenkinsop, whether I have offended him? I know,' he said, smiling faintly, 'that my views sometimes alarm the more timid spirits in my congregation, but I always welcome candid criticism.'

Gazing at Robert Corder, Hannah forgot Mr. Blenkinsop. This self-deception which, she could well believe, was sincere, had startled her into the fear that her opinion of herself was just as fond, and the world she had made for herself, in which she was wise and witty, of wide sympathies and an understanding heart, would have slipped silently into ruins if she had not found a desperate strength with which to prop it up. If it did not stand, she would go under with it; she would have to admit that Robert Corder was wrong in his dislike of her and one of her pleasures was the conviction that he was right, that she was too subtle for his comfort and too clear-sighted. It would be terrible to have to own that, however much they might differ, they had this bond of seeing themselves as no other person could.

'What is the matter, Miss Mole?' he asked suavely.

'I was – thinking,' Hannah said.

'You are doubting,' he said helpfully, 'whether you are justified in telling me.'

'No,' said Hannah, 'I'm afraid I'd forgotten all about Mr. Blenkinsop.'

'In other words, you were not listening to what I said.'

'Indeed I was, but it made me think of other things.' She looked at him with the bright intelligence she kept for him. 'Isn't that what conversation is for?'

'Not as I understand it,' he replied, and Hannah was smilingly silent.

'And now,' she said, feeling that this was her moment,

147

while he was angry, 'I hope you'll tell me what you've heard about me. For I can't bear suspense,' she added truthfully.

'No,' he said coldly, 'I prefer to try to forget it.'

'Oh, well, if you can forget it,' she said, rising as the door-bell rang, 'I shan't worry about it either,' but she was not so easy as she appeared. She fancied that Robert Corder's way of forgetting things was to put them in some safe place until he wanted them, and she knew that while she watched for an obvious danger, another, unsuspected, might creep up behind her. The obvious danger was Mr. Pilgrim. He was not the only person who knew Hannah Mole outside her professional capacity, but he was close at hand and that very night she was to feel that he was coming nearer, to hear his feet as she had heard them, ten years ago, padding up her little garden path. She had been angry then, but amused because she had been happy: she was angrier now because that happiness was only a little cherished dust, and it would need all her skill and energy to keep it from being blown away by the indignant breath of the sinless. It seemed hard that she should not be allowed to keep it without fighting for it; it was so frail a possession that, in the turmoil, she might lose it, and in its frailty, if she had been given to pity of her-self, she would have seen her tragedy. She had no memories which sustained her with their own strength; it was she who had to be tender with the weak. She could have faced the world with a glorious failure, but she must hide this one, which had ended meanly, and she was ten years older now and sometimes she was tired. She did not want to be sent roving again, just yet: she wished, as she had said, to make a good job of her undertaking, and the happiness of these people was becoming important to her.

When she opened the door to Doris, she looked at her sharply to see whether the course of her love was running smooth, and the sight of her face, rosy with the kisses of the grocer's assistant, was a pleasant one.

'Good girl,' Hannah said. 'It's just striking ten. Have you had a nice walk?'

'I've been to see his mother, Miss,' Doris said proudly. 'She was a bit stiff, but he says he thinks she'll get used to me.'

'Well, there!' Hannah said in congratulation, and watched one happy person go up to bed.

The voices of Wilfrid and Ruth, who came in soon afterwards, sounded happy too, and Ethel, following close on their heels, showed an excitement which roused Hannah's misgivings. Something had happened on which she would raise expectations not to be fulfilled, and the joyousness meant future trouble, but not until she began her confidences, when Wilfrid and Ruth had gone to bed, did Hannah understand that the chief part of the trouble might be for herself.

Mr. Pilgrim had been to the Girls' Club. The one in connection with his own chapel was ill-attended and badly managed and he had gone to see how Miss Corder managed hers. It appeared that he was delighted with everything, he had given the girls a little address, and he hoped Ethel would allow him to consult her again.

'So I must help him if I can, mustn't I, Miss Mole?'

'Practical experience is what he wants,' Hannah said briskly. 'Let him go to the club and watch you do it.'

'Yes,' Ethel said, a little doubtfully. 'But you see, Patsy Withers is generally there and she's so interfering. She wasn't there to-night, or she would have made Mr. Pilgrim think she runs the Club. And she's so silly with men. I thought I might ask him to tea one day.'

Hannah kept a silence which made Ethel anxious.

'Don't you think I might do that, Miss Mole?'

'Well,' Hannah said, 'you know what family teas are.'

'Yes,' Ethel agreed again.

'And your father and he would have so much to say to each other that I'm afraid you wouldn't be able to help him very much. And you wouldn't be at your best.'

'How do you mean – my best?'

'You wouldn't speak with the same authority in the bosom of your family.'

'Oh,' Ethel said, and she looked and sounded disappointed.

'But,' said Hannah quickly, easing her own conscience, 'you mustn't take my advice. You must do as you think best.'

149

'But I don't know what that is!' Ethel cried. 'I thought
you'd help me. You know, Miss Mole, it's dreadful, sometimes, not to have a mother.'

There were tears in her eyes and Hannah thought of Mrs.
Corder, who trusted Miss Mole to do what she could. 'Then
I'll tell you exactly what I think,' she said quietly. 'Do
nothing until he speaks to you about it again.'

'But, perhaps, he never will!'

'I know,' Hannah said, thinking now of all the women
who waited for the words they would not hear. 'But if he's
not in earnest about his work, it's not for you to remind
him."

'Isn't it? But that's just one of the ways where women
help.'

'Not at this stage of your acquaintance.'

'I feel as if I've known him for a long time. You do feel
like that with some people, don't you? He was so friendly
to-night. And I was wondering if we should have a Christmas party, for Howard, you know.'

'You'll have to speak to your father about that,' Hannah
said.

She went very slowly up to bed and her feet felt heavy. It
was no use running from Mr. Pilgrim: dodge and double as
she might, he was bound to catch her in the end, but if he
caught Ethel at the same time, the loss to one might be
balanced by the gain to another, and that, after all, was the
only way to reckon. The world would gain something from
a happy Ethel – if such a man as Mr. Pilgrim could make
her happy – and Hannah Mole would get something out of
it, in spite of him.

Her thoughts had carried her past Ruth's half-open door,
but Ruth's voice arrested them.

'Is that you, Miss Mole?' she called cautiously. 'I thought
it might be Father,' she explained. 'That's why I spoke like
that. It didn't sound a bit like you, Moley. You generally
run upstairs so much quicker than anybody else.'

'So I've been told before,' Hannah said.

'You're not tired, are you?'

'Yes I am, rather.'

'Oh, dear! And I'm afraid you had a dull evening. I

enjoyed the concert and Wilfrid was so nice, coming home, not trying to show off, or anything silly. He's like that when you're alone with him. And Ethel's in a very good temper and Howard will be here in a few days, but I don't like you to be tired. I do hope we're not going to be too much for you.'

'I hope not,' Hannah said, with a wry smile. 'I shall be all right in the morning,' she added cheerfully, but she stayed up for a long time, in the cold of her bedroom, working at Ruth's dress, repaying the child, whom she was afraid to kiss, for her first sign of thoughtfulness.

Chapter 21

THE arrival of Howard Corder unfortunately coincided with
the arrival of Mr. Blenkinsop's letter, and what should have
been a glad little family gathering had Robert Corder's
views of the younger generation for its entertainment. Mr.
Blenkinsop was the text of the discourse, but everyone felt
that illustrations from the home circle might be supplied,
and Wilfrid sat in lively, and Howard in patient, expectation of reproach. Mr. Corder spared them this, however,
and, breaking off suddenly, he remarked with a smile, that
he did not want to spoil Howard's first evening at home.

Wilfrid twisted an eyebrow in Miss Mole's direction and
Howard looked steadily at his plate. He seemed to have all
the patience the other Corders lacked and a capacity for
being contented if he were given the chance.

'Howard must tell us all the news of Oxford,' his father
said, generously resigning his position of spokesman.

'Oh – it's just the same as usual. We've had a lot of fog.'
Howard said, and suddenly, at a slight movement from the
head of the table, Wilfrid and Ethel both began to speak at
once.

Wilfrid waved a hand courteously. 'Go on. Your turn.'

'Oh, it's nothing. I was just going to say it's funny you
should have had that letter from Mr. Blenkinsop –'

'Funny!' Robert Corder exclaimed.

'I mean – queer, because I've had one from Patsy Withers.
She doesn't want to help me with the Club any longer.'

'Indeed? Well, no doubt Miss Withers has very good
reasons for her decision and I can see no likeness between her
and Mr. Blenkinsop.'

'Oh, no!' Ethel agreed eagerly, 'but she did promise to
help, and now she says Wednesday evening doesn't suit her.
Oh! Perhaps she likes going to the week-night service.'

'That would be very strange,' her father said bitingly.
'As a matter of fact, she was there last time. I told you it was
a mistake to have Wednesday for the Club.'

'But the girls wanted it then, and the Club's for the girls.'

'Then you must be prepared to lose your helpers.'

'I should think you'd be glad,' said Ruth. 'I hate Patsy
Withers.'

'Ruthie, Ruthie!'

'I do,' Ruth said stubbornly. 'She's like barley sugar, yellow and squirmy, and her voice is like it too, all sweet and
waggly, and she talks to me as if I'm about six.'

'If you were six I should send you to bed,' said her father.
'I won't have such remarks made at my table.'

'But you were making them yourself about Mr. Blenkinsop,' Ruth said sullenly.

'That's a very different matter,' he said, and he went out
of the room. This was his usual way of emphasizing a disapproval which he forebore to express in words, and possibly
he believed it left his family depressed. Ethel, indeed, looked
frightened, and Ruth looked glum until her next speech sent
Wilfrid into a roar of laughter.

'I don't think it's good for people to be ministers,' she
said, and Ethel cried, 'Oh, hush, Wilfrid, hush! Father will
hear you. And it's very wrong of you, Ruth, to say such
things. It's a noble profession. Isn't it, Miss Mole?'

'All professions can be noble,' Hannah replied gravely. It
was only a little while since Ethel had extolled the doctor's
calling in the same words, only a little longer since Ruth had
flushed in loyalty to her father when Miss Mole had discon-
certed him, and in these changes she measured the profund-
ity of Ethel's feelings and the extent of Ruth's trust. It was
Howard, to whom Miss Mole was a stranger, who looked
uncomfortable, and Ethel, glancing from one face to another, looking for support and thinking of Mr. Pilgrim, assuring herself she was right but wishing they would all agree
with her, saw her brother's look and misinterpreted it.

'And when your own brother's a minister, you'll change
your mind,' she said.

'Oh, shut up,' said Howard. 'Let's go into the other room
and play at something.'

'Coming, Mona Lisa?' Wilfrid asked.

Hannah shook her head and remained by the fire, under the hissing gas. As soon as Robert Corder heard the young people in the drawing-room, he would look into the dining-room to see if Miss Mole was doing her duty; in his present mood he would be more disappointed than pleased to see her there, and Miss Mole was willing to disappoint him, but what a pity it was, she thought, that he and she could not be companionable. Did it never occur to him, that she might crave for maturer society sometimes and need more relaxation than she got? From seven o'clock in the morning until half-past ten at night, she was busy in his service, dusting, cooking carefully, making beds, shopping economically, darning socks and stockings and his undergarments, superintending Doris, who was slow and stupid, and she got her little periods of leisure by her own speed and contrivance. If he had been a different kind of man, they could have had good talks by the fire when she took in his tea at ten o'clock. And, perhaps, he was thinking the very same thing, and wishing she were a different kind of woman and more like Miss Patsy Withers, and it seemed to Hannah that Lilla would have been cleverer if she had chosen her watchdog of the breed Mr. Corder admired. The angularity and asperity of Miss Mole simply served to show up the softness and sweetness of the other, but Lilla's thrifty turn of mind had seized on the opportunity of doing two good deeds in one, supplying Mr. Corder with a housekeeper and sparing herself the inconvenience of having a penniless cousin on her hands. She would have done better to have introduced Patsy herself into the family and let her see what she could make of it. Patsy would probably have found that a hero is more easily worshipped at a distance and Robert Corder would have learnt that flattery does not flavour food, and Hannah saw that the result of this combined ignorance might be as dangerous to her as Mr. Pilgrim, though not so disagreeable, and might be disastrous to Ruth. And Patsy had been at the week-night service and Mr. Corder had heard something which disturbed him. Now what could that be? Hannah asked herself, tapping her lips with her scissors.

Mr. Corder put his head round the door and Hannah

154

smiled at him as charmingly as she could. When he had disappeared, Ethel came in and fidgeted with the ornaments on the mantelpiece.

'Finished the game?' Hannah asked.

'No, but I have to stay out till they call me in. Miss Mole, don't you think it's rather funny about Patsy?'

'Is it? You're really glad to get rid of her, aren't you?'

'Yes. But still, I think it's funny.'

This was as near as Ethel would go to what was on her mind and Hannah would not give her the little push she wanted. 'Is she a great friend of yours?' she asked, instead.

'Well, sometimes I think she is and sometimes I think she isn't. That's what she's like.'

'I know. You tell her something and then you wish you hadn't. Have you ever told her anything about me?'

'Oh, Miss Mole, yes!' Ethel cried, for she was truthful and her deceptions were only for herself. 'But only about those mattresses.'

'Well, what else was there to tell?' Hannah asked grimly. 'You did all you could, it seems to me. Never mind, never mind! Don't cry. You cry far too easily and it's not becoming and they'll know you've been doing it when you go into the other room. Stop it!' Hannah cried.

'But you'll think I'm a sneak and you've been so kind to me lately.'

'I'll always be kind to you if you'll let me,' Hannah said.

'It wasn't that I wanted to tell tales, but I did want to talk to somebody.'

'Then talk to me in future.'

'Did she tell Father?' Ethel asked in a strangled whisper.

'I don't know.'

'Because, if she did – Oh, there! they're calling me. I'll come back next time I'm out.'

Wilfrid changed places with Ethel. 'There's trouble brewing,' he said.

'Man is born to trouble – And poke the fire for me, please.'

'What I like about you, Mona Lisa –'

'Yes, yes, I should love to hear it, but what's the trouble?'

'What I like about you is your allusive and elusive mind. There you are! The sparks are flying upward. And, of course, there are lots of other things I like.'

'What's the trouble?' Hannah repeated self-denyingly.

'Revolt's the trouble. Howard says he's chucking the ministry and all Mrs. Spenser-Smith's good gold will be chucked away too. What do you think of that? She sent him to the University to make a high-class little minister of him and he says he won't be a little minister. He's just broken the news, and they're arguing about it now instead of getting on with the game. So we're going to have a happy Christmas, and I shall go as early as possible to my poor dear mother and stay with her as long as she'll keep me. He'll have a hell of a time, but it's better than having it for life.'

Hannah sighed. 'Why do people want to give each other hell?'

'Because it makes them feel like God. And it's so easy. Now the uncle –'

'Be careful,' Hannah said. 'He's in the hall, getting the letters.'

'Yes, he likes turning over the letters. God, again! He has to know everything. And yet, Mona Lisa, to do the man justice, he's a benevolent deity in the chapel. But that's easy, too, when you come to think of it. His people get the reward of their obedience, and so would his children if they'd be what he considers good, which means admiring and believing in papa. Ruth's quite right. It isn't good for people to be ministers and there are times when I'm sorry for the poor devil. If you see yourself as the centre of the universe –'

'I should have thought that's what you do yourself.'

'Yes, but I know I'm doing it. That makes all the difference. Now the uncle –'

'I ought not to be listening to all this,' Hannah said, but she liked having the boy there, sitting on the hearthrug with his back against a chair and his arms hugging his knees. She could pretend that thus her own son would have dealt with her and she with him, while she knew that the very lack of those demands which a mother and son make of each other

156

was what constituted the charm of her relationship with Wilfrid.

'Oh, nonsense,' he said, 'you and I are the only reasonable human beings in the house. Howard's all right, but he's dull, and depressed, poor lad. Ethel's trying to make him change his mind and Ruth's persuading him to keep the bomb until her Uncle Jim arrives.'

'Ruth seems to think her Uncle Jim's omnipotent,' Hannah said, with the suspicion of a sniff.

'Well, he'll take part of the shock. It was silly of Howard to tell Ethel. She's bound to blurt it out. She can't see a difficulty without bumping into it, or giving such a jump that everybody else begins looking for it.'

He stopped speaking as Robert Corder came into the room, with a letter in his hand. 'This is for you, Miss Mole,' he said, giving it to her slowly, and he looked at her curiously and then at Wilfrid impatiently. 'I thought you were playing with the others.'

'So I am, sir. I'm waiting till they call me in. It's one of those games where there's more waiting than playing.'

Without examining it, Hannah had dropped the letter on to her knee, with the address turned upwards. ' And they begin talking about something else,' she said.

'Oh, yes,' Wilfrid returned her smile, 'they're doing that.'

'Well,' said Robert Corder, 'I hope you are not disturbing Miss Mole.'

'No, we're talking about something else too,' she said pleasantly. 'And I can sew at the same time. A woman can always do two things at once. If she couldn't, she'd have a dreary time of it.'

'I often envy women,' Robert Corder said. 'They have useful and not exacting occupation for their hands, and no labour need be dreary.'

To this, neither Wilfrid nor Miss Mole ventured a reply, and Robert Corder retired after another look at the letter on Hannah's knee.

'He wants to know who your letter's from, he wants to know what we're talking about, he wants to talk to somebody himself. You ought to have encouraged him, Mona Lisa.'

'Ought I?'

'Yes.' He nodded his head sagely. 'Just for the good of the community.'

'Why didn't you do it, then?'

'He hates the sight of me,' Wilfrid said. 'Too much like my father. But you want to read your letter.'

'I'm not sure that I do. I don't know who it's from.'

When she had read it, she realized that Robert Corder must have recognized the clerkly hand of Mr. Blenkinsop who asked her to tea with him early the next week. 'I haven't a hat fit to wear,' was Hannah's first thought, and the second was one of impatience that Mr. Blenkinsop could not manage his affairs without support, but there was something flattering in his desire to see her, and something touching, and, as she thought of him, who looked so self-sufficient, she was bound to wonder if Robert Corder, also, was not as much a baby as the rest of them. Mr. Blenkinsop was a solemn infant who asked for what he wanted and Robert Corder was a spoilt one who expected his needs to be divined.

Chapter 22

ROBERT CORDER's work took him out of the house for a great part of the day, but it also brought him back at times when a business man is in his office and knows nothing of domestic affairs until he returns to find a meal awaiting him and the work of the day apparently done. Robert Corder was conscious perforce of the doings of the household. He would swing down the garden path in the morning and meet the butcher's boy carrying a recognizable joint, and if the joint did not appear in a cooked condition that evening, he would wonder where it was and why Miss Mole had ordered it a day before it was needed, or he would come back and see half the drawing-room furniture in the hall and get a glimpse of Miss Mole doing something with a duster or a feather broom. His study was never disturbed in this manner. The fire was lighted before breakfast, and the room, presumably, dusted and swept, and when he was in the house he chose to sit there, but, even in that sanctuary, he could not be unaware of sounds and movements. He could hear the front-door and the back-door bells when they were rung and the thumping feet of Doris as she ran up the three stairs from the kitchen, and if she did not introduce a visitor into the study, he would, as likely as not, hear her voice, with its Radstowe burr, calling Miss Mole to settle some question with which she could not deal herself. He could distinguish Ethel's prancing step from Miss Mole's quick, even one, and sometimes, when he heard the front door shut, he would stroll to his window to see whether it was his housekeeper or his daughter who had gone out. When it was his daughter, he would have a slight feeling of discomfort: when it was Miss Mole he felt an active irritation. There was something wrong with Ethel's appearance and he could not give it a name, but he knew she did not look definitely feminine, like

159

Miss Patsy Withers, in spite of her bright colours, or completely unconscious of herself, as her mother had been, and she certainly was not pretty. That, perhaps, was a good thing. It would have been a great and highly distasteful anxiety to have had a daughter who attracted young men, and Ethel had given her heart to her work and seemed to be content. People spoke very well of her in the chapel and told him he should be as proud of such a daughter as she should be of such a father. This praise of her seemed to him somewhat exaggerated, but there was no doubt she was a good girl and her fits of passion seemed to be less frequent, but it was difficult to be patient with her nervousness and secretly he resented, while he benefited from, her protective plainness.

When he watched Miss Mole it was with definitely antagonistic feelings. The alert bearing of her head, her quick step, seemed to him unsuitable in a housekeeper, and arrogant in a woman who had no pretensions to good looks. If she had to be plain and thin, she should also have been meek, and he supposed it was possible to be domestically intelligent without looking as though she had some secret source of satisfaction in herself. That look had been growing on her lately and he could not but connect it with the visit and the letter of Mr. Blenkinsop. He had seen her as an unfortunate woman, undesired by any man, and he had despised her accordingly, and with the suspicion that Samuel Blenkinsop had found something in her which he had missed himself, he immediately set about searching for it and felt uneasy. He remembered, too, his discovery of Wilfrid, sitting on the floor and talking to her, not dutifully, but with enjoyment sparkling in his dark eyes, and it was increasingly evident that Ruth liked her.

Robert Corder did not understand that he was always jealous of those who gave to some one who was not himself and of those who received: what he did realize was that Miss Mole had some mysterious power to make certain people like her and that she did not like him, and as it was impossible for him to like a person first, he remained in his state of irritated interest and curiosity. Mrs. Spenser Smith had been wise in her choice of a housekeeper: his house was well kept, his food was well cooked, and Ruth looked healthier, but Mrs. Spenser-Smith probably had no experience of Miss Mole as an inmate of her house, of this personality which gave every promise of being properly negative and then developed signs of positive character. Not once, since her arrival, had Miss Mole asked Robert Corder's advice. The kitchen range, the gas, the hot water, might go wrong, and Miss Mole was equal to them or found some one else to manage them; she had no difficulty in keeping her accounts; she brought him no tales of dilatory or dishonest tradesmen. This peace from domestic care was what he wanted, what Mrs. Spenser-Smith had told him he ought to have and what Ethel had not been able to give him, but he would have been better pleased if he could have believed that Miss Mole was making determined efforts and overcoming her natural disabilities for his sake, instead of taking everything in her easy stride. He knew nothing of Miss Mole's real difficulties, of the constant caution necessary to prevent Ethel's jealousy when any two members of the family paid more attention to each other than they did to her, to give her encouragement without raising false hopes, to damp down her threatened returns to sentimentality about Wilfrid, to give her the position of mistress of the house while she did nothing to sustain it. Miss Mole had to intervene in the quarrels which sprang up so quickly between the sisters, to avoid giving evidence of the sympathy between Wilfrid and herself, to steer conversations into safe waters and, above all, to conceal the control she really exercised. It was exhausting work but it did not exist for Robert Corder. The family of the minister of Beresford Road Chapel should be, and therefore was, a happy one, and his own griefs, his consciousness of the different treatment he received in the chapel from what he received at home, were not allowed to mar the concord, but it seemed strange to him that while Mrs. Spenser-Smith should be ready, almost too ready at times, to help him and Miss Patsy Withers brought her rather touchingly simple little problems for him to solve, his own children should give him little and ask for less. There were no signs of Howard's improvement in this or any other direction. He showed no affection and no enthusiasm, and Robert Corder was confirmed in his opinion that it was a mistake to make things too easy for a young man: his father had fought for his position and kept it; Howard accepted his advantages and did not use them. Robert Corder could speak of these dissatisfactions to no one, now that his wife had gone, and while she lived he had hardly noticed them, and there had been no Miss Mole to add to them. To discuss Miss Mole with Mrs. Spenser-Smith would be to criticize her judgment; to deplore the faults of his children might be to admit failures of his own, and when Miss Withers referred to them in terms of praise he could not buy her sympathy at the cost of her envy of a life in which work of eminent importance was combined with the amenities of the happy home he had made, yet it comforted him that she knew of the little rift in the lute for which he could not possibly be blamed. She seemed to have an intuitive distrust of Miss Mole which agreed with his own, and it was increased, no doubt, by Ethel's story of the mattresses. It was wrong of Ethel not to have told him. It was a small matter, but it was indicative, and it was necessary for him to keep an eye on the stranger in the house. If it had not been Wilfrid's mattress, he would have taken action, but he could not pamper the boy, even in the cause of discipline.

Such thoughts as these underlay his life when he was in the house; outside it, they were forgotten if no one jogged his memory, and he strode about the streets, visited the sick, attended his committee meetings, with an energy and liveliness which gave him a reputation as a man of action. His actions were generally those of his committees, but his enjoyment of an authority which never presented itself to his mind as being safely diluted, his look of vitality, his handsome head, his conviction that he was of importance in the religious and civic life of Radstowe, had a suggestive value for others as well as for himself. To those who were sad or sick, his entrance was reanimating; knowing this, he was able to help them as he sincerely desired to do, and it was inevitable that he should suffer from a feeling of neglect and of misvaluation when he returned to his home, where his importance and his usefulness were diminished by the dullness or the wilfulness of its inmates.

He had no great power for concentration and no desire for

peace in which to meditate or to read and, unless he had callers to interview, he had little to do in the house when his letters were written and his sermons prepared, and he had time and willingness to listen to the sounds of voices, feet, bells and doors, to conjecture or to criticize. He would hear a murmuring from the kitchen as he passed through the hall and, sometimes, a burst of laughter, and making some excuse, such as the need for another pair of boots, he would penetrate into the kitchen regions and find Miss Mole and Doris mysteriously busy at the table or the stove, when he had expected to find one or both of them idle.

'The Christmas puddings are ready for stirring,' Hannah said to him on one of these occasions. 'Will you have your stir now?'

'My stir?'

'Everybody has to stir, for luck.'

Doris turned aside with a giggle. She was embarrassed by the presence of the minister in the kitchen and by Miss Mole's airy way with him, and Robert Corder, interpreting this sound correctly and reacting to it immediately, took the opportunity to prove his essential homeliness. He stirred manfully, circling the wooden spoon through the unwieldy mixture and an unmistakable scent, very pleasant but forbidden, rose to his nostrils.

'I hope there is no brandy in it,' he said seriously.

Miss Mole looked disappointed. ' I know some people prefer beer,' she said, 'but I think brandy's better. I ought to have asked you.'

He dropped the spoon. 'But Miss Mole, you must know we never have intoxicants in this house, and I happen to be the president of the Radstowe Temperance Society.'

'Does it count,' she asked meekly, 'when it's cooked and in a pudding? I'm so sorry. What can we do about it? I can't possibly eat all these puddings by myself.'

'Waste would only be an aggravation of the mistake,' he said sharply, 'but, another time, Miss Mole . . .'

He went away, very much disturbed. Surely the woman could not be as simple as she seemed, and if she was not, what was she? And this was the sort of thing which could be ignored in an ordinary household but was of real importance

163

in one like this. Doris would spread the story; it might have a far-reaching effect on the girl's attitude towards the drink question, and probably the brandy had been bought through that young man whose relationship to Doris had affected Robert Corder's own attitude towards the girl, as towards some one not quite unspotted from the world of the flesh, and it would be impossible to offer Christmas pudding to any visitor to the house.

He returned hurriedly to the kitchen.

'And the mincemeat?' he inquired.

'I'm afraid that is contaminated, too,' Miss Mole replied.

No, she was not simple, and he remembered the mattresses. He had an impulse to order the destruction of the savoury mess, to let the family go puddingless at Christmas, but he hesitated and the ardour of his indignation left him, and he did nothing. What he needed in his house was a little committee of people like himself which would frame and pass resolutions and give orders in which responsibility was shared. Alone, he felt that, in some way he would be baffled and his position worsened, but when the pudding appeared on Christmas Day he would quietly refuse to eat it and he hoped Miss Mole would feel ashamed. Then swiftly, with the glibness acquired by answering awkward questions at his class for young men, he arranged such tolerant, humorous comments as might be needed, on domestic accidents and the lenience which must be extended to others in affairs of conscience, but he felt very bitter towards a woman who put him to these shifts and, as the object of his suspicions and dislike, she became oddly fascinating: he liked looking at her and despising her for her lack of beauty, he enjoyed listening to her and silently sneering at her remarks: he was puzzled by the frankness which alternated with her slyness and he did not see how he was to get rid of her without less petty reasons to offer Mrs. Spenser-Smith, a practical woman who would make nothing of the little objections he could name and who would not understand that a mere personality could trouble his peace of mind. He saw himself permanently saddled with Miss Mole and, two days after the pudding incident, he found more causes for mistrustful speculation.

He saw her go down the garden path in what might be

taken for her best apparel and, as she went up the road, she waved a hand gaily towards the next-door house. It was growing dusk, but he saw her hand plainly in its light glove and the light glove offended him. She was not at the tea-table and when he asked where she was Ethel reported that she had gone out. He made a dubious sound and Ethel, tactlessly loyal to Miss Mole, said quickly: 'She has to go out sometimes.'

'I am quite aware of that, Ethel. Do you know where she has gone?'

'She said she was going to see Mrs. Gibson first,' Ethel said, and he allowed a sufficient pause to elapse before he made some reference to Mr. Samson. Had anyone seen him lately? Did he still live alone?

Ethel said she had not seen, and was not interested in, the horrid old man, but Ruth said, a little shyly: 'He isn't horrid. It's just his face and that's not his fault. Miss Mole says she thinks he's rather nice, like everybody else when you get to know them.'

'And how has Miss Mole discovered this?'

'Oh, she just knows things like that,' Ruth said contentedly, pretending not to notice her father's covert sneer.

Chapter 23

HANNAH accepted life as she found it, she accepted imperfection, but this did not prevent her from pondering on human existence in her own fashion. Finding pleasure and excitement in little things, because there were no others, seeing those about her doing the same, though, as she believed, with less intensity, she could still wonder whether more was not expected of human beings, or whether, in getting food and shelter and what happiness came their way, they were doing all that was required of them. Robert Corder could see himself as a man with a definite mission against evil; Wilfrid, perhaps, was somewhat shamefacedly hoping to alleviate the physical sufferings of men, but the mass of people was like herself, without her special advantages, living from one day of small things to another, grateful when sorrow was avoided and pathetically thankful for peace, and in a world which knew the procession of sun and moon and stars, the miracle of spring and the pageantry of autumn, the occupations of these two-legged creatures, running about the earth, seemed insufficient. They vexed themselves about things of no apparent moment, such as mattresses; they became excited over a mild entertainment, such as having tea with Mr. Blenkinsop; they wasted time, which ought surely to have been given to some higher purpose, in trying new modes of hairdressing for the benefit of a strange sailor who would not notice them. But what were these higher purposes and who pursued them, outside the special band of thinkers and creators? And to these people did their efforts sometimes seem as unimportant as hers to Hannah Mole? She envied artists with their definite objects and work which seemed to them imperative, but envy was one of the emotions she never allowed herself for long, and it vanished when she realized that she, too, should be an artist in her own sphere, that, indeed, she was already doing almost her best to be one, and that the results of her labours, if they were good, were no more to be despised than was a painting of a Dutch interior because it did not deal with gods and goddesses.

This decision to be a conscientious artist was an inspiriting one, particularly as it exacted the expression of her own, and not Robert Corder's, conception of what the housekeeper to a Nonconformist minister should be. It was comforting to think there would be disloyalty in pandering to his notions, for in her relations with Robert Corder she sometimes felt guilty. She who boasted that she could like anybody, had not tried to like him, yet Wilfrid had told her that a little encouragement would be for the good of the community. The artist, however, did not consider the good of the community. The best work was not done in that way, and Hannah felt perfectly free to go on disliking Robert Corder and to get from that exercise the peculiar kind of pleasure which, as she suspected, he was beginning to get out of his dislike for her. She was cleverer at disguising her feelings than he was, cleverer in every way, she believed, and her pleasure would increase in proportion to her concealment and his revelations. She must be allowed this joy, she told herself: moreover, nothing was more dangerous than going contrary to nature for the sake of an imagined future good, and, if future good must be considered, what could be better for Robert Corder and his family than the impact of an independent mind on his?

Miss Mole was feeling rather gay and conceited after her tea with Mr. Blenkinsop. She had made that serious young man laugh once and smile unwillingly several times, and, in a secluded corner of the tea shop, where the food and the tea were good, she had talked freely for the first time for many years. In her situations, she had listened more often than she had spoken, and though some of them had been lost through the sharp readiness of her tongue, that tongue had merely been restive with pent-up energy and lack of exercise, like a horse, not ill-natured, but riotous when it sees a stretch of grass. To have a listener like Mr. Blenkinsop was to have the grass and no punishment for bolting. There had been no need to pick her words – and when she did not pick them they were harmless enough – with a potential, if not an active fellow-sinner, and when she left him she was afraid she had talked too much for his convenience, though not for her own comfort. Voluntarily, he had not spoken of his affairs, and when, giving him his chance, she tried to tease him about the gilded gratings of the bank and the dangerous re-actions of his evening liberty, he had assured her that he was not an impulsive person. She had expressed amazement and this was one of the moments when he smiled, but he was solemn when he went on to say that due consideration was always given to his undertakings.

'Then you haven't my excuse,' she said, 'or my fun. It's a wonderful world, Mr. Blenkinsop, when you may find an adventure round any corner.'

'Yes, but one doesn't,' he replied crushingly.

'Of course one can avoid them. It's a startling thought that if I'd been of the avoiding kind, I should never have known you. I'm sorry this incident always crops up when we meet, but I suppose it's in both our minds. I'm referring –'

'I know what you're referring to.'

'And you regret the reference and the incident.'

'Not entirely.'

'Then you've changed.'

'Yes, I've changed.'

'Ah!' Hannah said significantly. 'And I don't regret it at all, for here I am, having an outing with a single gent, and but for that, I might still be in Mrs. Widdows' stuffy parlour. But that's not very likely,' she added honestly. She wished she had called him a technically single gent and seen what he made of that. Possibly she had talked so much that he had decided on reserve. She had told him about her child-hood in the country, about her situations and the kind of books she liked and what she would do if she had a lot of money. She felt tired by her own eloquence, but relieved, and she did not think she had given him cause to doubt her discretion. It would be a pity if she had. She liked Mr. Blen-kinsop and she wanted to know whether the stories she had made about him would come true, and when she looked back at her past and the men she had met, as her employers and their relatives and friends – for her life had been singularly barren of closer relationships with men and women – she decided that Mr. Blenkinsop was the one to whom she would tell a secret or go for help, and when, in a quick, frightened thought, she remembered Mr. Pilgrim, it did not need a great effort of her imagination to see the solid, bulky form of Mr. Blenkinsop overshadowing the narrow-shouldered, somewhat slinking figure of the other, like a policeman keeping an eye on a suspicious character.

Mr. Pilgrim, however, had come no nearer; Mr. Blenkinsop had given her nothing new to consider except a feeling of safety, and her mind was free to receive the impression of Uncle Jim. As Hannah always had her tongue in her cheek when she created romantic stories about herself, she could make them as extravagant as she chose, and she was hardly disappointed when she saw a man, in clothes which looked too tight for him, who had no likeness to her buccaneer. It was just as well, she thought, when she remembered the difference between the Miss Mole she had fitted to him and the one with which this plain Uncle Jim, who might have been a tax collector, was shaking hands. He had a close-clipped fair moustache in a short face, a pucker of wrinkles round his eyes which gave him an amused rather than a worried expression, and though he was bronzed enough to make Robert Corder look hectic with the colour on his cheekbones, he was not immediately suggestive of hurricanes and tropic sun. He was an ordinary looking man yet, in the slowness of his movements and speech and in his calm, apparently uncritical regard, there was something to make Hannah feel that here was another person who could be relied on. He had a dwarfing effect on Robert Corder, but this was Hannah's first opportunity of comparing the minister with a man who belonged to a wider world than that of Beresford Road Chapel, and it seemed to her that Uncle Jim in the pulpit would be less incongruous than Robert Corder on the bridge of a ship. Uncle Jim's authority was that of the man who knew his trade and had his position as a consequence and a matter of course, while, with Robert Corder, the position came first, and the authority derived from it was a constant source of gratification and made a constant demand for recognition. Hannah thought sadly that she was rather like him herself; she had no position to give her a fair start, but she was not

169

content to let her personality make what mark it could, without assistance; a sign, she feared, of a weak character.

She made another of her good resolutions and remained silent and observant. She saw Ruth looking with shining eyes at the imperturbable face of her uncle and glancing from him to Hannah, as though she wished to connect them in her happiness and to know what each thought of the other. Ethel, wearing an extra necklace in honour of the occasion, and a bright blue frock, rattled her beads and jerked in her seat at the supper table, but her glances had not the confidence of Ruth's. She could never forget the presence of her father, and her anxiety was that conversation should go amicably between him and Uncle Jim. Robert Corder did his best as host. He invited his brother-in-law to talk of his experiences and Uncle Jim was as unresponsive as Howard had been on the night of his return. He said something about the weather and Robert Corder lifted his eyebrows patiently. He was not really eager to hear another person talk, but it was exasperating to see such a waste of opportunity. A single voyage would have supplied the minister with anecdotes for countless supper tables and sewing meetings, with texts and illustrations for innumerable sermons, and this man, who had followed the sea since he was a boy and knew all the ports of the world, could produce nothing more illuminating than a casual reference to the weather. Opportunities did not come to those who could use them. Howard and Jim were alike in their dumb obtuseness, and what sort of minister Howard would make, his father feared to prophesy. He sank back in his chair and resigned his duties. He had done all he could.

Then Uncle Jim volunteered a remark.

'What's the matter with the gas?' he said, looking at the pendant light. 'It oughtn't to make a noise like that. I'll have a look at it to-morrow.'

'I've been looking at it for more than two months and it doesn't take the slightest notice,' Hannah said mournfully.

Ruth laughed and looked at her uncle. She had been hoping Miss Mole would say something to show she was not just an ordinary housekeeper who was afraid to speak.

Robert Corder frowned. 'Then, Miss Mole,' he said sharply, 'you should have called in the plumber.'

'But would he come, if I did call to him? And would he go, if once he came? Plumbers,' she said, 'are like everything else. You want them badly and, when you get them, you're sorry.'

'I think,' Robert Corder said in the bland manner of his annoyance, 'you must make a point of wanting the things you should not have.'

'That was implied,' Hannah said brightly. She had broken her good resolution and Uncle Jim had waked to the fact of her existence.

'We'll try combined tactics to-morrow,' he said, and then he created a timely diversion. 'I've got some Chinese silks upstairs. I'll bring them down after supper.'

Hannah stayed in the dining-room and Robert Corder lingered by the fire.

'You and I, Miss Mole,' he said, 'are not interested in the Chinese silks.'

'Aren't we?' Hannah replied. 'I expect they're beautiful.'

'Oh, no doubt, no doubt, but hardly matters of concern to you and me.'

Was he trying to remind her of her age and position and hinting that she should not follow the others to the drawing-room?

'Not of concern, certainly. That's why I'm staying here,' she said reassuringly. 'I wonder if Mr. Erley can stop these jets from hissing as well as the other one from bubbling. I thought I was getting used to the noise, but, as Christmas draws nearer, it sounds like all the geese and turkeys making a fuss at the thought of being killed.'

'What a very unpleasant idea!' he said, frowning quickly.

'Yes, isn't it?' Then she looked up at him and laughed. 'I've spoilt your Christmas pudding and now I've spoilt your goose.'

Mr. Corder suddenly condescended to jest. 'Or, as you might say, you have cooked it.'

Hannah laughed still more merrily. She was not going to be beaten by the ladies at the sewing meeting and Robert Corder might have found it necessary to withdraw in good-humoured dignity, before Miss Mole took advantage of his affability, if Ruth had not appeared, to say that Uncle Jim had given her a lovely silk with little flowers all over it, and

171

did Miss Mole think it could possibly be made into a frock in time for the Spenser-Smiths' party?

'We'll try,' Hannah said slowly. She was thinking of the little velveteen dress which was to have been a surprise and which would seem so humble in comparison with the flowery silk.

'I knew you'd say that!' In her excitement, Ruth turned to her father and exclaimed, 'she never says she can't do anything when she knows you want it! And do come and stop Ethel from choosing a bright pink. There are heaps of others and the drawing-room's like a shop.'

'Just a minute, Miss Mole. I suppose you have replied to Mrs. Spenser-Smith's invitation?'

'No,' Hannah said, 'your daughter has done that.'

'But I think it would be courteous to send a separate little note. It's very kind of her to ask you.'

'Yes, but I wasn't sure that I ought to go,' Hannah said meekly.

'But certainly, certainly! You could hardly refuse and you will find it quite a homely, friendly affair. Just write to Mrs. Spenser-Smith and express your appreciation.'

'In the first, or the third, person?' Hannah inquired.

'The first, Miss Mole, would be more suitable. Write it in the form of a note.'

'Very well,' Hannah said, and she began to plan her humble little letter, but Ruth had her by the arm to lead her into the drawing-room, and was asking if she had a party frock.

'Black silk and jet trimmings. It's the only wear for a housekeeper.'

'And Uncle Jim's got all those lovely things!' Ruth sighed.

'If you dare to say anything to him about me, I'll never speak to you again!' Hannah whispered vehemently, but Uncle Jim did not need a hint. He was looking at the mass of stuff he had bought and wondering how he was to get rid of it and Hannah's modest protests were useless when he thrust a roll of silk into her arms.

Ruth's happiness was now complete. 'And won't Mrs. Spenser-Smith be secretly vexed when she sees us all looking so grand!' she cried.

Chapter 24

HANNAH had the homeless and the childless person's dislike for Christmas. There were a few people from whom, in the course of her career, she had not been completely severed, and to these she wrote, but the paucity of her acquaintances and her lack of real intimacy wth them were very present to her at this time of the year and almost persuaded her of some failure in herself, but it was not easy, and Robert Corder had lately emphasized the fact, to make friends outside the house in which she was a dependent, and to most of the people she had served, often wholeheartedly, sometimes with misguided zeal, becoming absorbed in their affairs as though they were her own, she remained as mere Miss Mole, whose importance vanished with her useful presence. She was accustomed to this state of things but it still amazed her. A human being, to her, was a continuous wonder, a group of human beings made a drama of which she was half creator, half spectator, and she was baffled to know how people amused themselves without this entertainment which never palled and never ended. Hannah was not one of those who considered it a waste of time to lose a train and have to wait on a station platform, who shut their eyes, or read a paper, in railway carriages: she was thrilled by the sight of strangers and by the emanation of their personalities, and it was hard to understand that they did not get the same excitement from her neighbourhood.

When she considered the Corder family dispassionately, she could see that the material for her drama was not promising. The egoism of the Reverend Robert offered the most scope, for the egoism of a person whose abilities are mediocre must have a humorous element, but in Ethel, in Ruth, in the quiet Howard, in Captain Jim Erley, in his shirt-sleeves, as he busied himself about the gas, how could she find so much interest? Was her own egoism enlarging the significance of these who made her little world or was she really seeing the whole world in miniature, which was all the ordinary human eye could manage? The shaking of an empire was not more agitating than the imminence of Howard's disclosure about the ministry; the intrigues of diplomacy were not more complicated and needed no more skill than Mr. Pilgrim's intrusion into this life shared with the Corders, and the news of a great victory could hardly gratify its engineers more deeply than Uncle Jim gratified Miss Mole when he stepped off the dining-room table and said, 'You've done Ruth a lot of good. If I'd known you were here I might have stuck to the sea a bit longer.'

'Think of that!' Hannah said, concealing her pleasure under this light retort. 'But you might have been drowned on your next voyage and Ruth wouldn't have liked that. The reason she looks so happy is because you're here.'

'No, she's different. Not so jumpy. I'm grateful to you.'

'Well, I'm not a permanency,' Hannah said rather tartly, 'and she must learn to rely on herself.'

'You're not going to leave them, are you?'

'I don't know.'

'I shouldn't blame you,' Uncle Jim muttered indiscreetly. He put on his coat and Hannah felt that he would have said more if he had remained without it. She had lost her buccaneer, but the brother of Mrs. Corder, the brother-in-law of the Reverend Robert, was still there and her desire to know what the feelings of these three had been in connection with each other, was almost a pain.

She took a step at a venture. 'Is that a good photograph of Mrs. Corder, in the study?'

'It depends who's looking at it. My brother-in-law would say no, I should say no, and so would Ruth, but we'd all mean something different. She was something different with all of us, I suppose.'

'And what would Mr. Samson say?'

'Who's he? I've never heard of him.' He made a grimace. 'One of the deacons?'

Hannah laughed and did not answer. She had learnt another thing she wished to know, but she had not finished yet. 'You can't have had time to see much of your nephew.'

'Well, we stayed up rather late last night,' he said, and he and Hannah eyed each other calculatingly; he measured her trustworthiness and she his willingness to trust.

'I'm not supposed to know about him,' she said at last. 'I'm surprised Ethel hasn't told me, but she's rather preoccupied, perhaps.' She gave him a sidelong look out of eyes in which green was the predominating colour, but these words struck no response from Uncle Jim; he had not received Ethel's confidences as well as Howard's, and Hannah left this side issue. 'Family disturbances are very bad for Ruth,' she said.

'I'd like to adopt her,' Uncle Jim said suddenly, and, just as suddenly, Hannah felt a rush of enmity towards him.

'But that,' she said coldly, 'could not be arranged in a few days, within which time we're going to have trouble.'

'And I don't see how it's to be avoided.'

'The right words in the right quarter –' Hannah said thoughtfully. She did not believe that Robert Corder had any great desire to see his son a minister with a more valuable degree than his own and a social distinction he had missed. He would, of course, be able to make Howard feel his inferiority, but it would be less easy to suggest it, allied with fatherly love, to other people, and nothing else would satisfy him. A little flattery, a little comparative disparagement of Howard, would do much to mollify him, but who was going to offer it? There was no hope of that from Uncle Jim and it would come somewhat startlingly from Miss Mole. Even Robert Corder might suspect some motive in her admiration, and Hannah sighed audibly at the difficulty, the impossibility, of acting wisely for the future.

'The right quarter,' said Uncle Jim, 'seems to be this Mrs. Somebody who's financing the boy. It's very awkward for him. He's had two years of her patronage and that's what's going to worry his father most. Throwing her money in her face! And I gather she's a lady of some importance.'

A slow smile curved Hannah's lips. She had a sense of power which affected her physically, with a tickling feeling of pleasure. She was in haste to use that power, her mission

175

to the Corder family enlarged its sphere, she saw herself as an appointed agent, and, for the moment, she had finished with Uncle Jim.

'You'll see Mrs. Spenser-Smith at the party,' she said.

'Must I go to the party?' he asked in dismay. 'I haven't got any evening clothes.'

'They won't be missed,' Hannah assured him.

She dusted the table on which she meant to cut out Ruth's silk dress, and, looking busy, she spread out the material and fetched her pins and scissors, and Uncle Jim watched these preparations critically, for a few minutes, before he rolled away. Then Hannah ran upstairs to her room, enjoying her unnecessary stealth. She sat down by the wide-opened window with a pad of note-paper on her knee, and the energy she had meant to concentrate on a letter to Lilla was dissipated through the eyes which could see the coloured roofs of Radstowe, the plumes of smoke, the spires, the factory chimneys, the distant fields sweeping up to the high ground which blocked the view of her own country. For her, much as she disliked the day itself, the approach of Christmas was the approach of spring in the West country. There might be snow and frosts later, but always, at this season, there was a damp mildness in the air, a message telling her that the earth was being stirred by tiny pushing feet, pressing downwards so that spikes, eager to be green, might reach upwards, and she fancied she could smell primroses, that scent delicate as the flower's colour, soft as its pale cup. She knew a place where she thought primroses might be blooming even now, standing up among their strong crinkled leaves like some marvellously fine work on the rough palm of its maker, but from that thought and the view of Radstowe she turned aside. The primroses grew too near her cottage and innumerable reminders of other lives lessened the urgency of the task she had set herself.

This was to write her little letter of thanks to Mrs. Spenser-Smith, as Robert Corder had directed, in the first person, and to do it with a gratitude which would make Lilla flush in annoyance and conceal the letter from Ernest, and she meant to add a threat that if Lilla chose to make trouble about Howard, her loving cousin would know how to make

176

it for her, but this proved more difficult than she had thought and she tore up her attempt. Lilla might appear in Beresford Road, confident of her ability to right anything and demanding to know what it was. It would be better to go and see her, to suggest a probable cause of offence, to drop several hints from which Lilla could pick up the one she thought least objectionable, to leave her in no doubt that Hannah had a counter-stroke for any indignant thrust at the family whose welfare she had so much at heart, and to set Lilla wondering at this loyalty. Lilla would curb any amount of indignation rather than have her relationship to poor Miss Mole made known. She would have been wiser to have announced it, regretfully, as a distant connection, from the first; now she must face the accusation of snobbishness and suffer from the truth of it, the accusation of deceit and explain it away without convincing anyone.

Hannah had no time to spare, but she made enough of it for the expedition across the downs and an interview with Lilla which sent her chuckling home again, burdened though she was with Christmas presents for the Corders.

'As you are here, you may as well take them and save the postage,' Lilla said.

'And how am I to explain where I got them?'

'That's your affair, Hannah. I've never known you at a loss for a lie,' Lilla said severely.

Hannah pecked her cheek and wished her a happy Christmas. 'And you'll see us all at your party. I didn't mean to come and embarrass you, dear, but Mr. Corder insisted that I should. He implied that he wouldn't enjoy it without me.'

'You won't get me to believe that,' Lilla said, but she was puzzled. A woman who attended to a man's comfort could be a potent influence, and men were very simple. Perhaps she had reckoned too surely on the safety of Hannah's plain exterior. She was capable and Lilla could not deny her a peculiar kind of charm. Her arrival involved worry, but her departure took something exhilarating from the house and if she, who had disturbing doubts about the niceness of Hannah's conscience, could feel like this, how much more likely was Robert Corder to become dependent on her gay resourcefulness. And Lilla remembered that there were years

177

of Hannah's life of which she did not know the history, and it suddenly occurred to her that Hannah's anxiety for the happiness of the Corders could more naturally be interpreted as anxiety for herself, and this thought made Hannah's playful threats more dangerous, for, bad as it was to have a cousin who was a housekeeper, it was worse to have one with a past.

Willingly carrying the parcels, to save Lilla a few pence, Hannah hurried back. There was bound to be a storm when Howard broke his news, but she believed she had reduced its violence and curtailed it. She had done a lot for Ruth, according to Uncle Jim, she had done something for Howard, and, if she could secure a reasonable existence for Ethel, her life, she told herself dramatically, would not have been lived in vain ; but the last was the hardest of her undertakings and when she cast about for that middle-aged minister who might solve Ethel's problem, she could see no one but Mr. Pilgrim, bearing olive and myrtle for Ethel and a sword for Hannah Mole.

She threw a longing glance at Mr. Samson's windows as she passed. There was the old gentleman who might have been her salvation, but he had already told her that he lived on an annuity and had no dependents to consider except the cats and birds, and for their future he had made arrangements. 'Then what is the good of my coming to see you?' Hannah had asked, and sent him off into one of his throaty chuckles.

Undeterred by the thought of the annuity, she went to see him that evening when the family was gathered in the drawing-room. She had made him a new night cover for the canary's cage as a Christmas offering, and she hoped to give it to him and return before her absence was discovered, but Mr. Samson detained her. He had found among the jumble of objects he had collected in his travels, a fine piece of lace for Miss Fitt, and when she had thanked him and heard how he acquired it and how much less than its value he had paid for it, when he had draped it round her shoulders and said that that, at least, was not a misfit, it was nearly ten o'clock and time for Mr. Corder's tea, and Mr. Corder was hovering in the hall when she opened the front door.

He looked at her bare head, at the parcel in her hand, and

for the first time, he was openly angry with her, too angry to notice the tautening of her body and the lift of her head. He considered it most improper for Miss Mole to leave the house without warning; nobody had known where she was; they were all extremely worried, and had searched everywhere for her.

'Not everywhere,' Hannah said, smiling a little. The trump card was up her sleeve and she was going to bring it out. 'If you had called next door you would have found me with Mr. Samson.'

'Mr. Samson! I very much object, Miss Mole, to any member of my household visiting that disreputable old man.'

'Is he disreputable? I think he's lonely, and he misses Mrs. Corder. She used to go and see him regularly, you know – at least once a week,' Hannah said, and she went upstairs to lay away, like a magpie, her lace with her roll of Chinese silk, but she had not reached her room before her triumph left her. She had been unreasonably reprimanded and provoked, but was it worth while to hurt the man? Moreover, she had been hoping for this occasion and she was ashamed. She had rushed across the downs to do these people a service because it was one she would enjoy, and, indulging herself again, she had done more harm than she had prevented. She had imperilled the peace and goodwill for which she had pretended to be so anxious and planted a little barb, from which the wound might fester, in the heart of a man about whom she had chosen to know nothing but the worse.

Chapter 25

CHRISTMAS EVE had dawned long before Hannah went to sleep. She could not help thinking about Robert Corder and though, having learnt certain forms of self-control, she did not toss and turn on Wilfrid's mattress, she was unhappy and restless in her mind. She tried to keep back the persistent thought by recalling as many past Christmas Days as she could and vainly hoped sleep would overtake her before she had done. There were the Christmas Days of her childhood, like glorified Sundays, with the church bells ringing a livelier chime and the sounds of the cows and the horses in their stables and the feet of the farm hands and her father as they moved about the yard and did those jobs which no festival could interrupt, and when she was very young, Hannah would mentally transport one of their own cow sheds and some of their own cows to a distant land where palm trees grew, and imagine the infant Christ opening his eyes to see the soft brown ones of Daisy, Cowslip and Primrose. The church bells and the church decorations were all the gaiety Hannah got out of those early Christmas Days. She opened her stocking alone, in the darkness, received more than usually hearty kisses from her parents when she went downstairs, and solemnly walked with them to church, and she had not been aware of missing anything. After church and greetings among neighbours, which gave her a secret feeling of grandeur, of participation in a rite, there was the Christmas dinner of a turkey they had reared from babyhood, a nap for her father and mother in the afternoon and a quiet time for Hannah playing with her toys and those imaginary friends who lived in one of the kitchen cupboards, and came out and went back at her will. When she was at school in Radstowe, she heard about parties and pantomimes, and jogged home, at the beginning of the holidays, to that quiet place where such things were not, but by this time she had books and the people in them for her companions, and the friends who lived in the cupboard had been absorbed into herself, to issue as manifestations of Hannah Mole with all their beauty and ability, and such adventures, in embryo, as must befall the brilliant and the fair.

And here she was, a housekeeper in Beresford Road, at fifty pounds a year, remembering nearly twenty Christmas Days far from the big farm kitchen, with the tall clock ticking time away in the callousness common to all clocks, the smell of burning wood, the noises of moving beasts, of clinking pails and slow, heavy footsteps. Few later events were as clear to her as the details incident to that country life, and there came over her as she lay in bed, conscious of the widespread city outside her window, a hunger for quiet places and the conditions in which she had been bred. It would have been better for her if she had stayed in the farm when her parents died, struggling against debt, forcing a living out of the fields which responded with such faithfulness to care, with her own livestock about her and in time, perhaps, she would have married some young farmer who put capacity before good looks, and by him she would have had lusty children, clumping to the village school in their rough boots, as she had done, their little ears and noses whipped red by the wind. A good, hard life, that would have been, worthier of an active human being than this trailing from house to house, a dependent on the whims and tempers of other people and a victim of her own; she would have been spared her disillusionment about that love affair which had seemed so romantic until she discovered that a man might be a hero in battle and an essential weakling when the inspiration was removed; and there would have been no time for making drama of every look and word she met and heard, when she was wrestling with the enduring things, the fruits of the earth and her own body. But, at nineteen, a girl who had faith in a different future and saw every possibility of adventure and happiness in the world beyond, would have been wise, indeed, if she had taken up that heavy burden so that, at forty, looking back, she might escape this vision of herself dragging her skirts through other people's dust. Now it was with an effort that she remembered to believe in the goodness of things as they were, for the cruelty she had inflicted on Robert Corder was the first deliberately unkind thing she had ever done, and it had shocked her into a humility she sadly lacked and made her hope it would be a lesson she would not forget. Was he asleep, down there, in the room he had shared with the woman who had never breathed a word to him about Mr. Samson? It horrified Hannah to think of the grief that might be gnawing him at the first realization that he had not had all the confidence of his wife, the first suspicion that she had withheld it because of something unreceptive in himself, and if such suffering as this was beyond his power or did not fit the measure of his devotion to his wife or the devotion he had expected from her, he must be in a supreme state of irritation at having revealed his ignorance to Miss Mole. His words might be twisted into another meaning or explained as inapplicable to his wife, but his look of amazement, his dumbness, his perfect stillness, must be as memorable to him as to Hannah. He would not forgive her for possessing that information, she could not forgive herself for passing it on, yet she could not help maliciously wondering how he would try to punish her. She had learnt, by this time, that his actions did not match his anger, but he would probably find himself compelled to say something in an attempt to blur the memory of his sharp-cut silence and to put Miss Mole in her place.

She hoped he would; if he could show the wound she had given him, she would feel easier at having dealt it, but, by accident or design, he disappointed her, in the morning, and when she went into his study in the afternoon, while he was out, to see that his fire was burning, she thought Mrs. Corder looked at her reproachfully and she realized that indulging her spite against the husband had involved betraying the wife's little secret, with all the implications of Hannah's own invention, dissatisfaction, lack of confidence and a taste for a robuster companionship than Robert Corder could offer. Hannah felt almost physically sick. The consequences of her indiscretion were possibly less than she liked to think the consequences of any action of hers could be, but there was a special brutality in telling tales of the dead: nothing could have

182

induced her to tell them of the living, yet she had ignored a greater obligation in her desire to score a point, to get a cheap triumph over a man she despised. If she could do that, what could she not do?

She attacked the fire viciously, wishing it was her own body she was belabouring, and then she sat back on her heels with the poker still in her hand, and nodded at Mrs. Corder, whose face was fading away as the twilight deepened, assuring her that she would try to make amends for this offence, pleading to be forgiven for what life had made her, and again Hannah wished she had not left the country. She would have been too much occupied to be spiteful, and instead of kneeling in front of Robert Corder's fire she would have been busy at her own, and, as it was Christmas Eve, there would be coloured candles on the mantelshelf above the big kitchen fire, and coloured candles on the table spread for tea, with thick slabs of bread cut ready for the hungry children, with their reddened noses and ears, when they came in from playing about the farm, bringing with them a whiff of sharp air, of earth, manure and stables as they opened the door. The number of the children was indefinite. It was not a detailed picture Hannah saw framed in the kitchen where her own quiet childhood had been sheltered; it was an impression of arms and legs and faces, of voices which had not known the softening influences of a boarding-school in Radstowe, and of a vague man, the father of these children, whose temper varied with the weather and who had an unwillingness to take off his muddy boots until he went to bed.

At two fields' distance from the farm, its blind end facing a rough lane from which a path wound through the orchard to the front door, was the cottage she had refused to sell because of the craving for possessing earth which came of generations of farmers and returned to her strongly now. It was hers, yet she could not see nor touch it. Her common sense, partnered so strangely with her carelessness and a readiness to lose her property rather than emphasize her ownership, had forced her to tell her tenant, as she called him ironically, of each change of her address, for this was only fair to the cottage and the land, and if he cared to think she was asking for the rent he had light-heartedly promised to pay, she must

183

suffer that with the rest of her disillusions, but, as she sat on her heels in the firelight, thinking with nostalgia of the country she could often forget for weeks at a time, she decided that she must be done with a sentiment already ten years old and go and see if the roof had fallen in or the apple trees been pruned. She had more hope for the roof than for the trees. He would act if the rain dripped on him as he lay in bed, but the welfare of a tree would seem to him a fantastic matter to make a stir about, even though, or perhaps because, it was her tree and not his own.

The cottage had been let until the war came and emptied it, leaving it vacant for her wounded hero and herself, and what she had saved out of the rental she had spent in furniture and repairs and in starting the little poultry farm which was to supplement, with its profits, the hero's war pension. What had happened to those hen-houses? Were there any descendants of the original fowls? She pictured rotting wood and rusty wire and a few mournful birds wandering about the orchard, and she saw the refuge she had intended for her old age occupied by the man whose commerce with her had created the probable need for that refuge before her working days were over. She had lost her actual and her potential savings and, when she listened, she could hear the feet of Mr. Pilgrim, an echo of the sound she had heard so defiantly ten years ago, coming nearer with a menacing deliberation, and, as the study door opened and she looked round with a start, she was astonished to see Robert Corder's tall figure and gladder at his arrival than she could have believed possible, though she was discovered on the hearthrug, making free with his domain.

'Is that you, Ethel?' he asked, peering towards the figure by the fire which must have illumined it adequately.

Hannah smiled at the subtlety of this rebuke. 'I'm afraid it's me,' she said gently. 'I came in to see that the fire hadn't gone out, and fires have such a reminiscent effect.'

'A pleasant one, I hope,' he said, kindly making an excuse for the unwarrantable lingering.

'No,' Hannah said. 'Not at all. Perfectly horrid, in fact. But there, what does it matter? I'll light the gas. And when we're not allowed to have coal fires any more, there'll be a

184

lot of changes. We shan't be so much inclined to think about our sins, and babies bathed by electric radiators won't be the same as babies bathed by open fires, lovers won't be so romantic and, in the face of scientific improvements, we shan't think about the past.' She struck a match and shielded it while she looked at him. 'Do you think those will be changes for the better?'

It was obviously his duty to answer this question, which might just as well have been put without so much elaboration, but it was a duty Miss Mole should not have imposed on him and he answered coldly, and indirectly: 'I think we must always be prepared to suffer for our mistakes.'

'Oh, I'm prepared.' She lit the gas and turned to him again, and her face had a disconcertingly elfin look. 'Prepared,' she repeated, 'but not what I should call really satisfactorily equipped,' and she turned to go, but Mr. Corder, as usual, called her back.

'There will be the chapel waits here, this evening, Miss Mole. You have not forgotten that, I hope.'

'Coffee and cakes,' Hannah said promptly. 'I'm so glad you reminded me.' She would have been sorry to miss the opportunity of watching his Christmas geniality with the minstrels.

Chapter 26

ON Christmas morning, by candle-light, Doris brought an early cup of tea to Miss Mole, with an ornamental box of biscuits, from her young man and herself, on the tray.

'My friend says it's the least we could do,' she replied, when Hannah had made suitable exclamations. 'He thinks you're such a nice lady.'

'Does he?' Hannah sat up and the long plait of her dark hair fell across the front of her nightgown. 'And I think he's a nice young man and I'll eat some of your biscuits now, and when they're finished I shall keep the box on the dressing-table for all my little odds and ends. Thank you for the tea, too, Doris. It was a kind thought and you might make a precedent of it, if you know what that means.'

Doris did not know and was not concerned to learn. She was used to what she called Miss Mole's queer way of talking and she was burdened, at the moment, with a confession she had to make.

'It was Mr. Wilfrid who told me to do it, before he went away,' she said. 'And I told my friend and that's how we come to think of the biscuits. I was to make you a nice cup of tea, Mr. Wilfrid said, and give you this parcel on the quiet. I reckon it's something he didn't want the rest of them to see. And he give me ten shillings for myself,' she added with a sigh. She was more than satisfied with her young man, whose mother was so respectably stiff, but Mr. Wilfrid was her ideal of manly beauty and winsomeness. To keep Miss Mole's little parcel for him was an honour, but it was hard to go away and leave her to the discovery of what was inside, and among Doris's other reckonings, was the one that she would never know what she had been carrying in her pocket for the last three days.

It was a small parcel and a small parcel suggested something rare, and, turning it over and rattling it before she opened it, Hannah pretended she would find a ruby ring or a necklace of pearls, just as she had felt her stocking, thirty odd years ago, and imagined marvellous toys she knew would not be there, and when, at last, leaning towards the candle, she drew a brooch from the little box, tears started into her eyes and she could not see it clearly. She could feel that it was smooth and oval, with a narrow twisted rim, and she wiped her eyes on the sheet and had a good look before she began to cry again. Wilfrid, if he was awake at this moment, would think she must be laughing, and she did laugh while she cried, for that boy had tactfully chosen an old brooch which had a humorous reference to his avowed admiration and excused the nature of his gift. The brooch was held in a narrow twist of gold and under a shield of glass was what Hannah thought must be an engraving of the blind Cupid drawing his bow, the offering, no doubt, of some early Victorian lover to his lady.

Holding the brooch and crying, with childish abandonment, for pleasure in this pretty tribute, she wondered how much time he had spent before he found exactly the right thing, beautiful in itself, a whimsical comment on his liking for her, and an ornament which might, so conveniently, have belonged to her own grandmother. She would wear it at the Spenser-Smiths' party with Mr. Samson's lace; she could not wear the Chinese silk which was still rolled in its delightfully foreign paper, but her weeping ceased when she told herself that, with three charming presents in as many days, there must be something disagreeable waiting for her, to adjust the balance of fortune. But for that she was prepared and with Wilfrid's brooch pinned in her nightgown while she finished her tea and biscuits, she was better equipped than she had been. Wilfrid's affection was worth having and this ridiculous fit of crying had done her good. It was years since she had cried and it would be years before she did it again, and she determined to spend the rest of the day in cheerfulness if this family would permit it, if Ethel would not be injured by some fancied slight and if Howard would continue to hold his tongue.

The day began quietly. The present-giving in this house-
187

hold did not take place until after the morning service and the midday meal, and Robert Corder, who certainly had some force in his personality, created an atmosphere of peaceful thankfulness at the breakfast-table. The great day had dawned and he seemed to go on tip-toe, as though he felt the presence of the sleeping, sacred babe, and though he smiled readily, he did not do it broadly, and his good wishes were given like blessings, but, at one o'clock, when Hannah was basting the turkey, one of Mrs. Spenser-Smith's annual gifts, thankful, in spite of her red cheeks, for a duty which freed her from the chapel, she heard the loud tones of his voice like a fanfare authorizing joviality to begin.

At this signal, Hannah and Doris loaded the tray with turkey, greens, potatoes, gravy and sauce, and Uncle Jim appeared quietly from nowhere and picked up the burden. The sight of his brother-in-law's helpfulness was not altogether pleasing to Robert Corder; it might have been interpreted as a reproach, but he made a little joke about the handy man and Uncle Jim muttered that the tray was too heavy for a woman.

'But it's all knack, all knack,' Robert Corder assured him. 'Trained nurses – and what wonderful women they are – can lift a heavy man without an effort.'

'But you're not a trained nurse, are you?' asked Uncle Jim.

Hannah wanted to say that, no, unfortunately, she was not a wonderful woman, but she remembered that it was Christmas Day and simply shook her head. She tried to look weak and modest, the subject of contention between two strong men, and then, unable to resist asserting herself, she ruined this unique experience by remarking that she was used to handling turkeys, dead and alive.

'Alive?' Robert Corder said gently, giving her a chance to retract before she must be proved guilty of untruthfulness.

'And alive. I was born and bred on a farm.'

'Were you? Then you'll be able to give me some advice. I'm thinking of starting a little farm myself.'

'Come, come, let us take our places,' said Robert Corder.

188

'And I'll ask you to carve, Miss Mole, as you have such an intimate knowledge of turkeys,' he said, and Hannah, looking at him over the knife she sharpened, thought he had a positive genius for getting a note of disparagement into his voice. 'But where's Ethel? We can't start our Christmas dinner without Ethel.'

'She'll be here in a minute,' Howard said quickly.

'But where is she?'

'I don't know.'

'Then how can you say she'll be here in a minute?'

'Because she'll want her dinner.'

'Your remark was misleading. You made a statement which was nothing but a conjecture. If that sort of quibbling is what you learn at Oxford –'

'Oh, I've learnt a lot more than that,' Howard began, and two people held their breath for the few seconds that passed before Uncle Jim said good-humouredly:

'Well, well, let's load the tray up again and put the turkey in the oven. The skies won't fall because Ethel's a few minutes late.'

'I happen to be thinking of all the trouble Miss Mole has taken.'

'Don't mention it,' Hannah said, and wished she could look at Wilfrid. Mr. Corder's moments of consideration always arrived when he was annoyed with someone else.

'I suppose she was at chapel?' he went on.

'Oh yes, she was at chapel!' Ruth and Howard cried together, in an eager unanimity.

'Not in our pew.'

'No,' it was Ruth who started first and Howard did not try to catch her up. 'If Ethel sees one of her girls, she always goes and sits with her. I suppose the girl likes it,' she added thoughtfully, and Robert Corder gave a sharp glance at her innocently pensive face.

'Most inconsiderate,' he said, 'and Ethel must have her dinner cold. Let us begin. Ask a blessing, Ruth.'

Ruth obeyed in an unwilling mumble. She disliked addressing her God in the family circle as much as hearing her father do it from the pulpit, but this was not the moment to make more trouble and, as though even so slight a

189

communication with the unseen, and done by proxy, had cleared away his irritability, Robert Corder forebore to reproach Ethel when, flushed and breathless, she slipped into her place, just as Hannah, with the carving-knife poised in her hand, chose the spot for its insertion with great precision.

'And how did you think they sang the carols, Ethel?' her father asked.

'Very well,' Howard and Ruth said heartily in another duet.

'I was asking Ethel.'

Ethel was physically and mentally incapable of telling a lie: she could not prevaricate without blushing, yet now, in an inspiration of self-protection and in reference, as Hannah guessed, to some singing not heard by Robert Corder, she made the one remark likely to turn aside his questions. 'Not very well,' she said, with a roll of her eyes.

'I agree with you,' he said curtly, and he looked at Howard. 'I can only suppose you were not listening. But I would rather hear a disagreeable truth than a pleasant fiction. It was very bad. Half the choir was away.'

'Cooking their Christmas dinners, like Miss Mole has been doing for us,' said Uncle Jim. 'You've roasted this fellow to a turn. Any profit to be made out of turkeys, do you think?'

'Difficult things to rear,' Hannah said.

'Pigs, perhaps?'

'Prices are so variable. You get a lot of pigs and find everyone else has got them, too. We used our pigs for our own bacon and that was about all.'

'Then what would you start with?'

'Years of experience,' Hannah said.

'Oh, don't try to stop him, Moley – Miss Mole –' Ruth begged. 'It would be lovely if he had a farm near Radstowe and we could go and stay with him. He could try with a tiny little place at first and then he wouldn't lose much money. What a pity he can't have your little farm. Couldn't you let him have it?'

'It's let, and when it's empty I'm going there myself,' Hannah said, and because she knew that Robert Corder was suddenly attentive to a conversation he had been pointedly ignoring, she added rather grandly: 'People who own land ought to live on it.'

In a few moments of time, Robert Corder had to re-arrange all his ideas about Miss Mole. He had seen her as a poor, homeless woman who must be glad of the shelter of his house, and now he learnt that she had property of her own: he had wondered at her independence of spirit and this was now explained: he had resented her manner of speech which was better than his own, her evidences of having read at least as widely as he had, the charming notes of her voice, which he acknowledged for the first time; he had been seeking a way of getting rid of her and found she could go when she chose, and he felt that he had been duped. He cast back in his mind to those occasions when he had tried to snub her and hoped she had been as uncon-scious of them as she had seemed, and he thought Mrs. Spenser-Smith had treated him unfairly in not warning him of Miss Mole's real position in the world.

'Is it the farm you were brought up in?' he inquired.

'No, I sold that, but I kept a little place on the estate,' she said, and she began cutting second helpings for those who might want them.

'And where is this little property?' he asked genially.

'Over the river,' said Hannah, with a jerk of her head.

'In Somerset?'

'Yes, in Somerset.'

'And that's where Mr. Pilgrim comes from,' Ruth said, looking at Ethel.

'It's a large county,' said Hannah.

'A charming county,' said Robert Corder, giving Miss Mole the credit for it, and when the pudding came in, he ate his share. He had forgotten about the brandy. He had other things to think of.

Hannah went into the kitchen as soon as she could.

'Be off with you,' she said to Doris. 'I'm going to do the washing up. You can stay out till half-past ten to-night, but not a minute later, and be sure to thank your young man for the biscuits.'

She stacked the plates neatly, collected scraps for Mr. Samson's cats, washed the silver first and dried it before it could get smeary, and while she did this methodically but almost mechanically, she was thinking what a fool she was, a fool to come to Radstowe just because she loved the place, a bigger fool to have spoken about her cottage, and though she knew that her possession of it had impressed her employer, she also knew that his curiosity would not be content with the little she had told him.

'Fool, fool, fool,' she said, pushing the plates into the rack. She could not get into her cottage and, if she could, she had not a penny for food and firing. She was angry, too, at her ignorance of the conspiracy in which Howard and Ruth had been joined at dinner. They were protecting Ethel, but from what? And they had been so eager in it that they had almost roused their father's suspicions. Well, she would find out. She could always find out anything she wanted to know: her difficulty was in keeping her own secrets, and she, who cared little enough for money, but knew its freeing value for the spirit, wished the china under her hands would change to gold.

She heard Ruth calling her and she did not answer. 'If she wants me, she can come and fetch me,' she muttered. 'She can't tear herself away from that blessed man for a minute.'

But Ruth, divided in her affections, was not unfaithful. 'Are you there, Miss Mole, dear?' she asked, hurrying into the kitchen.

'Yes, and Miss Mole dear's very busy.'

'But we're waiting for you – to open the presents. Uncle Jim said why weren't you there, and Howard's got something for you that you'll like.'

'No, no. It's a family affair. I'll come in afterwards.'

'But I feel happier with you there, Moley, and safer. Ethel's such an idiot. She looks as if she's going to cry. I suppose she didn't get a chance to speak to Mr. Pilgrim, or else he wasn't nice to her. Or it may only be her way of being excited. That was a narrow escape at dinner, wasn't it? I don't know what Father would say if he knew she's been at Mr. Pilgrim's service, and on Christmas Day, too!'

Hannah did not know either, but what seemed to her of more importance was Mr. Pilgrim's view of this attention and Ruth's painfully clear vision of Ethel's weakness.

Chapter 27

MRS. SPENSER-SMITH's party was usually on the twenty-seventh of December, a date on which no hopeful member of the chapel would have made any other engagement until the chance of an invitation had gone past. On Boxing Day there was an entertainment at the Mission, demanding the attendance of the whole family and Doris, and Hannah was left alone in the house. Later, she was to look back at that solitary evening as at an oasis where she had rested between two stages of a journey and, as though she knew the one in front of her was the harder, she made the most of the interlude, sitting by the fire and reading one of the books which Mr. Blenkinsop had, most unexpectedly, sent her.

Uncle Jim and Howard had been for a long walk in the country and she supposed Howard's affairs had been discussed and they had arranged their plan of action. She could do nothing more in that business, but she had determined to try a new method with Robert Corder, to present herself to him as the person who understood, and so to take the burden of his indignation from those who were less able to bear it.

'But I shan't succeed,' she said sadly, knowing how far short her actions always fell of her intentions, and then, remembering the wrong she had done Mrs. Corder and the reproachful, half-humorous gaze she met when she went into the study, she rejected the idea of failure. Robert Corder himself was doing what he could to help her. He had been very affable since he learnt she was a lady of property and she had not thought it necessary to tell him how small and poor that property was, and perhaps he shared her own desire to be kind and was frustrated by the same cause, the insistent craving to be impressive, and as there was not room for two such people in the same house and one must make

193

way for the other, it was Hannah, who flattered herself on
her superior sight, who must stand aside while he went
blindly on. Nevertheless, he had his own kind of cleverness.
He had been silent about Mr. Samson until that very afternoon, when he had casually mentioned that he had called
on the old gentleman, and implied that Mrs. Corder had
always hidden her light under a bushel and been chary of
speaking about her good deeds, which he was glad to continue if he could, but that what the wife of a minister could
properly do was perhaps not quite suitable work for an
unmarried lady.

'I never thought of it as work, and he likes me,' Hannah
had cried.

'Is that a compliment?' he asked gently.

'He liked Mrs. Corder, too.'

'If you think it over, Miss Mole, I am sure you will see
the difference,' he replied, and it was all Hannah could do
to refrain from saying that Mr. Samson's affection for both
of them was grounded on his partiality for what he called
misfits, and that Mrs. Corder's good deeds, in his connection, had been a charity towards herself. Hannah was looking forward to Mr. Samson's account of the interview. She
would have been interested to know that Mr. Corder, who
was a follower though he thought himself a leader, had been
influenced, against his will, by the old man's high praise of
Miss Mole which fell into line with Samuel Blenkinsop's
attentions and the books which had not escaped Mr. Corder's notice, with Wilfrid's and Ruth's affection and Ethel's
dependence on her judgment, and with the little property
in Somerset. The fact that he continued to consider Mr.
Samson a disreputable old person with a loose tongue and
no respect for the status of a minister, did not affect his
changing estimate of the woman he could not help distrust-
ing. She was undoubtedly a woman of some character
and he hoped she would not show too much of it at Mrs.
Spenser-Smith's party. He was afraid she might be too
clever at the games or too lively in demeanour, for she was
his housekeeper, after all, and he did not want Mrs. Spenser-
Smith or Miss Patsy Withers to imagine she was more, and
he was sorry Mrs. Spenser-Smith's truly Christian hospit-

ality should have urged her to include Miss Mole in the invitation. This was the little shadow on the prospect of an evening towards which he looked forward as much as Ethel and more than Ruth did. He knew his people, loving him when he was in the pulpit, loved him still more when he was out of it, and there was a rich pleasure in letting them see him play at musical chairs with the eagerness of a boy, act in the charades, and dance Sir Roger de Coverley, with a slightly comic gaiety, before the party came to an end with the singing of Auld Lang Syne.

Ruth had her own troubles about the party. There was the usual trouble about Ethel who giggled and looked too pleasant and wore too many bits of jewellery and would probably have one of her tempers when they got home; there was the difficulty of pretending to herself that her father was always a jolly man and of trying not to feel half ashamed of him in his frock-coat; there was the disappointment that Uncle Jim would not be in evening clothes, and, worse still, had cheerfully confessed that he had possessed none for many years, and allied to this worry was Miss Mole's black silk dress with the jet trimmings. Ethel's Chinese silk had been made up hastily by an obliging little dressmaker who went to the chapel, and Miss Mole had finished Ruth's, and they were the nicest dresses they had ever had; Howard would be in his dinner-jacket, but the appearance of the contingent from Beresford Road would be completely spoilt by Uncle Jim's blue serge and Miss Mole's black silk. Her father's frock-coat did not matter so much. People were used to it and he was a minister, but a favourite uncle in blue serge, rather short in the sleeves, and Miss Mole, who had promised Ruth they would have all sorts of jokes about the party afterwards, so that the more they hated it, the more fun they would get in the end, Miss Mole looking housekeeperish and Uncle Jim looking all wrong, would make a mock of the beautiful new dresses; they would look like the accidents they were. Nothing was ever really right, Ruth thought miserably. This was the party dress she had wanted all her life and she longed to wear it, in spite of the background her elders would make for it, but she had not been deceived by Miss Mole's des-

cription of the velveteen frock as one to wear on occasions
for which the other was too gay. She knew Miss Mole had
made it in secret for the Spenser-Smiths' party and must
have sat up late at night to get it done. It was pretty, too,
of a deep coral colour which was kind to Ruth's pale cheeks,
and there was a hair ribbon to match, for Miss Mole remembered everything, and the present must have cost more
than she could afford. She felt she ought to wear it; she
could explain to Uncle Jim and, anyhow, he would not
notice, and Ruth laid both dresses on the bed and decided
first for one and then for the other. It was horrible, it was
treacherous, to think, as she could not help thinking, that if
Miss Mole had spent the time and money on herself, Ruth
would have been happier at this moment, and then, as she
stood in her petticoat, trying not to cry at the maddening
perverseness of this dilemma, Miss Mole looked in on her
way upstairs to dress and quietly took the velveteen frock
and hung it up.

'But Moley –!' Ruth exclaimed.

'No you don't,' Hannah said. 'I haven't been working
my fingers to the bone, as they say, for a dress that isn't
going to appear to-night.'

'But you worked them to the bone for the other one.'

'You can wear that at the Thingumbobs' party next week.
I ought not to have given it to you for Christmas, but I
hadn't anything else. I might have known your Nonconformist conscience would make you miserable about
it.'

'I haven't got a Nonconformist conscience!'

'Then wear your uncle's frock,' Hannah said.

That was settled, and Ruth sank on to her bed to enjoy
this moment of relief, to tell herself, once more, that Miss
Mole knew everything, to look back at those terrible two
years between her mother's death and Miss Mole's arrival
and find they were too black for contemplation. It was
mean, it was despicable, to mind about the black silk and
jet trimmings when they were worn by Miss Mole who had
thought about the night-lights, who had chased away fears,
without mentioning them by name, and been wonderfully
kind without encroaching on the rights of the mother for

196

whom Ruth still kept her caresses and the spoken expression of thoughts which Miss Mole was content to divine.

Ruth cast away all her cares except the one about Howard, who had the sudden indiscretions of the naturally discreet and might choose this very night for telling Mrs. Spenser-Smith he was not going to be a minister. It was no good asking him not to do it; if she put the idea into his head, it might pop out at any minute. That was the way things happened with Howard. He was good-natured and patient and easy-going and all of a sudden it would seem that he had been nearly boiling for a long time, and, at last, the lid had blown off. It would be awful when this particular lid blew off, for there would be more explosions than one, and Ruth gave a little shudder and a last look into the glass, before she went downstairs.

Uncle Jim was in the drawing-room. He was freshly shaven and he had put on a clean shirt, but he was reading the evening paper as though a party were no more agitating than staying at home, and Ruth envied, while she pitied, the calmness of middle-age. He looked up, however, and approved of her appearance, just as her father bustled into the room, looking at his watch and complaining that Howard was not in and would make them all late.

'Well, well,' this was Uncle Jim's usual soothing preface. 'Perhaps the boy doesn't want to go.'

'Doesn't want to go!' Robert Corder had banked Mrs. Spenser-Smith's Christmas cheque that morning and his voice was shrill with indignation.

'Well, well,' Uncle Jim tried again. 'Perhaps he's met a friend, or something.'

'Perhaps he's been run over!' Ethel cried, coming in with a rattle of beads, but no one encouraged this notion and she had all her anxiety to herself.

'It's a strange thing,' Robert Corder said more calmly, 'that with my passion for punctuality, I should be constantly vexed,' and he looked at Ethel, 'in this manner. And where's Miss Mole? And what friends has Howard that he should meet at this time of night and when he has an engagement?'

'Oh, for goodness' sake, Bob, don't make mountains out

197

of molehills. He'll be here soon enough and if he makes us half an hour late, let's be thankful.'

'If you feel like that, James,' said Robert Corder, who could hardly believe he had been reprimanded in the presence of his daughters, 'you'd better stay at home.'

'All right, I'll look after the house for you.'

'But Doris's adenoidy aunt has come on purpose to keep her company!' Ruth protested, because the cowardly, snobbish side of her half hoped Uncle Jim would stick to his decision.

'Her what?' Robert Corder demanded.

'Her aunt who has adenoids,' Ruth answered sullenly.

'I don't like to hear you using such expressions,' her father said mildly, and Miss Mole, entering at that moment with a slight rustle, knowing she looked nice and was going to surprise them, said levelly, using the beautiful middle notes of her voice.

'I'm afraid it's my expression, but really, when you've seen and heard her, you can't call her anything else.'

'But that isn't black silk, Moley!' Ruth exclaimed.

Miss Mole's dress was not fashionable and it was modest, with long sleeves and a small opening at the throat. It was made of a moire silk which changed from green to brown as the light fell on it, a varying colour which matched her eyes, and Wilfrid's brooch fastened Mr. Samson's string-coloured lace.

'No,' she said. 'This belonged once to my old lady with the wigs. I believe she had it in her wedding trousseau and it will last for ever. I've had it cleaned, and I've had it remade –'

'Fine old piece of lace,' Uncle Jim remarked.

'And what a quaint old brooch,' Ethel said, with a doubtful glance at her own beads.

'Yes,' said Hannah lightly, 'they've both been in the family for generations.'

Robert Corder went out of the room. There was no lace or old jewellery in his family, and where was Howard? He paced up and down the hall and, in the drawing-room, Ethel fidgeted and Ruth looked gloomily at Hannah. Her relief at Miss Mole's appearance was spoilt by this worry about Howard, and now Uncle Jim was saying he would come to the party, after all, so that he could treat them to cabs across the downs, to make up for lost time and keep the girls' hair tidy. Things were never altogether right, she discovered again, but they improved a little as Howard entered the house and, rushing past his father without apology, cheerfully shouted an assurance that he would not keep them waiting for five minutes.

Chapter 28

HOWARD ought not to have spoken in that cheerful manner or to have looked so unabashed when he came downstairs, so unusually lively and determined that the reproaches died on Robert Corder's lips. Miss Mole ought not to be wearing old lace and appearing calm at the prospect of being Mrs. Spenser-Smith's guest; in fact, her double masquerade of housekeeper and lady with a little property was disconcerting. It was irritating to be forced into a cab with her, while his children and his brother-in-law crowded into another. He objected to the cabs on principle: he could not afford these luxuries and, though he was not paying for them, he disliked the ostentation of such an arrival. And what was it that had cost Howard fifteen shillings? Nothing, he thought, should have cost him as much as that: the boy had too much money to spend: but what had he spent it on and why had he told Jim about it?

'I thought it would be something like that,' Jim had growled.

Robert Corder hated hearing snatches of conversation and remaining in ignorance of their context; he hated this familiar nearness to Miss Mole and he sat stiffly, looking out of one window of the cab, while Miss Mole looked out of the other.

'We'll soon be there,' she said in a small voice, as though she was comforting him, or was she really more nervous than she seemed and in need of a little encouragement? He saw her profile by the light of a passing car, and it was meek and drooping, her head was bare and the collar of her coat was turned up.

'Too soon?' he inquired kindly.

'Oh no. I've always wanted to see Mrs. Spenser-Smith's children.'

He squeezed himself further into his corner of the cab. 'I'm afraid they are not going to be the equals of their parents.'

'No, they never are,' Miss Mole said sadly, and he took another look at her.

'You don't happen to know where Howard was this evening, I suppose?'

'No idea,' she said in a sharper voice, and she thought of the bowl of Roman hyacinths he had given her for Christmas.

Robert Corder let down the window to see if the other cab was following, the wheels crunched the Spenser-Smiths' gravel, and Hannah stood in the porch, surrounded by gigantic chrysanthemums.

It was he who led the procession into the drawing-room, with Ethel at his heels: Ruth tried to get behind Miss Mole but she kept her place in front of Uncle Jim and had the pleasure of watching Lilla's greeting of the minister and his daughters before she stepped forward for her own welcome. This was an extended hand and a half-puzzled glance, quickly changing to one of recognition.

'Oh, it's Miss Mole,' Lilla said.

'How sweet of you to remember me,' Hannah replied.

Valiantly Lilla restrained a frown and her quick eye saw the lace, the brooch and the moire silk before Hannah felt her hand grasped in Ernest's and knew that only his duty to his other guests and the instructions he had received from Lilla prevented him from taking her into a corner and having a good cousinly chat.

Hannah found a corner for herself. She asked for nothing better than a point of vantage from which she could watch Lilla so skilfully varying the warmth of her smile for each new-comer and, by the slight changes in her cordiality, Hannah thought she could judge the worldly position or soundness of doctrine of each arrival. Lilla was perfectly dressed for her part; richly enough to do honour to her guests and remind them of their privileges, but with due consideration for the shabbily clad, and of these there was a good number, and Uncle Jim's was not the only blue serge suit. Hannah recognized many faces she had seen in the chapel, faces of matrons, of spinsters and of young men with thin necks. It was surprising to see so many young men with thin necks and large Adam's apples; it had something to do with Nonconformity, she supposed: perhaps Mr. Corder would be able to explain their association, but at the moment he was engaged by a gloomy deacon who could not forget the chapel in the party, and indeed, the party was the chapel on its lighter side, and Robert Corder, trying to get away from the deacon, was as anxious as anyone else to emphasize that side and to encourage the liveliness with which Mrs. Spenser-Smith's parties always went from the beginning. Already Ruth was biting her pencil as she earnestly took part in a competition, and Ethel was being very bright with the young men whose placarded backs she had to examine. Uncle Jim, to whom self-consciousness was unknown, was prowling round the room and volunteering advice about the competitions to people he had never seen before, and enjoying himself more than he had expected. It was easy to distinguish Margery Spenser-Smith, like a more sophisticated Lilla at that age, and to recognize sons of the house in a youth who had something of Ernest's quiet kindness in his manner, and a younger boy who looked more bored than any guest would have dared to be. These were Hannah's cousins and, if she knew her Lilla, they had not heard of her existence. As far as they, and most of the other people in the room, were concerned, Hannah was invisible, though Miss Patsy Withers had given her a sweet smile, and she was tiring a little of this advantage when she saw Mr. Blenkinsop approaching. There was an empty chair beside her and she pointed to it, hoping Lilla or Robert Corder would see this airy gesture, while she smiled up at him, a radiant Miss Mole, her face transfigured by the laughter behind it. Yet there was nothing comic in Mr. Blenkinsop's appearance. He looked very clean and his dinner-jacket was well cut; the little black tie and the winged collar became him; he seemed slimmer in the waist and broader in the shoulders; his neck was not thin and he had no convulsively working Adam's apple.

'I didn't expect to see you here,' she said. 'You're a black sheep, but perhaps Mrs. Spenser-Smith doesn't know it.

Thank you for the books, Mr. Blenkinsop. I've used up a lot of Mr. Corder's candles, reading them when I should have been asleep'

'You mustn't do that,' he said, with a little frown.

'Dishonest?'

'No. Tiring. As for dishonesty, I was going to telephone to Mrs. Spenser-Smith and say I'd got a cold –'

'I'm glad someone else can tell lies,' Hannah interjected.

'And then Mrs. Gibson told me you'd be here, so I came too.'

'Well, tell me all about it, quick! You'll be dragged away to play one of those idiotic games in a minute. What's been happening?'

'I spent Christmas Day with a sister of my mother's.'

'And when you got home – ?'

'And when I got home, I felt worn out,' Mr. Blenkinsop said simply. 'Sitting in a stuffy room, after a heavy meal, and trying to keep up a pleasant conversation.'

'Don't I know it!' Hannah said feelingly. 'I've spent years of my life doing that – years! At about fourpence halfpenny an hour. It's grim, isn't it? I'd rather have a suicidal husband. There's some excitement about that and the hope of ultimate release.'

'Not if people insist on being as resourceful as you were,' Mr. Blenkinsop said incisively.

'No,' Hannah said penitently. 'And yet you sent me those books! But go on, Mr. Blenkinsop. When you got home, worn out, in no state to deal with a difficult situation – what happened?'

'I went to bed, of course.'

'Oh dear,' Hannah groaned. 'If I laugh out loud, Mrs. Spenser-Smith will hear me and take you from me, and I can't spare you, but I'm longing to laugh! It hurts!'

He turned his mild, spectacled gaze on her. 'What's the joke?'

'Oh, nothing, nothing! I was prepared to hear the story of another rescue, and you merely went to bed!'

'I don't see anything funny in that.'

'Perhaps there isn't,' Hannah said amiably, and her lips twitched as she imagined his methodical retirement for the

203

night; she saw him winding his watch, laying his clothes aside neatly, getting out a clean collar for the next day and examining the buttons about which he was so nervous, and Mr. Blenkinsop's voice, more intense, reached her just as he was getting into bed.

'But there'll have to be a rescue, of another kind, sooner or later,' he said, and Hannah told herself that he had come to the party to talk to her about Mrs. Ridding.

'I'm afraid to offer to help,' she said, 'in case I do the wrong thing again, but if I can, I will.'

'The ridiculous part of it,' he confided, 'is that I believe he'd be just as happy without her.'

'Well, that's a comfort, isn't it?'

'I don't know. I think it makes it worse.'

'You're the best judge of that, Mr. Blenkinsop, but I should call it an extenuating circumstance.'

'These people simply suck the strength out of their relations – like vampires,' Mr. Blenkinsop said, becoming fanciful under emotion. 'I believe he'd be better if he had a thorough change.'

'Of wives?' Hannah asked flippantly.

'I shouldn't care to offer anybody the position,' he said bitterly.

'I may be wanting a job myself, before long,' Hannah said. 'I suppose you don't know any respectable old gentleman – but not too respectable – with a competency – and not an annuity – who would suit me?'

'Don't be silly,' said Mr. Blenkinsop and, when he looked at her, he missed the mocking curve of her lips.

'I'm proud to say I've never asked anyone for help yet,' she said, 'but the day may come. Yes, the day may come,' she repeated, and now he saw that she was smiling again, but not mockingly and not at him. 'Mrs. Spenser-Smith has got her eye on you,' she said, 'but stay here for a little longer if you can. It doesn't do to boast. You see, I'm asking you for help already.'

'Just sitting here?'

'Just sitting here,' she said, and Mr. Blenkinsop settled himself in his chair with an adhesive pressure.

He was observant, as far as he went, which was no further

than the person who held his interest at the moment. He had not the power to watch another group of people at the same time, to see the development of a situation or to feel slight differences in the atmosphere, which was Hannah's by nature and by training, and he had no clue to her strained look which quickly changed to one of quivering, half-merry determination. Mentally lost, Mr. Blenkinsop was firm in his seat. He knew not why he had to stay there, but stay there he would and, indifferent to everything but this duty, he endured the confusion of voices and laughter, the danger to his patent leather toes from all these young people pushing past him, carefully avoided the eye of Mrs. Spenser-Smith, and calculated that Robert Corder – now talking to another minister who had just arrived and who also wore a frock-coat and had a sleek black head – would ignore the presence of his deserter.

'Can't you talk about something?' Hannah asked sharply.

'Yes,' he said obediently. 'I was going to tell you that I'm looking for a little house in the country.'

'Good gracious! Are you going to start farming too?'

'Not exactly, but I want a little house with a bit of land.'

'And do you expect me to tell you where to find it? Are you going to live in it yourself?'

'Not exactly,' he repeated, and though he looked embarrassed, his confidences continued. 'You see, the present state of things can't last.'

'Which?' Hannah asked perversely.

Mr. Blenkinsop frowned again. 'With the Riddings. But we don't want to talk about it till things are settled.'

'They're never settled,' Hannah warned him. 'Take my word for it. If you want to be comfortable, don't do anything.'

'Not what I think is right?'

'That's the very worst thing you can do. What other people think right, if you like, Mr. Blenkinsop, but not what you do. That's the advice I give you out of my own experience.'

'Well, I've been doing nothing in particular for forty years and now that I've started I'm going my own way, and

205

it was you who laughed at me for living behind the gilded bars, you know.'

'Oh, don't blame me!' she cried.

'But it's no good being off with the old love before you are on with the new.'

'But aren't you on with it?'

'Getting towards it,' Mr. Blenkinsop said, smiling slyly. 'But first I want to find the little house.'

'And if you do,' she said, speaking slowly because she was thinking of two things at once and watching the owner of the sleek black head making towards her deviously but surely, 'it will bother you for the rest of your days – I know all about these little houses – for when it comes to hard tacks, Mr. Blenkinsop, if you know what they are, for I don't – but then, you've got what they call an independent income, haven't you?'

'I shouldn't do it if I couldn't afford it,' he said, a little stiffly.

'And that,' she said, 'is just the difference between you and me,' and Mr. Blenkinsop turned from her, who had spoken the last words on an upward and then a descending breath, to the man at whom she was looking with a little questioning lift of the brows.

This was the minister with the black head, and Mr. Blenkinsop took a great dislike to him. He was interrupting an important conversation, and he was objectionable in himself and in his unctuous smile as he addressed Miss Mole, saying he thought they had met before.

Miss Mole shook her head. 'I don't think so,' she said. 'I have a very good memory for faces, but if I've seen yours before I've quite forgotten it.'

'But you're Miss Mole, aren't you?'

'Yes, I'm Miss Mole.' Then she smiled with the vividness which always startled Mr. Blenkinsop. 'I wonder if you're thinking of my cousin,' she said. 'Another Mole.'

'Is her name Hannah?'

'No, Hilda. There's supposed to be a strong family likeness. Oh, don't go, Mr. Blenkinsop!'

'But we're going to play Clumps,' said the voice of Mrs. Spenser-Smith, 'and I want Mr. Blenkinsop to be one of those to go outside. Mr. Corder will be one, of course, and Mr. Pilgrim, perhaps you'll be another.'

She swept them both away and it was some time before Mr. Blenkinsop could see more of Miss Mole, for they were in different clumps, than a small steady head among many other heads, like those of bathers, bobbing above a sea of coloured dresses.

Chapter 29

AFTER supper, one of those little rumours, which start mysteriously and surprise no one so much as the people to whom they refer, began running about Mrs. Spenser-Smith's drawing-room. For a skilfully long time she pretended not to hear it, but the moment arrived, and it was hastened by Ernest's clumsy kindness; when it was impossible to resist the knowledge that Mr. Pilgrim could recite. Solo performances were against her rule. She knew what sort of talent the members of the chapel possessed, its devastating effect on the gaiety of her parties and the little jealousies that could arise, but Mr. Pilgrim was a new-comer, invited, as a lonely bachelor, at Ernest's particular desire, and though she doubted his ability and disliked singling him out for honour, she could not refuse the eager requests of those ladies, of all ages, who were thrilled by the presence of another and a new minister and begged her to let him recite, nor could she ignore Ernest's open persuasions of the apparently reluctant Mr. Pilgrim. It was noticeable that no other male voice joined in the solicitations, and that even the thinnest-necked of the young men, to whom a minister was a natural object of veneration, put his back against the wall and settled his features into an expression he hoped they would be able to maintain.

Hannah longed for Wilfrid, but, lacking him, she found some consolation in watching Uncle Jim's unguarded look of amazement and Robert Corder's earnestness to do as he would be done by, and when she met the eyes of Samuel Blenkinsop, who stood among the other young men against the opposite wall, she felt that she was more than compensated for the loss of Wilfrid. Mr. Blenkinsop was looking at her with a solemn dismay, as though she was his only hope in this calamity, and though she had not much time to give to anyone, being anxious not to miss a word or a gesture of Mr. Pilgrim's performance, or to lose one drop of her revenge for his persistence in dogging her with glances all the evening, it was very pleasant to know that it was her eye Mr. Blenkinsop had sought.

Mr. Pilgrim was a tragedian and he did not spare himself. The long poem he recited was all too short for the enraptured Hannah, and if the clapping at the end did not express a correspondence with her own feelings, Mr. Pilgrim was not a prey to doubts. He wiped his face with the freedom of the man who has obviously done his utmost, and Mrs. Spenser-Smith managed, with great adroitness, to start another game as she went forward to thank him. Ethel was thanking him already; she had no doubts either, but, for the first time in the history of Mrs. Spenser-Smith's parties, there were no charades. The games went merrily on until Miss Patsy Withers's elder sister was whispered towards the piano and the opening bars of Sir Roger de Coverley were played. Robert Corder partnered Mrs. Spenser-Smith. Ernest tucked the hand of the shabbiest of the spinsters under his kind arm and seemed to regret that he could not take care of all the other women who were not wanted, and Hannah, smiling gaily at him as he passed and trying to look as though she did not want to dance, saw Ethel beaming in her place opposite to Mr. Pilgrim and Ruth happy with her Uncle Jim.

'Could you bear it?' Mr. Blenkinsop asked her crossly.
'I should love it.'

'I generally get away before this begins, I feel such a fool, capering down the room with my hands out.'

'From *capra*, a goat,' Hannah murmured to herself. 'But if we're capering together –'

'That's what I thought,' he admitted gloomily. 'Is there any chance of walking home with you? It would do me good to talk to somebody about that recitation.'

'Somebody?' Hannah said sharply. 'Try Mrs. Ridding. Yes, try her as a sort of test. There ought to be a preliminary examination for every vocation, you know, and if she fails in the subject of Mr. Pilgrim, I should plough her altogether.'

209

'I don't know what you're talking about,' Mr. Blenkinsop said with a trace of sulkiness, as they took their places for the dance.

'And anyhow,' Hannah bent towards him to whisper, 'Mr. Corder doesn't approve of followers. It would embarrass me to be escorted across the Downs by a single gent. I have to pay for my pleasures, Mr. Blenkinsop!'

There was more annoyance than amusement in his smile. Apparently this sort of banter was not to his taste and, either in expression of his disapproval, or in deference to her wish, there was no sign of him when the Beresford Road party started across the Downs followed by Mrs. Spenser-Smith's regret that, for some unexplained reason, she could not send them in the car.

They went in pairs, like a girls' school; Uncle Jim with Howard, and Ethel and Ruth in an accidental companionship which left their father with Miss Mole.

'This is the first time we have not had charades,' he burst out, like a disappointed child. 'I can't remember one of Mrs. Spenser-Smith's parties when we haven't had charades after supper. We choose a word, Miss Mole, and as I am always expected to be the leader of one of the sides, I'd given a little thought to the matter, to save time. I don't grudge that and the whole thing is of no importance, but I must say I think the party was not quite so successful this year.'

'Mrs. Spenser-Smith is a clever woman,' Hannah said.

'Certainly. Yes. But I think she showed less cleverness than usual.'

'Clever – and considerate, to us and to Mr. Pilgrim. He would have expected to be the leader of the other side. We had seen him as a tragedian; we might have had to listen to him being funny. Considerate to all of us, but more considerate to him,' she added in a slow, droll tone, and Mr. Corder laughed so suddenly and loudly that his daughters looked round as they walked in front, and Howard and Uncle Jim, still further ahead, slackened their pace and turned to see who had joined the little company and made Robert Corder laugh as he seldom laughed in the family.

210

'So you didn't enjoy the recitation?' he asked with some eagerness.

'It was one of the brightest moments of my life,' she replied, 'but then, I'm afraid I am not charitable.'

There was a pause before Robert Corder, having digested this, said kindly, 'But I'm glad to find you have a sense of humour, Miss Mole. A sense of humour, I sometimes think, is as valuable a possession as brains.'

'Then I must try to cultivate mine,' Hannah said.

'However,' he said, following her into the tramcar in which the others already sat, four tired-looking people in the otherwise empty, brightly-lit conveyance, 'I am sorry we both had to exercise it to-night. I'm afraid Mr. Pilgrim made himself rather ridiculous and it was lucky for him that his own people did not hear him. Though,' he added with satisfaction, 'they might have missed the absurdity. They are not a highly-intelligent little community,' and putting his hand into his pocket, for the fares, he fell into talk with the conductor who, like most of the conductors in Radstowe, was an acquaintance.

Hannah saw that, to the young man clipping the tickets, Robert Corder was a fine reverend with no nonsense about him, and she knew it was not fair to judge him by the only side he showed her. It seemed to her that he had to be given a certain character before he could live up to it, and that if his children would see him as the conductor did, he would be the kind of father he thought he was. Perhaps everybody was like that, she mused, but when she looked at Uncle Jim, she saw a man unaffected by opinion and quite unconscious of himself as a possible object of interest to anyone. That, probably, was the happy thing to be, and it was what poor Ethel certainly was not. Like her father, but without his self-assurance and with less stability, and urged by her pitiful desire for love, she reacted violently to appreciation, and Mr. Pilgrim had taken her in to supper, he had chosen her for the dance, and the hard words just uttered by the father she admired were painful, but of no critical value, when she remembered the kind looks of the man who seemed to admire her, and she cast distrustful glances at the two who had been discussing him.

211

Looking at the young Corders, at Ethel with the flush of excitement on her cheeks and gleams of resentment in her eyes, and yet with a mouth willing to smile, at Ruth, tired and leaning contentedly against her uncle, and at Howard, sitting in the far corner of the tramcar, as though to mark his spiritual distance from his father, Hannah renewed her unreasonable feeling of responsibility for them all, and now it was not Ruth, but Ethel, who demanded most of her. This change might have been due to the knowledge that Ruth was safely hers and Ethel was still a half-conquered country, and Hannah would have been ready enough to accept this less creditable explanation if the truth had not lain in her conviction that Ruth was fundamentally less helpless than Ethel. She had some of Hannah's own qualities under the layer of nervousness her conditions had imposed on her, and Hannah could liken her, as she had so often likened herself, to the little ship in the bottle, sailing gallantly and alone, but towards a surer harbour than Hannah's, with her Uncle Jim for port in a storm, while Ethel rolled helplessly at the mercy of winds and tides, defenceless against piracy, starvation, thirst, and all those Acts of God which would be no less lamentable on account of their name. Hannah wondered if Mr. Pilgrim was a pirate or a pilot. Probably, he intended to be neither, but his intentions counted for little, in their emotional effect, compared with Ethel's wishes and ready credence. Poor Ethel, ready to make a hero of Mr. Pilgrim, Hannah thought, and her compassion turned suddenly against herself, and changed to scorn, for she had been as foolish and as pitiable as Ethel and she was as much Mr. Pilgrim's prey, and a little panic came over her, not for her future, though that was desperate enough, but for her sad little past, held and turned over in Mr. Pilgrim's soft, damp hands.

Nevertheless, her future had to be thought of and when they alighted at the end of Beresford Road, and the same procession walked up the street, she took advantage of Robert Corder's restrained but evident approval of the woman who had laughed at Mr. Pilgrim, to make her first request. She hoped Mr. Corder would be able to spare her for a whole day, before long; she had business to do in the country.

'Why, certainly, Miss Mole. We must manage as best we can without you, and if I can be of any help – But if your business has to do with the tenancy of your farm, you should consult a lawyer. Mr. Wyatt, one of my deacons, is a sound lawyer and he tells me ladies are generally too trustful in business dealings.'

'Yes, I suppose we are,' Hannah said, including herself among the trustful ladies.

'Too ready to make arrangements by word of mouth, and he would advise you well, I am sure, and make a nominal charge, at my request.'

'Thank you,' Hannah said. She had seen Mr. Wyatt, taking round the offertory plate: he did not slip past the poorer members of the congregation, as Ernest Spenser-Smith took care to do; she doubted his liberality of pocket or opinion and, as she glanced up at Robert Corder, striding beside her, sure of himself and his little world, stepping over crevasses he did not see, blind to the clouds confronting him, amiably companioning the woman whose virtue he took for granted, because all decent useful women were virtuous, Hannah's long nose took on its derisive twist. There were several shocks awaiting Robert Corder, but she thought his chief suffering would come from the memory of his gradual softening towards the bad Miss Mole.

Chapter 30

HANNAH's cousin Hilda had developed into a definite person before Hannah went to bed, but it was just as well to know everything about her and, when it was all settled, Hannah liked her very much and as good as believed in her existence. She had some of the characteristics of the people who used to live in the kitchen cupboard; she would come out when she was wanted and, in the meantime, it was nice to feel that she was there, for her own sake as well as for her possible uses, and as the creator is not satisfied until someone else has seen his work, so Hannah longed to produce her cousin for inspection. By the time she had dressed, the next morning, Hilda, that wayward, charming girl, impulsive, but sound at heart, was woven into the substance of Hannah's youth and it seemed a pity not to entertain Ruth with stories of their escapades: there was the time when they were chased by the bull, for instance, and Hilda had nobly diverted his attention from Hannah, but, as it happened, Ruth was in no need of entertainment that day, for she was confronted with an event which demanded all her horrified, trembling attention.

It was on this day that Howard vanished like a shadow, without a sound, or like some wild beast slipping into the forest without the snap of a twig for warning, and in the excitement that followed, the rage, the bewilderment, the demands for explanations, the grief and tears, Uncle Jim stood calm and stolid in his certainty that he had done right to let the animal escape. There was a story Hannah had often heard told in her childhood about some resident in their countryside – dead before her time – who had made himself famous and infamous for giving shelter to a hunted fox and withstanding the clamour of the hounds and the abuse of the huntsmen, and she thought of him when she looked at Uncle Jim. But it was hardly fair to compare

Robert Corder with a hunter: he was more like a man who had brought up, and thought he had tamed, some creature he half despised, yet took a pleasure in having about him, and he had lost it through the treachery of one of his own household. This, however, was far too simple a metaphor for a complicated position. He had been outraged as a father and, as a father, he was responsible for Howard's scurvy treatment of Mrs. Spenser-Smith. How was he to explain matters to her and how would she explain them to his congregation? Was he to repeat his brother-in-law's statement that he had advised Howard against dealing frankly with his father, had told him it would be a waste of time and would make bad blood between them, and had persuaded the boy to take the opening that had been offered to him on a South African fruit farm and leave his uncle to stand the racket? Those were Jim's words and Robert Corder was more enraged with him than with his son. He was genuinely and bitterly hurt by what he saw as a perverse cruelty, he was shocked at such an estimate of his sympathetic understanding, but it was inevitable that he should immediately calculate the impression this extraordinary behaviour would make on his world, of which the chapel was only a part. If he owned to a bad son, there would be people ready enough to imply that the father was to blame, yet with what other story was he to approach Mrs. Spenser-Smith? He could not conscientiously take the fault on himself, but when he rehearsed what he should say to her, his pride, and perhaps his love, forbade him to show her the picture of Howard which he saw himself.

He tried to shut his mind against the things Jim had told him quietly, as though they were accepted facts, unjust things about his character and his treatment of Howard and his incapacity to see another person's point of view. He had said, in so many words, that if the boy was to escape from the net Mrs. Spenser-Smith and his father had spun for him, it must be done on the instant, with a sudden break: he would never have been able to disentangle himself gradually from reproaches of ingratitude and that gentle bullying of which he had had too much. He would have stayed where he was rather than have struggled without dignity, but he had gone and Robert must make the best of it. It was bad now, but it would be better later on, and when the two met again they would find themselves feeling more kindly towards each other than they had ever done before.

It is difficult to quarrel with a man who refuses to be ruffled, but Robert Corder managed to do it with the man who was quietly insulting him, as the anxious listeners in the next room could tell, and at the end of this angry eloquence, Jim suggested, still mildly, that Robert might like to pay back what Mrs. Spenser-Smith had spent on Howard and, if so, he would let him have the money. He was willing to pay for his undertaking, he was glad to buy the boy what he wanted, what all the Erleys wanted, he added, and Robert, angry, resentful, in a quandary about this money business, and foreseeing his own compliance, was still curious enough to ask, unwillingly, what it was that the Erleys wanted. Uncle Jim became less articulate when his own feelings were in question. He mumbled that it was what had sent him to sea, and made his sister feel like a hen in a coop.

Robert Corder repeated these last words, slowly, as though he could not understand them, and then, realizing their cruel import, he struck his desk a hard blow so that Mrs. Corder's silver-framed photograph let out a little jingle, like laughter, and: 'You can leave my house!' he cried, in a great voice. 'You're trying to take my wife from me now!'

'Don't be a fool, Bob. I'm not saying she wasn't fond of you, but she was cramped. I'm sorry if I've hurt your feelings, but I still think I've done right – and what she would have wanted me to do.'

He left the room but he had no intention of leaving the house immediately. In his experience, the man who shouted his commands was not the one who expected them to be obeyed, and though he had enough imagination to divine the needs of those he loved – and his sister's children were dear to him for her sake – he could not picture the real distress of Robert Corder whose imaginative powers were concentrated on himself. His son! His wife! Mrs. Spenser-Smith and the chapel! The fellow-members of his committees, who all knew he had a son at Oxford! The ingratitude and cowardliness of Howard! And how could his wife have

216

been cramped when she shared her husband's life? Yet he
thought of her strange visits to Mr. Samson and he knew he
had consistently sneered at Howard. He admitted that he
was not perfect: no doubt he had made mistakes, but, where
his wife was concerned, he could see none, and he felt a
slight, unconfessed easing of his duty towards the dead.

His thoughts were too tumultuous, too painful and too
sad for clearness. He was more unhappy than he had ever
been before, and neither of his daughters had offered him a
word of comfort, but already he was adapting himself to
new conditions, hearing his own remarks and seeing himself
as he went about his work with undiminished spirit, disappointed but tolerant, and gradually acknowledging that
Howard had been right and quoting extracts from his letters.
But it was very lonely in the study that night, and when
Miss Mole came in with his tea he was glad to see her, but
he thought of Miss Patsy Withers who would have been
tenderly indignant for him and more helpful in her tearful-
ness and her pity than Miss Mole, with her swift, sure movements and her matter-of-fact face.

'I've cut you some sandwiches,' she said, 'as you didn't
have much supper.'

'That is very kind.'

'And I hope you'll eat them.' She was pouring out his
tea and remembering that he liked one big and one small
lump of sugar.

'This is a bad business, Miss Mole,' he said.

'Yes,' she agreed. She was, indeed, sorry for him and
thought he had been unfairly treated. She was sorry for
Howard too, for Ethel and for Ruth: she was suffering the
discomfort of seeing everybody's point of view and the impatience of considering it all unnecessary. 'But when you
think of the sun and the moon and the stars –'

'What have they to do with it?'

'Nobody knows,' she replied, 'but they do make our affairs
seem rather small beer, don't they? And if you compare
infinity – whatever that is – with three weeks, for in about
three weeks all this will be forgotten –'

'I shall never forget it,' he said, his head in his hands.

'No, but other people will, and that's what really matters.

That's our weakness – and our strength. There's no shame,'
she said, as though to herself, 'no disappointment, no disillusionment, we can't bear if we can keep it to ourselves.
It's the beastly curiosity and the beastly speculations of other
people that get one on the raw. But no,' she was faithful to
her creed, 'it's not beastly. It's natural. I'd do it myself.'

'Then,' he said, forgetting, in the relief of speech, to be
superior, 'you can understand how I feel.'

'I do!' she cried, and he said sadly, from the depths of an
experience denied to her, 'But no. You are not a parent,
Miss Mole.'

She gave him one of her sidelong glances. 'You take a
good deal for granted,' she said, trying to control the upward tilt of her lips. 'But you happen to be right,' she went
on with a calmness which left him displeased, but dumb,
'I'm not a parent. I'm not a minister, either, or a son, and
yet, somehow . . . Please eat these sandwiches. Minced
ham and turkey. They're very good. And it isn't so difficult
for you as it seems.' She spoke to him quietly, as though she
persuaded a child to its good. 'Your son had a sudden offer
in South Africa, an out-of-door life is really what he is fitted
for, he had to take it or leave it, so he cabled his reply and
went off at once and there was no time for explanations.'

'So that was what cost fifteen shillings,' Robert Corder muttered. 'And Mrs. Spenser-Smith, who has been so generous?'

'I should tell her as much of the truth as is good for her –
and you. That's only fair to yourself.'

'I shall pay back the money!' he said loudly and with
determination.

'Then she can't complain, and I don't believe she will.
Good night, Mr. Corder.'

'Good night, Miss Mole.'

This time, he did not call her back, but she returned.
She stood with her hands clasped in front of her, smiling
timidly and looking pleasingly diffident, and more like his
idea of what a woman should be than he had ever seen her.

'I wonder . . .' she began, and he said briskly, with a
defensive caution at the back of his mind, 'Well, Miss
Mole, what is it?'

'Could you pretend,' she said, 'not to be as angry as you are?'

'I'm not angry, but deeply hurt.' Her silence accepted the paraphrase and he added, with his usual authority, 'And pretence of any kind is against my rule.'

Her eyes widened, she looked remarkably child-like and that gaze made him uneasy. He was beginning to know her well enough to expect some retort in violent contrast to the expression of her odd, mobile face, but it did not come.

'I was thinking of Ruth,' she said. 'And Ethel. Yes, she has asked me to call her Ethel,' she said quickly, in answer to the slight contraction of his brows. 'They are very unhappy.'

'That is my son's responsibility. We must all suffer together.'

'But don't suffer at all,' she suggested. 'If you can't pretend, the only thing to do is not to feel. You can't have people thinking your son has done something wrong. In your position,' she added softly. 'And Ethel and Ruth are very much worried about you.'

'They've shown no signs of it.'

'Ah,' she said, 'they're a little afraid of you. You can be rather terrible, Mr. Corder, if you'll forgive my saying so. They are sitting in there, shivering and trying not to cry. Could you make them realize that you have the situation in hand, that there'll be nothing for them to do but follow your lead? Ethel is troubling herself about Mrs. Spenser-Smith and wondering what she is to say to her – and to everybody else.'

Robert Corder did not fail in his response. 'There is no need for Ethel to distress herself,' he said. 'She can leave it to me. I shall go and see Mrs. Spenser-Smith to-morrow. I suppose there are troubles in every family and some day she may have some of her own.'

'I should think it's more than likely,' Hannah said. She glanced at the clock. 'I must write a letter before I go to bed. I shall just have time to catch the post. Good night, Mr. Corder.' She hesitated and said, with the timidity he found very becoming in her, 'I shall tell your daughters they must try to be as brave as you are,' but as she left the study, she was telling herself that one of his children was free and she must do what she could to secure liberty for the others.

Chapter 31

To see Robert Corder reassuring his children, gravely taking this new burden on himself and shouldering it courageously, was, for Hannah, rather like watching a man palming off the work of an artist as his own, and she wondered he did not see the pathos, the tacit reproach, of Ethel's surprised admiration for him and of the relief which flushed Ruth's face, but, after all, it did not matter to Hannah why he acted well so long as he did it, and she remembered that her suggestions had been successful, not because she was skilful, but because they were practical. If he was to keep his picture of his broad-minded optimistic self, he must take Howard's departure and give it his approval in a wise, foresighted spirit; only so could he mount his pulpit on Sunday and feel that he still dominated his people. There are certain kinds of sorrow which add to a man's value, but that of possessing a bad son is not one of them, and Robert Corder decided not to have it. That, at least, was Hannah's criticism of his behaviour.

Ruth had her own comment to make, though she put it as a question which was not meant to be enlightening. She had the appearance, Hannah thought, as she lit the night-light, of a person who has had a severe bout of pain, and lies limp and contented in its cessation. Her face, which softened and hardened so quickly, seemed to have taken on childish contours, but her eyes, drowsy with comfort, kept their look of guarded intelligence.

'Isn't it wonderful,' she sighed, 'not to be as miserable as you thought you were going to be?'

'Is it? I don't know. I'm never miserable.'

'Well, you must have been, often, when you were young.'

'There was always something else,' Hannah said. 'There's always something else, when you look for it. But no, I wasn't unhappy when I was young. There were my boots, of course, but there were the feet inside them and, you know, if I'd had the kind of boots I wanted, my feet wouldn't have been so pretty now, and I suppose I realized, even then, that it was all for the best. I've always been good at that.'

'You're very conceited about your feet. And people don't notice feet much.'

'What does that matter to me? I notice them myself, and every night I have a little reception for them. They sit at one end of the bed and I sit at the other and I look at my nice straight toes and all the little bones of my feet and think of the manifold works of God. It's not conceit. I didn't make them.'

'But you like them more because they're yours than you would if they were mine.'

'Perhaps; they're such a surprise. My father and mother had honest yeomen's feet, and so has Lilla.'

'Lilla? That's Mrs. Spenser-Smith's name.'

'Did I say Lilla? I meant Hilda.'

'Who's she?'

'Oh, she's a cousin, rather a mysterious cousin. I'll tell you about her some day. She was better looking than me, but not much, and her feet were ugly. Nice hands, though, and she used to say that if she and I could pick out our best features, we might make one quite decent-looking woman of us.'

'Is she alive now?'

'Good gracious, yes, I hope so. Somewhere. She's no older than I am, but I haven't seen her for years. Elusive creature,' Hannah said, staring at the little flame of the night-light.

'Go on about her.'

'Not now. Good night.'

'Moley . . .' this was Ruth's question, 'was Father angry when you took in his tea? I know he was furious with Uncle Jim, because we heard him shouting, and I never thought he'd come in and be so nice to us.'

'But as it wasn't your fault, why should he be angry with you?'

Ruth made no reply to that; there was none to make and she did not refer to past experience. It was plain to Hannah that Ruth was giving credit where credit was due, and it was sad that she should have to look beyond her father's character for the cause of his unexpected gentleness. 'Well, I hope he'll stop being angry with Uncle Jim,' she said. 'I'll tell you what I've decided. I shall go out to South Africa, to be with Howard, as soon as I can.'

'And what about me?'

'Couldn't you stay and look after Father?'

'I'm here to look after you because you're such a baby and can't mend your own stockings. As soon as you can, I shall go.'

'Is that why you haven't tried to make me do it?' Ruth asked slyly. 'And why shouldn't you come too?'

'I don't know why I didn't go years ago,' Hannah said. 'What a fool I've been!'

'There was your little house.'

'Yes,' she said, 'perhaps that had something to do with keeping me, but there, I never had enough money to pay my fare and I never shall have.'

'That's because you're so extravagant about your shoes,' Ruth said pertly. 'And that reminds me. There's the story about breaking the window, and now there's your cousin Hilda. You're always promising and never telling.'

'I can't tell you about the window because the story isn't finished. Neither is the one about Cousin Hilda, for that matter. Stories don't finish. The window one is coming to what you might call a period, but not an end. No, indeed, I fancy that Part Two will be less exciting but more enthralling to the student of human nature than Part One. Really good biographies can't be written until the what-you-may-call-thems are dead. But I might tell you when we're in South Africa – far away.'

'Couldn't you just give me a hint about why you broke the window? Was it in Radstowe?'

'Not a hint,' Hannah said. 'Why can't you make up some stories for yourself? That's what I have to do.'

'But these are true, aren't they?' Ruth cried anxiously. 'Not like the burglar one?'

'Not in the least like the burglar one. And now, sleep. If you're going to South Africa, you must take a profession with you and you'll never have one if you stay awake till this time of night. Be anything you like, but be something. Simply being a useful woman like me isn't good enough.'

'You're good enough for me,' Ruth said, shutting her eyes on the awkwardness of this confession.

Hannah went upstairs and stood in the darkness of her bedroom. For the first time she heard her own true story with Ruth's ears and she did not like the sound of it, and Ruth did not repeat her assertion that Miss Mole was good enough for her. She was mute, stricken, all her faiths shaken, what she had seen as beauty changed to ugliness, her sight, perhaps incurably, dimmed or distorted, and this was Hannah's work. Apart from the consequences of her acts on the innocent, the undreamed of, her adult conscience was not troubled. Her regrets were for her lack of judgment, not for a chastity which did not seem to her to be sensibly diminished. She had loved her lover and expected to marry him, but she did not make that expectation an excuse. She did not need an excuse. Her values were not those of Robert Corder and Beresford Road Chapel and she was heartily thankful that there was no legal bond, but she was unhappy when she tried to exchange her own conscience for Ruth's juvenile one, and what Ruth made of the story would chiefly depend on who presented it to her. If it were her father or her sister, all these happy hours they had had together would be smeared by their disgust. And yet Hannah had a heartening belief in the independence of Ruth's mind and her natural tendency to go contrary to her relatives: moreover, they were not likely to tell her much. Miss Mole would disappear mysteriously, her name would not be spoken, and Ruth's silent loyalty might be strengthened by her secret defiance, yet she might be disillusioned, though she was still loyal. No woman, not even Hannah, who had made a practice of indifference to most people's opinions, could relish the prospect of being thought evil, but it was the effect on Ruth herself about which she was really troubled, and it seemed to her hard that what she had done ten years ago should have its influence on a child of whose existence she had not known, so hard and unreasonable that her sanity refused to take the weight of this responsibility and, as she stood there, meditating immediate flight, her common sense resisted a temptation which, indeed, was not very alluring, for where was she to go and what good would she be doing Ruth if she left the field to Mr. Pilgrim? And perhaps her cousin Hilda would save her from him as she had saved her from the bull. No, she told herself, undressing in the darkness which clarified her thoughts, the worst thing she could do was to waste the powers which had been signally proved this evening. Through her means, Ruth and Ethel had gone comparatively happily to bed and all her calculations were grossly wrong if Robert Corder did not return cheerfully from his interview with Lilla, for by the first post she would learn that the occasion for discreet behaviour had arrived. And, during the interview in which they tried to make things easy for each other, Hannah hoped Robert Corder would speak enthusiastically of his housekeeper. That would give Lilla something to worry about, she chuckled, as she got into bed, and she thought she would be almost willing to sacrifice herself maritally to Robert Corder, if she got the chance, for the sake of supplanting Lilla as leading lady of the chapel, a short-lived joy for a long martyrdom, but she knew that he would only praise her in flattery of Lilla and that he was in happy ignorance of his indebtedness to Miss Mole.

It was difficult to endure his look of self-satisfaction the next evening. A stranger would have thought he had planned his son's escape and made Mrs. Spenser-Smith a party in the enterprise, and Hannah had another glimpse into the life of Mrs. Corder, who, surely, must have wilted and perhaps actually died, under the blandly arrogant delusions of her husband. The face which looked out of its silver frame was that of a woman with delicate perceptions who would find more truth in Mr. Samson's extravagant inventions than in Robert Corder's interpretation of his acts and thoughts, but, no doubt, her chief desire, like Hannah's, was for the happiness of her children and she had borne with her husband as wives find it necessary to do.

This was Hannah's view of their relationship and Uncle

Jim had given her no cause to change or amplify it. He, at least, did not yield to Hannah's wiles. Under his matter-of-fact directness, he was not simple; he seemed able to guess the destination of Hannah's conversation, when it was Mrs. Corder, though she might start in the opposite direction, and she gave him up. When she saw him go, the next day, she would be almost as poor in information as she was when he arrived, and this was hardly fair, for he had constantly questioned her about farming and expressed his regret that he could not see her little place. He would be a good tenant when she wanted another one. The place would suit him very well, he thought; it was near enough to Radstowe and he wanted to keep an eye on Ruth.

'Well, one never knows,' Hannah said. 'You'd better leave me your address. I suppose,' she went on thoughtfully, 'I've got another twenty years of work left in me. My tenant may not last as long as that and, while I'm working, you could be paying me rent. And I'll charge you a high one too, for depreciation of my property. Then, at sixty, I'll turn you out and retire. But the difficulty is that if I lose this job, I may not get another.'

'Why should you lose it? But look here, if you do, you've got to let me know. I'm going to wander about for a bit, but my bank will always find me.'

'Are you thinking of kidnapping Ruth too?' Hannah asked coolly.

'I'll have a shot,' he said.

'And Ethel?'

'No, I don't think I need kidnap Ethel. I'm hoping she'll get married. Who was that black-haired chap who made such a fool of himself at the party? I thought they seemed pretty friendly.'

'Would you like her to marry him?'

'I'd like her to marry anybody, so long as he didn't drink or knock her about,' he said, and increased Hannah's respect for his astuteness.

'But perhaps it will be Mr. Corder who gets married. There are plenty of ladies in the congregation who would meet him more than half way.'

'Yes, I spotted one of those too,' he said. 'The fair, floppy

225

one. No use to Ruth at all. I wish to goodness,' he said, knocking his pipe out against the grate, 'you'd marry him yourself.'

'Anything to oblige you, of course,' Hannah said dryly, and then, flaring up, she cried: 'Upon my word, I think you're the most unscrupulous person I ever met.'

Chapter 32

In the few days that passed between Uncle Jim's departure and Wilfrid's return, there was an atmosphere of unnatural sweetness in the Corders' house. Ethel's gratitude to her father, for refraining from making her suffer for Howard's fault, transformed her into the sunny daughter of an indulgent parent, but Ruth, with the cynicism which both pleased and saddened Hannah, treasured these good moments because she did not believe they would last. Robert Corder, however, had adopted an attitude and he kept it, and Hannah, who found it impossible to attribute a good motive to him if she could find a bad one, saw this consistency as a result of his instinct of self-protection which warned him that if he was to play a part well he must play it all the time. Before many days were over he had merged himself into his rôle and she wondered whether there had been any real suffering at Howard's treatment of him and any response to its implications. His was a curious character and, for all his human weaknesses, she could not believe he was quite real. She would tell herself that he was a marvellous puppet, so much like a man that he could deceive most people, and then, when he came into the house, she had to admit her consciousness of his personality. Ethel was in a flutter to please him, Ruth was vigilantly critical, Hannah herself paid him the tribute of an irritated delight in watching him, in divining the meaning of his looks and foretelling his remarks, and these were the reactions to no puppet. He could absorb the suggestions that suited him as easily as water takes a colour, yet he must have had some suggestive power over other people or they would not have sought him out and gone away comforted. This was a puzzle which it would take a lifetime to solve and Hannah was afraid her sands were running out – for Ethel's good temper was not

227

all due to her father's leniency – and as she saw the silent slipping of the moments, she was alternately enraged and amused that, with a few words, Mr. Pilgrim could change the family friend into a person to be shunned, though her management, her economy, her cooking, her counsel, all that made her useful to these people, would remain unchanged. But there was her cousin Hilda and her own word against Mr. Pilgrim's; it became a matter of pride with her to frustrate him, and there was a strained alertness about her which no one but Mr. Samson noticed. It would have been comforting to tell him everything; he would have listened with a salutary lack of surprise, but, sane as he was, she could not unwrap her little secret to his gaze. He was, in fact, too sane to understand that what he saw in terms of natural harmless appetite had had a spiritual value for her which she still struggled to keep.

She admitted to being tired and Mr. Samson growled his anxiety about her; he had told that Bible-smiter she was worth taking care of and would have told him a good deal more, but for Miss Fitt and the peaky little girl. He did not want to make trouble that would fall on the family. And what had Corder wanted, poking his nose in and waking Mr. Samson out of his afternoon nap? If he had not thought it was the man with the cat's meat he would not have gone to the door, and there he was, smirking on the step and trying to look like a herald angel.

'But I let him know it's you that's the angel, just as his wife was before you. I'm a lucky old devil, finding two of you at the end of my days, and you wouldn't think I'd fancy your kind, to look at me, now would you? Well, I've fancied all sorts, to tell the truth, but it's the lively ones I like. A quick tongue's more use to me than a pretty face. Now, you take care of yourself. And what about a bottle of port to drink on the quiet?'

'No, no, it's a teetotal household.' Her laughter rang out. 'But Mr. Corder had to eat some brandy with his Christmas pudding! I don't want any port. I'm going to have a day's holiday and spend it in the country.'

'And that's a funny idea of a holiday,' Mr. Samson said.

It was certainly a euphemistic description of the expedition she had planned and for which, knowing that Ruth would beg to go with her, she had not settled on the day. It would have been better to wait until the beginning of the school term, but that was a long way off and she would have to refuse Ruth a pleasure which, for her, would be something like a day in Radstowe had been for Hannah; and Hannah herself, full of shrinking though she was, had a great longing to see her own country, to sit in the train and watch the city and its suburbs giving way to fields and woods, flat meadows cut by dykes and villages dominated by their stately Perpendicular churches, just as she had watched all these giving way to the promise of Radstowe, that fairy place of streets and towers, bridges, water and ships. She would get her business done as soon as possible, and then she would cross the fields to the old farm. She did not know who owned it now, but if they had any likeness to her own wary but kindly people, they would let her have a peep into the kitchen, where she ought to have been living with the red-cheeked children; they would let her stroll round the farm buildings and have a look at the cows and, as she sat in the Beresford Road dining-room, darning the everlasting socks and stockings, she fancied she could smell the sweet breath of the cows, and the sweetness of wallflowers, old man and pinks, in the little garden where the bear had lurked. There would be no flowers blooming now, unless there was a chance primrose on a sheltered bank, but the cows would be there, and she looked at Ruth, sitting on her feet in the old saddle-bag arm-chair, and reading with absorption, and thought it would be cruel to go without the child. Was this an excuse for procrastination? she asked herself, as there came a loud knock on the front door which made Ruth look up and say: 'Postman, Moley. It may be the fortune.'

'What fortune?' Ethel asked. She was trying to alter one of her many unsatisfactory dresses, but she was inept, and presently she would ask Miss Mole to gather her scattered pieces into some semblance of a whole.

'If it's the fortune,' Hannah said, going towards the door, 'I'll give you each – well, it depends, but I'll give you each something.'

'And she would, you know,' Ruth said, looking gravely at Ethel.

The knock had drawn Robert Corder from his study and he found Miss Mole, in the hall, holding a letter. 'The postman?' he asked.

'No. This came by hand, as they say, as though a postman hadn't got one.'

'For me?'

'No, for me,' she said, and she opened and read it while he stood there.

'Not bad news, I hope,' he said.

'Not at all,' she replied, smiling at him as she tucked the letter into the bosom of her dress, and returned to the dining-room.

The smile was still on her lips, though she did not know it until Ruth cried: 'And I do believe it really is the fortune!'

'Good gracious! Do I look as pleased as all that?'

'Not now. Now you're frowning a little. Isn't it something nice?'

'That depends on one's point of view,' Hannah said, and Ruth resumed her reading. There were times when she knew it was of no use to ask Miss Mole any questions.

Hannah wondered, and was half annoyed at her satisfaction, but a day in the country with Mr. Blenkinsop would be a day of inward and outward laughter: she could not look at him without a bubbling feeling of pleasure, even his handwriting made her smile and, if she gave him the day he asked for, she must postpone her own expedition. This, in itself, was a relief, and to be looked after as she knew Mr. Blenkinsop would look after her, to have her ticket taken for her, to be asked if she were tired, was an alluring prospect to Hannah, who had spent so much of her time in looking after other people. But Mr. Blenkinsop took a good deal for granted: he assumed, and no doubt she had given him cause, that her interest in Mrs. Ridding was considerable, but to take her into the country to inspect the little house he had found – that house, which, no doubt, was to be Mrs. Ridding's refuge from her husband – was a dependence on her judgment which that lady might resent, and it was a deliberate involving of Mr. Corder's housekeeper in an affair

230

which would do her reputation no good. This care for her reputation satisfactorily explained her slight feeling of irritation with Mr. Blenkinsop, but it did not influence her desire to oblige him. Such invitations did not often come her way and, irritated or not, she liked Mr. Blenkinsop, and the thought of his companionship, preoccupied though he might be, for a whole day in the country, with bare branches against grey skies and pale fields slipping into brown ones, and the chance of a primrose, was more than enough to make her smile.

Mr. Blenkinsop hoped the following Sunday would not be an impossible day for her. He was afraid it would be awkward but – he was quite playful in the excitement which had made him begin his note without any formality of address – he also hoped she would be able to produce the usual grandmother or aunt whose illness or funeral called her away. Hannah, however, did not need these ladies, for she had a tenant, and Mr. Corder's prejudice against Sunday pleasures would not be applied to business if she explained that it could be transacted on no other day. Her trouble was not Mr. Corder; it was lack of suitable clothing for this outing. She had the shoes, but she had no well-cut tweeds, no gay scarf and jaunty hat. Life was simpler for men. Their festive occasions were not brightened or dimmed by the clothes question; it was dull for them, but easy, and Hannah looked at her battered headgear and sighed. She counted her little savings and saw the coins as so many meals and so many nights of shelter: it would be madness to spend a penny, but why should she not be mad? There was not much difference between having food for a month and having it for a day, and she put her purse in her pocket and decided to go and look at the shops. The January sales had begun, and she might pick up a bargain: she might save a rich old gentleman from being run over and her future would be secured because she had dared to risk it, and she set off, believing the miracle was really going to happen, ready to squander, but possessed of the pleasant certainty that she could restrain herself if she chose. This was the right mood in which to go shopping. The smell of spring in the mild air, the thought of Sunday, and the purse held firmly in the pocket of her coat, were like wine to Miss Mole, who walked with her quick, light tread until she reached the shops, and then she walked slowly, gazing into the windows, but her exhilaration left her before she had gone far. She was born fastidious and the heaps of clothing, boldly ticketed, did not attract her. She knew it was better to be decently shabby than cheaply gay and she retraced her steps up The Slope, looking back now and then at the beauty she could get for nothing.

As she neared the top of the hill, she spied the figure of Lilla bustling down, and a new light came into her eyes. If she could not have a new hat, she could have some fun with Lilla, and she greeted her cousin so loudly and lovingly that Lilla looked round for a retreat.

'Come in here and have some tea,' she said, indicating the shop where they had met on that October evening when Hannah first saw Mr. Blenkinsop, and Hannah followed her into the most secluded corner.

'I've been wanting to see you,' Lilla said.

'You don't look a bit pleased, dear,' Hannah said sadly.

'I'm not pleased, but I wanted to tell you that I wish you'd mind your own business and leave me to mind mine. I don't need instructions about how to behave, Hannah, and your letter was quite unnecessary.'

'Not instructions, dear – only hints. You told me I was to bark when necessary, so I barked. You put me in that house to take care of Mr. Corder, and I'm trying to do it. I thought you'd be glad. Are you paying for this tea, or am I?'

'Never mind about that. I want to get to the bottom of this affair of Howard's.'

'But I do mind, Lilla. If it's me, I'm having a bun. If it's you, I'll have buttered toast to start with.'

'Have anything you like,' Lilla said grandly. 'I suppose that boy is running away from trouble, but of course his father wouldn't admit it. He talked a lot of rubbish about temperament and the open air, and I did my best to make things easy for him, but he ought to have trusted me. I've a great respect for Robert Corder –'

'Nothing to what he has for you,' Hannah said feelingly.

232

'I really believe the only thing that worried him about Howard was the fear that you would be hurt. He has a noble character, Lilla.'

'H'm,' Lilla said. 'I'm not satisfied, but I must say he seemed anxious to return the money I'd spent. Where he's going to get it from, I don't know, and, if he can pay it back, it seems to me that he can't have needed it. And that's not a pleasant thought.'

'Then don't think it. Just remember that you're a lucky woman. If Mr. Corder admired me as he admires you – '

'Now don't begin getting sentimental, Hannah. It's no good. He thinks you're a capable woman, but there he stops. I took care to find that out.'

'Oh, did you?'

'Yes, I did. There's too much nonsense about him in the chapel already, and really, Patsy Withers made me feel quite ashamed at my party. What with her and Mr. Pilgrim –'

'What was she doing?' Hannah asked quickly. 'I didn't notice her.'

'No,' Lilla said dryly, 'you were too busy monopolizing Mr. Blenkinsop, and I may tell you that Mr. Corder saw it. It wasn't fair, Hannah, with so many girls in the room.'

'I couldn't help it, dear. I've a fatal sort of attraction for him. Why is it, do you think? I was the belle of the ball for Mr. Blenkinsop, there isn't a doubt.'

'I invite young men for the sake of the girls, not for you to sharpen your wits on, but if I'd known, as Mr. Corder tells me, that he'd left the chapel, I shouldn't have invited him at all. And he wouldn't have been missed, as it happened, and that was your fault. Do you know where he goes?'

'Goes?' said Hannah.

'What place of worship?'

'Oh, here and there; here and there. He wants to take me with him on Sunday.'

'Stuff!' Lilla said, but she said it doubtfully. 'Well, Mr. Pilgrim isn't likely to get him, after the exhibition he made of himself – and that was Ernest's fault. What did you think of him?' she asked, and her bright eyes sharpened a little. 'He told me he'd seen you before, Hannah, and he seemed curious about you.'

'Naturally,' Hannah said easily. 'I'll never get you to understand that I'm a noticeable character.'

'And he used to live in your part of the country,' Lilla went on, 'but as you haven't lived there for years –' she sighed. 'I wish I could feel more comfortable about you.'

'Don't try,' Hannah said. 'I haven't split on you yet.'

'I'm thinking of your own good, Hannah. I didn't like the man's manner at all. If there's anything I ought to know, you'd better tell me.'

Hannah shook her head. 'I won't betray him.'

'Him!' Lilla cried.

Hannah smiled in the way Wilfrid loved and Lilla distrusted.

'It hasn't occurred to you that he might be nervous about his own little secrets, I suppose?'

Chapter 33

WILFRID was to return that evening and, as Hannah walked home slowly, she was glad to think she would see him soon. He, if anyone could, would restore her liking for herself. Her little outing had been a failure. She had not bought a hat; she had told Lilla what amounted to a lie about Mr. Pilgrim, and, until to-day, Hannah's excursions into fiction had always stopped at the injury of anyone else. Her offence was the greater because she did not in the least mind injuring Mr. Pilgrim: it was at her own peculiar kind of integrity she had aimed a blow, and it would not be the last one. It was a choice between her integrity and her treasure, and she had not been tender with her treasure for ten years to have it breathed upon by Mr. Pilgrim's outraged sanctimony and revengeful spite. She was tired and disheartened as she walked through the streets and she was careless, for once, of the life about her. She forgot to remind herself that hers was only a small part in a big drama and that all these men and women, going home from work or coming from the opposite direction in search of pleasure, felt the same overwhelming importance of their lives as she felt of hers: she forgot her little sermon to Robert Corder about infinity, the sun, the moon and the stars: she allowed her own affairs to cast a dun cloud over the whole world, and the tramcars, like noisy magic lantern slides, the shadows of trees on the pavements, the sound of her own footsteps which she had often heard as a sound of advance and adventure, had lost their significance and beauty. In her heart there was the unacknowledged belief that with her lies and evasions she was paying too big a price for what she was concealing; she would have had to pay no more for the memory of something perfect, something she would not have wanted to conceal, and, without actually making that confession, her mind went on

235

to imagine what a real love might have been. But such loves do not come in the way of the Miss Moles of this world, and now she was nearly forty. And thinking thus, she allowed the threatening wave of her loneliness, avoided for so long, to sweep over her, and she stood still in the street, helpless while it engulfed her. It fell back, leaving her battered, but on her feet, and longing for a hand to help her upward before she could be swamped again, but she longed in vain and it was a weary woman who walked up Beresford Road and found no comfort in the ruby glow of Mr. Samson's window curtains.

She assumed her usual look of competence as soon as she entered the house. Employers do not expect their servants to have visible emotions, and professional pride straightened her back when she went into the dining-room. Yet at the sight of Wilfrid, sitting by the fire and listening to what his cousins had to tell him, and leaping to his feet at her appearance, she felt as she had felt when she opened his Christmas parcel, tearfully grateful for a liking which was for herself and not for what she could do for him, and she put her hand on his shoulder and kissed his cheek, without a thought, as naturally as though he were her son.

'Miss Mole!' Ethel exclaimed. And in her voice, the rolling of her eyes, the gleam of her teeth and the checked spring of her body, Hannah recognized the colt she had been trying to tame, now scared, shocked and jealous.

'Yes?' Hannah said pleasantly, but she looked at Ruth who was smiling stiffly, and Wilfrid, laughing, seized Hannah's hand and said dramatically, 'We have betrayed ourselves, Mona Lisa, but no gentleman will compromise a lady and refuse to make honourable amends. You must marry me!'

'Wilfrid! She can't!' Ethel cried. 'She's old enough to be your mother!'

'Oh, not quite,' Hannah begged. She took off her hat and threw it down. 'Don't be so silly, all of you. Are kisses so scarce among you that you take fright when you see one? I'm sorry, Wilfrid. Absence of mind!'

'Don't spoil it. I'm grateful. Ruth didn't kiss me, Ethel didn't –'

'I shouldn't think of doing such a thing! I didn't even kiss my own brother.'

'Perhaps that's why he's gone to South Africa,' Wilfrid said.

'Oh, you know it isn't!' Ethel said helplessly, and Ruth gave a hard little laugh.

'Dear me, dear me, dear me!' Hannah said. 'What a fuss! The only thing I can suggest is that we should kiss all round and cry quits.'

'It isn't that. You know it isn't, but I think kisses ought to be sacred, and I don't see why you should take such a liberty with Wilfrid.'

'Then I'll tell you why,' Hannah said, her body as tense, her eyes as green and keen, as a watchful cat's, and a stillness fell on the little company in the presence of this new and formidable Miss Mole. She held them like that for a few seconds and then, satisfied with this small triumph, she dispersed the thoughts that had been crowding into speech and smiled benevolently at all three, remembering that they were children. 'Because he's a dear boy,' she said, 'and I like him.'

'Because he's a man!' Ethel said with stubborn courage, and Hannah looked him up and down teasingly and said: 'Yes, he'll be a man, some day.'

No one answered her smile, and she felt that there was an influence in the room of which she knew nothing, and she believed it was stealthy and malign. She glanced at Wilfrid and saw that he, too, was puzzled, seeking, behind that thoughtless kiss, some explanation of the atmosphere which Ruth and Ethel created between them, Ethel struggling between caution and the blundering candour natural to her; Ruth sitting on her feet, her back pressed against the back of her chair, perched there like a hard young judge, weighing unspoken evidence against some person unnamed.

'I think,' Ethel said at last, 'I ought to tell Father,' and even now she looked at Hannah for advice, and though she did not ask for it in words, her expression had a familiar appeal and a pathos in its offended bewilderment.

'Don't be a fool,' Wilfrid said. 'The poor man's got enough worry as it is. A son who runs away –! He doesn't

237

want to hear about a nephew who has kissed Miss Mole.'

'It was Miss Mole who kissed you.'

'Yes, but I kissed back, and jolly quick! Didn't you notice?' His speech fell into its provoking drawl. 'I call this exceedingly vulgar. Don't you, Mona Lisa?'

'No,' she said, 'nothing seems vulgar to me, not really. There's something wrong with me, I suppose. It's funny,' she went on, and she leaned forward eagerly, though she looked at nobody, 'it's funny that it's so easy to be positive about good things and so difficult about what are called bad ones. And d'you know why I think it is? It's because the good things exist and the bad ones don't.'

'Oh, but, Miss Mole –' Ethel could not resist a discussion in which she had a sort of professional interest, though her antagonist was Miss Mole, 'we know there are bad things like – like deceit.'

'Yes, yes, it has a bad name; but get to know the person, the cause and the circumstances, and it may deserve a good one.'

'Then you think I oughtn't to tell Father?'

'I'm hardly the person to advise you, and this is rather like a nightmare, but I'll try. Do you mean about the kiss?'

'Not only the kiss,' Ethel muttered, biting her tortured lips.

Ruth's voice came clearly. 'If you do, you'll have to tell him that Mr. Pilgrim came to tea.'

'Oh, has Mr. Pilgrim been? Did he recite?' Hannah asked, and there was no one in the world who knew her well enough to detect the anxiety under her careless tones.

Ethel turned to Ruth. 'Why shouldn't I tell him?'

'Because Father doesn't like him.'

'Father doesn't know him.'

'That won't make any difference,' Ruth said. 'Moley, you told me about your cousin Hilda, didn't you?'

'I didn't tell you much.'

'Ah, but you're going to. So there, Ethel! But of course you wouldn't believe me.'

'I don't know who to believe,' Ethel said, blinking away her tears.

'What on earth are you all talking about?' Wilfrid asked.

'And if there's nothing bad, what's the use of trying to be good?' Ethel asked.

'It isn't being good to be a sneak.'

'But how can you help being a sneak if you try to tell the truth?'

'You can hold your tongue.'

'But I'm worried!' Ethel cried. 'And what does a little girl like you know about it?'

'More than you know, anyhow!'

'Don't quarrel, don't quarrel,' Hannah begged. 'This is the queerest conversation I've ever heard. Why doesn't anyone else want to laugh?'

'Because we like listening to you,' Wilfrid said, 'and whatever your sins may be, you'll go to Heaven. They'll give you all the indulgences you need because they'll want you in the choir.'

'But I can't sing a note.'

'Then the choir will go on strike and say they'd rather hear you talking in your lovely voice.'

'Have I got a lovely voice?' Hannah asked.

'Has she?' said Ethel, and Ruth exclaimed: 'Oh, Wilfrid, how sickening of you! I thought nobody knew it except me,' and that remark, flattering though it was, seemed to Hannah indicative of the fiercely individual attitude of the Corders towards anything they considered good. They could see trouble in its effect on the family, as they had shown in the case of Howard's departure, which neither Ethel nor Ruth had mentioned as a personal loss, but they would not share their pleasures.

She had another proof of this in the information Ruth gave her, later, about Mr. Pilgrim's visit. She had been allowed to have tea with him and Ethel, but, afterwards, Ethel had got rid of her, and Hannah easily imagined her clumsy efforts at tact. 'And she needn't have bothered,' Ruth said. 'I didn't want to stay. I think he's a horrid man. He smiles too much and his teeth don't fit. They click too. And Ethel was so grinny and giggly, till Mr. Pilgrim began talking about you and saying he was sorry to miss you,' and here Ruth paused and looked at Hannah who

239

could not find it in her conscience to ask questions of this child and waited for her next words. 'And, of course,' she said reflectively, 'you did look specially nice at the party, almost pretty, Moley, when you were talking to Mr. Blenkinsop.'

'What next?' Hannah asked disdainfully. 'And I don't see much use in a face that's only almost pretty.'

'But it's so exciting. You don't know what's going to happen to it.'

'Well,' said Hannah, 'I never thought I should die conceited about my looks and, if they've pleased Mr. Pilgrim, I shall also die contented.'

'I don't know about pleasing him. At first I thought it was that and so did Ethel, and she stopped giggling, but afterwards, when he'd gone, I found out that he'd been more interested in your cousin. I was rather in a muddle about it all, and I told Ethel you had a cousin Hilda when she asked me, and then I rather wished I hadn't, in case there might be something about her you wouldn't want people to know. I suppose I ought to have stayed with them all the time.'

'Ought?' Hannah said quickly.

'Yes, and then I should have known why Ethel was so funny when you came in. It wasn't only kissing Wilfrid, Moley. I didn't like that myself.'

'You're rather a goose, aren't you? And look here, I don't employ private detectives, and my cousin Hilda is quite a match for Mr. Pilgrim, so please mind your own business in future.'

'It is my business,' Ruth said stubbornly. 'If people talk about you and your relations, I shall tell you what they say. Besides, I'm interested. What does Ethel want to tell Father? But you'll find out. She won't want to tell you, but she can't help it. And why did she begin altering her new hat?'

'She's always altering things. It's the reforming spirit. And I'm going to alter mine, the newest I've got, and that's three years old. I shall be out all day on Sunday.'

'How perfectly beastly! But you're not going into the country, are you?'

240

'Yes I am. I can't take you. I'm sorry. Some day we'll go together.'

'It's always some day with you,' Ruth complained.

'Yes,' Hannah said, 'it always has been and I suppose it always will be.'

'You're not unhappy, are you?'

'I should be happier if I could take you with me. In another month or two, perhaps we'll go across the river and find primroses and violets.'

'In the Easter holidays?'

'If we can,' Hannah said, wondering where she would be by that time.

'We can if you really want to.'

'Want to!' Hannah cried. 'I'd like to spend the rest of my life doing nothing else.'

'You'd soon get tired of that,' Ruth said wisely.

Chapter 34

HANNAH studied the sky carefully on Saturday night. It promised well for the next day, and when she had finished with the stars she lowered her gaze to the housetops and tried to decide from which of the chimneys in Prince's Road the smoke of Mr. Blenkinsop's excellent coal fire was rising. She thought there would have been more sense in an arrangement which allowed her to look after the baby while Mr. Blenkinsop took Mrs. Ridding into the country, but, fond as Hannah was of babies, she rejoiced in Mr. Blenkinsop's caution. A day spent in Mrs. Ridding's basement, or in pushing the baby about the streets of Upper Radstowe, could hardly be favourably compared with the plan he had made, and no one but a woman with Hannah's experience of living in other people's houses and of being perpetually on duty, could understand the rapture with which she looked forward to the morrow. If she had a wish it was that she might have gone alone into some place free of associations, where she could have walked whither she liked, and as fast or as slowly, thinking her own thoughts until, in wide spaces, she lost all pressing sense of her personality. But things were very well as they were, and in this mood she started the next morning, before the family had gone to chapel, leaving a Ruth who tried not to look neglected and a Robert Corder who was almost paternal in his good wishes for her undertaking.

She put away her cares. She would not think about Mr. Pilgrim and what he had told Ethel: she would not think about Ethel and her renewed manner of a distrustful colt, advancing, with suspicious glances, for favours, in such matters as altering a hat, and edging away as though it were Hannah, and not she, who had a tendency to bite. With such worries Miss Mole was not going to spoil her day:

Mr. Blenkinsop was waiting for her at the station, and the tramcar which carried her to that grimy portal was a processional coach, and the more it swayed, the better Hannah was pleased. She was determined to be, she could not help being, pleased with everything.

At nine o'clock that evening, Miss Mole walked slowly up the garden path. She did not turn and wave a hand to Mr. Blenkinsop at the gate, yet she knew he would stand there until he heard the front door shut behind her, and perhaps a little longer, and through all her other memories of the day she saw his stalwart figure, pursuing and protective; his solemn face, anxious but chivalrously incurious. She went through the hall and up the stairs, hardly feeling solidity under her feet, noticing things from the habit of observation, but indifferent to them. The drawing-room door was open and she could see that the blinds had not been drawn, an omission peculiarly irritating to her, and on any other night she would have drawn them quickly and had a sharp word for Doris: to-night she passed on. She knew Mr. Corder would be waiting for his tea and the knowledge flicked her mind and left no impression, and it was only when she came to Ruth's door, which was ajar, and heard Ruth's voice, that she halted in a march which seemed to have been going on for ever, through lanes, and fields, and woods and the streets of Radstowe.

'Oh, come in, Moley,' Ruth said. 'I've been waiting for you. Light the night-light. I thought you said you would be in to supper, and we've had such an awful day! Have you seen Ethel?'

'I haven't seen anybody,' Hannah said in a colourless voice. She stood at the end of Ruth's bed, gradually distinguishing the face from the pillow and the dark eyes from the face, and slowly, finger by finger, she drew off her gloves, making that business last as long as possible.

'I was afraid she would come upstairs before you did and begin banging,' Ruth sighed. 'I very nearly got into your bed. Why don't you light the light? I'd do it, but you always do, and I like you to.'

'In a minute,' Hannah said.

'I can't see you and you don't sound as if you're here

243

at all. You sound as if you're where you've come from.'

'Oh, no, no,' Hannah said faintly. And now Ruth sat up and asked anxiously, 'Have you had an awful day too?'

Hannah swept her face with her hands, trying to brush away its weariness and the stiffness of its control. A certain amount of mental warmth invaded her cold brain, telling her that here was Ruth, who had had an awful day, and who was afraid of Ethel, and she responded to the suggestion that she was needed. 'Where are the matches?' she said.

'Oh, that's right, that's right,' Ruth said, as the little flame budded and then flowered. 'That's better. Standing there in the dark, all frosty, as if you'd come sailing through the air and hadn't any breath left – it gave me a funny feeling. You're not unhappy, are you?'

'Tired,' Hannah said. 'I've walked for miles and miles.'

'And was the little house all right?'

'I don't know. I didn't go inside.'

'But I thought that was what you went for.'

'So it was, but I had a good long walk instead.'

'Then I wish you'd come home earlier, if that was all you were doing. You managed Father about Howard,' and at these unexpected words, Hannah's brain became normally active, 'and you might have managed him about Ethel. But it would have been better if you hadn't gone at all.'

'No doubt,' Hannah said sourly.

'For you, I mean. Because Father thinks you didn't go to see your little house, and you haven't seen it properly, have you? But still, if you meant to –'

Hannah heard this careful balancing of her deeds and intentions, this calculation of consequences, with a surprise which changed to indignation that Ruth should have them to make and then should offer them to her, and she said sharply, 'Don't talk like that! You can tell me about Ethel, if you like.'

It was seldom that Miss Mole spoke severely and there was always humour in her acidity, but there was none tonight and Ruth was silent for a few moments before she said, 'I do hate people to talk after chapel, across the pews. I believe that's what they go for.'

Hannah did not know a depth of misery from which she could not rise for the discussion of human impulses and motives. 'No,' she said, 'it's the psychological what-d'you-call-it of the varnish. Something adhesive about it, I suppose. And then, with the bright blue firmament overhead, you must expect geniality.'

'I wish I could go to a beautiful church where nobody speaks until they get outside, and then not much. I can't bear the way they ask each other to tea, and talk about who's got influenza, and what the doctor said. They look so holy before the service, and, as soon as it's over, they're just like Jack-in-the-boxes, nodding their heads and being so pleasant to each other.' Ruth paused. 'So pleasant, but not really nice,' she said slowly. 'And that's how Ethel got into trouble.'

Hannah sat on the end of the bed, looking at the floor, and through the vision Ruth had conjured up of yellow pews and the matrons of the congregation in their Sunday best of amiability and garments, with roast beef and batter pudding waiting for them at home, she saw herself in a lane sunk between high banks topped by trees, and heard the whistle of a robin. If she had been standing on higher ground, if the robin had not whistled with that sweet detachment, she might not have run away, but she had felt that she was in a pit of her own making, and the robin gaily mocked her.

'You're not listening, are you?' Ruth asked.

Hannah raised her head. 'Yes. Ethel. Trouble. Who made it?'

'Barley sugar Patsy. And Mrs. Spenser-Smith made some more, but you won't let me tell you about that. And it was partly Mr. Pilgrim's fault, too, because somebody must have told Patsy that Ethel went to his chapel on Christmas Day, and I should think he's the kind of man who would. And she let it out to Father, on purpose, when they were talking after the service, just so that Mrs. Spenser-Smith shouldn't think she knows more about us than Patsy does. And then Mrs. Spenser-Smith had to let Patsy know that she knew something that Patsy didn't, but they both talked to Father and pretended they weren't talking to each other.'

'It sounds complicated.'

'It was worse when we got home. Father and Ethel had a quarrel and she's been to Mr. Pilgrim's chapel to-night and says she'll go as often as she likes, and I don't know whether she's come back yet. So that's the kind of day we've had. Do you think,' Ruth asked wistfully, 'you could finish it up a bit better? It was so wonderful about Howard, but that's always the way. The horrid things happen all of a sudden, and we were so peaceful, weren't we?'

It seemed to Hannah that all her work was undone. Here was Ruth, as nervous and unhappy as she had been three months ago, Ethel had bolted from her stable in search of Mr. Pilgrim, and Lilla's spite, too great for her caution, had shaken Robert Corder's growing trust of his housekeeper in some way yet to be discovered. And Mr. Blenkinsop had had a fruitless errand and never again would he come to Miss Mole for help, or give it to her in asking for it. She had seen him for the last time, perhaps. He had been good and kind, but he must have despised her and compared her unfavourably with Mrs. Ridding who was self-controlled. And how was he explaining her behaviour? He had asked no questions, but they must be knocking at his brain and he would have to answer them. She was indifferent about his answers, for who was he to criticize? It was a sense of loss that oppressed her when she went down the stairs to do what she could for Ruth. She had lost Mr. Blenkinsop, she had lost the remnants of her romance and some of her self-esteem, and she did not know what else she was going to lose when she encountered Mr. Corder. She had, too, a sense of shame from which she had been running all day, and she must turn and face it when she was alone, stare it out of countenance, until it dwindled and then vanished. This she had not been able to do while Mr. Blenkinsop was near. His pained solemnity and mute desire to help had confused her mind, for he was connected with the shame, his presence had increased it, and she longed for the solitude of her bedroom, a hiding-place for her wounds, towards which she had been making when the habit of thinking about Ruth had stopped her. And Ruth's need had come at a fortunate moment: she realized that, in spite

246

of her misery, and up sprang her resilient hopefulness. The disasters of this day might have their value – all things had their value if they were properly used – and who could handle them better than Hannah Mole? And whatever Robert Corder's cause of complaint might be, she was ready to do battle with him.

'We have had a very unfortunate day,' he said sternly when she entered. 'I found the fire out when I came back from evening service.'

'Ah, what's why I never go to it,' Hannah said, and she said it with more roguishness than was quite suitable.

'I have reason to know that some people find superior attractions elsewhere,' he said loftily, 'and naturally, I must be the last to blame them, but when one of them is my own daughter . . . By the way,' he said, and she approved the carelessness of his manner, 'I hope your business was done satisfactorily.'

With her head calculatingly on one side, Hannah looked at him. She was not going to be trapped, and she saw safety in the truth, which, for her, had been accidental and dreadful, but was already proving useful. 'Well, no, it wasn't,' she said.

'But you saw your house?'

'Yes, I saw it. But then a robin sang –' There was a delicious pain in speaking of the robin and already the power of that memory was lessened. 'He sang, and I didn't go any further, not in that direction, but we went a long way in another.'

'We? You were not alone?'

'Oh, no! I was with Mr. Blenkinsop.'

'If it was only a walk with Mr. Blenkinsop, I think it was a pity you chose a Sunday. And I wish you had told me before,' he said in a lower tone.

'How could I know you would be interested?'

'I don't like to be informed about my domestic affairs by outsiders.'

'Then you knew?' Hannah asked innocently, and she decided that if he could thus deceive her, she was justified, if she needed justification, in deceiving him.

'No, I – well, I had a suspicion.'

247

'Then it was lucky that I told the truth!' She laughed and seemed to expect him to laugh with her. 'And why shouldn't I? But will you tell me who forestalled me?'

'It was Mrs. Spenser-Smith.'

'How on earth – Oh, yes, I told her myself.'

'But she gave me to understand that Mr. Blenkinsop was taking you to some other place of worship.'

'Only to Nature's cathedral, as they call it. That's a painful expression, isn't it?'

'Is it?' Mr. Corder replied vaguely, and she thought he was wondering how often he had used it, but he put that aside. 'And it hurt me, Miss Mole.'

'It would,' she said sympathetically.

'Coming, as it did, after more troubling news of the same kind.'

'And perhaps there's just as good an explanation.'

'I'm afraid not. I'm afraid there is no doubt that my daughter had been attending Mr. Pilgrim's chapel, not regularly, but noticeably. How can I explain a desertion like that? And it's not – it's not modest, Miss Mole. She won't listen to reason. She defied me this afternoon.' He shaded his eyes with his hand. 'This is worse than Howard,' he said in a muffled voice, and she thought that in this reference to his son, the man himself was speaking, and past his shoulder, on the desk, she saw Mrs. Corder listening.

She took a breath and said, 'You must ask him to the house.'

'But why? I dislike the man. He is not a man with whom I have, or could have, any sympathy. Ignorant – and rather absurd. And if you are suggesting that I should do it for Ethel's sake, I must refuse. I don't wish her to be friendly with him.'

'The more she sees him, the less she may like him, and stolen fruits are sweet – so they say. It isn't everybody's experience.'

'And I have never encouraged young men to come to the house.'

'If you had, she might not have been interested in Mr. Pilgrim, and he's middle-aged, but I think a middle-aged man would suit her.'

248

'I'm disappointed, Miss Mole. I was hoping for your support, but it seems as though no woman can see a man who is not married without prejudice in his favour.'

Hannah controlled a smile and gave what was almost a sniff. 'I don't call Mr. Pilgrim a savoury object myself, but that's neither here nor there. Make a bargain with her. She doesn't go to his chapel, but he comes here if he wants to. If she's going to tire of him, she'll tire the quicker; if not, what can you do? No, she must not go to his chapel. It's a fierce light that beats on those thrones of yours.'

'Could you –' he hesitated, 'would you speak to her yourself? She won't listen to me. I used some strong expressions about Mr. Pilgrim.'

'I'll keep mine to myself. *Suaviter in modo.* I'll do my best.' She looked at Mrs. Corder and hoped she was feeling grateful. 'And, Mr. Corder, it's a pity for Ruth to hear about things like this.'

'It's a pity for the things to occur. And – er – Miss Mole, you'll forgive me, but I think you will agree I ought to know – is there any – any attachment between you and Mr. Blenkinsop?'

Hannah cast down her eyes and her lips twitched, but, suddenly she wanted to cry. She had lost Mr. Blenkinsop: the only use he had for her was gone, and the one she had for him, which was no more than the sense of a strange kind of fellowship, was growing greater as Mr. Pilgrim approached. She had meant to equivocate and tease Mr. Corder with the prospect of another amorous situation, even to raise her value in his opinion, and she found she could not do it. She looked up and she was afraid there were tears in her eyes. 'No, none,' she said firmly.

Chapter 35

HANNAH went into the cold, dreary dining-room. Long ago, she had removed the dejected fern from the middle of the table and Uncle Jim had improved the behaviour of the gas, but now the fire was nearly out and nothing could change the aspect of a room which had not a single article of beauty in it, except the chrysanthemums in a shallow bowl of Hannah's purchasing. She put her face against the flowers and drew in their bitter scent before she took off her hat and coat and knelt down to stir the fire, and she cast a grim look at the hat as it lay, upside-down, on the chair. She was glad she had not bought a new one for her happy day in the country, yet there would have been an excellent irony in spending her savings on adornment for the occasion, and, from the artistic point of view, that would have been the finishing touch, the master stroke, to this comic tragedy, for undoubtedly there had been something comic about it, and that, perhaps, was what made it harder to bear. There would have been consolation in seeing herself as a purely tragic figure, and that relief had been denied her.

Nothing had been further from her thoughts than tragedy when she reached Radstowe station. The sun was shining. Mr. Blenkinsop was watching for her from the entrance, the tickets in his pocket. He had secured seats in the waiting train, and Hannah sat in the corner of a first-class carriage with her feet on a foot-warmer that was really hot, too hot for the welfare of her shoes, which she was willing to jeopardize rather than disregard Mr. Blenkinsop's efforts for her comfort. Mr. Blenkinsop sat opposite to her and he wore the kind of country suit she did not imagine he possessed, and she had a passing regret for her own shabbiness and then forgot it. She was too busy looking out of the window to think about herself, and when she looked at Mr. Blenkinsop it was only for response to her pleasure and the knowing remarks she made about the fields, what was to be sown, or had been sown in them, and how the ploughing had been done.

When she remembered the journey, and it was a slow one, giving her plenty of time to look at the winter landscape, more exquisitely coloured than a summer one, she thought Mr. Blenkinsop had treated her as though she were a child; he answered intelligently, but seemed preoccupied, as grown-ups will be, but once he broke a silence by announcing that the house they were going to see was not to be sold, but to be let.

'So much the better,' Hannah said. 'A house can be a millstone round your neck. But I think you'll find the train service inconvenient.'

'So much the better,' he echoed with a smile that vexed her in its complaisance, and the child he was taking into the country became the alert Miss Mole, who asked if he intended to resign his work at the bank.

At this, Mr. Blenkinsop had the grace to look a little embarrassed. 'I'm thinking about it,' he confessed.

Ah, she thought, things were easy for people with an income they had not to earn; they could take risks; they need not be afraid of being found out; yet she had compensations; no day, for instance, could ever be for Mr. Blenkinsop, with his inheritance from his mother and as many holidays as he liked, what this day was for her, and he, who was potentially free, could not get the full flavour out of a brief and lovely pause in a perpetual state of dependence on the whims and prejudices of other people. The sense of space, the fields, rippling gently into a distance where they lost their colour in the pale blue of hills so dimly outlined that they might have been clouds, were giving Hannah a liberty of spirit which made her material bondage unimportant, and she did not envy Mr. Blenkinsop; indeed, she felt a sort of pity for him. His material bonds might be nothing, but what spiritual ones was he forging for himself? She looked at him, trying to keep that question from shaping itself into words, and he smiled at her, rather shyly, as though he knew what was in her mind and wished to reassure her.

251

It was at the junction, when they changed to a still slower train, that Hannah began to be uneasy for herself, and now there was another question she dared not ask him. This train looked old enough to be the very one in which she had journeyed to Radstowe for those wonderful days with her parents, the very train which had taken her part of the way to school and back again, and every field they passed, every spinney and farmhouse, was familiar.

She said, a little breathlessly, 'But this is my own part of the country!' And she was not surprised; she was resigned to the ruin of her day, when, at her own station, Mr. Blenkinsop told her that it was here they must get out. She stood apart while he asked directions of the porter, so fearful was she of hearing the impossible words she dreaded, and then, defying her premonition of evil, she took the broad road to the right, instead of the one that led towards home.

'No, it's this way,' Mr. Blenkinsop said, pointing with his stick, and he set off at a good pace.

'Not so fast,' Hannah begged. Her mind was like a map in which she saw every house and cottage in the district reached by this road. 'How many miles?' she asked.

'About two.' She stood still and Mr. Blenkinsop anxiously inquired if that was too much for her.

'No, no.' There was still a little hope and a good deal of courage in her heart. 'Tell me about the house,' she said, as they walked on.

Mr. Blenkinsop had not applied to any agencies for the cottage he wanted. He had heard of this one in a roundabout fashion which ended in a customer at the bank, and back again, through this customer, he had made his appointment with the owner, a procedure which suited his own desire for secrecy.

'And I think those must be the chimneys,' he said.

It was then that Hannah stopped dead. She had a physical feeling of sickness, a horrible, shrivelling feeling in her breast, as though her heart, with all its generosity and courage, had been squeezed in a hard hand to the size of a pea and, for a moment, she felt murderous at this outrage. Then shame swooped over her like a great flapping, threatening bird, and the robin piped his gay derisive note.

In the sunk lane, in sight of her own chimneys, she looked about her for escape. She could not face the man to whom she had given everything she had, she would not look at him and see the full folly of her surrender and her treasure broken at his poor feet of clay. The black bird hovered, the robin piped, and she knew she had been befooling herself for years, making excuses for him, clinging to every memory that had beauty in it, and now the fingers, which had so quickly grown flaccid in hers, were insolently snapped in her face. This was the man she had loved! Her shame lay in his character and her misreading of it, not in the physical intimacy which, though it was misery to remember it, was comparatively unimportant, and no power could have dragged her, accompanied by Mr. Blenkinsop, into his presence.

'I can't go,' she had said. 'I can't go. You must go alone,' and she had scrambled up the steep earthy bank into a little wood, and there, as she heard the breeze very softly singing in the pine trees and felt their needles under her feet, she knew that the black bird had not followed her and she felt no shame, only a purely human grief that anyone could have hurt her so cruelly.

At this point in her memories, Hannah stopped and dropped her face into her hands. The rest was a confusion of woods and fields and lanes, with Mr. Blenkinsop at her side and the bird shadowing them again. She did not know where she had gone, or what she had said, or whether she had been silent. Kind Mr. Blenkinsop, had he but known it, was retarding her recovery from shock. She longed to be free of him. Alone, she could have steadied herself and concocted more of her excuses, striving to find something not altogether dishonourable in this sorry business, but Mr. Blenkinsop persisted, and a funny pair they must have made – a distraught woman pursued by a solemn gentleman who vainly hoped for a clue to this mystery, and the longer she left her behaviour unexplained, and she might so easily have invented something, the more impossible explanation became, but, in truth, she hardly thought of him, except as someone she did not want, and someone who subtly made the conduct of the other more abominable.

She realized, and she grew hot, that he had treated her as the mental case she actually was, and, but that he had made her eat and drink, he had let her have her way which was that of physical exhaustion, until at last he had found a station and a train, and back they had jogged, in a darkness that hid the beauties she had rejoiced in earlier in the day.

Her weariness and her poverty in friendship assailed her now. For the first time in her career she had behaved like a baby, and she was denied the luxury of having someone who would bear with her in that state and think no worse of her, and that, at the moment, was the greatest luxury she could think of. There was Mr. Samson and there was Wilfrid who both, in their different ways, would have offered sympathy and comfort, but Mr. Samson was not sensitive to human emotions and Wilfrid was too young to be made a confidant. On the shoulder of neither of these two could she lay her weary head. There was no one to look to beyond herself, and after all, this despondency would pass. She had had enough experience of unhappiness to know that it need not be permanent if she willed otherwise, and she willed it now with all her might. She told herself it was a good thing she had finished with the remains of her sentiment about her cottage and its occupant, and if she had lost her first motive for frustrating Mr. Pilgrim, she had found another in the simple necessity of earning her bread, yet, like a fool, she was encouraging Mr. Corder to have him to the house! That was the fault of Mrs. Corder who could hear every word spoken in the study and could do nothing more. It would be cowardly and cruel not to help her, moreover Hannah knew that what was not worth risking was not worth keeping, and while she was prepared to risk, she was also prepared to fight.

She sat there, waiting for Ethel to return, but it was Wilfrid who came in first, and, at once, she said, 'You did well to give me that brooch and remind me that Cupid is blind.'

He hesitated for a moment and if, like everybody else, he knew of her excursion with Mr. Blenkinsop, he made no reference to it. 'In wounding Ethel?' he asked. 'Is this

254

Pilgrim fellow as bad as that? We had the hell of a Sunday dinner, Mona Lisa. What did you want to go out for?'

'You may well ask that! But all things work together for good.'

'To those who love God. I've always told you God's the uncle and no one loves him at present, so there's not much hope. Why couldn't he take Ethel into the study and give her a wigging, instead of poisoning the food? But he wouldn't have enjoyed it so much without an audience. I did my best. I tried to look bored, but he went on and on. Streams of indignant eloquence! I wonder he had any breath left for the evening service. I found I had an engagement for tea and supper, and I think I'll change my lodgings. My poor dear mother doesn't pay three guineas a week to have her son's nerves shattered. I want a nice, comfortable landlady and peace in which to pursue my studies.'

'You'd better try Mrs. Gibson. She may have some rooms to let before long.'

'But then, I don't want to leave you, Mona Lisa. You are the extenuating circumstance.'

'I don't extenuate indefinitely.'

'Ah, you're wanting to change your lodgings too! Now, if you'd start a boarding-house of your own –'

'I've thought of that, but I've no money and I've been told I'm too young. That surprises you, doesn't it? But it shows you what some people think about me! And now they'd add that I haven't enough sense! No, I can't bother with a boarding-house. All I want is a little hole to crawl into – a nice dry cave – but people aren't allowed to live in caves nowadays, are they? Everything always belongs to some one else. When I leave my present situation, I'm going to be a charwoman. A home of my own, if it's only an attic, and no questions asked so long as I can scrub. I ought to have done it years ago, but I suppose I had some ridiculous notions about gentility. You'd better go to bed. I'm waiting up for Ethel and it will be no help to me if she finds you here!'

255

Chapter 36

SITTING by the fire and waiting for Ethel's arrival, Hannah was almost annoyed to find that the acute stage of her suffering had passed before she had had an opportunity to lie on her bed and cry until she could cry no longer. That was what she had meant to do, but first Ruth and then Robert Corder had made demands on her and the contact with their minds and Wilfrid's, had diverted her thoughts into several channels and the strength had gone from the main one. 'And a good thing too!' Hannah said to herself. She was able to analyse the emotions she had no need to control and did not wish to express in an extravagance of weeping, and she could wonder how much the presence of Mr. Blenkinsop had contributed to her pain and whether, meeting the circumstances alone, she could have dealt with them more sanely, with her usual acceptance of human frailty. She ought to have gone on and got what humour she could out of a situation in which her lover offered her house to Mr. Blenkinsop, but she was not callous enough for that, nor cruel enough to put the offerer to such confusion. And his shame would have been hers; the worse he proved himself, the greater was her folly and, at once, she began to find excuses for him. Perhaps he wanted to let the house for her sake and intended to send her the money; perhaps his conscience had begun to prick him after ten years of somnolence, but even to Hannah's eagerness, these explanations were unsatisfactory, and she knew it was more likely that he was weary of the place and wanted to get rid of it, and saw no difference between living there for nothing and taking the proceeds of someone else's tenancy. There was the chance, and Hannah unwisely clung to it, that Mr. Blenkinsop's information, received in such a roundabout fashion, had been distorted in transit, but all these speculations were useless. Though she had cured Mr. Blenkinsop of wishing to see her again, though she had given him food for curious thought, she was not otherwise much worse off than she had been before, and she would be actually better off if she could be ruthless with her memories and face the fact that the man she had loved, with a recklessness due to a hero who had risked death and been grievously wounded, had not been worth loving at all; that he, at least, had had no romantic notions of a life-long attachment; that he had merely seen her as a young woman, enamoured, like many others, of a soldier, who had offered him a home when he had none. He had taken her as part of the house, like the furniture and the fowls, and it was horrible to think that probably at no stage of their intercourse had he considered her as more than a temporary and amusing convenience. If there had been any other sentiment, at any time, any realization that a woman of her character was not one for easy alliances, or that she had imperilled her future while she made the present secure for him, he could not have treated her to years of silence and to this final insult.

Yet it was well that this had happened, Hannah thought. She was bare, she was bereft, but she was no longer trying to be blind, and she was the stronger to meet Mr. Pilgrim. She could transform herself into Cousin Hilda without any sickening qualms of disloyalty to a memory and, given a little time, she could put these hurts so far from her that she would persuade herself it was really Cousin Hilda who had endured them.

The expedition to her house had been an odd coincidence and, with the imminence of Mr. Pilgrim, it would have persuaded some people that God approved of the laws men had made, and ratified them with cunningly contrived punishments for offenders, but this would be to make God responsible for Mr. Pilgrim, who had spared a little time from his exhortations to the troops encamped near Hannah's cottage, for reproaching a woman for her care of a man broken in doing what Mr. Pilgrim had no intention of doing himself: it made God responsible for Mr. Pilgrim's conscience, then and now, a state of things inconsistent with Hannah's conception of her Deity. No, no, men made the laws and, impatient at seeing them broken, they devised the punishments, and their representatives, in the persons of Mr. Pilgrim, Robert Corder and Ethel, in Hannah's case. would see that the penalties were rigorously administered, And no doubt it was God who suffered most, at the sight of His creatures making each other miserable. Hannah was sure He was more tenderly tolerant of her than she was herself, that He grieved for her in having mistaken her man, but knew her love had been largely compounded of pity, like God's own; that, in her act, He saw a rashness emulative of deeds of another kind, not permitted to her sex, and, as He had watched, presumably in some wise helplessness, the torture of brave men, so He observed her lesser agonies, so small compared with theirs that Hannah was ashamed to dwell on them.

It was comforting to know that God and she understood each other, she told herself, with a cynical smile for her presumption, and it was strange to think that Mr. Pilgrim was probably as sure of God's nature as she was, and, like her, made it fit his prejudices; strange that a God who had as many characters as the men and women who sought Him in times of trouble and forgot Him in their happiness, should yet have the power of giving peace to bewildered spirits; strange, too, that the dreary dining-room felt like a home. The resuscitated fire babbled its cheerful inanities, Uncle Jim's corrected gas did its best to do as it had been told, the almost inaudible ticking of the marble clock had a faintly friendly sound. Hannah's peace might only have been that of exhaustion, but she believed it was something more, and, in any case, it would serve her turn which was to fit her to waylay Ethel before she could rush upstairs and begin the process known to Ruth as banging, and persuade her to accept her father's bargain.

In the meantime, Hannah likened herself again to her little ship, becalmed after a storm, and using the calm for overhauling her condition, in readiness for the next misadventure. The misadventure would come. Small lonely ships which set out on perilous voyages, must be prepared for worse treatment than bigger ones receive, especially when they are hampered by bad records, but, changing the metaphor, Hannah refused to be the dog with a bad name who, foreseeing hanging, waits passively for his punishment. There was work for her to do, and though there was humour in the thought that she would not be allowed to do it if Robert Corder knew about her past, and that the time might yet come when he would look back with horror at the confidences he had made to the unscrupulous Miss Mole, she was not going to lose her pleasure while it lasted, and she was proud of her little triumphs, culminating, on this day which had seemed so unrelievedly black, in Robert Corder's asking of a favour, and its inevitable effect of making Hannah like him rather better.

She was thinking that she might even learn to like Mr. Pilgrim, when a sound at the front door drove her into the hall, and there was Ethel, with a new stubborn look on her face. The study door opened a minute later, but it was discreetly shut by an unseen hand, for Hannah was asking Ethel if she had had any supper, saying she had fasted herself since five o'clock, and proposing that they should go into the larder and see what they could find.

This was the sort of greeting Ethel had not looked for and, braced to meet abuse, she collapsed under kindness to the extent of accompanying Miss Mole into the kitchen. 'I've been to Highfields Chapel,' she said, anxious to sustain her attitude of independence, 'and then I went to see Patsy Withers.'

'But she's the one who's been telling tales about you.'

'That's why I went.'

'H'm,' said Hannah, 'people who tell tales seem to have an attraction for you. And just look what they've done to the joint while I was out! Mangled it! And wasted,' she eyed it calculatingly, 'at least half a pound, I should say.'

'It may have been wasted, but it wasn't eaten,' Ethel said, and Hannah looked at her with quick appreciation, but Ethel was not trying to be funny; she was merely stating a fact. 'And that reminds me,' she went on, and now it was she who looked at Hannah, 'I met Mr. Blenkinsop just now.'

'Why does it remind you? Oh, I suppose he made part of the midday meal. Well, what was he doing?'

'Having a walk, he said.'

259

'I should have thought he'd walked enough.'

'You never told us you were going out with him.'

'You never told us you were going to Mr. Pilgrim's chapel. I don't think we'll have any of this reminiscent mutton. I'll warm some soup. And was Miss Withers pleased to see you?'

'She was more pleased to see me go,' Ethel said with her unconscious humour. 'Mr. Blenkinsop was walking up and down on the other side of the road.'

'Dear me! I'm afraid I've wound him up and he can't run down. And did Mr. Pilgrim preach a good sermon?'

'Yes,' Ethel said unwillingly, 'but that's quite a different thing.'

'I don't follow you,' Hannah said politely as she stirred the soup.

'I mean, going out with Mr. Blenkinsop is quite different from going to a service.'

'That was what I hoped,' Hannah admitted.

'And I don't see why I shouldn't go where I can get – get what I want.'

'Ah, don't try too hard for it,' Hannah said, and she spoke dreamily because she was thinking of Mr. Blenkinsop, walking up and down the road. Did he think she meant to do something desperate? And would he walk up and down all night? It seemed to her that the kindest, the most painful, and yet the pleasantest thing she could do was to run out and tell him all was well.

She put a bowl of steaming soup in front of Ethel. 'Drink that,' she said. 'I shall be back in a minute.'

Mr. Blenkinsop was turning slowly and coming towards her when she reached the pavement, and she hurried across the road to him.

'It's all right, it's all right!' she exclaimed, half laughing, and putting out a hand, she said, 'Forgive me. I've spoilt your day, I've spoilt everything, but it was only a temporary insanity. Now I'm in as right a mind as I ever had.'

'I can't leave it at that,' Mr. Blenkinsop muttered, holding her hand firmly.

'But it's too late to get me certified to-night.'

'Can't you be serious, just for once?' he begged.

'I've been serious for hours. That was the mistake. One's self is the wrong subject for seriousness, Mr. Blenkinsop.'

'But I'm serious for you.'

'I was afraid so. That was why I came out. To tell you there was no need, and to say good night.'

'I shan't have a good night,' he said testily.

'That will be a change, won't it?' she asked, and giving his hand a parting pressure and freeing it with some difficulty, she went back into the house.

Ethel was making large eyes over the bowl of soup. 'Wherever have you been, Miss Mole?'

'Turning Policeman X off his beat. It's time the poor man had some supper, and I'm hungry too. Didn't Miss Withers offer you anything to eat?'

'Yes, she did, but I wouldn't have it. Of course I wouldn't! What did she want to interfere for?'

'Why does anyone want to interfere? If we could all live and let live, we should be happier.'

Ethel grew restive. 'I know what you're hinting at, and nobody wants to do you any harm, Miss Mole.'

'They can't,' Hannah said stoutly.

'But we have to do what's right.'

'I'm sure Miss Withers used those very words.'

'But it's so different! I've done nothing to be ashamed of. It's not wrong just because it vexes Father.'

'That's true,' Hannah said, 'but what does Mr. Pilgrim think about it?'

'He says it helps him to have me there.'

'So you're trying to help him, and Miss Withers is trying to help your father.'

'No, she isn't. She's trying to make him think we need somebody to look after us. She said she felt like a mother towards us, Miss Mole, and that's what she'd like to be. I told her you could do everything we needed, and we didn't want anybody else.'

'That was very nice of you,' Hannah said, 'and one in the eye for Patsy!'

'And that's what worries me,' Ethel said. 'One of the things. You're so kind, Miss Mole, and so unselfish, but Mr. Pilgrim says he doesn't see how you could have a cousin

261

so exactly like you. And there's Ruth to be thought of.'

'Ruth!' Hannah controlled herself and waited.

'He says you and your cousin would have to be twins.'

'So we are – spiritually. Poor Mr. Pilgrim! Poor Miss Withers! How anxious some people are for the welfare of some of the others! And I'm anxious about yours and that's enough to make you suspicious, I'll admit, but I really mean it. Listen. If Mr. Pilgrim finds you such a help, he'll come and look for you when he wants you.'

'But Father doesn't like him.'

'Perhaps he'll learn to,' Hannah said hopefully, 'but he won't if you desert the chapel. It really isn't quite fair to him, you know. Now, don't start crying! What are you crying for?' she asked and she regretted the sharpness of her voice when she heard Ethel's answer, pathetic in its distrust of herself and in her helpless readiness to confess it.

'Because Mr. Pilgrim may not come.'

'Oh, he'll come,' Hannah said. 'Why, he'll come if it's only to have another look at me! Has he told you why he's so curious about me?'

'No, he says it isn't fit for me to hear.'

'Then you may be sure he'll tell you,' Hannah said encouragingly.

Chapter 37

SHE ought to have told Mr. Blenkinsop to give up all thoughts of the little house. It was ill-omened, it was a place in which no happiness would be found. She ought to have told him that, and to have asked him to think again before he acted, to have pointed to herself and told him that the world would be against him, and the world had a nasty way of making its displeasure felt, but she had been thinking of her own misery, she, whom Ethel called unselfish, and she had not warned him of his dangers, the disillusions which are worse when they come to unlawful lovers, the bonds which tighten irksomely when there is only chivalry to prevent their being unloosed. And Mr. Blenkinsop would have replied that this was no concern of hers, just as Hannah would have replied to any friend who had tried to interfere with her. Mr. Blenkinsop would much prefer being left to look after himself; he was as old as she was, as he had taken care to tell her, and it was odd that he should have taken her into his confidence at all, but, for some reason or other, that was what people did. Ruth, Ethel, Robert Corder, had all done it and perhaps Mr. Pilgrim would find he had to ask her how he had best deal with the duty pressing on him in connection with herself! That would not surprise her; nothing would surprise her after the events of this day, and it seemed impossible that it should be only a few hours since she had stood in the lane and seen the chimneys of her house.

She lay in bed, and the peace she had felt in the dining-room would not stay in a mind busy with pictures of that house. She saw it as it was when she saved it from the sale of everything else her father had possessed, a four-roomed cottage washed in a pale pink which was stained with drippings from the roof: there were overgrown, weedy flower-

263

beds under the windows, but the true cottage flowers were there, and there were apple trees, with whitened trunks, in the rough grass of the orchard. She was a girl then, resisting the advice of her elders against keeping a property she could not use, and she had kept it and let it to the young farm hand who already occupied it, and who had gone to the war and not returned. She tried not to see it as it was when she had made it ready for her own soldier, the flower-beds weeded, the rooms re-papered with her own hands, the outside walls washed anew and the stains hidden, and a blue feather of smoke rising from the chimney, like a banner in honour of her happiness, but, try as she would, she could not help remembering it. She remembered how the pink of its walls had been coarsened against the lovely pink of the apple blossom, and how all the colours, the green of the grass, the new green of the trees, the blossom, the waving tassels of the larch trees beyond the house, the red-brown plumage of the new fowls, had seemed more brilliant, more delicate and more wonderful than any colours she had seen before, and she remembered the absurd, pretty things she had said to herself about them all, and had said to no one else.

That silence was a comfort to her as she turned restlessly in her bed. She had given him everything she had except the tenderest and most foolish of her thoughts, restrained from giving those by some instinct which she had not acknowledged, and for which she now thanked God. And again she found excuses for him. She had never been sentimental, never shown herself sensitive; she had been gay and practical and energetic and when the time came for parting, she had gone off with a light word, pretending, in her pride, that his conception of their relationship was her own. He had not understood that she could be hurt: that was it: he had not understood.

She pressed her fingers against her eyeballs and, as though she had pressed a button, the pictures moved away, leaving nothing but a blur of darkness, shot with gold and blue and purple, and this passed, too, and there was the orchard again, in the sun, and Mrs. Ridding was hanging washing on a line swung between two apple trees. Hannah saw her quite clearly, with the sunshine on her fair head, her arms raised, a clothes peg in her mouth, and the baby crawling in the grass, clumsily and carefully fingering the daisies and pulling them off at their heads, and Hannah cried 'No, no!' in a voice that startled the narrow quietness of her bedroom. They should not have her cottage. It would be ill for them and, somehow, ill for Hannah. They must go somewhere else; yet, when she pictured them elsewhere, she had the same sinking of the heart.

What did this mean? she asked, starting up in bed. Propped against her pillows, she stared for a long time at the oblong of her window, with nothing but air and trees and hills between it and the lane where she had stood that day, and when she lay down she did it stealthily, as though any noise, any quick movement, would rouse into activity, into reality, a suspicion of herself which must be allowed to die. Surely she had enough to bear without this new, absurd, hopeless pain, but this was one which it was in her power to stop, and she would stop it. She lay, rigid under this determination, and suddenly, unawares, she began to laugh, quietly, with her mouth against the bed-clothes. Mr. Blenkinsop had always made her laugh and she would laugh now if she never did it again. It was queer to love a man because he made you laugh without intention, or was the laughter born of love and the love of a conviction that you could trust him to the end of time? She did not know, but her laughter ceased, and the suspicion had become reality, and it no longer hurt her.

'It is more blessed to give than to receive,' she said aloud, and she raised dubious eyebrows above her closed eyelids and turned down the corners of her mouth, for she had made previous trial of giving and not receiving. 'But it depends on the person you give to,' she said, and with surprising quickness, with more surprising happiness, she went to sleep.

But a happiness that comes at night, when all things, both good and evil, are possible, is harder to sustain on a cold winter morning, and though Hannah woke to the knowledge that some beneficence had lulled her to sleep and given her dreams of a vague felicity, she rose in a stern state

265

of mind and, as she twisted up her hair before the mirror, she looked disdainfully at a face which was sadly yellow in the gas-light. That look expressed her opinion of herself and her realization of how she appeared to other people; and during the next few days, she went about her work in a passionate earnestness, quite different from the leisurely manner in which Miss Mole usually fulfilled her duties, a manner which shirked nothing, but was not designed to impress the rest of the household with her superior energy and ability. Now she washed and ironed curtains, dusted books, turned out cupboards which had been comfortably neglected for months, overlooked the linen, got out the sewing-machine which was an instrument she detested, and made the dining-room uninhabitable while she tore sheets asunder, turned the edges to the middle and rapidly machined them together.

Perched in her chair, out of reach of these white billows, Ruth watched this activity disapprovingly. 'I don't like this at all,' she said.

'And do you think I do? If there's anything I loathe it's making this nasty little needle hop along the hems. It's like a one-legged man running a race. I hate to make him go so fast, yet I can't bear to let him go slowly, and I know the cotton in the spindle will give out before I get to the end, and I detest the noise, and I hope you'll all be very uncomfortable when you're lying on these seams. I'm not taking any particular care to get them flat.'

'Well, I suppose it won't last.'

'No, nothing lasts. That's why I'm doing it.'

'You mean – to save the sheets from wearing out?'

Hannah stopped her turning of the handle and let the one-legged man have a few moments' rest. 'Exactly,' she said. It had been on the tip of her tongue to say that in saving the sheets from wearing out, she was trying to wear out her emotions, but that was not an answer for Ruth, and she knew Ruth's questions often had more purpose than a desire for direct information. Nevertheless, she supplied the information. 'When sheets get thin in the middle, the careful housewife turns the middles to the sides. Unsightly, sometimes uncomfortable, but economical.'

'But the cupboards were not getting thin in the middle, or the books.'

'Most of the books were thin all through,' Hannah said with a chuckle. 'I had a good look at them. Dusting books is one of the lesser evils, and cooking's another. You can pause for refreshment on the way.'

'And it seems to me,' Ruth went on, 'that you're either worried about something, or –' her voice changed its note, 'you're putting everything in order, in a hurry. Rather like making a will and paying your debts when you think you're going to die. It isn't that, is it?'

'I'll tell you what it is,' Hannah said with a great effect of frankness. 'I'm bad tempered.'

'Oh! Not worried? Not worried about Ethel?'

'Ethel? Why?'

'You've been so busy, I suppose you haven't noticed, but she's been very pleasant for the last few days. And after that row with Father! I expected she'd be awful.'

'It must have done her good,' Hannah said.

'I'd rather she wasn't quite so nice, though, and I wish you wouldn't be so busy about things that don't really matter. You see, I'm afraid you'll miss something important.'

'Well, if I do, you won't. Don't be so fussy. I'll tell you what we'll do to-morrow. We'll have our walk.'

'But the spring isn't here.'

'Then I'll have it alone.'

'No. I didn't mean that, but it's rather like the cupboards and the books, isn't it?'

'I don't see the resemblance,' Hannah said, turning the handle of the sewing-machine again, but Ruth had found the right reason for Hannah's suggestion. They must have their walk while they could and if they were together when spring came, well, then they could have another.

Ethel was amiably ready to look after Doris and the house. Not a single gleam of her eyes betrayed any jealousy that Miss Mole and Ruth were going off together with sandwiches in their pockets and no expectation of returning before dark; she showed no further anxiety for the moral welfare of her young sister, and Hannah and Ruth both silently came to the conclusion that their absence suited her.

267

This was unfair to Ethel who had her own consolations and who was doing her best to be pleasant to Miss Mole, preferring her, in the capacity of housekeeper in spite of her dark past, to the possibility of Miss Patsy Withers as a stepmother, and Ethel knew no more than they did that this was the day Mr. Pilgrim had chosen for ingratiating himself with her father, obeying the instinct which recommends a piece of scandal shared for the sound knitting of a bond.

Unconscious of this danger in the rear, Ruth and Hannah started, and if the trees had been in bud they could have fancied it was April. There was a lovely mildness in the air and it was a day on which something delightful ought to happen as, indeed, it did, for instead of going through Albert Square and reaching the bridge by way of The Green, Hannah dived into a narrow, twisting lane, with mysteriously untidy gardens on one side of it and the backs of houses on the other, and, twisting and turning in their descent, they came into a square where dirty children played on the steps of Georgian houses, and when they had passed through this and a narrow street, they were on the road running parallel with the docks. These were places which Ruth, living all her life in Upper Radstowe, had not seen before, nor had she crossed the docks by the footbridges Hannah knew, some of them, to an adventurous imagination, hardly wider than a plank, with a hand-rail on one side only.

'Bad places on a dark night,' Hannah said solemnly.

'And very exciting now,' Ruth replied appreciatively.

It took them some time to get across the docks and stand in another county, for everywhere there were ships; big ones moored alongside warehouses and loading or unloading; sailing-ships piloted by tugs and looking, Hannah said, like sad widows in their pathetic dignity under their bare masts and yards, and the tugs were like the undertakers, in a fuss about the funeral. There were dredgers with endless chains of buckets, picking up the river mud, and there were rowing-boats and men shouting and locks being opened and shut. The sky was blue and bluer when the gulls struck across it, and on the right, high up, the suspension bridge was like a thread, and the carts crossing it were the toys of midgets.

'We might stay all day,' Ruth said.

'We might, but we're not going to. We've got to have our walk.'

'Oh, don't say it like that, as though it's the only chance!'

'For the benefit of our health,' Hannah said. 'Why didn't you wait and let me finish my sentence?'

They had their walk, up a long winding hill until they reached the level of the bridge, along a pleasant road bordered with the woods that sloped down to the river, across fields and through copses, to the Monks' Pool where the red trunks of firs were mirrored in the water. There, rather late in the day, they ate their lunch, and dusk seemed to be deepening round them though the sky was a pale blue circle like a reflection of the pool, and the tops of the trees which circled the water made a fringe for the patch of sky, and when they had thrown their crumbs for the age-old carp which were said to live in that water, they walked home slowly, saying very little, happy in each other's company, and passed over the spangled bridge and saw the docks, spangled too, far below them on one side and the dark river on the other.

'It's been a lovely day,' Ruth said, on a deep breath, when they stood outside the door in Beresford Road, but when they entered the dining-room and saw Ethel sitting by the fire, they knew it had not been a lovely day for her.

Chapter 38

IT was fortunate for Hannah that Robert Corder heard her story from Mr. Pilgrim. From another, he might have listened to it receptively, but from Mr. Pilgrim whom he disliked, who had spoilt Mrs. Spenser-Smith's party for him, who had lured Ethel to his chapel and who was creating trouble of the kind Robert Corder dreaded most and felt, in some obscure way, to be indecent, he heard it with studied incredulity. He was not the man to let Mr. Pilgrim think he could supply information of any kind to the leading Nonconformist minister in Radstowe, and he would have seen this approach as an insult to his household and his own acumen if his vanity had not assured him that Mr. Pilgrim had worldly, as well as sentimental, reasons for performing what he called an unpleasant duty, though it was one which might be the means of putting him on familiar terms with Ethel's father. Robert Corder was not, and never had been, quite comfortable about Miss Mole, and, while he listened and showed Mr. Pilgrim a forbidding face, he remembered all his suspicions and irritations, forgotten lately in his reliance on her, but his chief impulse, at the moment, was to be as different from Mr. Pilgrim as he could, and he read him a little lecture on tolerance, generosity, tenderness towards women and the duty of Christians to accept sinners who had repented, which was as good as the best of his sermons. He did not commit himself to a belief in Miss Mole's innocence: he was too wily for that, and he preferred to present himself as a man who was ready to fit his practice to his theory, but if Mr. Pilgrim had had a tail, it would have been between his legs when he left the house, and that was why Ethel wept alone.

'Oh, what's the matter now?' Ruth exclaimed. 'It's always the same. We can't have anything nice, in this family,

without having something nasty afterwards. Is it because
Moley and I have been out together?'

'I don't care what you and Miss Mole do!' Ethel cried. 'I
wished she'd never come here!'

'Oh – you beast!' Ruth said with vicious slowness. 'If she
wasn't here, I wouldn't stay. No, I wouldn't. I'd ask Uncle
Jim to let me live with him, and I know he would. But
you'll stay, won't you, Moley? Don't listen to her. She
doesn't mean it. She'll be sorry, soon, but she hasn't any
self-control.'

'Be quiet!' Hannah said sharply. 'Why, in the name of
goodness, can't you be kinder to each other? I tell you this –
and I hope you'll remember it – I believe unkindness is the
worst sin of all. Yes,' she said, looking at Ethel, 'the very
worst.'

'I'm not unkind to Ruth,' Ethel said sullenly.

'But you were to Moley, so I was to you. What's she done
to you, anyhow?'

'That's not for a child like you to know,' Ethel said.

'Then I don't believe you know yourself.'

'Well, I know more –' Fearful, Ethel caught her lip on
what she was going to say, but daring and careless, in her
wretchedness, of consequences, she let it go, and said in a
strained, weak voice, 'I know more than Mr. Blenkinsop
does,' and she looked at Hannah from between shoulders
raised as if to ward off a blow.

It was the table Hannah struck with a single smart rap,
calling attention, if it had been necessary, to her white face
and sombre eyes, and Ruth's murmured, questioning repeti-
tion of Mr. Blenkinsop's name sounded, in all their ears, like
the last effrontery. There had been dark rings round Hannah's eyes for days and now they showed, like bruises, on
her pallor, and Ruth and Ethel, looking at what seemed to
them the very symbol of fury and, waiting for fierce, de-
nunciatory tones, heard her say quietly, in a movingly sweet
and weary voice, 'You have no manners, either of you.
What's to become of you? You can't go through life biting
and scratching like this.' The sadness went out of her voice
and, in the one they were used to, she said, 'I don't flatter
myself that mine are good, but they ought to be, for when I

271

was at school in – when I was at school – I used to look at a motto on the wall and I thought it was rather silly, but I've never forgotten it. And that just shows that when you're a school, or anywhere else for that matter, there are people who know better than you do. And, in this room, I'm the one who knows, and I'm going to tell you, as the motto told me, that manners are not idle, but the fruit of a loyal nature and a noble mind. Yes,' she said emphatically, 'a loyal nature and a noble mind. As for you two, you remind me of nothing so much as a pair of monkeys in a cage.'

'Oh, Moley, that's not manners!' Ruth expostulated, half laughing in her relief at escape from something much worse than this, but she obeyed Hannah's significant look at the door, while Ethel moaned piteously, in excuse, 'I'm so unhappy.'

Hannah checked a movement of impatience. She knew the unhappiness of a girl could be as poignant as that of a woman, perhaps more poignant, but the doors were still open for the girl and she had time to wander and find what she wanted, while, for the woman, the doors were shut and barred and she had to find, not what she wanted, but what she could get, inside. 'What's the matter?' she asked gently, and Ethel cried, 'Oh, Miss Mole, Mr. Pilgrim's been, and Father was furious with him – about you!'

'How do you know it was about me?'

'Because I – I saw Mr. Pilgrim afterwards, and he told me.'

'Well, it's very obliging of you to pass on the news,' Hannah said, and she went out of the room to the sound of Ethel's protestations that her father's anger was not going to affect her actions.

In the hall, Hannah rubbed her cheeks vigorously and blinked her eyes to rid them of their stiff, glaring feeling. Her indignant, sore anger, too bitter for relief in words, had changed into a lively, almost gay, one, and she knocked at the study door and showed Mr. Corder a face which, he immediately decided was not the right one for his housekeeper.

He was in a noble state of scorn for Mr. Pilgrim, but he was ready to see suspicious symptoms in Miss Mole and the consciousness that he knew something to her possible detri-

272

ment and meant to keep that knowledge from her, gave him a sense of power which was expressed in the cold blandness of his manner. 'Can I do anything for you?' he asked. She did not look like a guilty person, but the guilty were often shameless.

'Yes, please,' Hannah said. 'I want to know what Mr. Pilgrim has been telling you.'

This vexed Mr. Corder. He always shrank from a direct attack and his feeling of power was sensibly diminished. 'It was a confidential interview, Miss Mole.'

'Of which Ethel knows some of the details.'

'I am not responsible for that.' He did not want to repeat Mr. Pilgrim's remarks. He had a fear that this woman, who was like no other he had met, would corroborate them, and force him to some action about which he could consult no committee, and he took refuge on that height from which he had addressed Mr. Pilgrim.

'I think I can guarantee that he will say no more. I consider his behaviour unmanly, Miss Mole, and even if I did not doubt the truth of his statements, I should ignore them. We have all sinned, in some way, at some time –'

'Oh, not all of us,' Hannah interpolated, and she tried to look at him admiringly.

'In greater or lesser degree,' he said, 'and I, for one, am willing to let bygones be bygones. I judge you as I know you, Miss Mole. I ask you no questions. I wish to hear nothing from you.'

If he had wanted Hannah to tell him everything this was the way to do it. His condescension was almost more than she could bear. Every feeling of antipathy she had had for him returned in force. She wondered what influence her little property was having on his leniency and his wish to hear nothing from her was the strongest of motives for disobliging him. It would be worth a good deal to see him floundering in the embarrassment of her confession, and she was in a mental condition which craved the satisfaction of desperate measures. She believed that most of her soreness would be healed if she could tell him what she had done, and assure him that she did not care a damn. Yes, if she could use that word it would do her all the good in the world.

273

But after that – what? She had nowhere to go, she had very little money, and even Mrs. Gibson's house was now closed to her. She could not go there and, wherever she went, she must leave Ruth behind.

The tightness of her body slackened, her hands came together in front of her. 'You are very generous,' she said, and some of her pleasure in offering that tribute was lost in her fear that it might be true, but her fear was not great: his generosity would cease when other people became aware of it. 'One has one's family pride, and after all, there wouldn't be much sense in punishing me because of poor Cousin Hilda. I've always been friends with her and I always shall be. I haven't Mr. Pilgrim's fear of contamination and I have none of his reforming spirit. And I'm very fond of her. There must be some reason why the naughty people are so much nicer than the others, and Hilda is one of the naughty, nice ones. But then, perhaps I'm prejudiced,' she added with a smile.

'I'm afraid I don't know what you are talking about,' Robert Corder said with his quick frown.

Hannah's eyebrows went as high as they could. 'You don't know what I'm talking about? Then what on earth has Mr. Pilgrim been saying to you? Tell me, please, Mr. Corder. I must know.'

Mr. Corder reddened above his beard. 'He was talking about you,' he said reluctantly.

'About me? About me? Oh, I see,' she said slowly. 'Yes, we're very much alike. Poor Mr. Pilgrim! How disappointing for him!'

'Why should it be disappointing for him?' Robert Corder asked with an acuteness she had not been prepared to meet.

'He's that kind of man, isn't he? And you are even more generous than I thought.'

'Too generous, I am afraid,' he said, for he was not sure that he was wise in associating himself with what proved to be Miss Mole's own views, and he could not forbear expressing his doubts and his general uneasiness by adding, 'It must be a remarkable likeness.'

'It is,' Hannah said, and with that she turned to go, and again, a bad sign, he called her back.

'Just to clear things up, Miss Mole –'

'But I thought you didn't want to!'

He frowned again. He was not used to having his words brought up against him. 'For your own sake,' he said, and her enigmatic smile was a goad, quickening his temper. 'Your cousin seems to have been living in her own little house in a part of the country known to Mr. Pilgrim. It's an odd coincidence that you should both have a little house in the country.'

'Not at all. She was in mine.' All Hannah's desire to enlighten Mr. Corder had gone. This was better sport, and the rules of the game demanded that she should take risks, but save her life. She had an exquisite enjoyment in watching for the feints of her adversary, and into her mind, stored with detached, incomplete pieces of information, there darted all the fencing terms she had ever heard, those bright, gleaming words with the ring of steel and the quick stamping of feet in them. She had the advantage of him. She knew what she was going to do, and she knew that he had no plan of action and she felt that she had him on her point, but, behind the temporary excitement, there was waiting for her the moment when she would have to tell herself that, for all its outward gallantry, this was a sorry, sordid business.

Robert Corder brought it to an end with an unconvinced inclination of the head. 'Thank you, Miss Mole. I don't think you will have any more trouble with Mr. Pilgrim,' he said, and Hannah became aware of Mrs. Corder's candid gaze. Whether she approved of these prevarications, Hannah could not be sure. In saving the younger of her daughters, Hannah was embarrassing the other, but would Mrs. Corder look favourably on Mr. Pilgrim as a husband for Ethel, and had Mr. Pilgrim any intention of asking for the privilege of the post? There was no knowing with Ethel. A kind word was enough to set her heart beating faster; she had probably built high hopes on the unsteady foundation of such compliments as would trickle easily from his lips, and Hannah found comfort in the thought that, if they really cared for each other, Robert Corder's antagonism would not separate them for ever.

275

That night, when she sat on Ruth's bed and they discoursed on their favourite topic, which was where they would go when they had money and could travel, Hannah felt that, on the whole, she had done well. It was possible to be too careful about one's own soul and, in trying to help two people, she might help neither. Moreover, Ruth's queer, selfish affection was dear to her: it was worth lying for, and though there was the chance that some day, and perhaps soon, Ruth would hear about those lies, the chance had to be taken; and the saying of an old woman she had known in childhood came back to her, telling her that, in times of trouble, wisdom lay in living for one day at a time, but even that one day was more than Hannah felt she could endure.

Chapter 39

RUTH had had one lovely day, marred, it is true, by Ethel's outburst, but mended, afterwards, by the talk of those voyages she was to make with Hannah, and on the next day Wilfrid had a surprise for her. Hannah was informed of it in a paraphrase designed to protect her in case of trouble and, at the midday meal, Wilfrid mentioned, in an off-handed manner, that he and Ruth were having a little excursion that afternoon. In answer to questions, he was prepared to say that they meant to examine some of Radstowe's public buildings, but, in the absence of Howard, Robert Corder made a practice of ignoring Wilfrid's remarks when he could not find fault with them, and he said nothing, and Ethel's concern with her own affairs deadened her to those of others.

The changeable nature of Robert Corder's views made these precautions necessary. He had never been in a theatre in his life. He had been trained to a distrust of everything connected with the stage and though his mind had broadened with the times and the opinions of eminent fellow-ministers, he had remained aloof. Thus he was spared the awkwardness of deciding what plays were fit for him to see and the danger of making unfortunate mistakes. Ethel also remained aloof, for the sake of her girls who might be misled in those questionable haunts, and pastoral plays in the Zoological Gardens were all she and Ruth had seen. The Spenser-Smiths always went to the Radstowe pantomime, and if Ruth had been invited to accompany them, no doubt her father would have let her go, but it was a different matter when Wilfrid carried his young cousin off, and she had all the excitement of this longed-for experience, yoked to the difficulty of wearing her velveteen frock, in honour of Wilfrid and the dress circle, and getting out of the house before

277

Ethel could see the significant finery under her concealing coat.

This was safely accomplished while Ethel was noisily closeted in her bedroom, and Hannah hoped she was dressing for some pleasure of her own. She felt incapable of dealing with more of those mad interviews in which the accused was consulted about the prosecution. Her mind was dull with a weariness demanding solitude and, when Ethel had looked in to say she would be out to tea, Hannah told Doris she had a headache and was not to be disturbed, and she went upstairs slowly, feeling old and strangely deserted, now that she had her wish of being alone.

She had not long for the indulgence of this rare self-pity. She fell into that daytime sleep which, for the exhausted, can be profounder than any that comes at night, and she sank into it as though she floated on subsiding water, without consciousness of the drop, and, accompanying the descent, there was the promise of an oblivion which came upon her before she had had her fill of waiting for it.

Out of this timelessness, this absolute ease from care, she woke with a thumping heart, and with an effort, like a physical wrench, to remember where she was. Darkness had filled her bedroom, the noise she had heard, on the point of waking, as that of horses thundering up the stairs, resolved itself into heavy, hurried footsteps, and her door was flung open to the sound of Ethel's voice calling for Miss Mole. A fire in the house, or in the theatre, Ruth run over, an accident to Mr. Corder or Mr. Pilgrim, were possibilities rushing to Hannah's mind as she put her feet to the floor and felt Ethel's presence in the room, and before she could light the gas, she heard Ethel saying in breathless catastrophic tones, 'I've been to see Mrs. Spenser-Smith!'

The match-box slipped from Hannah's fingers and while she fumbled for it, her legs aching sharply with her fright, she muttered angrily, 'I thought someone was dead, at least.'

'It's worse!' Ethel cried shrilly.

Hannah lit the gas and, looking at Ethel, she thought she saw what Mr. Blenkinsop had seen ten days ago, for strong emotions have faces of their own, and those which had command of Ethel had blotted out the individuality of her

278

features and she might as easily have been taken for Hannah Mole or any other woman in distress, as for Ethel Corder, the competent leader of the Girls' Club. It was no wonder Mr. Blenkinsop had prowled up and down the street, when he had the memory of such a face; it was no wonder he had not risked further communication with a woman who could look like that; but Hannah had responsibilities towards Ethel which were not Mr. Blenkinsop's towards her, and whereas she had been incapable of speech, Ethel's was torrential under the encouragement she received.

She had been to see Mrs. Spenser-Smith in search of comfort and advice. Who else was there she could go to? She had no mother, her father was angry and Miss Mole, to whom she told this story, was the cause of half the trouble, but Mrs. Spenser-Smith, who ought to have been consoling and maternal, had shattered what happiness Ethel had.

'She was cruel to me, Miss Mole,' Ethel said, with tears streaming down her face. 'So cold and haughty. She said Father was quite right; she didn't like Mr. Pilgrim herself. She said – But it can't be true! If it's true, I shall die!'

'No, you won't die,' Hannah said soothingly.

'But I shall want to!'

'I'm afraid that won't make any practical difference. Men have died and worms have eaten them, but not for love.'

'Oh, Miss Mole, what do you know about it?' Ethel cried. 'And it wouldn't be dying of love. It would be dying of – shame! For having loved him.'

'You won't even die of that,' Hannah said, very low.

'It isn't that I care what he's done. I could forgive anything – only not lies, not lies! I couldn't love anyone who told me lies.'

'Then you'll have a remarkably narrow choice,' Hannah said dryly. 'But, it seems to me, the important question is whether he loves you.'

'But of course he does!' The flow of Ethel's tears stopped and went on again.

'Has he said so? In so many words? Was it what they used to call a declaration? Unmistakably?'

'Yes,' Ethel said, dropping her head. 'He told me yesterday – but I knew before that.'

279

'Then why in the world were you crying last night when Ruth and I came in? You ought to have been jumping for joy, girl!'

'But Father came and said awful things about him, and Mrs. Spenser-Smith says he isn't a good man. She says he's telling tales about you because he's afraid you'll tell them about him. She says you know something against him. You don't, do you, Miss Mole? You said you'd never seen him till the Spenser-Smiths' party – he told me so, but who am I to believe?'

Hannah sat on her bed, looking at her folded hands and for a few minutes she was more occupied with thoughts of Lilla than of Ethel or herself. 'So you told Mrs. Spenser-Smith what you had heard about me, did you?'

'Yes. I didn't mean to, but it came out.'

'It would!' Hannah said, and she smiled as she pictured Lilla's horror, her immediate belief in her cousin's guilt, and her equal quickness in protecting her own reputation by using the hint Hannah had dropped about Mr. Pilgrim's little secrets.

'And oh, Miss Mole, don't tell me lies to comfort me,' Ethel begged.

Hannah had already made her decision, but these courageous words ennobled the task she had set herself and though she doubted Mr. Pilgrim's worthiness of the girl who had uttered them, she would not allow the doubt to influence her. 'You can go on loving him,' she said. 'He hasn't told you any lies, not about me, anyhow, and I don't suppose he has ever committed what he would call a sin. That's what's the matter with him. You see, he's got a grudge against me. I shut my door in his face once, and I'd do it again, and, worse still, I believe I laughed at him. He can't forgive that, and then, if he loves you, he has an interest in looking after you and trying to get rid of me. He wouldn't like me to do you harm. I don't blame him. I don't blame anybody. What's the use?'

'Then wasn't there a Cousin Hilda?' Ethel asked timidly, making sure of Mr. Pilgrim's perfections before she gave way to her joy.

'Not in the flesh,' Hannah said, 'but in every other way

280

there was, and now she has vanished and her works follow her. The evil that men do –' Her words slipped into silence and after a moment she added, very softly, to herself, 'But it was not evil.'

She was not looking at Ethel, but she could feel her fascinated stare at this new species, at a woman who seemed good, who had never failed to give help when it was wanted, and yet confessed to wickedness, without apology or excuse.

'I shall have to tell Father,' Ethel said with difficulty.

Hannah raised her head sharply. 'I don't see the necessity,' she said, and she thought of Ruth, laughing at the pantomime and proud of Wilfrid's company.

'But don't you see, I must. It's only fair to Mr. Pilgrim, and to me. Mrs. Spenser-Smith will be saying things about him. Why, it might ruin him!'

'Then tell him,' Hannah said wearily.

'I'm sorry, Miss Mole, I really am. It seems mean, I know, and I've always liked you, but you see, don't you?'

What Hannah saw most clearly was her own shabby, homeless figure, and it amazed her that Ethel did not see it too, but she said, 'Yes, yes, I see it all. Don't tell him until Ruth's in bed. And don't tell her at all. I'll send her to bed early, and I'll go out. It would be uncomfortable for you, wouldn't it, to know I was in the next room? Wouldn't it?' she persisted.

'Oh, yes, Miss Mole, it would. You think of everything, and I'll do my best. I'll ask Father to forgive you, and you've been so good to us, I'm sure he will.'

'Well, leave me now,' Hannah said.

She counted her money. She would not stay to be blessed by Mr. Corder's forgiveness. She would go to-morrow. She had no intention of going without giving Robert Corder an opportunity to repeat his generosity and herself the unlikely pleasure of refusing it. She had made her choice. She had sacrificed Ruth to Ethel's chance of happiness, but she could not sacrifice all her dignity to Ruth, who had her Uncle Jim to care for her, and to Uncle Jim Hannah wrote before she went downstairs, and, turning to look at the little ship which had been her companion for so long, she decided that Ruth should have it in exchange for Hannah Mole.

Years seemed to pass over her head while she waited for Ruth and Wilfrid to come in, and while she listened to all they had to tell her. The evening meal, strained by Robert Corder's general disgust with uncalled-for circumstances, Ethel's nervous excitement and Ruth's carefulness to let fall no revealing word, seemed everlasting, and then there was the night-light to be lit for the last time, and there were more of Ruth's confidences to hear, before Hannah could leave the house, bareheaded and wearing her old ulster.

She hesitated at Mr. Samson's gate, but she did not open it. She was afraid she would cry if anyone spoke kindly to her, and more afraid that the signs of this weakness were on her face. And why was she so miserable? She had foreseen all this and been prepared to meet it without a murmur. Was it because she was leaving Ruth, because her secret was being discussed in the study, or because she had no money and no home? It was because of all of these, but they were only part of her distress, for she could no longer trust that spring of hope which, hitherto, had always flowed for her, sometimes feebly, more often with iridescent bubbles which might break as she put her lips to them and change their shape, but kept a quality that refreshed her. The spring had run dry and, as though she went in search of another, she hurried up the street in a drizzling rain and followed the route she and Mr. Blenkinsop had taken when they had walked together at night and found nothing to say to one another. It was strange to remember that she would have been as happy, then, without him, and now, with each step she took, her desire to speak to him increased, not to tell him anything, just to speak to him, before she went away.

She went round the hill with no regard for the cliffs and the dark river and the sparkling docks she loved so well. She knew they were there and, in a way, they comforted her, but she did not look at them. She hurried down the sloping ground, across The Green and across Albert Square, and she did not slacken her pace until she reached Mrs. Gibson's door. The door was open, and Mr. Blenkinsop, in his coat and hat, was turning to shut it for the night.

282

Chapter 40

'I HAVE just come back from Beresford Road,' he said. 'They told me you were out.'

'They?' Hannah said anxiously.

Mr. Blenkinsop smiled. 'A loose expression! I only saw the servant. How did we miss each other?'

'I've been for a walk,' Hannah said, watching Mr. Blenkinsop hanging up his coat and hat.

'You oughtn't to do that, at this time of night. And nothing on your head! It's quite wet,' he said in annoyance.

'What time is it?' They spoke in low tones, careful for the slumbers of Mrs. Gibson and the little maid and the people in the basement.

'Ten o'clock.'

'Then I oughtn't to be here, either. I must go back.' The smile of the alert Miss Mole was weak and wavering, like a nervous child's. 'I don't really know why I came at all,' she said, and she looked at him as though she expected him to explain her action. 'I shall be locked out. I forgot to bring my latch-key.'

'Then we shall have to trouble Mr. Corder to let us in,' Mr. Blenkinsop said.

That pronoun had an extraordinarily friendly sound in Hannah's ears and she repeated it. 'We'd better go now.'

'No. Come upstairs. I'm going to make some tea. You're cold and wet.'

'But –' Hannah began, and Mr. Blenkinsop said severely, 'Just try to forget there are any such people as the Corders. I'll go up first and turn on the light.'

Mr. Blenkinsop's room was warm and glowing with fire-light and a shaded lamp, and there was not a sound in the house but the lapping of the fire and not a sound in the street. A dreary peace stole over Hannah, an indifference to duty and disaster, and she went towards one of the deep arm-chairs in an unreasonable conviction that if she could once get between its arms she need never get out again.

'Take off your coat, first,' Mr. Blenkinsop said. He was busy at a cupboard, getting out cups and saucers and a canister of tea.

'My poor old coat!' Hannah said with a vague laugh. Months ago she had promised Ruth not to wear it. 'But it will have to last for a long time yet,' she said to herself. She leaned back and shut her eyes and listened to Mr. Blenkinsop's movements, to the change in the notes of the kettle, and then the hissing sound as tea and water met, and she did not open them until he said, 'There, drink that.'

Suddenly she was awake, remembering when she had last seen Mr. Blenkinsop, and urgent with all the things she ought to say to him before she went away. 'Have you taken that cottage?' she said.

'No. I was going to ask you if you'd like to sell it.'

'Not to you,' she said quickly.

'I don't want it. I've found another that will suit us better, I think.'

'But how –' She was realizing that she had not told him the house was hers. It was natural for him to know, and right, but she had not told him. 'How do you know it belongs to me?' she asked, and thought it was right for him to know, her eyes were wide and her mouth dropped piteously.

'I've been there again,' he said with a slight embarrassment, but a steady look. 'I don't like breaking appointments,' and at this description of the chase she had given him, she laughed without much mirth.

Mr. Blenkinsop responded with a smile and then, quietly, looking at his well-shod feet, he said, 'I've turned the fellow out.'

Like an arrow from a bow, Hannah's thin body darted forward, a hand on each arm of her chair, and the last embers of her loyalty leapt into a blaze under the indignant breath with which she cried, 'How dare you? How dare you? What business was it of yours to interfere?'

Without raising his head, Mr. Blenkinsop turned it towards the fire. 'Somebody had to do it,' he said mildly. 'You see, when it came to talking business, he couldn't produce a deed or a lease and he isn't a very competent liar. In the end, he had to refer me to the owner so I just told him he'd better go.'

'Then you can just go back and tell him he can stay.'

'Oh, he's gone by this time, and the man who owns the farm is willing to buy the place. Somebody has to look after you,' he explained patiently.

Hannah stood up and reached out blindly for her coat. 'But not you,' she said, and her voice seemed to come from the very source of sorrow. 'Isn't there anybody in the world who won't trample on the few things I've had?' she asked plaintively. 'All these people – why must they? And you – I didn't think you would do it.' Her anger took hold of her again. 'What right had you to interfere?' she repeated. Then pure pain overcame her anger and she said, 'It doesn't matter. It doesn't matter, but I didn't think you would do it. I didn't think you would try to find out why I ran away.' Again she put out her hands for her coat, but they did not meet it and she sat down again, as though she had forgotten what she meant to do.

'What else could I do?' he said simply. 'I told you I couldn't leave it at that. You were in trouble and you wouldn't tell me what it was. I see now that I ought not to have gone without asking you, but I'm glad I did. No, I ought not to have gone, but when I went I thought there might be something I could do for you. All sorts of queer ideas came into my head and I never thought, I never thought for a moment –'

Hannah dropped her hands from her face and he saw the familiar, teasing smile. 'And yet it ought to have been the first thing that occurred to you.'

'Ought it? I suppose I'm stupid. You'll have to forgive me. I saw he was trying to rob you, or not caring whether he did or not, but I didn't turn him out until – until –'

'No, no,' Hannah mourned. 'Don't tell me. Don't tell me anything he said. Is there no end to it? I didn't mind your knowing about it, but I didn't want you to see him. That's why I ran away. I didn't want you to see him and

285

now you've seen him and talked to him. You've seen the kind of man I loved – and lived with. It was the only thing, the only thing about me I didn't want you to know – the kind of man – and even that I couldn't keep. I can't keep anything! Oh, let me go back. I must go back.' With a tremendous effort at self-command she changed her voice to cne of acid amusement. 'It seems to me that your affection for one woman has made rather a busybody of you, Mr. Blenkinsop.'

'I'm afraid that's true,' he said. 'Drink your tea. There's no hurry. I want to tell you about the other cottage we've got hold of. It belongs to Ridding's brother-in-law. He's a farmer and he'll be able to keep an eye on Ridding and help him with his fowls.' He was looking at the fire, avoiding her eyes, and he did not see astonishment gradually spreading over her face. 'Ridding will be better in the country. An office isn't the place for a man like that, and Mrs. Ridding thinks it will suit the baby. They'll be going in about a fortnight and it's a great load off my mind,' he ended with a deep sigh.

'Take my cup,' Hannah said in a strangled voice. 'Take my cup. I shall spill the tea. I'm going to laugh. But I can't!' she cried after a moment. 'Oh, what's going to happen to me if I can't laugh any more?'

'You're tired out,' he said.

'Yes, but it isn't that.' She looked about her, seeking an explanation. 'It must be because it isn't really funny,' she said in a low, puzzled voice. 'You see, I thought you were in love with Mrs. Ridding. I thought the cottage was for you and her.'

'Good God!' Mr. Blenkinsop exclaimed in horror, and again Hannah had the sensation that her heart was shrinking to the size of a pea. He was kind to her, as he was kind to Mrs. Ridding, but this was what he thought of such love affairs as hers, and now she stood up with a deceptive briskness.

'And that,' she said, in a hard voice, 'just shows you what kind of a mind I've got. I suspect everybody else of what I did myself! And now I must go back, for Ruth may want me.'

'She can't want you as much as I do,' Mr. Blenk[insop]
said quietly, in unmistakable accents.

Hannah stood quite still. She clung to her coat, bu[t it]
dropped out of her hand, and she said slowly, address[ing]
the wall in front of her, 'This isn't true.'

'Yes, it's true,' he said. 'That's why I've been botherin[g]
about the Riddings, to do something I thought woul[d]
please you. And if you're going to say you don't care about
me –'

'But I'm not!' Hannah cried, with a wide, tremulous
smile. 'I'm not! Don't talk to me for a little while. Don't
say anything,' she begged, and Mr. Blenkinsop was obediently silent while she lay back in her chair, telling herself
that the miracle she had believed in had really happened,
it had really happened, it was here, in this room, but in a
moment she started up again. 'I'll tell you what we'll do.
We'll sell the cottage and give the money to the Riddings.'

'As a thank-offering!' he said.

'Yes,' she said, rather wistfully, 'if it seems like that to you.
Well, you know everything about me.'

'No,' he said, 'and I don't think I ever shall,' a speech
more satisfying to Hannah than any more lover-like
protestation.

It was twelve o'clock when they walked down Beresford
Road, and Hannah had no latch-key, and Mr. Blenkinsop
was looking forward to his interview with Robert Corder.
And, after all, Ruth need never know, Hannah thought, in
great content, and Mr. Corder would be relieved of the
responsibility of taking action, and Ethel would marry Mr.
Pilgrim, and, surely, Uncle Jim would rescue Ruth, and
Robert Corder would marry Patsy Withers and find her
somewhat dull after the incalculableness of Miss Mole, and,
for this misfortune, Lilla would find compensation in the
disappearance of a cousin who would cause her no more
anxiety. The miracle had happened and though, through
the wonder of it, there were regrets for Ruth, Hannah had
never been less inclined to doubt that everything was for
the best.

Can this be me? she asked herself. She had run up the
road, two hours ago, in a drizzling rain and an unbear-

had hold of Mr. Blenkinsop's
...ning.

...saying, and she glanced up at him
...erself, he saw something whimsical
...ove. She hoped he did not. She could
...t with other people's eyes and laugh,
...t doing it any injury, but, for him, she
...piness to be too solemn and beautiful for

...away,' he said. 'I'll leave the bank. You've
...ather ashamed of the bank. It's too safe.'
...want safety now! That's the worst of happiness –
...s you want safety. We mustn't want it. I've always
...afraid of wanting too much,' she said.
...Oh – my poor heart!' Mr. Blenkinsop exclaimed in a
...oken voice, and stopped and stooped to kiss her.

'She can't want you as much as I do,' Mr. Blenkinsop said quietly, in unmistakable accents.

Hannah stood quite still. She clung to her coat, but it dropped out of her hand, and she said slowly, addressing the wall in front of her, 'This isn't true.'

'Yes, it's true,' he said. 'That's why I've been bothering about the Riddings, to do something I thought would please you. And if you're going to say you don't care about me –'

'But I'm not!' Hannah cried, with a wide, tremulous smile. 'I'm not! Don't talk to me for a little while. Don't say anything,' she begged, and Mr. Blenkinsop was obediently silent while she lay back in her chair, telling herself that the miracle she had believed in had really happened, it had really happened, it was here, in this room, but in a moment she started up again. 'I'll tell you what we'll do. We'll sell the cottage and give the money to the Riddings.'

'As a thank-offering!' he said.

'Yes,' she said, rather wistfully, 'if it seems like that to you. Well, you know everything about me.'

'No,' he said, 'and I don't think I ever shall,' a speech more satisfying to Hannah than any more lover-like protestation.

It was twelve o'clock when they walked down Beresford Road, and Hannah had no latch-key, and Mr. Blenkinsop was looking forward to his interview with Robert Corder. And, after all, Ruth need never know, Hannah thought, in great content, and Mr. Corder would be relieved of the responsibility of taking action, and Ethel would marry Mr. Pilgrim, and, surely, Uncle Jim would rescue Ruth, and Robert Corder would marry Patsy Withers and find her somewhat dull after the incalculableness of Miss Mole, and, for this misfortune, Lilla would find compensation in the disappearance of a cousin who would cause her no more anxiety. The miracle had happened and though, through the wonder of it, there were regrets for Ruth, Hannah had never been less inclined to doubt that everything was for the best.

Can this be me? she asked herself. She had run up the road, two hours ago, in a drizzling rain and an unbearable loneliness, and now she had hold of Mr. Blenkinsop's hand and the stars were shining.

'We'll go away,' he was saying, and she glanced up at him and wondered if, like herself, he saw something whimsical and unlikely in their love. She hoped he did not. She could trust herself to see it with other people's eyes and laugh, with them, without doing it any injury, but, for him, she wished this happiness to be too solemn and beautiful for mirth.

'We'll go away,' he said. 'I'll leave the bank. You've made me rather ashamed of the bank. It's too safe.'

'But I want safety now! That's the worst of happiness – it makes you want safety. We mustn't want it. I've always been afraid of wanting too much,' she said.

'Oh – my poor heart!' Mr. Blenkinsop exclaimed in a broken voice, and stopped and stooped to kiss her.

EMILY HILDA YOUNG

(1880-1949) was born in Northumberland, England, the daughter of a ship-broker. She was educated at Gateshead High School and Penrhos College, Colwyn Bay, Wales. In 1902, after her marriage to a solicitor, J.A.H. Daniell, she went to live in Bristol, which was to become the setting of most of her novels. Her first, *A Corn of Wheat*, was published in 1910, followed by *Yonder* (1912), and *Moor Fires* (1916).

During the First World War Emily Young worked in a munitions factory and as a groom in a local stable. After her husband's death at Ypres in 1917, she left Bristol for London and lived with Ralph Henderson, a married man and Head Master of Alleyn's school in Dulwich. She continued to write. *The Misses Mallett*, published originally as *The Bridge Dividing*, appeared in 1922, preceding her most successful novel, *William* (1925). Then came *The Vicar's Daughter* (1928), *Miss Mole* (1930) — which won the James Tait Black Memorial Prize, *Jenny Wren* (1932), *The Curate's Wife* (1934) and *Celia* (1937). She lived with the Hendersons in South London until Ralph Henderson's retirement at the time of the Second World War, at which time he and E.H. Young moved to Bradford-on-Avon, Wiltshire. Here Emily Young wrote two children's books, *Caravan Island* (1940) and *River Holiday* (1942), and one further novel, *Chatterton Square*, published in 1947, two years before her death from lung cancer at the age of sixty-nine.

Both *The Misses Mallett* and *Miss Mole* are published as Virago Modern classics.